ONE

Susan Edwards packs carefully for her family's August vacation. She prides herself on being sensitive to details and anticipating their needs. But this year she's concerned with her own needs.

Deep within a large carton, hidden from her husband Jeff's view by the usual array of board games, is her French dictionary, the heavy manuscript entombed in the rigid, oatmeal-colored box favored by the Parisian publisher, and her laptop. She knows that she has violated the long-standing agreement between Jeff and herself – that there will be no work on during the month of their vacation. But this year is different. She will wait until they arrive at the inn, until Jeff is relaxed and in a forgiving mood, a glass of wine in his hand, a smile on his face. Then she will explain why she could not turn down the opportunity to translate Juliette LeBec's novel, the literary sensation of Paris, certain to be the literary sensation of the States. Its very title intrigues. *Pierre et Jacqueline: L'histoire d'un marriage.*

'Ace this – and I know you will – and you'll win the PEN translation award which will mean you can name your own price, choose your own projects,' Leonie, her agent, had told her, and Susan knew Leonie to be right.

She had worked steadily on it, seduced by the story of Pierre and Jacqueline, complex personalities struggling through the labyrinth of a complex marriage. The story gripped her and after working her way through the first few chapters she realized, with a shock of recognition, how closely it matched the current pattern of her own marriage, the sudden inexplicable interludes of sadness, her irritability with Jeff, his irritability with her. Intrigued, immersed in the story, obsessed by the challenge of her translation, there were times, as she worked, when she imagined herself to be Jacqueline and saw Jeff as Pierre.

Eager to capture the nuances of LeBec's elegant French and

fashion it into an equally elegant English, her progress had been slow and the deadline for the first draft in late September looms. If she is to meet it, she will have to spend some precious vacation time in New Hampshire working on the manuscript. She dared not mention that to Jeff, especially after he told her that he had refused an invitation to attend a prestigious conference being held in August.

'Family first, right?' he had said ruefully, and she had nodded. No need to upset him. He has been moody enough over the past months. She will manage her time, set a pace, melding work and leisure. And when she explains, he will understand. She is not being deceptive. She is being realistic. This is a once-in-a-lifetime commission and she has fallen in love with the work. Her heart beats faster as the narrative accelerates, love and lust commingling, desire and destiny chasing each other in LeBec's amazingly poetic prose. Meticulous translator that she is, she works and reworks every sentence, puzzles over subtleties, lost in the language of her dreams, the language she has made her own.

She reassures herself. Jeff will have plenty of companionship at the inn. He and Simon Epstein often go fishing together and he occasionally joins Helene and Greg on their endless antiquing excursions. In any case, the carton is sealed. Jeff will not check its contents.

She turns her attention to the clothing they will need, adhering to the list she printed out in large, bright primary color-coded fonts, chosen to indicate holiday light-heartedness. She checks items off as she glides from bureau to bed, her arms laden with her undergarments and his, her nightgowns and his pajamas, his jeans and tops and her own, his worn khaki swimming trunks, her shapeless and faded blue bathing suit. She places his double ply pale green cashmere sweater (her birthday gift to him), and her own pink fleece-lined silk jacket (his birthday gift to her) in the zippered compartment. She smiles to think of the similarities of their wardrobes, the similarities of their tastes. They have grown into each other through the years of their marriage.

The thought pleases her. She reads through her list again and, satisfied, she shreds it and buries the strips of paper at the bottom of the wastepaper basket. She knows that her compulsive list making, a habit which Jeff had found amusing and endearing during their courtship and the early years of their marriage, now irritates him. She has seen him crumple the pastel-colored Post-its that litter surfaces throughout their home, each numbered notation reminding her of an errand – stops at the post office, the supermarket, the library, calls to be initiated, calls to be returned. 1, 2, 3, each number checked off.

'Can't you manage to remember all this crap?' he has asked with a muted anger she does not recognize. She attributes it to fatigue, to the adjustments of new demands as the children grow older and the patterns of their lives shift. But of course, all things change, she assures herself. It is inevitable that small habits become small annoyances. She herself is unnerved by his constant humming as he pays bills or balances the check book although once she had found it so charming that she would hum along with him. Such trivial irritants are inconsequential. *Sans* importance. She retreats into French, the calming language of her profession. She smiles as she recalls the recently completed translation of a chapter in which Pierre and Jacqueline have a fierce and furious argument over Pierre's failure to replace the cap on a tube of toothpaste. Of course, irritants are inevitable, but marriages do not end over toothpaste caps (as Pierre reminds Jacqueline) or over scattered Post-its (as she reminds herself). They are, she and Jeff, much as they have always been, a couple in love, in sync, happy in their work, in their home, loving partners, loving parents. A list in itself, she realizes, as the words run through her mind in a well-rehearsed mantra, repeated often, perhaps too often, in recent months.

The unbidden thought unsettles her and she slams the valise shut, opening it again because she has forgotten to pack the gifts for her sister, Helene – a black smock daringly patterned in magenta geometrics, triangles and circles converging. She has bought a soft leather folio designed to hold sheet music for Greg, Helene's musician husband. The sisters struggle each August to find clever gifts to be offered on the first evening of their shared vacation, a studied ritual to compensate for the deprivations of a childhood when birthday gifts were too often packets of cotton underpants, and celebratory cupcakes (never a cake, never a party) were plucked from the day-old shelf of the supermarket. She and Helene have earned the right to spoil each other, to spoil themselves, Susan thinks, as she carefully folds the smock.

The bickering of her older children drifts up from the kitchen and she wonders for how long she can ignore their quarrel. Annette's voice, shrill and self-righteous, rises above that of her twin brother, Jeremy, who is, in turn, blustering and accusatory, but Susan is reluctant to go downstairs and mediate. Instead, she wanders over to the mirror and stares critically at her reflection. She takes stock, with unflinching honesty. Admittedly, obviously, she is no longer the slender bride who blushed too easily and worked too hard, often falling asleep over a manuscript in progress, her French dictionary open, her head resting on her desk. She was reluctant, during the early days of her marriage, to go to sleep while her new husband was still at the hospital. She awaited Jeff's return home from a long rotation. He would wake her, kissing her brow, tousling her curls with tolerant affection, encircling her in a tender embrace as he led her gently to their bed.

She has, of course, over the years, learned to manage her time, ration out her energy. There are no more nocturnal naps, no more sweet awakenings. Her dark curls themselves have been subdued into a sleek layered helmet fringed with encroaching silver. She is no longer slender, she acknowledges ruefully. Three children, delivered by caesarian section, rendered her waistline non-existent – not unusual, Jeff the skilled surgeon had assured her, although she realizes that it is a long time since he has repeated that embrace or any embrace at all.

That realization does not unduly disturb her. Of course, intimacy eludes them. She knows that. He knows that. It is because they have so little time together, beset as they are by the demands of the children, the demands of their work, this meeting, that deadline. They have said as much to each other in the darkness of the night, in the half light of the morning, wearily, apologetically, tentatively touching hands and then withdrawing.

'We need time away.' His words, her thoughts.

That time away, so precious to both of them and to their children, has always been the month of August, an expanse of

GUESTS OF AUGUST

Gloria Goldreich

SEVERN HOUSE

For Sheldon – of course!

First world edition published 2019
in Great Britain and 2020 in the USA by
SEVERN HOUSE PUBLISHERS LTD of
Eardley House, 4 Uxbridge Street, London W8 7SY.
Trade paperback edition first published
in Great Britain and the USA 2021 by
Severn House, an imprint of Canongate Books,
14 High Street, Edinburgh EH1 1TE.

British Library Cataloguing in Publication Data
A CIP catalogue record for this title is available from the British Library.

ISBN-13: 978-0-7278-8972-0 (cased)
ISBN-13: 978-1-78029-663-0 (trade paper)
ISBN-13: 978-1-4483-0360-1 (e-book)

Typeset by Palimpsest Book Production
Falkirk, Stirlingshire, Scotland.

golden leisure as the rainbow-colored flowers of summer slowly yield to the earliest blossoms of autumn. She thinks of those weeks at Mount Haven Inn as a magical refuge, an annual renewal for Jeff and herself, and for their family. It is doubly precious because it is then that she and Helene share an extended period of time, leisure in which to balance their distant childhoods on the uneasy seesaw of mixed memories.

Helene and Greg are already en route to New Hampshire. Susan smiles at the thought. Tomorrow she and her family will pile into the car and drive northward to mountains and lakes, to Mount Haven's verdant rolling lawn and wide-windowed dining room.

The LeBec translation will not interfere, she assures herself. She will manage. Early-morning hours, late-night sessions, the pile of manuscript pages growing smaller as she taps out carefully composed sentences on her laptop, her English rendition catching the exact cadence of the French. Her apprehension diminishes.

'We will have a wonderful time,' she tells herself sternly and, for no reason at all, she applies a fresh coat of lipstick and hurries downstairs as the twins' voices rise dangerously and little Matt, always frightened by his siblings' odd and inexplicable rages, begins to cry.

Helene and Greg Ames begin their journey to New Hampshire two days before their scheduled arrival at Mount Haven Inn. Unlike Susan, they have packed carelessly, almost recklessly, tossing their things into two huge burlap bags, one dyed purple and the other orange, both hastily purchased at an Istanbul bazaar during what they refer to as their 'wandering years'. Helene, however, has taken great care to cushion the stained-glass pieces she crafted as gifts for her sister's family. The car windows are open and a gentle breeze riffles Greg's thick dark hair, although it is so warm that he rolls up the sleeves of his plaid cotton shirt and Helene slips off her sandals and lowers her peasant blouse, baring her shoulders.

The two days which will carry them from their Maryland home, through New England, are, they agree, the best part of their vacation, a leisurely odyssey during which they are without obligation, free to linger in antique shops, eat their packed lunches in the car and order two or three drinks for dinner at upscale restaurants. Wine as well, if they are in the mood. No raised eyebrows, no knowing glances, no sly smirks. Time enough for that when they arrive at Mount Haven, when after the first rush of affectionate greetings, Susan's subtle appraisals will begin.

The sisters, Helene and Susan, will take stock of each other with equal parts affection and malice. Helene will think Susan's haircut too stylish, her inevitable pastel sweat suit too studied, too casual. She will indulge in false pity for her sister who never seems to relax.

Susan in turn will judge Helene's hair to be too long, falling as it does in a tangle of knots to her shoulders, dark roots already sprouting beneath the rose-gold rinse she applies herself. She may finger the gauzy fabric of Helene's long turquoise skirt and murmur, 'pretty', meaning, of course, 'too young for you'. And, as she does, each year, she will lean forward, to brush stray tendrils of hair from Helene's brow, the gesture at once monitory and maternal.

Jeff will shake hands vigorously with Greg and fire off a barrage of questions without waiting for answers. 'How's it going? Good trip up? Good year? Did you bring your instruments? Think we'll catch anything at the lake?'

Greg wonders why it is that they have repeated this New Hampshire vacation year after irritating year. He glances at Helene, seated beside him, studying the map, but says nothing. He knows the answer. She has said it often enough. She wants to spend time with her sister, her sister's family. Susan and her children are her only blood relatives. Their parents are dead and their few cousins are widely scattered and indifferent. Scrawled messages on Christmas cards are their only signs of life. Susan and Helene are each other's history, their lives forever linked by the commonality of their childhoods, their melded memories. They struggle, each August, to reinforce that linkage, to reconnect at Mount Haven, to deny their separateness, their disparate lifestyles, their disparate interests.

And each August, year after year, their husbands struggle to forge a fraternal friendship, laughing too heartily at each other's jokes, speaking too loudly, fearful of silences unbridged by words. Greg will play his violin during one evening at Mount Haven, a modest solo performance for the adult guests, and on a subsequent evening he will strum his guitar for the hootenanny, always organized for the teenagers and the children. Jeff and Susan will clap vigorously.

'You really ought to perform professionally again,' Jeff will say, and Greg will nod and refrain from telling his brother-in-law that he realized long ago that he is good but simply not good enough. So he teaches music in a small rural high school and Helene, who is an artist – also good but not good enough – teaches art and they are managing. Their summer session checks pay for the Mount Haven vacation and bring their dreams of leaving their rented apartment and owning a home closer. Not a house as big as Susan and Jeff's five-bedroom Colonial, but of course, Greg is not an upscale surgeon and Helene is not a world-class translator. But then they don't need a house that big. They are childless, by chance rather than by design.

'Our talents are our children,' Helene has said breathlessly more than once, and he does not contradict her. A careless housekeeper, their linens often sour smelling, the kitchen floor often sticky, Helene manages to keep the small room in which she paints as immaculate as a nursery. Her easel is wiped clean, her brushes soak in cleansing turpentine, her paint tubes are meticulously scraped and ranged on scrubbed-down shelves.

And he, like an attentive father, swaddles his instruments in soft flannel before placing them in their hard leather cases. Even now, as he drives, he glances back at the rear seat where he has placed his violin and guitar, to make certain that they have not slid down, that the battered leather briefcase that contains his sheet music has not snapped open. He would have welcomed children, but he learned long ago to take life as it comes.

They stop at an antique shop just over the Massachusetts border. Helene spies a small night table of golden oak, passes her hand across its smooth surface, opens and closes the single drawer which sticks slightly. She imagines it next to the sleigh bed still to be discovered, in the bedroom of the cozy cottage they have yet to buy. The price is reasonable and the proprietor, a white-haired woman, her body pretzeled by osteoporosis, hovers, a clear sign that she is prepared to bargain if necessary.

'I think I can fix it,' Greg says, sliding the drawer back and forth.

He holds a dart board, its cork surface punctured, a sure sign of authenticity. The darts themselves are lightly feathered and newly sharpened.

'You're buying that?' Helene asks.

'Yup. I played a lot of darts when I was hitching through England. I was good at it. We'll set it up in the rec room at the inn. I'll play with Jeff.'

He smiles, certain that he can beat his brother-in-law at the game. Jeff, always goal-oriented, had never wandered with back-pack and guitar through the hills of Scotland and small Irish villages with unpronounceable names. He relishes the thought of challenging Jeff to a game, or perhaps setting up a tournament which he will surely win. The thought of that certain small triumph, of doing something, anything, better than his successful brother-in-law, invigorates him. He might also triumph over the other guests at the inn – smug Simon Epstein and Mike Curran, that stock market obsessive. His prowess will surprise them.

'It won't be dangerous to play darts? With the kids around?' Helene asks.

'We'll be careful. That's a Susan question,' he replies irritably.

She turns away and reconsiders the night table. It may be too low, or perhaps too high. It depends on the size of the bed, which, of course, they will not buy until they have a house. This year, maybe next year. She shrugs and wanders out of the shop. The old woman sighs, turns to Greg and, vengefully, asks a higher price for the dart board than the one marked. Greg does not argue.

'We're going to have fun,' he assures Helene as they drive away.

'I hope the cast of characters has changed. Do you think the Epsteins will be back? And what about the Templetons? They are so weird.'

'Why should this year be different than any other year? Everyone will be back. It's sort of reassuring, in a way.'

He laughs. He is, finally, actually looking forward to their

Mount Haven stay. When late-afternoon shadows fall and they stop for dinner at a quaint inn, he orders a double Scotch and a bottle of wine. They drink half of it with their excellent seared halibut and carry the rest of the bottle up to their room because of course they will stay the night. They are briefly indifferent to expense. Their vacation has begun.

Mark Templeton, his khaki trousers sharply creased, a freshly ironed handkerchief in the pocket of his lemon-yellow broadcloth shirt, waits on the patio while Andrea finishes their packing. Preparing for a long journey always unnerves him and since that business with his heart ('an episode', the cardiologist, who is young enough to be his son, called it) he is careful not to become unnerved. Besides, he knows that he can rely on his wife to select the clothing he favors for their usual August holiday in New Hampshire. She will surely remember the lightweight sweaters he ordered from the L.L. Bean catalog, the periwinkle blue V-neck a perfect match for his eyes. Elderly and gray-haired he may be, but he clings to the vanity of his young manhood, oddly proud of the penetrating blue of his eyes. A great color, he thinks dispassionately, remembering how pleased he had been that his son's eyes had been of the same shade. Even in death, Adam's face blanched, a ribbon of dried blood across his forehead where his head had impacted against the windshield, his eyes had retained their color, that piercing electric blue. How long, after breath had ceased, did eyes lose their coloring? Mark had thought to ask but of course he had remained silent and turned away when the mortuary attendant gently, almost apologetically, pulled the lids down. The memory saddens him and he veers at once to thoughts of his grandson.

Donny – clever, lithe Donny – has inherited his mother's coloring. Like Wendy, he is olive skinned, dark haired and dark eyed. A pity that he did not take after Adam, Mark thinks and has said as much to Andrea, who nodded in agreement but did not reply. His wife does not often mention their dead son's name, although she keeps a small red leather photo album on her bedside table. It was a gift from Wendy, oddly enough, presented on Adam's birthday a week before his death, an affectionate offering from a loving wife to her husband's mother.

Andrea has filled it with photographs of Adam and newspaper clippings, reviews of his novel, his obituary. She studies it now and again during the melancholy pre-dawn hours when she thinks that Mark is sleeping or as she sips a glass of vodka, yet another glass of vodka, quietly poured when she thinks that Mark is watching the evening edition of the financial news. Vodka, Mark knows, has long been her drink of choice, because it leaves no odor and can often masquerade as clear water.

Mark sighs and watches a red-winged blackbird raid the feeder. He will have to remind Carlos, their gardener, to keep it stocked with seed while they are away. Damn it, there is so much to remember before they leave. He wonders irritably if Andrea has stopped the mail, if she has cancelled their newspaper delivery. But, of course, Rosa, Carlos's wife and their housekeeper, will manage any oversight. Still, he is troubled by trivia, a certain sign that he is getting too old for this annual pilgrimage to Mount Haven Inn.

He lifts his face to the hazy California sunlight and hopes that Andrea will hang his linen jackets in the garment bag so that they will not crease. He is partial to those jackets, especially tailored so that the silk-lined front pockets are both wide and deep. He will place a packet of spearmint gum and a bag of M&Ms in each pocket as soon as he unpacks at Mount Haven. It is, after all, a vacation ritual. As a child, Adam had delighted in plunging his small hand into the pocket and dashing off, playfully pretending that his father would chase after him and reclaim the treat. And Donny had, in turn, played the same game and plays it still, although he is growing too old for it. He humors his grandfather, with Wendy's encouragement, Mark supposes.

'Mark, what books do you want to take?' Andrea calls down to him, leaning over their bedroom balcony.

He stares up at her, shading his eyes. She is dressed for the journey, her mauve silk pant suit at once sensible and elegant, a white scarf draped over her shoulders, her silver hair coiled into a smooth chignon.

'The Einstein biography, I suppose. And the new Le Carré.'

He always selects thick volumes for the New Hampshire vacation, insurance policies against hours of idleness and boredom. Unlike Andrea, he has no interest in socializing with

the other Mount Haven vacationers. They are not of his generation, all of them at varying stages of overly absorbing parenthood
except for those childless pseudo bohemians, Helene and Greg,
for whom he feels an inexplicable dislike. It surprises him that
he remembers their names from year to year.

He is, admittedly, not a total hermit during his stay. He has,
now and again, given scraps of business advice to young Michael
Curran and there have been occasional decent conversations with
Simon Epstein who manages to combine his career as an
academic economist with corporate work, an achievement that
Mark, frozen in place in the corporate world, envies. Still, he
draws the line at spending time with Simon's wife, Nessa, a
woman who talks too much and laughs too loudly. She is, Mark
thinks, reluctantly, too Jewish. It is not a perception he would
share with Andrea or Wendy.

They think Nessa interesting, a woman whose reading is
eclectic and whose opinions are often surprising. They play
Scrabble with her and with Susan Edwards, that doctor's wife,
a translator, whose name he was surprised to see on a new
Sartre biography. Scrabble is popular as an evening activity at
Mount Haven Inn, given the lack of television. It annoys Mark
that he must get all his news from the radio and financial updates
from the *Wall Street Journal* which Michael Curran buys each
day. Michael drives into the village every morning to purchase
it, a journey which Mark supposes he welcomes because it gets
him away from Liane, his pushy, whining wife, and Cary, their
annoying son, a boy who trails after Donny like a small dog.

'I think young Michael welcomes the chance to get away
from the inn,' Mark observed to Wendy, the previous summer
as Michael pulled out of the driveway.

'You don't really like coming here either, do you?' Wendy
had countered gently and, as always, his softly spoken daughter-
in-law's perception surprised him.

The truth is that he is not a great fan of Mount Haven Inn,
which prides itself on its rustic simplicity. He would actually
prefer some elegance, some luxury. Still, he and Andrea have
vacationed there every summer since Adam's death. It is, after
all, so conveniently located, within miles of the Tudor home
where Andrea, with occasional assists from him and from

Smirnoff, had raised Adam. It was an arrangement that had suited them well enough during those years. It was Andrea's sanctuary, suited to her solitude and to her secret, their marriage's safe haven. That house, which Andrea will not enter, is now home to Wendy and Donny – Adam's widow and his son. Wendy sleeps in Andrea's bedroom and Donny has his father's boyhood room, the maple furniture unchanged, although Wendy has replaced the plaid curtains and bedspread with wooden shutters across which she painted fanciful birds and covered the bed with a brilliantly colored serape. She has an eye, he must admit, this odd girl whom his son married so suddenly.

Another advantage of the inn is that it is but a short drive to the cemetery where Adam is buried. It is also helpful that the same families return to the inn for the same August weeks, so that Donny has playmates and Wendy and Andrea renew casual and non-intrusive friendships.

So they travel across country each August, the month of Adam's birth, and of his death, to spend time with his widow and his son, to tend to his grave and to his memory. The limousine that will carry them to the airport pulls up in the driveway. The chauffeur honks lightly, discreetly, and Andrea glides toward him, her huge soft leather carry-on bag dangling from her shoulder, her make-up so smoothly applied that all lines of age and grief are concealed, although her gray eyes shimmer with a nacreous gleam. She is one of those women, always pleasant looking, who blossom into beauty as they age.

'All set?' she asks him and motions to the driver who obediently enters the house and carries their suitcases and, yes, the garment bag (she has remembered to hang his linen jackets correctly) into the car. It is remarkable, Mark thinks, how liquor never blurs her memory or her efficiency.

'All set,' he says.

'It will be fine,' she reassures him. 'The foliage in New Hampshire will just be beginning. You always love that.'

'Of course it will be fine,' he agrees.

They slide into the car and wave goodbye to Carlos and Rosa who stand in the doorway and wave back at them. Their leave-taking is complete; they are on their way.

*   *   *

Wendy Templeton packs very little for their stay at Mount Haven Inn. Three changes of clothing for herself, three changes of clothing for Donny – including, of course, those shirts and sweaters sent as gifts by Andrea, Donny's grandmother. Wendy has stopped thinking of Andrea as her mother-in-law – if there is no husband, can there be a mother-in-law? It is the sort of question that irritates her therapist, that very thin, very patient man with thinning corn-colored hair.

'That's not what you're really asking,' he might interject, if he interjected at all. And, of course, he is right, although the question she should be asking eludes her.

She cuts the tags off the two silk scarves Andrea sent for her birthday and the pale blue cashmere shawl that came at Christmas. Andrea has exquisite taste and her gifts to Wendy are well chosen, but Wendy has had neither the inclination nor the occasion to wear them.

She places them in her suitcase and wonders if she should add another sweater but decides against it. They will only be a few miles away and she will, of course, drive home now and again to collect additional clothing for herself and for Donny. That is what she has done in years past, welcoming the excuse to leave Mount Haven for a few hours, to escape Andrea's elegantly controlled sadness, Mark's carefully phrased questions, rephrased and repeated over and over through the days they spend together.

'Is Donny doing well at school?' Mark inevitably asks. He is already plotting his grandson's educational future just as he had plotted Adam's.

('I was Harvard-bound in the hospital nursery,' Adam had told her, his voice still edged with bitterness.)

'Does Donny have many friends?' Andrea will ask, as she does every year, her gray eyes focused on her needlepoint as though she fears to meet Wendy's gaze.

Wendy understands the grandmotherly concern that barely masks the unresolved maternal guilt. Andrea worries because Adam was a solitary child, because she did not do enough to relieve his isolation, because it was her choice to live in rural New Hampshire at a remove from a more appropriate environment for her only son. Andrea is a self-accuser, a woman who hugs her guilt both real and imagined. She should have arranged more sleepovers, more after-school activities.

Friends would have relieved the sadness that haunted her son for so much of his life. She has said all this to Wendy but never has she mentioned the real reason for the choice she and Mark made.

Wendy wants to assure her that it was not sadness that killed Adam, but she cannot because she and Andrea never talk about Adam. Donny is their focus, the live child who sleeps in his dead father's boyhood bedroom. Occasionally when Wendy tiptoes into that bedroom at night and looks down at her sleeping son, she imagines she can hear a hint of fading laughter, as though Adam, who so seldom laughed in life, laughs now to comfort her. The recurring thought is irrational, she knows. She has not even shared it with her therapist and she surely will not speak of it to Andrea.

Each year, as they sit side by side in their Adirondack chairs on the lawn of Mount Haven Inn, she assures Donny's grandmother that he is a popular child, that she does arrange play dates and sleepovers. There has been a great deal of development in their New Hampshire town since Adam's childhood and other children live within walking distance. He rides his bicycle with a pack of friends, text messages the two boys who share his passion for Harry Potter, and is always picked first for class teams. Donny is fine, just fine.

Wendy wanders into Donny's room now to check on his progress, to remind him that they want to reach Mount Haven Inn and settle into their rooms before his grandparents arrive from the Concord airport. She has already packed his clothing in the new khaki duffle bag (a gift from Andrea, of course) and he is filling his oversized backpack with the things he will bring with him to the inn. There is his current Harry Potter book, which he has already read twice despite the chapters that he did not understand. Paul Epstein will explain them to him as he has explained the other books in the series in summers past, his voice grave as he turned the pages and found the passages that confirmed his interpretations. Donny thinks Paul Epstein is the smartest person he knows, smarter than his English teacher, smarter than Peter and Denis, his best friends, the smartest kids in his class who, with Donny, have formed a club called the Potterites.

Donny is sorry that he only sees Paul during August, although this year he and his mother might accept Paul's mother's invitation to spend Thanksgiving with them in New York.

'We'll see,' Wendy had said softly, which sometimes means *yes*.

Donny stuffs his collection of action figures, the superheroes he used to call his 'guys', into his backpack. He is too old for them now, although he still plays with them occasionally. He will give some of them to Cary Curran and some to Matt Edwards, the two younger boys who trail after him, just as he trails after Paul. But he will give more to Cary than to Matt because Cary's mother is such a bitch. Donny will not say the word aloud (except to Paul who taught it to him) but he relishes thinking it.

'I need a rubber band for my Uno cards and a box for my markers,' he tells Wendy, who remains in the doorway watching him. He is not surprised when his mother hands him both items. He knows that he can rely on her to anticipate his needs.

'Put everything in your backpack,' she says. 'I'm going to start loading the car.' She carries her valise and Donny's duffle bag downstairs and goes to her studio to collect her collapsible easel, watercolor box, brush container and two oversized pads. She shoves everything into the trunk beside the large canvas bag which contains an anthology of modern poetry, the most recent 'Best American Short Stories' and two novels. It occurs to her that, like Donny, she has built a small arsenal against the onslaught of boredom.

The thought depresses her. Perhaps it is time to rethink this annual August odyssey. Adam has been dead for a decade. Time enough for Andrea and Mark to have come to terms with the loss; time enough for her to battle their insistence on this melancholy ritual of birthday and deathday observance. She did not need her therapist to point this out in his kindly, non-committal voice. Her sister and her friends have said as much and she knows them all to be right. It was generous of Mark and Andrea to offer her and Donny their home after Adam's death. She had not wanted to return to the Cambridge apartment she and Adam had shared, a nursery for Donny carved out of the room he called his studio, and she was not sure she could afford the rent. In turn, Andrea and Mark could not bear to live in the house that their son had called home. His voice lingered in every room, his shadow darkened every stairwell, every doorway.

And although Mark spent most of his time in New York, his short stays in New Hampshire during the fall and winters were difficult, especially 'the episode', as Andrea insists on calling his rather serious heart attack. California beckoned with its days of golden light, its orange trees heavy with sun-brushed fruit. They chose a house not far from the ocean, its rooms spacious, its garden a riot of color that receded into pools of shade cast by low-branched palms. They furnished it anew, all vestiges of the past banished. There is no memory of Adam in the sharply angled, white-walled home. Andrea selected Danish furniture in the palest of woods, upholstered in gay batik. Sheer draperies flutter at shimmering windows, and they awaken each morning to sea-scented air. They placed the silver-framed photo of Adam, his arm around Wendy who held Donny in her arms, on a low table in a recess of the living room. It is not in their field of vision when they sit in the living room or when they pass through on their way to the garden.

They deeded the New Hampshire house, fully furnished, to their son's wife and their grandson in a revocable trust. An arrangement was made for an allowance. It was a generous offer and one Wendy did not refuse. Nor did she refuse their request that they would all come together in August in the neutral setting of Mount Haven Inn. She would have agreed to anything during those first sorrow-seared days, and she was grateful, truly grateful for their generosity.

But now, at last, she herself is slowly, very slowly, struggling out of the web of grief. There have been new friends, pleasant men seated beside her by well-meaning hostesses at dinner parties. Some of them extended casual invitations which she did not accept. She did, however, go out to dinner twice with Kevin, a gentle widower, the father of one of Donny's classmates. After the second dinner she invited him in and, wordlessly, she led him upstairs to the master bedroom, to the huge double bed once shared by Mark and Andrea that she has made her own. They made love, slowly, sadly, as though adhering to the rhythm of their separate sorrows, each thrust beating back a memory.

It occurred to her after Kevin left, tiptoeing down the staircase with his shoes in his hands, that she had made love to another man on the very bed on which her dead husband had, in all probability, been conceived.

'A ludicrous thought,' she had confided to her therapist, pleased that she had something, at last, to tell him.

'Perhaps a healthy one,' he had responded quietly. 'Perhaps you are telling yourself that it's time to move out of the shadow of Adam's past, to tell his parents that you want your own furnishings, your own home, your own life.'

She wonders now if she will be able to say as much to Mark and Andrea and, with quiet honesty, acknowledges that it may not yet be possible. She remains too dependent on their approval, their support, too complicit in their grief.

'Donny,' she calls. 'It's time to go.'

It will take them an hour to drive to Mount Haven, an hour and a half if she drives very slowly, two hours if they stop for lunch. Which is what they will do, she decides suddenly.

Donny tosses his backpack into the car and she backs out of the driveway, on to the sun-spangled road. He looks back at the house but she does not turn her head. She is already focused on the weeks to come.

Nessa Epstein moves slowly through the appetizer section of the Fairway supermarket, crowded as all the supermarkets in New York's Upper West Side are mid-morning. She should be hurrying, she knows. Simon reminded her before she left the apartment that the trip to New Hampshire might take longer than usual because, as always, he has consulted a mysterious site on the internet which reports road conditions. Simon is a hoarder of time, scavenging minutes by avoiding traffic jams and lights, veering off the road if the voice on his GPS offers an alternative route. Minutes add up to hours, he reminds her, and hours add up to days. He is an economist who translates his professional skills into his daily life, determinedly multi-tasking, his phone at his ear, his eyes on his computer. Nessa wonders what he will do with the surplus hours he has accumulated. Perhaps they are entered into the credit column on some giant celestial ledger. Perhaps he will live forever. She smiles at the thought and always ignores his advice.

She herself neglects to make entries in the register of her checkbook, is often late for appointments (but never for work) and wanders the city at her own pace, even pausing now and again at a street corner to stare up at the sky, to revel in a sunset of muted colors, a cloud formation tinged with gold. She certainly will not rush through Fairway, not on a day like this when there is so much she must buy. Besides, it is her vacation and vacations mean that the demands of working life are vacated. She will take her time since Simon will, of course, leave before she returns with her purchases. It has long been their habit to drive to New Hampshire in separate cars, Simon in the small yellow sports car, newly washed and polished for the journey, its soft leather seats impeccable, its radio set to the FM station he favors, his hands-free phone checked and rechecked because he will make and receive at least five calls during his drive. She and Paul will drive north in her ancient van, the luggage that would not fit into the trunk piled on to the rear seat, Paul's CD player and his collection of discs precariously balanced on the oversized shopping bag in which she packed her sweaters because she could not find her large valise. It is Paul who arranged the luggage earlier that morning, sweeping the empty cardboard coffee containers and crumbled bags of chips off the front seat. He has already assumed a proprietary attitude toward the van which will become his own when he receives his driver's license. Nessa is relieved that he still has only a learner's permit. She is not eager to surrender her only son into adulthood.

Her cell phone rings as she stands before the display of olives. Simon reminds her to buy Stilton, to inform her that he is now leaving the apartment, to hope that she is almost done with her shopping, to caution her to drive safely.

'Yes. Fine. I will,' she says, putting a wrinkled Greek olive into her mouth and trying to remember if these are the olives that Paul favors. 'I love you,' she adds as she moves on to the huge green ones stuffed with pimento that Simon prefers, but he has already hung up. She shrugs and fills the largest of the plastic containers to the brim.

'Shopping for a party, Nessa?'

It is the mother of one of her nursery-school students who asks the question. Nessa struggles to remember her name and, when she fails, she compensates by smiling brightly and remarking on the beauty of the infant, strapped to the young mother's chest, a weeping appendage whose wails are muffled by the Baby Bjorn.

'No. Not a party. Just food for our vacation.'

'You're going camping?' There is envy and admiration in her voice. She too would love to go camping but her children are too young, her husband too reluctant. Lucky Nessa Epstein to be so free and so daring, to have such an accommodating husband.

Like many of the mothers whose children attend the Magic Mountain Nursery School she is in awe of Nessa Epstein, its founder and director. All the mothers know that Nessa is so marvelous with their children, magically coaxing forth hidden talents, gentling a raging boy into smiling calm. The children's books she writes are whimsical and unpredictable, sweet messages hidden in unlikely stories of skunks and spiders. The mothers buy them for their children, shyly ask Nessa for her autograph and send them as gifts to nieces and nephews, proudly confiding that they know the author and she is just marvelous. Even Nessa's appearance intrigues them. Her auburn hair is almost always in disarray, her color high although she wears no make-up and her nails are painted in wild hues – sometimes in varying shades, her thumbnails mauve, her middle fingers scarlet, which they take to be a mark of her daring, her wild courage. She is a large woman, comfortable with her height and her girth. Rainbow-colored skirts flare about her ample hips, her oversized shirts of rough and colorful weave hang loosely, offset by glittering beads which delight the children who grasp them with sticky, paint-smeared fingers. The toddlers, whom she calls her magic mountaineers, do not cry when she playfully brushes their small hands away.

The mothers envy her because she is no longer burdened with maternal servitude. She has graduated from the years of temper tantrums and insistent whining, of endless laundry and pureed food that still hold them prisoner. Nessa's son, Paul, is an adolescent, a tall and talented boy who sometimes comes to the school to play his guitar at a holiday celebration, and her stepchildren, Tracy and Richie, are away at college.

Simon, her husband, who sometimes waits outside the school building for her in his bright yellow sports car, is a grave-eyed man, his well-trimmed beard threaded with the silver strands that also weave their way through his thick dark hair, expertly layered by an expensive barber. Unlike Nessa, he is always impeccably dressed, his clothing the uniform of the upscale academic, tweed suits with leather patches at the elbows, dark shirts, woven ties, cable-stitched sweaters. The mothers have traded scraps of information about him. Nessa is his second wife. An unlikely match considering that his first wife, Charlotte something (not Epstein, of course) is the editor of a high-end fashion magazine.

They know that he is the chairman of the economics department at the university to the north of the city and that he is quoted now and again in the Business section of *The Times*. He has even appeared on the PBS Evening News, offering learned advice on the ups and downs of the stock market. He, like Nessa, is much admired.

The young mother in the cheese aisle of Fairway, her baby happily and stickily asleep against her chest, has often thought that Simon Epstein is the sort of man she should have married, a successful intellectual who is also rugged enough to enjoy hiking and camping.

'No, we're not going camping.'

Nessa laughs at the thought as they move on through the cheese section. Simon could not put up a tent if his life depended on it. She tosses a brick of cheddar, a loaf of Feta and a package of Muenster cheese into her wagon and searches for the Stilton, remembering Simon's monitory call.

'We go to this small hotel in New Hampshire every August, a wonderful place but kind of spartan. No air conditioning, no television, three meals a day – nourishing, of course, and boring. Still, they give us a shelf in the refrigerator and I bring nosh stuff for our family.'

'Oh. I see.'

The young mother is disappointed. She would have expected Nessa Epstein to plan a more daring or exotic vacation than a small hotel in New Hampshire that offers only plain cooking.

'Have fun,' she adds as she moves on, her envy dissipated.

Nessa heads for the appetizer counter and places her order of white fish, lox and pickled herring. She remembers to include the olive tapenade and bruschetta that her stepchildren Richie and Tracy favor. Simon will be pleased with her selection. He will, as he has done every year during his older children's visits, arrange the delicacies on the large plate that he cajoles from Louise Abbot, the inn's proprietress, who disapproves of their cocktail hour picnics on the lawn. Her in-laws, the first Mount Haven innkeepers, had also disapproved of the pre-dinner drinks Simon's parents had set out each afternoon.

Simon's family is the second generation of Epsteins to vacation at Mount Haven and Louise Abbot is grateful for his loyalty. Fewer and fewer vacationers are drawn to the very basic accommodations of the inn.

Simon will set the food on the small wooden table in the center of a circle of Adirondack chairs, adding it to the bottles of Aquavit and vodka and the wicker basket that contains their cocktail glasses and small plates, the tiny silver spoons and the long stirrers.

Nessa will not participate in these arrangements. The wicker basket, a wedding gift to Simon and Charlotte, which he carried into his second marriage, seems pretentious to her but she does not criticize it. It makes Simon happy and it has become part of their Mount Haven ritual. It has long been their tacit agreement to accept each other's small conceits. Those who find Nessa and Simon an unlikely match, which of course they are, do not understand that their very differences, and their acceptance of those differences, are the glue that cements their marriage.

Her shopping completed, Nessa returns home. Paul is waiting for her, his guitar slung over his shoulder. His denim shorts are ragged at the seams, his T-shirt, once orange, faded to an odd shade of rust, oversized and frayed at the neck. Unlaced sneakers cover his bare feet. She thinks to tell him to put socks on but does not.

'You didn't bring your guitar last year,' she says instead.

'I wasn't as into it last year,' he replies. 'I want to teach some chords to Donny Templeton and I got an email from Annette. She's bringing her mandolin and I thought that maybe we could work up some duets.'

'Good idea.'

Nessa likes Annette Edwards, who has, through their many shared Augusts, blossomed from small girl awkwardness into a strangely confident adolescence. Sweet-faced, lithe and narrow waisted, with silvery blonde hair falling loosely to her shoulders, she speaks so softly that her listeners must bend closely toward her in order to discern her words. Nessa had seen Paul's head lowered as she spoke, his auburn hair brushing Annette's pale cheek. She had watched them walk together down a mountain path, kicking stray acorns, and then suddenly break into a run, two teenaged children, racing their way out of childhood. Their friendship, vested with innocence, survives through the winter months with email and phone calls. But Nessa knows that it will soon be more than a friendship. Perhaps during this very August. Hormonal juices are flowing. She prays silently that they will not hurt each other, her gentle son and slender, wispy-voiced Annette. Annette's twin brother Jeremy, as dark and muscular as she is fair and fragile, does not like Paul. She senses something ominous in Jeremy's hostility but, immediately, she dismisses the thought. It has been a long winter. Perhaps Jeremy has changed. Perhaps they have all changed.

'We'd better get started,' Paul says. 'Dad left like an hour ago.'

'I think he's going to stop at Camp Kenakee, to see Tracy and Richie,' she replies as she places her purchases in the battered cooler.

The children of his first marriage are another subject on which she and Simon have tacit agreement. They do not discuss them although Tracy and Richie drift through their lives at will. They are very much Charlotte's children, blonde and fine-boned like their mother, always at the head of the class, effortlessly leading the pack in any race they choose to run. Richie is a junior at Harvard, Tracy a sophomore at Swarthmore. Dean's List, of course, high achievers, children of divorce equipped for battle. They each have a bedroom in the West End Avenue apartment, keys to the front door, foraging rights to the refrigerator and, although they are cool to Nessa, they are always polite. Their warmth against all odds is reserved for Paul, whom they treat as younger brother, younger friend.

Nessa is grateful to them for that. It ensures that Paul, an only child, will never be alone in the world. As she is without Simon. As Simon is without her.

'Yeah, I forgot,' Paul says. 'Tracy and Richie are going to come up to the inn, aren't they?'

'They always do.'

She does not add that the camp was chosen because of its proximity to the inn. Chosen originally by Charlotte, when Tracy and Richie were campers and she and Simon, a married couple then, vacationed at the inn. Simon is pleased that they have chosen to return to the camp as counselors. It gives them time together, time with Paul. They are, however briefly, a family. Nessa does not resent his pleasure although she tends to go off on her own when they visit. Long walks with Susan and Helene, the sisters who are so unlike each other. Perhaps she will plan a trip into Portsmouth with Wendy Templeton or even a solitary drive into the White Mountains.

'OK. Let's go.'

Paul is impatient to get started, impatient to see Annette Edwards again. He wonders if she will kiss him on the cheek in welcome as she did last summer. He remembers still the butterfly brush of her lips against his skin.

'We're off,' Nessa agrees.

She arms the alarm system and then they are out the door, which she double locks behind them. She remembers that there are no locks on the doors at Mount Haven Inn and the thought cheers her. How wonderful it will be to fall asleep beside Simon in their unlocked, white-walled bedroom and waken at dawn as the first rays of sunlight brush the mountain's foothills. She and Paul smile at each other and dash to the car. They are eager for the journey to begin, and eager for the journey to end.

Liane Curran has packed the night before their departure for Mount Haven Inn, hoping to get an early start so that they can claim one of the better suites that overlook the lawn. Louise Abbot, that sour-faced bitch who barely looks at Liane when she speaks to her, always maintains that she assigns the rooms on a first-arrival basis, but Liane does not believe her. The Abbots, Louise and Evan, clearly have favorites. They are certainly partial to the Templetons, the money dripping oldsters, their wraith of a daughter-in-law, Wendy and her weirdo son, Donny. The Templetons are never denied the suite of rooms on the second floor, with the remodeled bathrooms. And those Epsteins always arrive early, grabbing the room with French doors that open to the wraparound porch that Liane would have preferred. But of course people like Simon and Nessa Epstein know how to manipulate their way through life. Their kind always does. Pushy New Yorkers, both of them.

But now of course they will not get an early start. Michael has screwed up again, regardless of his promise that they would be on the road right after breakfast. He left for his office early and promised to return within the hour but then he had called, his voice quivering with apology. A client, his major client actually, was in Boston for the day and had insisted on meeting with him that morning. There was no way he could say no. He needed the account.

'And I need to get the hell out of here,' Liane had retorted. 'What am I supposed to do with Cary all morning?'

She did not expect Michael to offer any suggestions. Does he even know that their ten-year-old son is not a kid who has to be amused, thank God. Cary has his books, his computer, his email correspondence with other Harry Potter geeks like Donny Templeton, Matt Edwards and Paul Epstein, their summer friendships resuscitated throughout the winter months by their internet lifeline. It bothers Liane that Paul, who is almost ready for college, spends so much time with the younger kids. He seems different to other kids his age, but that doesn't come as a shock to her given who his parents are and New York and all that.

She is not surprised that Michael never mentioned it. Her husband moves like a zombie through their home, through their marriage, through Cary's life. The confident young man she had married, the man who promised her the house of her dreams, European vacations, charge accounts in Neiman Marcus and Nordstroms, has morphed into a stoop-shouldered worrywart who checks their credit card bill, questioning her about every item. Only last night as he paid bills, he had asked, in that tired, whining voice that really, really annoys her, if Cary needed all the new shorts and shirts she had bought for their Mount Haven stay, and why she needed two new bathing suits and the outfits she had purchased for herself.

'If I bought them we needed them,' she had replied irritably and watched as he wrote out the check.

She fingers the new clothing in the neatly packed suitcases, Cary's T-shirts with fashionable logos and his shorts with cargo pockets like the ones that Matt Edwards and Donny Templeton wore last summer. She unpacks and repacks her own new skirt of pale blue polished cotton and the sleeveless top the color of sunlight that the saleswoman at Nordstroms had insisted was just made for her, given her golden hair and blue eyes. The feel of the fabric comforts her. This year she will be as well dressed as snobby Susan Edwards and mousey Wendy Templeton whom everyone is supposed to pity because her husband had died so tragically. Liane reflects that Wendy, who is widowed, lives a whole lot better than her own family. Of course, she has those posh in-laws and Helene, snotty Susan's weird bohemian sister, who is an art teacher herself, told her that Wendy sells those wishy-washy watercolors of hers to collectors all over the country. All right. It is sad that Wendy's husband died so young and Donny, who is really a sweet kid, was left fatherless. And Susan and her sister can be really friendly, Liane can admit that. But she had never imagined when she married Michael that their vacations would consist of two weeks in a New Hampshire hotel that had seen better days.

So much for all Michael's promises that their life together would be nothing like her lousy childhood in that crummy Natick apartment, the hallway rank with the odors of other tenants' cooking, her parents' stale and angry arguments echoing through the tiny cluttered rooms. And she had believed him because she was a file clerk in the office where he was a department head. She ate lunch in a cubicle with two other girls while he worked at a large desk behind a closed door. He had gone to college, his framed Boston University diploma hung above his desk, and he wore dark suits and silk ties and shirts as white as newly fallen snow. She remembered how he had fingered the flimsy sheer white collar of her pale blue nylon dress the night he asked her to marry him. 'I'll dress you like a princess,' he had said, and of course she had believed him. She had been stupid to believe him, stupid to encourage him to start his own software firm, stupid to agree to the purchase of this house which is nothing more than a cracker box. True, it isn't a crowded apartment, but it isn't a palace either. She has been told that Wendy, the poor widow who is not poor at all, lives in a huge house, mortgage-free and fully furnished, a gift from her dead husband's parents.

Cary wanders into the room, his new sneakers untied, his blue and white shirt unevenly buttoned and hanging half in and half out of the waistband of his new navy shorts. His large eyes are red rimmed, his dark hair is an unbrushed knotted tangle and his long thin face is pale. The urban day camp he attended hadn't emphasized outdoor play. Well, he'd get enough of that at Mount Haven Inn. No television, no air conditioning, but fresh air and sunlight are always in plentiful supply, Liane reflects bitterly.

'When's Dad coming?' Cary asks petulantly, wandering to the window.

'Who knows?' she replies. She snaps the valises shut. The new clothes are no longer a source of comfort to her. Rather they are a reminder of all that she does not have, of all that she craves.

'Here he is now. He's just driving up to the house.' Cary's voice is no longer petulant. It throbs with excitement and he dashes down the stairs and throws the front door open.

'Dad!' he shouts. 'Are you ready? Can we get started? Did you get the quarters?'

Michael smiles wanly up at him. His shirt is still as white as newly fallen snow, but the collar is wilted. He has loosened his gray silk tie. Sweat trails down the back of his neck and his back aches from the hours spent staring at the computer screen, writing and rewriting the damn program until it worked.

'I have the quarters,' he says and hands Cary the roll of coins.

Quarters are the currency of popularity for the August kids at Mount Haven who feed them to the pinball machines with wild excitement.

'Gee, Dad, thanks,' Cary says. 'So we can load everything into the car?' He is anxious for the summer adventure to begin, anxious to reconnect with his friends.

'Just give me a chance to change.'

Slowly, very slowly, Michael walks upstairs, reluctant to confront Liane's annoyance, her barely disguised contempt.

'How did it go?' she asks as he enters the room. Her question is indifferent and she does not turn from the mirror. He watches as she carefully applies her make-up. She reminds him, as always, of a doll, a pretty painted doll, a doll that had caused his hands to tremble and his heart to turn the very first time he saw her. He had despaired then of enticing her. Blue-eyed, golden-haired girls with narrow waists and plump luminous cheeks were rarely drawn to men like himself, men who were short and narrow chinned, who squinted at the world from behind thick-lensed glasses. But Liane had surprised him. Yes to the first date, yes to the second, yes to his hands moving across her smooth skin, yes to his lips pressed against hers. Her acceptance had bewildered him then but soon, very soon, he came to understand it.

He moves toward her now but she evades his reach and busies herself at the window, slamming it shut and drawing the blinds so that sunlight will not fade the mauve carpet and the matching upholstery of the chaise lounge on which she has never reclined and for which he has not yet paid.

'It went all right,' he says, relieved that it is the truth, that he was able to debug the program that was the source of his client's irritation and thus retain the account. He is safe for another month and that month will give him time to consult with Simon Epstein and perhaps with Mark Templeton during their stay at Mount Haven. His new software is good, really good. He just needs some capital to launch it. Mark Templeton will recognize its potential. He is a clever investor and Michael's project interests him. He had offered some valuable advice the previous year, even suggested contacts.

It has occurred to Michael that the retired financier might help secure the venture capital he needs to keep his fledgling software business alive. He is dancing perilously close to the edge, barely meeting his overheads, borrowing from one credit card to pay the balance on another. Too often he wakes in the night, drenched in sweat, and wonders why he left the firm where his job had been secure, his health insurance covered, bonuses, however modest, paid into his account at the end of each year. But of course he knows why. A salaried man, even a department head, at a small firm, could not earn the kind of money he needed to fulfill all the promises he had made to Liane before they married. Those promises – the trip to Europe, the great house – were the insurance he had vested in his marriage and that policy is slowly coming due. He wonders what Liane would say if she knew that he will barely be able to pay the bill at the inn. Of course he knows. If he fails, really fails, she will leave him. That knowledge settles like a hard rock at the pit of his heart. And will she take Cary? he wonders. He shivers at the thought and pulls on his khakis, which fit too loosely because he has lost weight during the year. He shrugs into an old soft blue cotton shirt, laces up his sneakers, grabs the valises and hurries downstairs.

'Into the car,' he calls to Cary. 'We're off.'

'This is going to be a great vacation,' he tells Liane as she slides into the passenger seat. She is wearing a new perfume. He savors the scent, then wonders how much it cost. The car fills with the clink of coins as Cary drops the quarters one by one into his leather change purse.

'Let's hope so.' Her voice is tight and she does not look at him, but keeps her gaze fixed on the road ahead.

'Liane.' Her name upon his tongue is a plea, a prayer.

She turns to him and her eyes soften. He really is such a good guy. She has to remember that. She should remember that. She places her hand lightly on his.

The unexpected gesture lifts the heaviness from his heart. He will seek Mark Templeton out as soon as possible. All he needs is a new injection of cash, some time. Everything is salvageable. His marriage, his business. He lifts Liane's hand to his lips and she does not turn away.

'OK. A great vacation,' she says as he maneuvers the car on to the highway that will carry them northward to Mount Haven Inn.

Daniel Goldner washes his Harley motorbike early in the morning, although he had been determined to leave for New Hampshire at sunrise. The delay does not disturb him. Why shouldn't he change his mind? His time is his own for the first time in years and he revels in that bittersweet freedom. He concentrates on scraping away the scabs of sand that adhere to the bike's silver trim. It is not that they will corrode the metal but he does not want any reminder of that last weekend in the Hamptons. He rubs vigorously, his eyes squeezed shut against the memory of Laura kicking viciously at the small hillocks of sand with her bare feet, indifferent to the storm of pale grains that adhered to the cycle and pelted his own outstretched hands.

He wipes the metal dry and polishes the handlebars and the hubcaps, grimacing at his own reflection, his too narrow face unshaven, his pale green eyes watery. It occurs to him that he might grow a beard again. He had been fond of his silken chestnut-colored goatee, accustomed to curling it about his fingers as he lectured, but Laura had disliked it, claiming that it irritated her skin, that it was an affectation. He had reluctantly shaved it off. The thought of allowing it to grow again is vaguely comforting. He no longer has to worry about pleasing a wife who would not be pleased.

He packs his panniers, shoving his windbreaker, his toilet kit, a long-sleeved shirt and the heavy sweater Laura had bought him as a surprise during their Nova Scotia honeymoon, into the soft leather bags. August nights are cool in New Hampshire and the rooms at Mount Haven Inn are not well heated. That was another thing Laura had complained of during the few vacations they had spent there, although that had been the last and the least of her litany of complaints.

The phone rings as he goes back into the house. He glances at the caller ID. It is Laura, of course. He considers not picking up but allows it to ring three times and then answers it, as he had known he would.

'Daniel.' Her voice is uncharacteristically hesitant, and he imagines her crouched on the futon in the barely furnished studio she had rented on the Upper West Side, clutching the receiver, probably wearing her leotard because she will be just leaving for her early-morning class. Ridiculously, he wonders if she is wearing the pale blue leotard or the black one that hugs her small well-shaped breasts and he chides himself for the absurdity of the thought.

'What is it, Laura?' he asks, struggling to keep his tone cool. 'I'm just about to leave.'

'I wanted to know if I could come by the house to pick up my jewelry box. You know the teak one that was my mother's? It's on the top shelf of the bedroom closet and I forgot it when I moved my stuff.'

He thinks, with a sudden surge of hope, that she might have left it there so that she would have an excuse to come by, but almost instantly he realizes that that is not Laura's way. She is incapable of that kind of calculation. She is motivated by impulse, rarely considering consequences. Which is why they are where they are on this August morning. She had simply forgotten it. Forgetfulness and carelessness are in her DNA.

'You have your key,' he replies drily, relieved now that he did not follow his brother Leo's advice and ask her for the key back. Leo views the world through the prism of his legal training. Every divorce is a battlefield, he had told Daniel, and keys are powerful weapons. 'Come in and get it. Whenever you want. I'll be away for a couple of weeks.'

'Where are you going?'

She is more composed now, her voice steady. He has acquiesced and she no longer fears his refusal.

'Up to Mount Haven Inn. On the bike.'

'Why?'

He hears the hint of incredulity in her question and his face grows hot, the familiar unforgotten reaction to her derision.

'Because I always liked it there. You didn't but I did.'

'But it's August. Probably that same crowd will be back. All those cozy families off to go blueberry picking with the kids or packing up for picnics in the White Mountains. Deadly. And you'll be alone.'

Her voice trails off. The impact of her words has shamed her. He will be alone because he is no longer with her and he is no longer with her because she has made it impossible for them to be together.

'Not deadly,' he responds flatly. 'And I don't mind being alone. I'll be reading the proofs of my novel. Pick up your jewelry box whenever you want.'

He hangs up, angry at himself for reacting so defensively,

angry at her for passing judgment when she has rescinded all right to pass judgment on him, on his life, on the choices that no longer affect her.

He thinks of her words as he locks the house, as he mounts the motorbike and speeds northward, the helmet heavy on his head, the sun so bright that he stops to put on his goggles.

'The same crowd,' she had said so dismissively when he, in fact, is looking forward to seeing that crowd. He has missed them during the years he deferred to Laura who insisted on beach vacations, the Hamptons, the Cape, even one very long August on the Jersey shore where she had been invited to teach a dance workshop. The rush of the ocean distracts him, cascades noisily against his thoughts. Plot lines evade him as waves crash across the jetties and he hates the grit of the sand, the oozing dampness at the water's edge where Laura insisted that they walk at sundown, she dancing always ahead of him, pirouetting and bowing to the foam-crested surge of salt-scented water.

It is mountain country that soothes him, shadowed glens and meadows, clear and quiet lakes, trails ascending to windswept summits and thick-leafed trees, their branches arching skyward. He had followed those trails as a boy, he and Simon Epstein, both of them the only sons of school-teacher parents who vacationed together every August, bonded by their love of the landscape, the rugged simplicity of the inn and gratitude to the elderly Abbots who, unlike other New England resorts, accepted reservations from families named Goldner and Epstein.

Those Abbots, the original innkeepers, had died years ago, as had his own parents and Simon's, but the inn is managed, with very few changes, by their son Evan and his wife Louise. Simon and Daniel, loyal to memory, mindful of history, continued to vacation there. Simon, early on, with his first wife, Charlotte, whom Daniel had never liked, and later with his second wife, Nessa, whom Daniel admires enormously. But Laura, although she joined him a few times during the early and more conciliatory years of their marriage, had disliked the inn, had disliked what she called the forced camaraderie of the veteran August vacationers, had resented the journey to Portsmouth to attend the nearest dance studio that offered practice space. In the end Daniel submitted to her discontent. It is some years since he has been a guest at Mount Haven Inn, but Louise Abbot had assured him when he phoned that she had a room for him.

'On the same corridor as the Epsteins,' she had added, an unusual addenda from a New Hampshire woman who was frugal in all things, including conversation. But then she had always been partial to Daniel, oddly deferential and protective, perhaps recalling his own kindness to her during that difficult summer when the future she had planned came crashing down upon her.

He wonders, as he crosses the Massachusetts border, who else will be there. Surely the Edwards family, because when he met Susan Edwards at a Modern Language Association meeting she had told him they had already made their reservations. And Susan's sister Helene and her husband Greg would also be guests. Daniel loves Greg's music, the gentleness of his singing voice. He remembers how Wendy, that waif-like, frail young woman who was surely too young to be a widow, had lifted her sweet voice in a sudden unexpected harmony as they sang 'Foggy Foggy Dew.' The lyrics flooded back to him and he gave them full voice, singing them out into the wind.

'Now I am a bachelor, I live with my son, we work at the weaver's trade.'

His spirits lift. It is a long time since he has been surrounded by familiar faces, since he has sung the songs of his youth. Laura was wrong. He will be neither alone nor lonely. There is nothing strange about his decision to spend these particular August weeks in New Hampshire. He is simply reclaiming his past, girding himself to face a future newly uncertain.

He leans closer to the handlebars, floors the accelerator, eager for the journey to be over, eager to arrive at Mount Haven Inn.

Louise Abbot checks the inn's register and glances nervously at her watch. Her brown hair is pulled back from her avian face in an austere knot, and an oversized white butcher's apron covers her well-pressed black linen dress. Bought on sale in Portsmouth during the early spring, the dress, with its white collar and cuffs, now hangs too loosely. She has, unwillingly, lost too much weight over the past several weeks. The summer so far has been a difficult one. The July guests had been overly demanding and the chambermaids and waitresses, indifferent to the menial jobs they had taken simply to fill the weeks between school terms, had been unreliable and inefficient. Only Polly, pretty Polly – too pretty for her own good, thinks Louise, who once was too pretty herself – has been a consistently hard worker, arriving early and staying late. Polly is an honor student, improbably and, perhaps impossibly, pre-med working her way through the state university. Louise wonders how Polly imagines she will ever be able to put herself through medical school, but she has little time to ponder Polly's problems.

Throughout the summer, she has had to run up and down the stairs, replenishing towels and soap. She had even changed light bulbs herself, perilously balanced on a rickety ladder when Evan seemed to have vanished, a not unusual occurrence. More than once she has had to strip the beds and get a room ready for new arrivals because one of the girls called with a lame excuse or simply did not bother to show up.

She had never taken such liberties during the long summers of her high-school years when she worked at the inn. She had considered herself lucky to have a job, to collect her pay envelope each week with her name, Louise Wallace then, neatly printed in Joseph Abbot's fine hand. Evan's parents had always paid her in cash, had always factored in any overtime. They were fair and more than fair. She had never resented working for them and had even felt a frisson of pride to bike up the inn's wide circular driveway and slip on her blue and white checked gingham uniform, the stiff fabric always smelling of Clorox.

Mount Haven Inn had been a refuge, a world at a remove from the shabby farmhouse where her mother sat gloomily at a kitchen table littered with crumbs and unwashed dishes, turning the pages of grease-stained magazines, and her father slammed doors as he rushed in and out, now grabbing a beer, now cursing because a cow was sick, or because his combine needed repairing. He reeked of sweat and bitterness. Because he never bothered to wipe his boots, the faded linoleum was streaked with manure until Louise wiped it up but the smell permeated the house, mingling with the sour odors of her mother's cooking.

At Mount Haven, simple and functional though it was, everything was spotless.

Fresh flowers filled the vases, the fragrance of freshly baked bread and simmering stews wafted from the kitchen to the reception area. Floors were washed before the first guest stirred in the morning. Louise would scurry through her work in those days, listening to the cadence of Prudence Abbot's voice and imitating it softly as she ran the vacuum cleaner or pushed the broom. She had carried dishes into the dining room and lingered at each table, straightening a saltshaker, filling a water glass as she listened to the guests' conversations. They spoke of books they had read, plays they had seen, a much-anticipated concert. The Goldners and the Epsteins, schoolteachers from New York, discussed integration, civil rights. Their sons, Daniel and Simon, lanky college students, slyly and affectionately imitated their parents, now and again winking at Louise, inviting her complicity. She always smiled back, shyly, tentatively.

And in the evening, when Louise had finished helping with the dishes, there was Evan, the Abbots' son and Louise's high-school classmate, waiting for her. His own chores were done, croquet mallets and balls in place, the vast lawn mowed, the battered rowboats and unpainted canoes tethered to the dock. At day's end his dark hair was damp and his sun-tanned face aglow. He stood beside his bike which leaned against her own. Side by side, they rode through the town in the soft evening air, pausing always in the wild meadow near the cemetery where the grass grew high before they reached her parents' farm. There, Evan removed a thin blanket from his bicycle basket and they lay down beneath the huge oak that obscured them from view. His hands were gentle upon her skin, his lips soft and sweet against her mouth. Leaves danced overhead as their bodies moved toward each other.

Later they talked, spoke mockingly of the guests whom they both actually admired, traded plans for their separate futures. The year of their high-school graduation, they realized that this would be their last summer together. Louise had saved her money and enrolled in an evening secretarial course in Portsmouth. During the day she would be salesgirl in the Five and Dime store, a job she had been promised by a friend of her aunt's. She would perhaps work there for a year and then move to Boston. She had heard that a pretty girl with office skills could get a really good job in a classy office. And she *was* pretty, long-legged and slender, her light-brown hair falling in silken folds about her heart-shaped face. Evan was Dartmouth-bound, a tall handsome boy at the top of their high-school graduating class. His father wanted him to be a lawyer, his mother wanted him to be a doctor, but all he wanted to do was read and read and read.

'I'd be happy just sitting in a library for the rest of my life,' he told Louise, who nodded in understanding. He would change his mind, of course, but that would never be her problem.

When autumn came they would say goodbye and embark on their separate futures.

And then, suddenly, their futures were not separate at all. She missed one period and then another. Her breasts swelled and the doctor in Portsmouth, to whom she gave a false name, confirmed her worst fear. She was pregnant. They were going to be parents, Louise Wallace and Evan Abbot, two months out of high school. Her parents were enraged. The Abbots were pale with shock but quietly quiescent. They knew where their duty lay. Disappointment was not alien to them. Their son would, of course, do the right thing. He would stand by Louise and so would they.

Evan and Louise were married at the inn, late in October, after the last of the guests who checked in to admire the foliage departed and before the hunters and the skiers began to arrive. Louise understood then that her life would always conform to the seasons of the inn. Her parents did not come to the wedding. They sold the farm to a developer and moved south, never giving her their new address. Evan enrolled at the University of New Hampshire, praised its library and commandeered a prize carrel in the stacks. In the end their baby was stillborn. Perhaps he could have then gone to Dartmouth and perhaps she could have retrieved her Portsmouth/Boston agenda, but neither of them made a move. They were married; all past plans were forfeit.

Evan retreated into his books. He had realized his dream. He could and would read for the rest of his life. Year after year, he selected courses randomly, studying for his own pleasure. Louise learned then that he did everything for his own pleasure. He had neither academic or professional goals, and nor did he require any. The inn was his birthright. It would be his home forever. Just as his parents had managed it, doling out his allowance, so Louise would manage it, doling out whatever money he might need. Her ideas for the inn's betterment did not interest him although he listened patiently as she suggested possible changes, new upholstery for the lounge, a ping pong table, pinball machines to amuse the children and bring in extra revenue. Quarters added up.

Her ideas pleased his parents, with whom she had forged an affectionate closeness.

They appreciated her interest in the inn. It compensated for their son's indifference. Prudence taught her the intricacies of the business, the ordering of food, the laundering of linens, the mysteries of billing, of juggling reservations and dealing with staff. Joseph Abbot gave her a book entitled *The Hospitality Profession.*

'We are more than innkeepers,' he said. 'We are hosts. And like all good hosts we value and welcome our guests, regardless of race, color or creed.'

He was a serious church-going man who read deeply and translated his thoughts into action. Alone among the innkeepers in that part of New Hampshire, he and Prudence judged their guests only on their proper behavior and their ability to pay. Louise Abbot understood him to be saying that Negroes and Jews would never be denied reservations at Mount Haven Inn and she accepted his words as a mandate.

'You see, it's all worked out for the best,' Prudence told Louise one day. 'Evan would never have been able to manage the inn on his own. He's simply not interested. And you catch on so quickly. And you care. I recognized that when I hired you.'

Louise nodded, although she knew that when Prudence hired her to wait tables and clean bedrooms, she could not have anticipated that she would marry her son or that she would hold Louise's hand as she suffered one miscarriage after another. She could not have foreseen that Louise would, one day, shorten the skirts of her own dark dresses, pin Prudence's brooch to collars bleached to a snowy whiteness, tie her hair back and stand behind the reservations desk smiling her welcome at incoming guests.

Prudence Abbot died of pancreatic cancer a week after Evan graduated from the University of New Hampshire. At the end of that summer Joseph Abbot suffered a heart attack as he sat at his desk neatly writing his employees' names on the envelopes that contained their wages. Evan and Louise Abbot were the new owner/proprietors of Mount Haven Inn. With great foresight Evan's parents had made certain that he and Louise inherited jointly.

But it is, of course, Louise who manages the inn, darting from the reception desk to her small office, dashing to the kitchen and racing upstairs to see to the bedrooms. Evan does exactly the same chores that he had done as a boy; he mows the lawn, keeps track of the sports equipment, smiles engagingly at the guests and then disappears with a book. Dartmouth had been denied him but he remains a perennial student. He earned his bachelors at the University of New Hampshire and then a masters in economics and another masters in philosophy. He thinks of studying linguistics, perhaps learning Arabic. He is a swimmer, afloat on a sea of learning with neither the need nor the intention to come ashore.

Louise, small wrinkles carving their way about her eyes and at the corners of her mouth, her feet fitted for orthopedic shoes even before she reached middle age, has accommodated herself to the role thrust upon her during that summer of carelessness. She accepts reservations, assigns rooms, consults with the kitchen staff about the menu, the seating in the dining room. It is Louise who will greet the August guests due to arrive that day. It pleases her that they are, almost all of them, regulars who have been coming to Mount Haven Inn since the days when Prudence and Joseph stood in the doorway to welcome them. She is especially pleased that after an absence of some years, Daniel Goldner is returning. Without his wife, which also pleases her. Laura Goldner had never wiped the mud off her feet when she entered the inn, had never thanked a waitress or a chambermaid, had stayed in her room when the other guests socialized on the lawn. She may be a good dancer – Nessa Epstein had shown Louise a glowing article about her in a magazine – but she had not been a good guest and Louise doubts that she is a good wife to Daniel. Not that it is any of her business, although she admits that she has always had a soft spot for Daniel. He had taken time out each summer to walk with her, to listen to her modest ambition, to speak of his own determination to become a writer. He had understood that something had gone terribly wrong during those last August weeks of her too swiftly abbreviated girlhood and when he heard of her marriage to Evan, he wrote a sweet note which she placed in the album that contains too few such notes. Really, he deserved a better wife than a woman who seldom smiled and spent a great deal of time looking in the mirror. Louise shakes her head in self-admonishment. She has no business speculating about someone else's marriage.

She glances again at her watch and wonders which of the August contingent will be the first to arrive. She ticks off their names, checks them again against her register. The Templetons to whom she has assigned the adjoining suites; the Edwardses who requested a larger room this year for their children; Helene and Greg always content with the cheapest room without a private bathroom; the Epsteins who need an extra parking space for their cars; the Currans who are always so late to pay, and, of course, Daniel Goldner. Poor Daniel.

She sighs and goes to the door, opening it just as the Edwards' car pulls up. Hastily, she removes the white apron and sets her lips in a thin smile.

'We're here!' Susan Edwards calls to her as she opens the door of the car.

Louise Abbot nods. She repeats the words Prudence Abbot had murmured to each new arrival, words she has made her own.

'Welcome to Mount Haven Inn,' she says and walks slowly down the steps, her hand extended.

TWO

Polly Syms watches the arrival of the Edwards family from the kitchen window. She braces herself, anticipating the hiss of Louise Abbot's voice, alert to the rapid clack of her employer's steel-capped shoes against the hard wood of the reception area. She has often thought that Louise should be advised to wear sneakers so that she might better take her staff by surprise, but it won't be Polly Syms who tells her that. She needs this job which she has, by some miracle, held for three years and she is going to need it every summer until she finishes college. Two more years. Six more months. Twenty-four more weeks. The count soothes her and she summons a smile when Louise taps her way into the kitchen and shrilly calls her name.

'Polly. Guests are here. Get out there and help them with the luggage,' Louise commands.

Polly nods, knowing that there is no point in telling Louise that she is employed as a waitress and sometime chambermaid and not as a porter. It is Louise Abbot's creed that all her employees are created equal and endowed with the inalienable right to do whatever job needs doing at any particular moment. She has explained to her staff, at less stressful moments, that she does not ask them to do anything she did not do herself when she waited tables and cleaned bedrooms and bathrooms at Mount Haven, reminding them that she still does her share whenever necessary. Another thing that Polly will not tell Louise Abbot is that the village girls quit without notice or arrive too late and leave too early because she is so irascible and so demanding, her sermonizing so irritating. 'And so damn boring!' one brief hire had protested before she quit to work the check-out counter at Hannaford's Market. She might add that it would also be helpful if Louise occasionally said 'please' or 'thank you'. But of course, Polly will not say that either.

'I'm on my way,' she assures Louise and hurries to the door.

'Polly – do you happen to know where Mr Abbot is?' Louise calls after her.

'I haven't seen him,' Polly lies.

She knows full well that Evan Abbot raced through the kitchen, a thick book in his hand, and disappeared into the small brick outbuilding beyond the swing set as soon as he heard the Edwards' car pull up. Not for him the unloading of luggage, the cacophony of greetings.

'Well, maybe when you've helped with the luggage you can see if you can find him. Is the lemonade ready?'

'On the counter,' Polly says, pointing to the large crystal pitcher with slices of lemon and fresh mint floating atop the pale yellow liquid which is, in fact, made from a mix. Louise is, as always, concerned about appearances and it is important to her that newly arriving guests be greeted with glasses of fresh lemonade even if the lemonade is not exactly fresh.

The Edwards children are already clambering in and out of the huge SUV, its stereo system still blasting the music from 'Hamilton' as they unload.

'Hey, Polly!' A friendly, casual greeting from Annette, always amiable and why shouldn't she be? What is there to disconcert that slender, clear-eyed girl whose very clean, soft brown hair falls to her shoulders in shimmering swaths, the braces newly removed from her very white teeth, her features even, her skin smooth? Polly has seen girls like that at university, girls from prosperous families aglow with wealth and unchained to part-time jobs, free to ski every weekend. Such girls do not work summer jobs, nor do they worry about an anemic mother and a father who lives in fear that the plywood factory that employs him will close. Polly knows that if she and Annette Edwards attended the same school, they would eat at different tables or, more likely, Polly would be ladling food on to Annette's plate as she moved down the cafeteria line.

Polly extends her hand out to soft-voiced, handsome Dr Edwards, noting that his dark, thick hair is graying at the temples, almost exactly matching the smoky grayness of his wide set eyes. Broad-shouldered and muscular, he moves slowly, carefully, avoiding sharp-edged cartons and suitcases, piling the brightly colored soft duffle bags into a mound. She understands his caution. He is a surgeon, always conscious of his hands. He shakes Polly's hand, his skin very smooth against her own.

'How's school coming?' he asks. 'Did you ace organic chemistry?'

'I did.' She blushes, pleased that he remembers that she is pre-med, pleased that he recalls how nervous she had been about organic chemistry.

'Good for you.' His congratulatory smile creases his craggy face and Polly trembles with pleasure.

Susan Edwards, her arms laden with clothing, moves toward them and stands between Polly and her husband. She brushes a stray tendril of silver hair from his forehead, an affectionate and proprietary gesture.

'It's good to see you, Polly,' she says.

'Thanks. I'm glad you're back, Mrs Edwards,' Polly replies.

'Oh, please call me Susan. Can you take these?'

Polly takes the load of jackets and sweatshirts, swaying slightly under their weight.

'Hey, Polly. Great to see you.'

Jeremy Edwards jumps off the car's tailgate. He tosses two soccer balls on to the path and hefts three tennis rackets and a croquet set entombed in its battered carton which will be set up on the lawn, played with once and promptly forgotten. He makes his way through the maze of suitcases and backpacks, trips over the largest carton and drops the croquet set.

Wooden balls, their colors faded, careen down the path and he races after them as Annette rolls her eyes, inviting Polly to share her contempt for her impossibly clumsy twin. Polly shrugs to indicate her complicity and notes that Jeremy must have grown almost four inches since last summer and that Annette herself is both taller and thinner, her features newly sharp, her forehead high above pale, carefully plucked and arched brows.

'Hey, didn't you cut your hair, Polly?' she calls. Polly nods and touches the golden layers of her new bob. She wonders if Annette can tell that she used a rinse and is suddenly sorry that the beautician persuaded her to choose a color that is really too bright.

Laden with clothing, she turns as Matt Edwards, always her

favorite of the August kids, jumps out of the rear seat clutching his two fat Harry Potter books and hurls himself at her.

'Polly, Polly, we're back. Isn't that great? We're back! Is Donny here yet? What about Paul?'

'No. You guys are the first to arrive,' she says but even as she speaks another car pulls up and Helene and Greg Ames tumble out.

'Hey, Susan. Hey, Jeff. Hey, you kids!'

There is a rush of hugs, a trading of kisses, exclamations of pleasure and excitement.

'Gee, you guys have really grown.'

Helene, ever the adoring aunt, hugs her niece and nephews who remain indifferently rigid.

'Jeff, how the hell are you?'

Greg claps Jeff on the back, shows him a dart board, its cork surface fraying, the targets brightly and unevenly painted.

'Helene, I love that skirt.' As Susan Edwards' fingers pluck at the gauzy fabric, her sister's blush mounts.

Helene's crimson lipstick kisses streak Matt's cheeks and Jeremy winces as Greg pumps his hand up and down and up and down.

Polly disappears into the inn and races up the stairs to deposit the jackets, avoiding Louise Abbot who has pasted her welcoming smile on to her face and is on her way out carrying a tray loaded with the lemonade and clear plastic cups.

'Welcome to Mount Haven.' The familiar words fall from her lips in the accent learned from her mother-in-law. They all turn and greet her. Obediently, each guest fills a glass.

'So glad to be here,' Jeff Edwards says, the quasi toast of appreciation which he repeats each year at the onset of their holiday.

And then the Edwards' and Ames' luggage is carried inside just as car after car pulls up. The Templetons' limo cruises to a dignified halt. Nessa Epstein grinds the brakes of her ancient station wagon and Paul emerges and playfully directs traffic. Michael Curran sounds his horn and Cary tumbles out and he and Matt rush toward each other with yelps of delight. The women embrace, offer their cheeks for butterfly kisses as the men thump each other's backs. The air is electric with excitement and anticipation. The rituals of vacation are in place.

Louise refills her pitcher and circles the new arrivals as Polly and two other waitresses pressed into reluctant service scoop up suitcases and trail after Hank, the handyman who effortlessly heaves up the largest cartons, cursing under his breath, and carries them upstairs to the bedrooms. The children tumble over each other in their eagerness to help, plucking up backpacks and books and dropping them, their laughter rising, their voices tremulous with joy.

It is the chauffeur who drove Andrea and Mark Templeton from Concord airport who carries their matching luggage to their room, returning for their two garment bags and grunting when Mark Templeton curtly asks him to be careful of them.

'My linen jackets crease easily,' the elderly silver-haired man says.

In his room, Mark supervises the placement of the luggage, gives a ten-dollar bill to the chauffeur who lingers until a five-dollar bill is added. He does not say thank you when he leaves, slamming the door behind him. Mark Templeton has never been a man who endears himself to service staff but neither can he be accused of stinginess. He makes no move to unpack but goes to the window and looks down at his fellow guests as though he is an indifferent theatregoer observing an uninteresting performance. The cast of characters thins out as he watches. The children have vanished, probably clustered around the pinball machines. Jeff Edwards and his brother-in-law, Greg Ames, are striding toward the lake, practicing their unaccustomed roles of men newly at ease.

Jeff pauses and lights a pipe. Mark finds this interesting. He cannot remember Jeff smoking in previous years. After all he is a doctor, a surgeon, aware of the hazards of tobacco. 'Mid-life crisis,' Mark thinks and wonders if he should not resume smoking himself. Late-life crisis, he might call it, but of course Andrea would never tolerate it.

He spots Andrea now, seated on the lawn in an Adirondack chair, the plastic glass of that undrinkable lemonade perched on an arm rest. He has no doubt that she has laced it with vodka from the small bottle she purchased on the plane. He marvels at his wife. Although she has been traveling for hours, her mauve silk pant suit is without a crease, the white scarf is still elegantly looped about her neck, and not a single strand of silver hair has escaped her chignon. She leans slightly forward, her eyes never leaving the driveway. She is waiting for Wendy and Donny, he knows, and he feels a surge of anger at his daughter-in-law's thoughtlessness. She should have been at the inn when they arrived. She must know how unnerved Andrea will be. Wendy is driving down the very road where Adam's car crashed and became a coffin of twisted metal and soft leather. But Adam of course was driving in the opposite direction, speeding from Cambridge toward his mother's home, the house Mark deeded to his widow.

Mark closes his eyes against the memory of the fat state trooper who had described his son's death to him, telling him how Adam's body had been wedged so tightly between the driver's seat and the steering wheel that even with the jaws of life he had been extricated only with difficulty.

'He was speeding. They clocked him at ninety a couple of miles back. And probably drinking. I could tell by the smell, but I'll leave that out of the report. I don't want to mess up his insurance claim. Not when he's leaving a wife and kid. The insurance companies are a bunch of bastards, you know. I'm still trying to collect from a kitchen fire. But where the hell was he rushing to, a young fellow like that?' the officer had wondered as he licked his pen.

And Mark, who knew the answer, had remained silent. There was no need to tell the trooper about his last conversation with his son. Adam was dead but he would protect Andrea, as he always had, as he always would. He had explained the accident to Andrea and Wendy, creating a scenario that he almost came to believe.

'The sun was in his eyes. The troopers think that a deer may have skittered across the road. There's a "deer crossing" sign right where he crashed. You know how Adam felt about animals.'

With a few well-chosen words he transformed his son from a reckless drunken driver into a martyred lover of wildlife. Numb with grief, they had accepted his explanation.

He banishes the memory, opens his eyes and sees that Andrea

has risen from her seat and is walking toward the newly arrived Wendy and Donny. Her arms are outstretched and the mauve silk sleeves of her jacket flutter in the gentle wind, beneficent wings of welcome. Wendy waves her cherry-red straw hat and urges Donny forward. The dark-haired, dark-eyed boy hesitates and then lopes clumsily into his grandmother's embrace. Mark knows that Andrea's eyes are bright with unshed tears and his own eyes burn. As always, he is relieved that Donny does not look like Adam. That would have been too much to bear.

He turns away from the window as Simon Epstein's shiny yellow sports car pulls up and Simon uncoils his long, lean body, shades his eyes from the sun which has become dazzlingly bright, waves to Wendy, Andrea and Donny, calls his wife's name and strides into the inn.

'Nessa! Nessa!'

Simon's voice reverberates down the corridors as doors open and close and conversations drift through the hallways. Mount Haven Inn throbs with chatter and noise, a din of pleasure now and again tinged with annoyance.

The door to the Currans' room is open and Liane Curran's complaints are audible.

'This room is so damn small. Why do we always get the smallest room?' she asks angrily. Michael closes the door.

There is the musical sound of coins falling on the hard wood floor. Matt Edwards has dropped a cache of quarters and they all rush to retrieve them, laughing and chattering.

Outside a motorcycle brakes noisily. The rider dismounts, removes his helmet and turns to Louise Abbot who has hurried down the path to greet him. Mark recognizes Daniel Goldner, the writer, a very occasional Mount Haven guest. Adam had appeared on a panel with him and spoken admiringly of his short-story collection, published a few months after Adam's own well-received novel. Goldner's second book, also a novel, appeared about a year ago, Mark recalls. A splashy debut, a handsome jacket, dark blue with the title and the author's name imprinted in spiraling silver. Andrea read it because Wendy sent it to her as a Christmas gift, but Mark, who has read no fiction since Adam's death, ignored it.

'Daniel, I was beginning to worry,' Louise says, her pale

cheeks flushed as she leans toward him, touches the black
leather of his jacket and lifts her face toward him. He kisses
her cheek with casual affection.

'Why would you worry?' he asks.

Their words drift up to Mark, who closes the window. Andrea
favors this room because it adjoins the rooms she reserves for
Wendy and Donny each year and because its French doors open
on to a wrap-around balcony that offers a view of the verdant
mountains and a shining sliver of the lake. Mark dislikes it
because every utterance in the hallway and on the lawn below
travels upward and passers-by can easily see into their room.
It is enough that he must vacation with these people. He does
not want to overhear their conversations or endure their glances
into the privacy of his own room.

He sighs and unzips his garment bag, carefully removing the
pale blue linen jacket he will wear to dinner that evening,
waiting all the while for the door to open. He turns when it
does, his smile in place. Wendy and Donny, framed in a patch
of fading sunlight, stand very still for the briefest of moments.
Mark registers that Donny has grown taller, that Wendy has
grown thinner and that she allows her dark hair, once worn
short, to frame her oval face in a cluster of curls. Donny's own
hair, a match for his mother's, is too long for Mark's taste,
almost brushing his narrow shoulders. Wendy wears a sleeveless
white sun dress that emphasizes her deeply tanned skin. Donny's
T-shirt is pale yellow, ripped at the neck, and his shorts are
cut-off jeans, ragged at the hems. His sneakers are brand new
but unlaced and he does not wear socks. They move toward
him, the lithe mother and son who look so like each other. They
place their hands in his and brush their lips across his cool
cheek.

'Isn't it wonderful to be here together again?' Andrea asks.

There is neither wonder nor welcome in her cool voice and
her question remains unanswered as they all move toward the
window and gaze down at the lawn where Annette and Jeremy
Edwards, studiously ignoring each other, are carefully setting
up the croquet hoops.

'Dinner in two hours,' Andrea reminds them.

As always, she is their hostess, reminding them of schedules, calmly and coolly guiding them through these weeks of forced togetherness.

'I'll unpack,' Wendy says. 'Donny, go and see if you can find your friends. I saw Matt and Cary going down to the game room.'

'And Paul? Paul Epstein?'

'He's probably with them,' Wendy answers and smiles at her in-laws. *If my husband is dead, are they still my in-laws?* The recurring thought teases her even as Donny dashes out of the room.

'Be back to change before the dinner bell rings,' she calls after him.

The dinner bell is sounded before each meal by a different child, a schedule meticulously choreographed by Louise and consulted on arrival by each family. Tonight it will be Matt Edwards who proudly marches up and down the inn's corridors, energetically jangling the huge brass bell Prudence Abbot purchased decades earlier from a bankrupt farmer.

THREE

Evan and Louise Abbot, who prefer to think of themselves as the gracious hosts of a country house rather than innkeepers, stand side by side at the entrance to the dining room and greet their guests. Although the seating rarely varies from year to year Louise, who now wears a wide-skirted dress of floral design, holds a seating chart and refers to it with officious concern, waving each family to their set places.

Evan, his chestnut-colored hair still thick, his face ruddied by the mountain sunlight, wears a V-necked pale blue cotton knit sweater, a soft collared shirt and khaki slacks, the outfits of his adolescence unchanged. He has many such sweaters, all in pastel colors, and he alternates them carefully. Louise remembers still the lime-green sweater he placed beneath her head when she lay beside him, all those years ago, on the swaying, sweet meadow grass, but she does not dwell on that memory. She watches as he greets the men with a handshake. He bends to pat Cary Curran's head, indifferent to the fact that Cary, now eleven years old, is too old for such a gesture. He flashes his charming smile at the women, all of whom tell him how well he looks, how pleased they are to be back at the inn, as they glide past him to their tables.

Each year Helene tells her sister Susan that she cannot understand how a woman as dowdy and uninteresting as Louise managed to marry a man as attractive and intelligent as Evan. It is a thought that recurs as she and Greg follow her sister's family into the dining room.

The wide-windowed dining room is split into two sections, the dividing doors long since removed. Transient guests, those who have booked for the first time having discovered the inn on the internet or reserved their rooms through a travel agent, or are simply passing through, are relegated to the smaller section which has no view of the lawn and opens on to the kitchen. The long tables in that area are covered with unmatched plastic cloths of odd geometric design and the seats are steel folding chairs. The regular guests of August share the larger room and sit on ladder-backed wooden chairs around oval tables covered with carefully mended snow-white cloths and set with heavy cutlery and thick white china plates. A slender glass vase filled with the late pink and yellow full-petaled roses of summer, cut from the bushes that border the garden of the inn, is placed at the center of each table. Louise herself arranges the flowers in the vases which she purchased when a hotel in a distant town closed its doors. She thinks that they lend the dining room a touch of class.

Jeff Edwards supervises the seating of their children, careful to place himself between the twins, Jeremy and Annette, whose constant bickering unnerves him. Once inseparable, a small boy and girl who played sweetly with each other, inventing games, sharing secrets, they have rocketed into an adolescence of caustic enmity. Their evening quarrels erupt without cause, a spontaneous combustion of latent anger.

'Nerd,' Annette hisses at her brother.

'Slut,' Jeremy shouts.

Matt races from the room, frightened by their fury. Susan attempts mediation, Jeff shouts. On such evenings he closes his study door, sits at his desk, his head in his hands. He wonders when his children changed. He wonders when his own marriage changed, why Susan sometimes seems to be a stranger at a remove from his life, uninterested in his work, perhaps even repelled by it.

'We stink of death,' a surgical nurse once told him as she tossed away her sweat-stained mask and bloodied gloves.

Does Susan think he stinks of death? Is that why she retreats into the book-lined corner of the bedroom and sits hunched over her manuscripts and dictionaries, vanishing into another world, now whispering in French, now in English? The slender girl he married is now a woman who makes endless lists, often in a language he cannot understand. The twins, those gentle children in whom they delighted, now spew anger at each other.

He comforts himself with rationalizations. Everything changes. He of all people should know that. He is a doctor, charged with monitoring changes within the human body. The beat of the heart changes, the intake of air changes and relationships change.

And of course he and Susan both are exhausted, unnerved by the demands of their daily schedules. He is hopeful that the peace of these weeks at Mount Haven will vanquish their fatigue, will resuscitate their family. That hope soars as his children take their seats at his direction without protest, as Matt waves happily to his friends. He smiles at his wife, whose cap of golden hair glistens in the weak light of the dining room.

Greg produces a bottle of very good wine and asks Polly for four wine glasses.

'The good ones,' he says and grins because they all know that Louise Abbot hoards what she calls her 'good' glassware.

Susan and Helene, seated next to each other, glance around the room and exchange the secret judgmental smiles of sisters who anticipate each other's thoughts. Helene's many bracelets jangle as she reaches for the bread.

The Epsteins are at a window table, seated opposite Liane and Michael Curran, an arrangement that annoys Liane. She has nothing, absolutely nothing in common with Nessa. Liane is freshly showered, her rose-gold curls lacquered into place, the turquoise eyeshadow that matches her new watered silk dress, smoothly layered across the lids of her narrow eyes. She has dressed carefully, unlike Nessa, who wears orange plastic flip-flops, and whose toenails are painted in outrageous colors. Nessa's lack of makeup, her un-ironed tie-dyed halter dress, the mass of auburn hair that tumbles to her shoulders, annoys Liane.

Resentfully, she observes that Michael and Simon are pleased to sit opposite each other and to effortlessly continue a conversation that began a full year ago. *Is a recession imminent? Might small businesses like Michael's actually benefit from such a reverse?* Simon talks theory. Michael talks experience, explaining that the new software he is developing has the potential to predict economic trends. They agree that this is an idea that will surely interest Mark Templeton who spent his career monitoring and predicting market upswings and downswings. Michael, very hesitantly, asks Simon if he might take a look at the initial program, still in a pilot stage.

'Sure. Why not?' Simon's reply is both shrewd and generous. Michael is a hardworking, bright guy and he may be on to something.

He smiles encouragingly and rests his hand on his wife's head. Michael feels a flutter of optimism. Simon's input and suggestions could be invaluable and if he tells Mark Templeton that Michael's concept is workable there may well be an injection of venture capital. All is not lost. All is far from lost. Michael wipes his thick glasses energetically with a linen napkin.

Nessa asks Liane how Cary is doing in school and Liane shrugs. Paul and Cary engage in an avid discussion of Harry Potter. Liane glares at Paul who barely notices her, so intent is he on discussing Hogwarts.

Daniel Goldner, the Templeton family and Louise and Evan Abbot share the table that affords the best view of the lawn. It is, Louise knows, a temporary arrangement. Before the first week is over Mark Templeton will ask, very politely, if his family could possibly have their own table. They have matters of some privacy to discuss and Louise will graciously acquiesce and conceal her disappointment. Mark and Andrea Templeton always maintain a pleasant aloofness from the other guests although they smile and nod politely. Their replies to Louise's questions this evening are monosyllabic. Yes, their room is fine. The plane ride was pleasant enough. The weather in California is lovely.

Andrea places the napkin on her grandson's lap and Donny scowls. Wendy, a tangerine-colored shawl covering her shoulders because the evening is cool and her white sun dress is of the lightest of linens, shoots her son a reproving look and his scowl becomes a dutiful smile. Mark Templeton, not for the first time, observes that the inn would do well to stock a wine cellar and Louise makes no response. She is content on this first evening, pleased to be seated between Evan and Daniel.

Daniel. She rolls his name over in her mind. *Dear Daniel.* The alliterated words fall together easily as well they might. She has known him since his boyhood, when she was a teen-aged waitress busy at her chores but pausing to watch as he and Simon Epstein raced across the lawn to the lake. Simon the elder, swift and long-legged, was always the first to plunge into the calm, sunlit waters. But she had noted Daniel's grace and appreciated the softness of his tone, the gentleness of his understanding. He was such a good friend, such a good boy.

And then he was no longer a boy. She remembers still his

return to the inn after an absence of several summers. On that bright August day he emerged from his car, the youth now a tall, bearded man, his shoulders broad, his thighs muscular, his voice deep and confident. His graduation into manhood had startled her and she had stood naked before her own mirror that night and saw that she herself had, with equal mystery, morphed into womanhood, her waistline thickened, the breasts that would never nurture an infant high and firm. They had, both of them, passively and inevitability, drifted into maturity.

Daniel had achieved his ambition. He was a published writer. His small novel had made a small splash and he presented her with an autographed copy. The inscription, *For Louise, my August Friend, Sharer of Dreams*, pleased her, although she herself had long since abandoned the modest dream she had shared with him. There would be no secretarial course in Portsmouth, no job in Boston, no cute apartment shared with laughing room-mates. She was, instead, a childless woman, the summer serving girl become an innkeeper. But then things happen, things change. Boys become men, girls become women, parents die. Life moves inexorably and often unexpectedly forward.

She had never expected to sleep in Prudence Abbot's bed, to supervise village girls at the tasks she herself had undertaken, the employee now an employer, her future defined.

Only Evan, her husband, remains unchanged, his face unlined, his hair thick and tousled as it had been all those summers ago. He still mounts his bicycle with boyish grace, the perennial student earning degree after degree, now mastering Spanish, now Italian, writing papers, taking exams with no purposeful end in sight. His mother Prudence had been prescient. Evan never would have been able to manage the inn, never have been able to sustain his own whimsical life. His courses never would have steered him into a profession, a career. He had needed Louise who doles out the money he needs for his courses, his books, his expenses, accepting it as an adolescent carelessly accepts an allowance.

Louise glances at Evan now who is excitedly telling Daniel about a summer course he is taking entitled 'Novels of Death and Darkness'.

'We'll be reading fictional studies of loss and illness. Have you ever thought of examining that aspect of literature?' he asks.

Daniel nods wearily.

'Hard not to. It's the stuff of life and that's what absorbs novelists.'

He looks nervously at Andrea and Mark Templeton, recalling that their son Adam's novel had concentrated on the theme of a boy obsessed with the loss of his parents. Fortunately, they are not listening to the conversation, absorbed as they are in a murmured conversation with Wendy about Donny's grades, which, he gathers, were fortunately excellent.

It is Louise who winces at his reply. She wonders if Daniel recalls that she sat behind him at his father's funeral. She and Evan had traveled south to New York for the service, proving yet again that the Abbots were more than innkeepers, that their guests were also their friends.

It was at the funeral that she had seen Laura, then Daniel's fiancée, for the first time and had taken an instant dislike to her. Laura had sat beside Daniel at the funeral, wearing her flaring black skirt and long-sleeved black leotard, her hair fashioned into a tight dancer's knot. Louise had thought her outfit inappropriate for the synagogue service. Later, she had thought their marriage inappropriate. Laura was not good enough for Daniel, not smart enough for him. She had overheard Simon Epstein say as much to Nessa. It neither surprises nor dismays her that Laura and Daniel have most probably separated, that they may, in fact, have divorced. She sighs imperceptibly and lifts the silver bell that will signal the waitresses to carry the trays in as Wendy Templeton struggles to keep the conversation afloat, launching Evan on a discussion of 'The Magic Mountain.'

The waitresses, four sullen village girls whom Polly has coaxed into service, work in tandem, one setting the huge bowl of mashed potatoes on one end of each table, the other positioning the platters of meat and vegetables on the other end, while the wooden bowls of salad are handed to a diner who dutifully passes them around the table.

'Family style, as usual,' Louise says brightly. 'So much nicer to be informal, don't you think?'

They nod obediently although Mark Templeton frowns.

He prefers formal service and his table mates are definitely not his family.

Andrea recognizes his irritation but ignores it. She knows that these days of August, spent in proximity to their vanished life, to their son's grave, in false intimacy with Adam's widow and his son, ignite Mark's anger and fuel his fury. She knows that he, who is always in control, is frustrated because he cannot comprehend how their son's life rocketed so inexplicably into disaster. His inability to solve that impossible riddle enrages him. Andrea prefers her husband's anger and fury to the wildness of his unspent grief. She has learned, since their son's death, to weather Mark's moods. She numbs her own pain with vodka, the colorless liquid that has been her life's companion, her anodyne.

Adam's birthday will come and go as will the anniversary of his death. They will place new plantings at his grave. Wendy his widow will weep and Donny, the son who barely remembers his father, will stare unhappily at the austere marble gravestone. She herself will murmur a prayer or perhaps recite a fragment of poetry. Perhaps Dylan Thomas. 'Do not go gentle into that good night.' Such rituals are important.

Polly wanders about the room with her tray of gravy boats and salad dressings. She too has changed for dinner. Her cheeks are aglow and her too-blonde hair is brushed to a high gloss. She wears a bright pink sweater, so loose and low cut that when she leans over the table to pass the gravy boat to Jeremy Edwards, her breast brushes his father's bare arm.

'I'll take that,' Susan Edwards says, her gesture so swift that drops of gravy spatter across the white cloth.

Polly blushes. Jeff turns and smiles at her apologetically and Helene Ames stares reprovingly at her sister. How could Susan have been so insensitive, so stupid? The poor girl didn't mean anything. Or perhaps she did. The possibility tantalizes.

The meal is swiftly over, dessert plates left half empty because no one likes the tapioca pudding Louise makes herself following the recipe handed down by Prudence Abbot. Only Evan scrapes his dish clean, the obedient son become the obedient husband, the boy-man licking morsels of his mother's pale yellow pudding from his lips.

FOUR

The children and the teenagers scatter before coffee is served. The adults linger over their second cups of the bitter beverage and watch as the mauve shadows of evening curtain the mountains and splash puddles of darkness across the lawn. Slowly they drift out of the dining room. Polly watches them, noting with satisfaction that Jeff Edwards does not take his wife's hand.

The youngsters have already carved out their territory in the sprawling room which Louise calls the lounge and they call the rec room because it is dominated by a ping pong table and a pool table, placed too close to each other. It is furnished with an assortment of cracked brown leather couches and easy chairs. Matt, Cary and Donny, each clutching a hoard of quarters, are hunched over the pinball machine which stands in a corner, strategically placed near the rest rooms, its lights flashing, as the metallic cars race down the winding electronic paths.

Polly, her chores done, sits at a small table in the corner, the molecular biology text open in front of her. She bought the book cheaply from a pre-med drop out, determined to study it over the summer and get a head start on the demanding course. She needs an A if she is going to get any financial aid in med school, if by some miracle she gets that far. She moves her lips as she reads, slides her tongue across the cherry-colored lipstick she applied so carefully.

Paul Epstein and Jeremy Edwards play ping pong, the white ball bouncing with tympanic speed over the sagging net. Annette has settled herself at a table, her long bare legs tucked beneath her as she desultorily works on a jigsaw puzzle, her soft brown hair falling about her face in graceful waves as she turns her head now this way, now that way, in search of an elusive puzzle piece.

The guests of Mount Haven are partial to jigsaw puzzles which they purchase at a shop in town and work on in the evening. Their lives may be fragmented, their present uneasy, their future uncertain, but at least the small, oddly shaped puzzle pieces so disjointedly spread across the splintered table can be fitted into place. There is, after all, something that they can control.

Annette is working on a puzzle of United States Presidents, purchased by Simon Epstein the previous year, completed by Paul on the day they left and then disassembled by Louise, the pieces scooped into a box for the following summer. Annette has, so far, managed to isolate all the straight-edged bits and to join several together to form a fraction of the frame. The ping pong game over, Paul slides into a chair beside her.

'Can I help you with that?' he asks, and she nods.

Together they slip one piece and then another into place, their hands touching as they sort through the pile in their search for matching colors. Annette frowns as her twin leans over her shoulder and reaches for a piece that does not fit. Why can't Jeremy ever leave her alone? *He's not a brother, he's a leech. A goddamn annoying leech.*

'Hey, these two fit,' he insists.

'No. They don't. You're forcing them,' Paul corrects him and Annette snorts derisively.

Matt, Cary and Donny, having tired of the pinball machines, are at the pool table, struggling to manipulate the poles that are too long for them.

'Hey, let me show you what to do with them,' Jeremy says and Annette's sigh mingles relief and annoyance as he joins the younger boys and shows them how to set up the balls, how to chalk the stick.

'Show-off,' she thinks and turns back to the puzzle, back to her study of Paul's long and graceful fingers.

Nessa Epstein sprawls across the couch, a copy of Bruno Bettelheim's *Uses of Enchantment* unopened on her lap, her gaze fixed on the window which overlooks the path that Simon and Daniel are following down to the lake. She supposes that Daniel is telling Simon about his marriage, if indeed he is still married. Simon is the father confessor of unhappily married men, an example that divorce does not mean the end of the world, that life does offer a second chance. Haven't he and

Nessa, against all odds, found each other? He will, she supposes, tell Daniel as much, as they stand lakeside, puffing on their pipes.

Simon has always been Daniel's wise, older friend, a big brother to the boy who had so disliked Leo, his own biological sibling. The Goldner boys and Simon had grown up together. Their parents had been colleagues, all of them teachers at the same high school, their friendship close enough to be familial. They played bridge together, argued politics passionately, traded books which they discussed with enthusiasm, and vacationed together each August at Mount Haven Inn. Nessa has scrapbooks filled with snapshots of those distant Augusts, given to her by Charlotte, Simon's first wife, who had no fondness for Mount Haven and is always generous with discarded memories.

Simon and Daniel vanish from her view and she opens her book and closes it again.

'I hate fairy tales,' she says to Wendy Templeton and tosses the book aside. 'I don't even have them on the shelves at my nursery school. All they do is set the kids up for disappointment. Nobody lives happily ever after.'

'But fantasy does offset sadness,' Wendy replies softly. Her tangerine-colored shawl is wrapped tightly around her thin shoulders and she is curled up in a deep leather chair, her sketchpad open, her drawing pencils spread on the low table beside her although her hands are clasped. She is grateful to sit quietly and watch her son at play, grateful that her in-laws, wearied by the long day of travel, have elected to go to their room after dinner, grateful that Nessa, whom she likes very much, will again share these August weeks with her. There is an instinctive understanding between Nessa and herself, the rare rapport of women who sense each other's feelings and speak in rapid emotional shorthand.

Wendy wanders over to the bookshelves that line the wall and wonders if she will find Adam's novel. It had a very brief life in paperback but she does not have the heart to search for it. Besides, she imagines Louise would have removed it. Louise is sensitive to such things as an innkeeper must be. She turns away, sorry that she trespassed in this literary boneyard.

Liane Curran, her pretty painted face frozen into a mask of boredom, listlessly turns the pages of an ancient *Vogue*, wondering what Nessa and Wendy are talking about. They are strange, she thinks, not for the first time. Their conversations are so weird. Liane glances at her husband who sits in a corner of the room studying the spreadsheets that shroud the top of the wobbly bridge table. Damn it, doesn't Michael realize that they are on vacation? Can't he abandon his stupid project even for a few weeks? She shakes her head impatiently and looks across the room to the corner where Greg Ames is hammering a dartboard into place. His wife, his sister-in-law and his brother-in-law watch him warily.

'You're sure it's safe?' Susan Edwards asks. 'I don't want the kids throwing darts. You hear all these stories.'

'Perfectly safe,' Greg assures her. 'I'll put the darts on that high shelf when we're done.'

He opens the wooden box of darts, selects one, takes aim and throws. It lands right on the bull's eye and they all clap.

'Want to try?' he asks Jeff.

'I'll pass,' Jeff replies.

'I'll try.' Liane springs forward. Darts had been a big thing in Natick, a Saturday night activity in the local bar, and she had been a pretty good dart thrower, always chosen first for a team, even when the team was all guys. Greg hands her a dart and she fingers its sharp steel point, admires the colored feathers and presses them to her cheek, the seductive gesture of her high-school years. She steps back, pauses, narrows her eyes and throws. Her dart lands right beside Greg's and there is another round of applause. She blushes.

'Hey, Ma, I didn't know you could throw like that,' Cary calls.

'There's lots you don't know about me,' she replies.

She waits for Greg, whose dart lands outside the bull's eye and then throws again and again hits her target.

'Well, I'm going upstairs,' Susan says. 'I'm really tired. Jeff, make sure the kids don't go near those darts.'

'All right. Fine. I may be up late. Simon talked about a chess game,' he says without looking at her.

'Good luck with that.' Simon and Jeff are equally matched and equally competitive.

She waves to her sister who is waiting her turn at the dart board and sprints up the stairs. She has at least an hour, perhaps two, to work on the translation. Five pages. Perhaps even seven or eight because this section of the book is largely conversational. LeBec's dialogue is mostly monosyllabic and easily rendered into English.

Simon and Daniel light their pipes in the shelter of a copse of conifers which protects the fragile match flame until the bowls are safely aglow. Companionably puffing on their briars, they sit on the battered bench on which, during their boyhood years, they had whittled long branches into makeshift swords.

'Nice night,' Simon says.

'Beautiful,' Daniel agrees, but his voice is flat.

'Good year?' he asks Simon, realizing that although he spoke to his friend several times during the course of the year, they have not seen each other. The well-intentioned plans they made to meet for a drink or for dinner were always canceled by one or the other.

'Not bad. What about yours?'

'Lousy. Bordering on horrific. Or does horrific border on lousy?'

'The book?' Simon asks, although he knows the answer.

'No. The book's fine. The editor's happy with it. The marketing people are happy with it. I'm sort of happy with it. Even Laura read it and liked it, great literary critic that she is.' Daniel's laugh is an angry bark.

'So it's Laura.'

'Of course it's Laura. As though you hadn't guessed.'

'I guessed.'

'I think we're done. In fact, I know we're done.'

Simon is silent. He waits and remembers arriving home one evening to find Nessa and her friend Meredith, who was edging toward divorce, sitting in their darkened living room, their heads bent close, their voices soft but their exchanges rapid and audible.

Women, he conjectures now, have the gift of intimacy while men are emotionally handicapped. He wishes that he had a handkerchief to offer Daniel. He even wishes that Daniel would weep.

'What happened?' he asks at last.

'I guess what's been happening for a long time only I was too dumb to see it. Or maybe I just didn't want to see it. I could blame it on my writing, on my so-called gift. Fiction writers create imaginary worlds for their characters, which is only one step away from creating imaginary worlds for themselves. So there I was, married to Laura and writing our love story, the great romantic coming together of the beautiful dancer and the talented novelist walking through life hand in hand. So the beautiful part was true. She was – is – beautiful and I guess the talented part was sort of true. I do have talent; not genius but talent. But we were hardly on the same life path and our hands really didn't touch a lot. I was just too stupid and self-absorbed to see it.'

Daniel's voice thickens. His pipe is cold and he empties the bowl angrily, banging it against the bench, and reaches for his tobacco pouch. Simon lights a match, holds it out to him and sees, in the weak flicker of its flame, that although his friend's head is tilted skyward, his eyes are closed. He puffs at his pipe and exhales a soft cloud of gray smoke that drifts off into the inky darkness.

'Anyway,' Daniel continues, 'I was pretty good at fooling myself. Mostly because I was so crazy about her. From the minute I met her it was as though I'd been blinded by fairy dust. I'd sit in the audience and watch her perform and I'd shiver with wonder to think that that gorgeous creature gliding across the stage was coming home with me, that she was my wife, my own. She was my miracle even when our age of miracles had passed. It had vanished maybe two, three years into our marriage.'

'Two, three years,' Simon repeats. 'But Daniel, you've been married for twelve years.'

He knows the exact date because they had celebrated Paul's fifth birthday at the wedding and Laura, her bridal dress a white dancer's skirt and long-sleeved white leotard, had danced with Paul. The bride and the birthday child had been surrounded by applauding friends until the music stopped and Laura curtsied and gave Paul a white iris plucked from the coronet that crowned her dark dancer's knot.

'Twelve years,' Daniel acknowledges. 'I fooled myself for a long time. I kept writing new chapters for us. We'd grow. We'd work it out. We'd develop. We made do. We compromised. At least I compromised. Laura hated coming to Mount Haven so we gave that up and went to the shore. She hated the writers' conferences so I went alone but I tagged along to her dance workshops and wrote or tried to write while she was at rehearsals. When I took a teaching gig I told myself that it didn't matter that she didn't come with me. She had rehearsals for a performance, she was teaching a master class, she was working with a new choreographer. She had her career and I had mine. It was not always easy, but it was the bargain we had made with each other. We each had our freedom. No kids. An unspoken pact. Pregnancy does terrible things to a dancer's body. Kids screw up a writer's schedule. We had agreed to that from the beginning. So we were in sync. That's what I told myself. I repeated it so often that I began to believe it.'

Daniel stood and walked to the edge of the lake, bent to pick up a smooth stone, sent it skidding across the calm waters and then returned to the bench, biting down hard on his pipe.

'And that's what you told me,' Simon said, remembering the night Daniel had told him that he and Laura would marry, stating, with grave certitude, that they had worked out the kinks, that they wouldn't fall into any of the sand traps that had wrecked the marriages of so many of their friends.

'It turns out that Laura thought that the bargain we had made with each other went beyond our careers,' Daniel continues. 'She wanted freedom in all things. Financial freedom. She had her own bank account, her own checking account. I had no problem with that. Freedom of time. No need to tell me where she was going, how long she'd be away, what she'd be doing. OK. I dealt with that. But her agenda for sexual freedom was a shock, a big shock, a deal-breaker shock. I don't even know how to tell you this.' His voice quivered.

'Just tell it,' Simon said. 'Take your time.' He speaks in the tone he uses to encourage nervous graduate students before they begin an oral presentation.

Daniel breathes deeply. 'OK. Here goes. A couple of weeks ago, we go out to the Hamptons. There's a dance festival going on and she's involved in the programming. A lot of big names. Dancers, choreographers, impresarios, donors. Some I recognized. Some I didn't. I wasn't really interested but I said I'd go. She took the car and went a day or so ahead of me and I rode my bike down. I took the proofs of my novel and told her I'd work on them while she went to her meetings. Two nights later there was a big cocktail party at one of the mansions out there, a fundraiser, the kind of thing I hate. Lance something, one of these young millionaires who combines culture and philanthropy, was hosting it. I hate guys named Lance and I guess now I'll hate them even more. So anyway, we agree that she'll go alone and when she gets back we'll go out to dinner. So I work, I get caught up in making some edits in the manuscript and when I look at my watch it's almost nine – way past dinner time even for the Hamptons. I call her cell phone and there's no answer, not even voice mail. I get worried, really worried, because she has the car and she's a lousy driver.'

He pauses, breathes deeply and continues.

'But I knew where the party was, so I put on my running shoes and jogged over to the house. There were no cars except hers in the driveway and the house was dark but the door was open so I went in. You can guess the rest. It's kind of classic, I suppose. There, on the living room floor, on the goddamn oriental carpet, were my wife and Lance, both of them naked and flushed, Laura's skin kind of gilded, the way it gets after love making. And they look at me, the two of them, as though I'm the one who should be explaining, and apologizing. Lance kind of smirking and Laura with that aggrieved expression I know so well, the look she gets if another dancer gets a role she thought was hers or if I bring home pistachio ice cream when she had specifically asked for almond chip. I kind of lost it then. I yelled, I knocked over a lamp, I grabbed Laura's clothes from the couch and tossed them at her and while she was still buttoning and snapping, before she could even put her sandals on, I pulled her out of the house. We screamed at each other all the way back to our motel. She wanted to know what I thought I was doing. We had an agreement, didn't we?

Freedom. Sexual freedom. She thought I understood that, that I had understood it for years. I looked at her as though she was crazy, as though she was someone I had never known, this woman who had been my wife for a dozen years, the center of my life, the center of my dreams.

'"How many Lances have there been?" I asked her. "Lots," she screamed. She shouted names, men I knew, men I'd never heard of. There had, after all, been weeks and weeks over the years when our work separated us, when she was traveling with repertory dance groups and I was doing book tours. She was still screeching, spewing out names, places, when we got out of the car and I slapped her. Slapped her hard, across the face. She threw her sandals at me and began kicking my bike. A dancer's kicks, high and then low, dancing legs and flying sand, the sound of gravel against the bike's metal frame, the sound of our marriage crumbling. I picked her up and carried her into our room. By this time both of us were crying. I put her on the bed, grabbed my stuff and rode the bike back to the city. She drove back two, maybe three days later, and moved her things out of the house. A week later we had dinner, a restaurant in the city, neutral territory. We talked, cried, both of us, again, but it was over. We knew that. Probably it had been over for a long time only I had been too dumb to realize it. Or maybe I just didn't want to. You know I'm the kind of novelist who never wants to write an ending.'

Daniel's voice grows hoarse and he coughs harshly as though his words had injured his throat.

'Sometimes endings write themselves,' Simon says quietly. 'Sometimes marriages just end. But lives don't end. Lives go on. My marriage with Charlotte ended. Two kids, a six-year slice of my life, and then it was over. As it should have been. We were veering off in different directions. The magazine had become the center of her life, the glitzy parties photographed for her glossy pages, the junkets here, there and everywhere while I lectured, conferred with my grad students, went to meetings and got home in time to pay the nannies and baby sitters. It wasn't working. We didn't like each other's lives and we were beginning not to like each other. We parted before that could happen and that was best for the kids, for Tracy and

Richie. It wasn't easy, not for me. I lost about twenty pounds that first year and it was months before I could sleep through the night. Dreams scared me. Loneliness scared me. And it was pretty hard for Charlotte too. She's not a bad woman, you know. Just a bad wife. Or at least she was a bad wife for me. So the Charlotte and Simon chapter ended but it was only a chapter. What followed was a year of lousy sleeping, lousy blind dates, TV dinners or no dinners. Then I met my Nessa, messy, nutsy, wonderful Nessa.'

'How did you meet? I forget,' Daniel asks. He is relieved that the conversation has veered away from Laura, exhausted by his own revelations.

'Nessa was Tracy's nursery schoolteacher and I was supposed to confer with her about Tracy's small motor skills. She had play dough under her fingernails, a streak of carmine magic marker on her cheek and flakes of silver in her hair the first time I saw her.

'"We're making costumes for a play," she told me, and I reached up and brushed the tinsel away.

'Two weeks later we were concentrating on our own large motor skills and there was a new chapter in my life. The Nessa and Simon chapter. Just like there'll be a new chapter in your life.'

He puts his hand on his friend's shoulder and Daniel reaches for his fingers – the awkward gestures of men who are wary of touch.

'I hope you're right.'

'I know I'm right. Just watch out for Louise Abbot. She still has a thing for you, you know.'

They laugh, remembering their adolescent Augusts when Louise had evoked their reluctant sympathy and Evan had earned their casual contempt.

Even after her marriage to Evan, Louise had somehow managed to trail after Simon and Daniel, darting up at them as they hiked through the woods, sitting beside Daniel on the lawn, bobbing up between them when they swam in the lake. They became skilled at evading her, laughed as she plunged into a thicket chasing after them, but still, at dinner she brought Daniel extra desserts, at breakfast she offered him the small pitcher of whole cream. If he sat on the lawn she pulled a chair over and sat beside him. Daniel was always kind to her, and he and Simon agreed that she should have divorced Evan after that first year of accidental marriage. The guy was a creep, a self-absorbed bastard who hid in the stacks of the university libraries when he should have been pulling his weight at the inn. Louise was just a kid and she worked her ass off.

Even when his parents died, Evan did not step up to the plate. Instead it was Louise who ran the place, the summer waitress become the innkeeper, her ear to the phone, her eye on the books. Her face was drawn, her forehead furrowed. There was now neither the time nor the inclination to follow Daniel into the woods, to sit beside him on the lawn. She was a busy woman burdened with responsibility.

Daniel would always be grateful to Louise for coming to New York for his parents' funerals. Her decision, he knew. Evan could not have cared less. He knew that Louise worried when there were too many guests and worried when there were too few. She framed the cards guests sent at Christmas and in June she sent cheery notes to the guests of August reminding them to make reservations. The note she sent to Daniel was addressed to him alone even after he and Laura had been married for years.

His novels, duly inscribed, were prominently displayed at the inn's reception desk, the jackets laminated.

'I'm not afraid of Louise.' Daniel grins. 'I'll say this for her – she never liked Laura.'

'What a surprise,' Simon mutters and Daniel realizes that his friend had also disliked his wife. Soon to be ex-wife, he corrects himself. There must be another way to think of her. He is a writer. He will find the words.

Together they stride back to the inn. Simon looks up and sees that the light in his room is on. He hopes that Nessa is still awake. There is a contagion in Daniel's loneliness that infects him with the febrile memory of his own desolation when he and Charlotte separated. He is overcome by a need to lie close to his wife, to pass his fingers through the fiery folds of her thick, irrepressible hair and assure himself that he has reached the safe harbor of happy endings.

*   *   *

In the rec room of the inn, the dart game expands. Liane urges Helene to play but her darts land far off the mark. Wendy and Nessa laughingly take turns and fare even worse than Helene. The teenagers, Paul, Jeremy and Annette, line up to test their skill. Greg advises them on their stance, the proper distance to be maintained from the dart board, the correct thrust of wrist. Paul catches on immediately and coaches Annette. He lifts her arm, arranges her fingers, thrilled at the touch of her skin on his hand, at the smooth softness of her flesh. Jeff Edwards looks at them and turns away. He realizes, not for the first time, that Annette is no longer a child. His daughter has drifted into the far side of adolescence.

Jeff wants to stand between her and Paul Epstein, to protect his child although he knows that she has no need for his protection. He recognizes the absurdity of his impulse. Instead he goes upstairs to share his irrational urge with Susan, to invite her laughter and her indulgence.

Their room is dark except for the small desk lamp. Susan is asleep, her head resting in the golden cone of light. Her open laptop lies next to a neat pile of manuscript pages but her battered Cassell's French dictionary, the first gift he had ever bought her, is closed. He understands that the fatigue of the day defeated her, that she fell asleep at her work, as she so often did during the early years of their marriage.

A grim anger steals over him like a gossamer veil. She was not supposed to weary herself with work. This is their vacation, sacred to leisure. They had agreed that these August weeks would not be shadowed by the demands of their careers, neither his nor hers. He stands in the doorway feeling oddly betrayed and then that foolish sense of betrayal curdles into disappointment. He leaves the room, closing the door very softly behind him and returns to the lounge.

It is newly quiet. Everyone has left. He guesses that most of the guests are in the kitchen where Louise Abbot leaves a carafe of decaf coffee and a tray of sticky buns. But across the room Polly is still seated at the bridge table, her textbook open, her pink highlighter, which almost exactly matches her sweater, sliding across an illustration of molecular linkage.

'Shit,' she says, and he laughs and moves toward her.

'Having trouble, Polly?' he asks.

'I'll never understand this,' she says, and pushes the heavy book away.

'Let me help you.'

He pulls up a chair, sits beside her, glances down at the text and slowly, softly, explains the mystery of molecular morphology to her, all the while inhaling the strangely familiar scent of her bath powder, some of which clings in infinitesimal granules to her very graceful neck. Of course. It is Jean Nate, Susan's favorite during the distant days of their courtship and now used too lavishly by Annette. The young girl's aroma of choice, he supposes. He takes the highlighter from Polly's hand and underlines the key points of the text. She leans closer to him and her breath is soft upon his arm as he moves it slowly across the closely printed page.

FIVE

Morning comes slowly to the foothills of the White Mountains. The milky light of dawn is slowly gilded by trembling shafts of sunlight that expand with an exquisite slowness. Finally, a golden radiance hovers over wild woodland, across cultivated lawn and beams down on the quietly flowing waters of lake and brook. It penetrates the sheer white curtains that hang in every bedroom of Mount Haven Inn and sends rhomboids of light dancing across the pale wood floors. Gently, that first light brushes the faces of the sleeping guests, some of whom waken at once while others squeeze their eyes shut and seek the refuge of a few more moments of precious sleep, of sheltering darkness.

Louise Abbot, of course, springs to wakefulness in the pre-dawn darkness. Still in her high-necked white nightgown, thin slippers shielding her bare feet, she wanders into the dining room and checks that the tables were properly set the previous evening. She plugs in the percolator and ignites the oven so that it will be hot when the chef arrives. She pulls in the cartons of bread left by the bakery truck, shivering against the chill. Only then does she return to bed, her face turned to Evan who smiles in his sleep, briefly resembling the youth who had pillowed her head against his body in the high sweet meadow grass.

Sadness threatens but she does not weep. She is a careful woman who rations her moments of sorrow.

Simon Epstein, always an early riser, rests his head against his wife's bare shoulder, envying Nessa her ability to sleep so deeply and delighting in the musical rhythm of her dream-bound breath. He knows that Paul is awake. He hears his son moving through the adjoining room singing softly to himself, an old Steven Foster ballad laced with sadness that Nessa often sings as she cooks. Suffused with pity for Daniel, he tries to think of how he might divert him from his sadness. Perhaps a hike into the mountains or an afternoon of fishing. He weighs the possibilities and dismisses them. He has no talent for compassion. Nessa will know what to do, what to say. He relies on her instinctive wisdom, on her generous warmth and marvels at his luck, at the urban miracle of their coming together, an unlikely couple, a fortunate match. He curls a strand of her hair about his finger and kisses her eyelids, coaxing her into tender response.

Jeff Edwards, still drowsy after a fitful sleep, is unsurprised to find Susan already gone. Her laptop, French dictionary and manuscript have disappeared from the tabletop, cleared away the previous evening before his return to the room after the hour spent with Polly. Susan had been in bed then, wearing a new nightgown of periwinkle blue silk, her freshly shampooed hair capping her head in a sleek golden helmet. She sat up and held her arms out to him, but he shook his head wearily.

'I'm tired, Susan, really tired,' he had said and turned away, unwilling to read either the disappointment or the relief on her face.

'All right.'

She slid back beneath the blanket and did not edge closer to him when he stretched out beside her.

And now she is gone from their bed and he knows that she has carried her work downstairs, that she spent the pre-dawn hours working on her translation, perhaps at the same table where he and Polly had sat the previous evening. A wave of annoyance sweeps over him. He is surprised by the intensity of his irritation. But her bringing work along on this vacation isn't what really angers him. True, they had agreed that the August vacation worked best for them, best for their family, if they were free of all obligations. Still, he knew how proud she was to have been offered the LeBec translation and he would have understood if she had told him that she needed time to work on it. It is her deception that outrages him. They have always been honest with each other.

Why is it, he wonders, that she could not tell him about it? How is it that they have fallen out of the pattern of ease? Their conversations are scripted, stripped of the passion and the laughter that had once animated them. They speak of their children, of the adolescent tensions between Jeremy and Annette, of Matt's timidity. In the darkness of the night, when once they read each other's lips with their fingers, they now worry that their neighborhood is growing over-gentrified, that their roof must soon be replaced, that they may have to buy a car for the twins to share. Words, unspoken, lie heavy upon his heart. He does not tell Susan that the shadow of boredom has fallen across his days, that he sometimes feels himself an automaton in the operating room, that he has, more than once, stopped listening when a post-operative patient complained of pain. Sometimes, driving home during the twilight hour, he pulls over to the side of the road, opens the car window and watches the scudding clouds tumble across the cobalt sky. He envies those untethered clouds and wonders, at such moments, how he came to be on that road and if there is any way he can change direction. He wonders too if other men share such feelings with their wives. Midlife crisis, he supposes. It happens. It passes.

He wonders if a similar toxic silence had poisoned Daniel Goldner's marriage to Laura, the slender, blonde-haired dancer who had never bothered to conceal the boredom she felt at the inn. Jeff recalls that when Daniel spoke she clasped and unclasped her hands impatiently. Once Jeff had watched her as she danced alone beneath a giant oak, her feet bare, her arms hugging her breasts, only to fall still when Daniel approached. Have he and Susan become like Daniel and Laura, solitary dancers on a shadowed lawn?

Immediately, he chides himself for the absurdity of the comparison. The two marriages do not remotely resemble each other. Daniel and Laura always seemed adrift, riding the tides of their separate and separating careers. He and Susan are firmly anchored. They will be all right. They will be fine. They will talk. They will have to talk. This new certainty soothes him and he picks up her nightgown, fingers its silken folds and inhales the familiar commingling scents of her body.

'Hurry up,' he calls to Jeremy and Annette who are bickering in the adjoining room, but he does not wait for them. Instead he hurries downstairs to join his wife at the breakfast table as

Donny Templeton, followed by Matt and Cary, marches importantly through the inn, jangling the breakfast bell.

Daniel Goldner hears the bell and the shouting children, but he does not go down to breakfast. His sleep, such as it was, had been troubled; unremembered dreams had filled him with inexplicable fear and an odd trembling.

'It's not the end, it's only a chapter,' he told himself, struggling to capture the calming cadence of Simon Epstein's voice and shamed at all that he had revealed to his friend. He shivered as a cold sweat slithered across his body, then pulled the cover closer and slept again.

Now he was adrift on the large double bed, Laura beside him, floating across sun-streaked waters. He wakened, weeping, because she had vanished and he feared that she had danced across shimmering wavelets and allowed herself to sink below their surface.

'No, no,' he cried in a sleep-strangled voice. He pounded the pillow where her head should have rested and opened his eyes to the reality of the night's darkness and his own irrational terror.

He remains in bed then, as the boys and their bell disappear down the corridor, and closes his eyes in pursuit of rest, in pursuit of forgetfulness.

He does not stir when Louise Abbot tiptoes into the room and places a tray containing a carafe of coffee and a plate of toast on the bedside table. Such pampering is a rarity at Mount Haven Inn, generally reserved for sick children and indisposed guests. But, of course, that is how Louise must perceive him, as a convalescent in need of beneficent coddling. He opens his eyes as she leaves the room and glimpses the swirl of her denim skirt against her legs as she softly closes the door. Louise always had good legs, he remembers. He and Simon had agreed on that. He takes a sip of coffee and is surprised at how good it tastes. Hungry, for the first time in weeks, he gobbles up the toast.

He goes to the window and looks down at the emerald-green lawn across which Evan is very slowly guiding a mower. The aroma of newly mown grass hangs sweetly on the summer air.

Daniel inhales deeply and decides that it was, after all, a good idea to come to the inn.

Polly, standing at the kitchen window, waiting for the dishwasher to complete its last cycle so that she can unload it and then fill it with the rest of the breakfast dishes, watches as the guests glide across the lawn. She knows that they usually stay close to the inn on this first vacation day, still testing the waters of their new leisure, still uneasy with the empty hours that stretch before them, so newly bereft of reassuring schedules and crowded calendars. She supposes that the absolute quiet of Mount Haven Inn is unnerving after the turmoil of classrooms and offices where phones ring, and urgent emails summon them to meetings and consultations. But, of course, they are relieved to have abandoned their work lives for these few weeks. Polly notes that they leave their cell phones in the drawers of their bedside tables and the only visible newspapers are those Michael Curran buys each morning.

No television, no radios intrude on this peaceful respite. Wars are fought in another world, stock prices rise and fall on distant continents, all a matter of indifference to these guests of August. They are on leave from the larger world as well as from their own small frenetic universes. They have shed their urban uniforms in favor of the light fabrics and vivid hues of summer.

They scatter across the emerald green lawn after breakfast, veering in different directions, like brightly colored wild flowers driven by a gentle wind. The small boys race to the play area, as though flying on the wings of their own laughter. Annette, Jeremy and Paul, with gaily patterned beach towels draped over their shoulders, their long legs lathered with glistening sunscreen, head for the lake. The twins break into a run but Paul moves at his own pace, now and again gazing skyward. He spots a hawk, flying low and then soaring out of sight. He regrets not bringing his birdwatching diary but he was afraid that Annette might think that nerdy and he does not want Annette to think him nerdy. Impulsively, he sprints ahead, seizes her hand and, laughing, they race past her brother who, taken by surprise, stares after them and slows his gait to a walk.

Mark Templeton leads his wife and daughter-in-law to the

three chairs he arranged earlier. Obediently, the two women settle into the wide-armed, low-backed white wooden Adirondack chairs which Evan Abbot painted during the long winter months.

Andrea Templeton, wearing oversized sunglasses, tilts her large straw sun hat, fingers its band of apple-green linen that exactly matches her shorts, and removes her needlepoint from her carrier bag, also apple green. The long silver needle glitters in the sun and she draws a thread of crimson silk through the taut fabric and works her pattern in rhythmic stitches. She reaches into her bag for her scissors, which she finds without any difficulty. She seems a woman in control of her life, in control of her possessions, but Polly is not deceived. She has already cleaned and straightened the Templetons' room and discovered the three bottles of vodka, buried beneath a gray cashmere stole in the elegant black leather case with the monogram AM. They are exactly where they were the previous year only last year the stole was red and the brand of vodka was different. Grey Goose has replaced the Stoli.

Polly is familiar with secret drinkers. Her own mother sips very cheap bourbon from a teacup; her father keeps a flask in his tool chest. But neither of them are as careful as elegant Andrea Templeton who always places a bottle of very expensive mouthwash in the medicine cabinet and who never ever slurs a word.

As though she's fooling anyone, Polly thinks, and watches as Wendy drops her sketchpad and pencils on to the grass, closes her eyes and turns her face upward toward the sun. Wendy loosens the straps of her lavender sun dress, kicks off her sandals and releases her hair, dark as a raven's wings, from a tortoiseshell clip and allows it to fall about her face. Polly thinks her very beautiful.

The dishwasher stops and Polly unloads it, begrudging the minutes lost at the window.

She is waiting for Jeff Edwards. She is free for an hour after finishing the dishes and she is hopeful that Susan will go walking with Helene as she usually does on their first morning at the inn.

'We hardly see each other during the year and we need to catch up,' Helene had said apologetically to Polly the previous summer, as though an explanation for that early-morning walk was necessary. 'You know how it is with sisters.'

Polly had nodded agreeably. She, in fact, does not know how it is with sisters. She is an only child. Her mother, who suffers from a rare anemia, had been warned that another pregnancy might threaten her life. Despite her caution, despite her regimen of drugs and vitamins, and the bourbon which she insists is medicinal, she sometimes appears half dead to Polly who often shakes her awake when she returns home, to assure herself that her mother has not died in her absence. She did not, of course, tell this to Helene whom she distrusts because she laughs too often and stares too closely at her older sister.

If the sisters do go off together and Dr Edwards is alone, she will ask him if he wouldn't mind going over part of yet another chapter with her, perhaps in the brick outbuilding which Evan Abbot has turned into a kind of study, its walls lined with books, an old sofa and a rickety desk placed in a corner. Evan, she knows, is at the university library in Durham and she and Jeff Edwards will be undisturbed in his sanctuary. Such privacy is necessary. Louise Abbot would, of course, disapprove of her intruding on a guest and she does not want to risk angering Louise. She needs her job.

She is still at the window when Helene and Susan pass by. She smiles, waits for them to disappear down the road, and then swiftly removes her apron, runs her fingers through her hair, grabs her textbook from its hiding place behind the sugar and hurries out just as Jeff Edwards begins to cross the lawn.

'Dr Edwards,' she says breathlessly, 'I wonder if you would mind going over another chapter with me?'

He smiles, the non-committal practiced smile of a man who has spent years reassuring the families of post-operative patients that things went well, that everything will be fine, and nods.

'Of course, Polly. I'll be glad to.'

Together they make their way to the red brick building, their passage marked only by Nessa Epstein who stares after them before turning back to her book.

Liane Curran wonders if she can persuade anyone to go to the outlets with her. New Hampshire does have terrific outlets. Or maybe she could go antiquing. That is something Greg and Helene Ames do a lot and it might be fun. Greg bought that great darts set in an antique shop. Helene is with her sister, that snobby Susan who barely said hello to Liane. Maybe she and Greg could go alone. Greg might want the company and Michael wouldn't mind. She waits for the sisters to vanish down the road before approaching Greg Ames who has carried his guitar out to the lawn. Michael is safely sequestered with Simon Epstein who has agreed, somewhat reluctantly, Liane thinks, to look at his spreadsheets.

'Hey, Greg,' she says in the lilting voice she cultivated as a young girl. 'I just love that dart game. You were lucky to find it. You know, I've never gone antiquing. Are there any good antique places around here?'

'A couple,' Greg says.

'I'd love to find a nice old bookcase for Cary's room. Michael's busy. Would you have time to drive me to one of those places?'

'I'd love to, Liane, but I want to practice this morning. Helene and I may go after lunch. You could join us.'

'Oh, thanks. Maybe.' She flashes him a smile that shows no hint of disappointment and watches him walk across the lawn toward a chair at a remove from the other guests.

Annoyed, she turns back indoors. She will find a book or perhaps start a puzzle. Instead she heads for the box of darts, set on a shelf out of the reach of the smaller children. She selects one, blows on its feathers, stands at a distance from the board and aims at the target with angry ferocity.

Helene and Susan, as always, follow the road that leads from the inn to Middleton, the very small hamlet only a half mile away. Although they do not look alike, they walk with similar energy, with matching grace, bearing down hard on the balls of their feet and sprinting forward. Greg and Jeff have noted their shared gait and smiled at each other, admiring husbands of women who are sisters.

The two women continue on in companionable silence until they reach the last acreage of the property belonging to the inn. They pass a clapboard house sinking into disrepair, its paint peeling, a slab of wood substituting for a pane of glass in a downstairs window.

'Polly Syms' house,' Helene says absently. 'The family's on hard times. Her father hasn't much work and her mother is really sick. You have to admire her for plugging on.'

Susan nods.

'It's tough,' she says. 'But she'll manage. Girls like her always do.'

Helene looks at her quizzically but says nothing. She will not tell her sister how much she sounded like their mother.

They reach the small white house which has always charmed them.

'They painted it last summer,' Helene observes. 'We looked at a house very similar to that one but decided against it.'

Susan nods. She has heard those words before. Greg and Helene are forever searching for a house, finding one that seems possible and then rejecting it. She and Jeff speculated about their hesitancy back in the days when they, the contented couple, secure in their home, happy with their family, their careers, sat lazily over glasses of wine and mused on the vagaries of their friends and family. They were certain in that bygone time that their own lives were secure enough to escape such idle scrutiny.

Jeff had posited that Greg and Helene were aiming too high, seeking out homes that were beyond their means. Their incomes were modest, given the burden of their student loans and the fact that they were latecomers to their careers, having spent so many years traveling the world. Greg catches gigs in small clubs and Helene exhibits her paintings in even smaller café galleries, now and again making a small sale. Over the years, picture postcards from Spain and Greece, from Turkey and Ireland had arrived at irregular intervals at the Edwards' home and were briefly displayed on the mantelpiece, talismans to be envied and derided.

'No pension plan, no real savings, no equity.' Jeff had ticked off their financial missteps in the self-congratulatory tone of a man who has planned his own life carefully, and yet Susan detected a trace of wistful envy in his accusation.

'It might be that they don't really want a house, like

they don't really want children. Maybe that kind of permanence is just not for them. They're still gypsies at heart,' he had said.

'Helene even dresses like a gypsy,' Susan had countered.

And indeed, Helene is in gypsy mode today, in a rainbow-colored dress, its ragged hem swirling at her knees, the bodice baring her shoulders, all but exposing the rise of her breasts. Her bright hair, so carelessly tinted, is, as always, too long and too unruly. Susan pats her own golden helmet and adjusts the collar of her impeccably ironed pale blue shirt.

'Maybe you ought to scale down your expectations,' she tells her sister cautiously. 'Small houses can be very cozy, very easy to maintain.'

Helene shrugs. 'Your kids look great,' she says, too swiftly changing the subject.

She forgives herself. She does not want Susan's advice and she does have a deep fondness for her niece and nephews. There are framed photos of them on her bedside table and snapshots in her wallet.

'Yes. They're OK, I suppose,' Susan says.

Helene is surprised at the uncertainty in her sister's voice.

'But Annette and Jeremy are at a funny stage,' Susan continues. 'They were once so close and now they bicker constantly. They're so mean to each other that they actually scare Matt.'

'Adolescence isn't easy,' Helene says carefully.

She and Susan seldom discuss their own teenage years, a time riddled with sadness and tension, with melancholy memories of their ineffectual father who died of a heart attack the day before Susan's sixteenth birthday, and ambivalent feelings about their mother who was diagnosed with uterine cancer when Helene entered college and was dead within a week of her graduation. They do not speak of the years of her illness, of their own uneasy balance on the seesaw of remission and recurrence, relaxing in her brief optimism, fleeing her fury at the onset of too familiar pain, breathing easy only when they stood side by side at her funeral, safe at last from her roiling rage. They are sisters, sharers of a painful past, who remain firmly armored in the tacit silence of survivors, defending themselves against secrets they will not articulate.

'No. It's not,' Susan agrees. 'What did Shakespeare call it
– the heyday of the blood. A difficult phrase to translate into
French. All that sexual juice begins to ferment and the poor
kids don't know how to handle it. The twins are only seventeen,
but I have a friend who teaches at their school and she claims
that lots of the kids in their grade are already sexually active.
It scares me, Helene.'

'Have you talked to Annette about it?'

Susan smiles wearily. 'I tried. She just laughed at me and
asked what century I was living in. Jeff finally left one of these
books that a gynecologist wrote specifically for teenage girls
on her bed. If she read it, she didn't mention it. But I didn't
worry too much because she hangs out with a nice crowd of
kids at school and there was never any special guy. They go
everywhere as a group. But you know there's always been a
kind of chemistry between her and Paul Epstein and here at the
inn they're together constantly. We've been here for a day and
already they're off together. I don't want to be the paranoid,
nagging mother, but in fact I am frightened and I do want to
nag. She's so young, so vulnerable. Helene, did Mom ever talk
to you about things like that? I mean sex stuff, the dos and
don'ts.'

The question is hesitant and takes Helene by surprise. Her
heart beats faster and she struggles to find an answer that will
not be laced with the bitterness she has struggled for years to
overcome.

'Our mother?' she asks at last and amends the question with
a laugh she knows to be too harsh. 'Susan, you have to be
kidding. I'm not the daughter she would have discussed something like that with. She wouldn't have cared enough. Don't
you remember how it was with us? With Mom and me?'

'I remember. Of course I remember,' Susan says softly and
Helene wills herself to accept her sister's words as an apology
of a kind although of course it is not Susan's fault that she was
the favored daughter.

Neither of them can forget their mother but it is only Helene
who cannot forgive her. She is haunted still, in dream and
memory, by that long-faced, narrow-eyed woman, her features
distorted by an irrational anger which she vented only on her

younger daughter. Even in the days before her illness, Helene, the child she had never planned to conceive, had been the target of the wild rages that erupted without warning. She shrilled that it was Helene who had caused her father's death, burdening him with financial worries, always asking him for extra money for her art supplies, her art lessons, always cloying at him with her hungry need for attention. So spoiled, so selfish. It was Helene's arm that she twisted when a plate was broken, Helene's face that she slapped when a bed was left unmade, Helene whom she forced out of the house without a coat during a blizzard because she had forgotten to buy milk on her way home from school. Susan, calm and golden haired, was mysteriously exempt from her abuse, favored only with her fierce admonitions. The world was a dangerous place. No one could be trusted. Friends betrayed you. Men had secret and dark agendas. Her own husband had deserted her when he died. All men lacked fidelity. Susan, so beautiful, so trusting, had to be careful. Susan had retreated into her bedroom, closing the door firmly against her mother's fury and her sister's misery.

Later, when cancer darkened her life, their mother accused Helene of causing the carcinoma, shouting, in the delirium of pain, that even in utero Helene had been a restless, demanding baby, kicking angrily against the wall of the womb throughout that difficult, unwanted pregnancy.

'Cancer-giver!' she had shouted, writhing in agony, and the hospice nurse turned to the sisters and whispered, 'Don't be upset. It's not her talking. It's the pain.'

But the sisters knew her to be wrong. It was their mother's voice they heard. The words had preceded the pain.

It is her voice that resonates in memory, even in these happier days of their womanhood as they walk on in sorrow-rimmed silence. Before they reach the cemetery at the end of the road they pause, as always, in the wild meadow to pluck bouquets of flowers. They fill their arms with the last brave blossoms of summer, long-stemmed asters, sprays of golden rod, small clusters of dark-hearted rogue roses. Holding their floral offerings close, they open the rusting cemetery gate and walk slowly down the rows of graves. They pause before a headstone, new since their visit the year before, its ground cover of dark soil studded with nubs of plantings that will not sprout for another year. Helene reads the inscription aloud.

'*Miles Henderson. Beloved Husband, Father and Grandfather. Protector of His Nation and His Family.*' They are silent in deference to Miles Henderson whose life has been reduced to these few words by chisel and mallet.

Helene stoops and places a scarlet wild rose on the grave. Granules of moist earth cling to the hem of her colorful skirt. Susan brushes them off. They are both mindful that they do not visit their mother's grave, that they brought no flowers to her burial. This tender offering to an unknown stranger somehow assuages their odd guilt. They continue on their way, their shadows falling darkly across the sunlit slabs.

'What does Jeff say about Annette?' Helene asks.

It is a cautious query. Her sister's husband, she senses, has never quite approved of her or of Greg. She supposes it is because their careless lives, their carefree pasts, are an affront to his own calibrated agenda. That thought, unbidden, etches her question with acidity.

'Jeff?' Susan repeats her husband's name as though it is foreign to the emotional equation she has asked her sister to solve. 'He's hardly ever home. His schedule at the hospital, his meetings, his research. And when he is with us, he's exhausted. I talk but I'm never sure he's listening. Sometimes I feel as though I'm living with a ghost. I know that it's the craziness of our schedules, the constant demands of the kids – most of which I take care of because he's at the hospital and I'm at home. But I can't complain. I opted for translation because I could do it at my own pace and in my own home. It was my choice and I don't regret it. I promised myself, when I became pregnant, that I would be a mother who was there and who cared, a good mother. Because I knew what it was like to have a bad mother. Mom couldn't help it, I suppose. She was who she was. I try to understand. She was bitter, disappointed, angry, always at war with the world, at war with herself. I'm sorry for her now, the way I was sorry for her then, but there's no avoiding the truth. She was a bad mother.'

Helene nods but she remains silent.

They reach the far end of the graveyard. The dead of centuries past are buried here, the veterans of distant wars who fought on southern battlefields and across distant oceans buried now in the New Hampshire town of their birth. Small, faded American flags, remnants of Independence Day or perhaps death day visits, are planted in the friable earth. Here too are the graves of women, mothers and wives, sisters and friends. Aged cedars shelter weathered gravestones, their granite worn thin over the decades, pocked by onslaughts of hail and sleet, gently brushed by low-hanging pine trees. The sisters read the fading epitaphs. Susan braids her long-stemmed asters and places them atop the grave of *Gertrude Thompson, 1801–1860, Beloved Mother.* A smaller gravestone, abutting Gertrude Thompson's, reads *Prudence Thomson 1820–1821. Our Beloved Babe.* Susan scrapes away the dirt that encrusts the cursive carved letters and Helene, stooping to crown the tiny headstone with a spray of goldenrod, sees that her sister's eyes are bright with tears.

'You are a good mother, Susan,' she says softly. 'A wonderful mother. You were brave. I'm a coward, you know. Afraid to have children because I didn't want to be like her.'

'But it's not too late,' Susan says softly. 'And you don't have to worry. You could never be like her. Trust yourself, Helene.'

Kneeling then, before the grave of Lesley Green, *A friend who was like a sister* according to the inscription, the sisters, themselves so newly bonded in friendship, join hands, and slowly, fingers linked, they make their way back to the inn and walk across the lawn, shading their eyes in search of their husbands. Helene spies Greg, strumming his guitar, and waves to him.

'Jeff must be in our room,' Susan says, but even as she speaks Jeff and Polly emerge from the red-brick building, both of them smiling, Jeff's head lowered as though to better hear what Polly is saying. Susan stares at them and walks away, her cheeks burning, her heart heavy. She does not turn as Jeff hurries after her, almost colliding with Simon Epstein.

'What's his hurry?' Simon asks, sliding into the chair next to Nessa, who sits with her legs curled.

'I haven't a clue,' Nessa replies. 'Are you done dispensing sage advice?' Michael Curran, she notes, is still carrying his briefcase, a ludicrous burden for a man dressed in ill-fitting plaid Bermuda shorts and a faded red tennis shirt.

Michael waves to her and heads toward the play area where the small boys are building a fort using stones and fallen branches. He smiles at his son and Cary, without breaking pace, waves to him and sets a large rock in place. Michael sets down his briefcase and claps. Nessa, the early childhood educator, accustomed to reading parents' faces and gestures, nods approvingly. Michael Curran is clearly a man who loves his son.

'Curran's a bright guy,' Simon replies. 'He moved too fast but he's on to a good thing. He just needs some capital infusion. I'm going to talk to Mark Templeton about it. Hey, I got a call from Tracy. She and Richie are driving up for lunch. They both have the afternoon off. That OK with you?'

'Of course. Why wouldn't it be?'

His question surprises her. She has never found it difficult to deal with Simon's son and daughter and even her relationship with Charlotte, their mother, is untinged by anxiety. She considers Simon's failed first marriage to be a closed chapter, a remnant of his discarded past which, except for Tracy and Richie's occasional visits, barely impacts on their shared present. He has told her, and she believes him, that when he and Charlotte meet, he feels only indifference. She thinks of her friend Myra, long divorced, who confided that she had encountered her ex-husband in a restaurant and had difficulty recalling who he was and how their lives had been linked. Marriages end, relationships wither, some ex-wives, ex-husbands, become barely remembered specters.

It is entirely possible, she thinks, that their friend Daniel Goldner, so newly wounded, his shoulders bowed beneath the weight of a loss still fresh and raw, will one day see Laura and, like Simon, he will feel neither pain nor pleasure. She has always been fond of Daniel, has always felt protective of him. She resists the urge to hold him close as she often does with a nursery school child who has suffered a grievous hurt, real or imagined. The thought amuses her; she ponders the weight of his head against her body and laughs at the absurdity of the image.

She straightens her legs and Simon reaches out and tickles

her toes, mischievously stroking each varicolored toenail until she collapses with laughter.

Mark Templeton looks up from his book and Andrea Templeton sets down her needlepoint. They turn in their chairs and stare at Simon and Nessa, mystified by their merriment, not unlike bemused tourists from a silent world where spontaneous joy is unknown. Wendy, however, shakes her head so that her dark hair brushes her cheeks and smiles approvingly. As does Daniel Goldner who emerges from the inn, pauses for a moment and then walks toward his friends, straining to think of a comment that will evoke amusement and easy rapport.

SIX

They assemble for lunch, newly relaxed, eased into their new leisure. Louise Abbot flutters about the sun-filled dining room smoothing tablecloths, rearranging place settings, centering the vases of freshly picked flowers.

The room hums with murmured conversations, now and again punctuated by bursts of soft laughter. The kitchen door swings open and shut as dishes are carried in and out, bread baskets replenished, fallen silverware replaced. The guests of August are content on this first day of their vacation. They wear the mantle of their new leisure lightly.

Plans are being made for the weeks ahead. A day trip to the White Mountains. A sail on Lake Winnipesaukee. Blueberry picking. Whitewater rafting. The Concord outlets. Familiar names and activities emit frissons of anticipatory pleasure. Greg Ames unfurls a map of New Hampshire and Jeff opens a guidebook and studies it, avoiding Susan's gaze.

Matt looks anxiously at his father and then at his mother. He wants them to talk to each other. This new silence between his parents makes him as uneasy as the constant bickering of his older sister and brother who, even now, are glaring at each other. But Jeremy and Annette, as brother and sister, are bonded forever while husbands and wives, he knows, often part ways. Matt has three classmates whose parents have divorced. They come to school on Fridays, lugging bulging knapsacks. They are gypsy children, migrating from one parent to another. Matt does not want to be such a child. He struggles to engage his parents, to build a conversational bridge between them.

'Mom, Dad, come and see our fort after lunch.'

'Mom, what's the French word for "fort"?'

'Hey, Dad, were there hospitals in forts?'

They offer monosyllabic answers.

'Yes. Maybe.'

'*Fortresse*. The French is almost like the English.'

'Not hospitals. Maybe sick bays.'

His parents do not look at each other as they offer their separate answers. Jeremy and Annette spar briefly over the last remaining roll. Defeated, Matt finishes his meal, pushes his chair back and joins Cary, who is racing toward Donny's table.

The small boys chatter about the fort they are building, putting forth new ideas.

Wendy is grateful that Donny has these friends, that they are engaged on this project. She appreciates Daniel Goldner's entry into their conversation as he tells them about the fort he and Simon built years ago, how they fortified it with stones carried up from the lake. He is a kind man, she decides, and she flashes him a smile.

'You could paint the stones,' Wendy tells Donny as Matt and Cary are summoned back to their parents' tables for dessert. 'That could be fun. Shall I drive to the craft store with Grandma and Grandpa and pick up some paint?'

'Gee, that would be great.' Donny's face lights up and he is again out of his seat and off to share this new idea with Matt and Cary.

'I couldn't do that today.' Andrea's voice is dry. 'I feel a headache coming on.'

'I've already arranged to meet with Simon Epstein,' Mark adds.

Wendy feels the stirrings of anger at their indifference. These August weeks that she and Donny spend with Adam's parents, this orchestrated celebration of her husband's life in the month of his birth and of his death, is a stupid pretense, a sentimental charade, an on-demand drama crafted by her manipulative mother-in-law, that well-groomed mistress of secrets and lies.

Louise, sensing the tension, excuses herself and goes into the kitchen. Evan does not excuse himself but simply leaves the table. Mark pours a second cup of coffee for himself and smiles grimly at Andrea.

'Why don't you go upstairs and lie down, my dear?' he asks.

'In a few minutes,' Andrea says very softly, as though the sound of her own voice will trigger pain.

Daniel Goldner peels a green apple, his gaze wandering from the haughty older couple to their gentle daughter-in-law. He is puzzling out the strange dynamic that impels their annual ritual. They are clearly not bound by affection or a commonality of interest. They are, simply, mutually bereft. Adam Templeton, he knows, died when Donny was a toddler. For how long then, he wonders, does the sorrow of loss linger, enmeshing abandoned survivors? He realizes, with surprise, that for the first time in days, he has not thought about Laura and his own loss. It is Wendy Templeton's controlled anger, the soft sadness of her eyes that intrigues him.

'I'll drive over to the craft store with you,' he offers. 'My bike or your car?'

'My car. I'm kind of afraid of bikes. But then I'm a bit afraid of cars as well. Although accidents can happen anywhere,' she replies, and realizes she has said too much.

Andrea pales, stares at her daughter-in-law and rises from her seat. How insensitive of Wendy to speak of her fear of cars, to spirit them so heedlessly into the sphere of Adam's death.

'Please excuse me. I really must lie down.'

She does not look at Wendy. Walking too swiftly, she nearly collides with Tracy and Richie Epstein who burst through the door in a whirl of movement and laughter.

Shrugging with annoyance, Andrea continues on her way as the two young people dash to their family's table, laughing and talking, their faces brushed with summer's brightness, their voices electric with excitement.

Tracy's many silver bracelets jangle. Richie's long legs are a flash of bronze against his snow-white tennis shorts. Their energy – their frenetic greetings, exuberant hugs for their father and for Paul, their half-brother, dutiful affectionate cheek kisses for Nessa, their stepmother – changes the ambience of the room but there is no annoyance in the glances that are trained on them. The children of Simon Epstein's first marriage, his handsome son and his beautiful daughter, leaping so gracefully toward adulthood, are not strangers at Mount Haven Inn and they are welcomed with admiring affection.

Extra chairs and place settings are brought to the table and Richie and Tracy fill their plates, nodding pleasantly at Louise Abbot who hurries over to their table, beaming her pleasure at their arrival.

'So nice that you could come for lunch,' she says.

'Hey, we're here for more than lunch,' Tracy says. 'We didn't have time to call, Dad, but the camp shut down. Three cases of measles. Richie spoke to Mom and she's tied up with runway shows or something, so she told us to drive straight up here and she'd be in touch. It's OK for us to stay, isn't it?'

She asks her question of Simon but she turns to Louise, her smiling face radiant with the certainty that she will not be denied.

'Louise?' Simon asks apologetically.

He knows that the inn is full, that Louise managed to accommodate Daniel only because of a cancellation. (And, of course, because he was Daniel.)

'We'll manage something,' she replies. She is already calculating the extra income that two more guests will bring and assessing her options. There are two tiny bedrooms and a small bath in the loft of the red outbuilding that Evan considers his study. They can house Tracy and Richie there. Evan will not like it, but she no longer cares about what Evan likes or does not like. She hurries off to speak to Polly about cleaning the rooms and making the beds. And towels. She sighs. Adolescents use so many towels.

'It's great that you're able to spend some time with us,' Nessa says easily.

She gets along well with her stepchildren although, with her usual unflinching honesty, she acknowledges that she does not love them. She anticipates that sometime in the future she and Tracy will be friends but that is something they will have to grow into. She is less certain about Richie who reminds her, for no discernible reason, of the handsome boy who was president of her own high-school senior class, a boy with a talent for adolescent cruelty. Anonymous notes left in the locker rooms of less popular girls. Insinuations about boys who listened to music and read classics. In secondary school Richie had been accused of bullying but he has, apparently, moved on. And he has always been kind to Paul who, in turn, admires his older half-brother. Her Freudian friends might claim that their bonding is simplified because they do not have to share the same mother, but she thinks that they are simply boys who like each other enough to be friends, despite the disparity of their ages. After all, Daniel is years younger than Simon and they have always been like brothers to each other. She really should not worry about the friendship between her son and her stepson.

'We love having you here,' she adds.

'It'll be great, really great.' Paul amends her words.

Lunch is over, chairs are being pushed back, napkins folded, watches consulted. The long afternoon awaits them. The guests move slowly, sated by their meal, anticipating hours of drowsing in the sunlight or retreating into the cool silence of their rooms, the delightful luxury of a midday nap. Their alternatives are numerous. Perhaps a drive. Perhaps a short walk. Books dangle from their hands, smiles linger on their lips.

The small boys race to their fort. Richie and Tracy, dragging knapsacks and duffle bags, trail after Polly who carries a load of linens and towels.

Wendy and Daniel head for her car and drive off. Nessa stares after them and smiles. A perfect fit, she thinks. A soap-opera dream. The lovely young widow and the soon-to-be-divorced novelist. Definitely the ingredients of romance. Simon, who worries about Daniel, will be pleased when she shares her news with him, but that will have to wait. Simon has arranged a meeting with Mark Templeton and Michael Curran.

She watches from the steps of the inn as Simon sets three chairs in a circle. He is soon joined by Michael Curran, who has discarded his Bermuda shorts in favor of khaki slacks and a well-pressed shirt, although he still clutches his attaché case. He wears the uniform of a man concerned with business. Minutes later Mark Templeton strides toward them and claims the chair in the middle.

'Do you want to take a walk, Nessa?' Helene Ames asks.

Nessa turns. She had not heard Helene come up behind her. 'Sure. I'd love to,' she says, and the two women follow the tree-lined path that leads to the lake.

Wendy and Daniel discover that the craft shop in town is closed but will reopen within the hour. They do not mind. They wander the quiet streets of the small town, pausing at shop windows, stopping outside the bookstore to examine the used books that are ranged on sidewalk racks.

'I'm always afraid I'm going to find a copy of one of my books in a place like this,' Daniel says.

He shoves books aside and actually finds a short-story anthology that he has been meaning to read. He glances at the price – less than a dollar – and winces, pitying the editor whom he knows.

'And I'm always afraid that I'll find Adam's novel in a remainder pile,' Wendy says.

'It was a good book. You know, Adam and I were once on a panel together. I had forgotten.'

'I sometimes forget myself,' she replies and falls silent. How could she explain that Adam, his work, his angular melancholy face, his long lithe body, was slowly fading from her memory? It was as though his death, in all its tragic finality, obscured his life.

Daniel pays for the anthology and they walk on, pausing at a small café.

'A cappuccino?' he asks.

'Why not?'

They find a corner booth in that intimate room, its newly painted walls hung with watercolors by local artists, and African violets in brightly colored ceramic pots centered on each blond-wood table. Daniel looks around appreciatively, captivated by the café's modesty and charm, so unlike the trendy cafés of the Hamptons with their faux seashore ambience that Laura favored. He stares at a delicate drawing of a weeping willow tree, casting its shade across an intricately drawn flower bed.

'I really like that one,' he murmurs.

Wendy blushes. 'It's mine,' she confesses.

He looks at her in surprise.

'I live only an hour away,' she explains. 'I like this café. Ellen, the owner, is a friend. She's a portrait painter herself and her café doubles as a gallery for her own work and the work of local artists. I gave her that one because I thought she might be able to sell it and earn a commission. I know things are a little tight for her. But she says she likes it too much to sell it so there it hangs.'

'You're good. Really good.'

'I have to be. It's what I do for a living.' Her words are matter of fact, seeking neither approval nor surprise.

'I didn't know that.'

'We don't know each other very well, do we? Hardly at all. Strange, considering that we've seen each other at the inn now and again over the years.'

He nods. She is right, of course. During his infrequent visits with Laura, they had scarcely spoken to other guests, spending all of their time with Simon and Nessa. He had noticed Wendy, of course, had gleaned a few facts about her, crumbs of information offered by Nessa who somehow always seems to know everything about everyone.

'Here's what I do know,' he says reflectively. 'I know that you're a widow; that your husband, who had just published his first book, was killed in an automobile accident and that you and your son live in his childhood home. I didn't realize it was so close to Mount Haven. Now I discover that you're a very talented professional artist. I also know that your in-laws live in California and that you meet each August at Mount Haven Inn, a ritual reunion that I don't quite understand. And I have the feeling that your husband's parents are not your favorite people,' he adds daringly.

'You're right about that,' she admits and wonders why she is being so honest. She is relieved when Ellen approaches their table, kisses Wendy on the cheek and waits for their order.

'You'll want your usual decaf cappuccino, won't you, Wendy?' she asks.

'I'll have the same,' he says.

Ellen nods, smiles agreeably and he turns back to Wendy.

'And what do you know about me?' he asks.

She hesitates and then decides to match his candor with her own.

'I know that you're a novelist and critic. Historical novels. I read the first one because it was set in New Hampshire and I read the second one because it wasn't. And, of course, I know that you've been coming to Mount Haven Inn since you were a kid, that you and Simon Epstein have been friends forever and that Louise Abbot is your biggest fan. And I was here during the occasional August when you came with your wife who is very beautiful and who always seemed bored to death. Now you're here alone so I assume you're separated or divorced or maybe she's just dancing somewhere. She is a dancer, isn't she?' she asks, although of course she knows the answer.

'Laura. Her name is Laura. And it's possible that she is dancing somewhere even as we speak. I wouldn't know. We were married for twelve years and now we're separated and in the process of getting divorced, whatever that process may be.'

He relates this in a monotone and is astonished by the brevity of his revelation. How is it that his marriage, his life with Laura and its lonely aftermath, can be reduced to so few sentences? He wonders if he will ever be able to weave the strands of those cursory melancholy words into a fictional tapestry.

'Laura.' She says slowly, measuring out the syllables. 'My husband's name was Adam but you probably know that. We were only married for two years. I fell in love at twenty, out of love at twenty-one and I was widowed a month before my twenty-third birthday. Rather precocious of me, don't you think?'

She looks up as Ellen serves their coffee and places a bowl of biscotti on the table.

'Almond. Fresh baked. I know you like them, Wendy.'

'I do. Thanks, Ellen.'

Daniel watches her bite into the pastry and wonders what it would be like to live in this small community, to be coddled by a café owner who doubles as a portrait painter and greeted with affection by passers-by. He imagines himself resident here – he is, after all, in search of a new life. He might write all morning, glance now and again at the mountains beyond his window and then stroll down the quiet street to this café where Ellen will greet him by name, as she greeted Wendy. The anonymity and solitude of his work hours might be briefly banished, his writerly loneliness briefly sated. He smiles at this improbable fantasy, dismisses it and focuses on Wendy.

'I don't know if "precocious" is the word I'd use.'

'Oh. What word would you use?'

He thinks for a moment. 'Sad,' he replies simply. 'What

happened to you was sad. Falling out of love is sad. Confronting death is sad. Being left with a small child is sad.'

'Yes.'

All flippancy is drained from her voice which becomes so faint he must lean across the table to hear her.

'It was sad and hard, very hard. Sometimes I think it might have been easier if I had loved him during those last months, that last year. I would have earned the grief of a mourner. I would have been entitled to the sorrow of loss. Instead I felt abandoned and frightened and, of course, sad, so very sad.'

'When did you stop loving him?'

The intrusiveness of his question startles him. It was a question he had thought to ask Laura. *When did you stop loving me?* But he had feared her answer and settled instead for the congealing bitterness of silence. Yet now he has thrust these words at Wendy. He chastises himself. This intimacy between them is too sudden. It is riddled with danger and yet he waits expectantly for her reply.

She sighs. Their conversation has ambushed her. She has never before spoken so openly about her relationship with Adam and it startles her that she has offered Daniel Goldner, whom she hardly knows, such intimate revelations. And yet the words come easily. She answers his question without hesitation.

'It's easier to think about when I started loving him. I came to Cambridge from the Midwest, a small Ohio town, because I'd won a scholarship to the Art Institute. I was so far out of my league I might have been in another country. Some friends in my watercolor class dragged me to a party, which turned out to be one of those mob scenes in a small, smoke-filled grad student apartment that stank of liquor and pot. I was sorry I'd come the minute I walked in and sorrier still that I'd worn my new blue sweater. People were talking about writers whose names I'd never heard, places I'd never been to, poetry readings in cafés, experimental theatre in church basements. Reefers were being passed around, beer cans were popping and, crazily enough, in all that din, a baby was crying. Some couple had brought their infant and just tossed it on top of the pile of coats in the bedroom. I had one beer and then another, then two or three puffs on a reefer. My first weed and yes, I inhaled. My head was spinning and I was trying to work my way across the room, thinking that maybe I'd just leave, or maybe I'd find the baby and cuddle it, when I bumped into this tall thin guy.' She pauses and takes a sip of coffee which Daniel assumes must be tepid by now.

'Adam?' he asks. 'Adam was the tall thin guy.'

'Of course. Adam. He was carrying a glass of beer and it spilled all over me, all over my new blue sweater. I looked up and I began to cry. The crowd around him looked at me and laughed but Adam didn't laugh. He took me by the arm and led me into the bathroom. He locked the door, patted my sweater dry, sat me down at the edge of the tub, washed my face with a corner of a dirty towel, took a comb out of his pocket and combed my hair. He asked me what had made me cry and I told him about the baby and how it was crying. 'OK. Let's get the baby,' he said but instead he sat down beside me, put his arm around me and we kissed and kissed, the two of us clinging to each other on the edge of that scummy white tub until people began banging on the door. So Adam unlocked it and we went back to the party, which was winding down. The baby was gone and so were most of the coats.

'"Adam, let's find a bar on the Square and really celebrate your book," one of his friends called to him. So I knew that his name was Adam and that he had written a book and it had been published. It occurred to me that maybe the party was in celebration of its publication, and that turned out to be true. But Adam didn't go down to the Square. Instead he took me back to his apartment and we made love once and then again. We laughed and took a shower together and then we lay down on his bed and marveled at how swiftly and easily we had fallen in love.'

She laughs bitterly.

'You were twenty,' Daniel reminds her.

'Yes. I was twenty. A very young twenty. A Midwestern small-town twenty. I wore pastel sweater sets and matching head bands and I never cut a studio class and I worked the reception desk at the Fogg so I'd have expense money. In my small town a girl like me didn't get into bed with a guy she had known for two hours. Adam was twenty-seven, a sophisti-cated twenty-seven. He'd graduated from Harvard, lived in

Europe, trekked through India, written a novel and gotten it published. He bought his clothes at J. Press, mostly chinos and soft collared shirts. I knew, I suppose, that there was money lurking in the wings. He told me that his father kept an apartment in New York because that's where his business interests were and his mother lived in a house in New Hampshire, the house he'd grown up in, because she hated the city. But I didn't ask any questions. I decided that I was in love. I moved into his apartment but I kept my job at the Fogg and, good girl that I was, I never missed a class or a workshop. We played house, those first couple of months. Adam bought the food and I cooked it. His friends came over and drank beer and talked about who was writing and who just said they were writing and who was selling out which meant that someone had taken a job, and of course, how rotten the government was and how great some new restaurant in Somerville was. We always had bottles of gin and vodka and Scotch and bourbon that always seemed to need replenishing way too soon, but I didn't think much about that. It didn't occur to me that Adam was drinking. I was out all day and I assumed he wrote all day. Wasn't that what writers were supposed to do?'

'Ideally,' Daniel agrees. 'But it often happens that they don't.'

He thinks of his own days too often spent in moody silence, in desperate fear of the blank computer screen.

'Anyway, I got pregnant. We decided to get married just as easily and swiftly as we had decided to move in together. No discussions. No weighing of options. I called my parents who were suitably horrified. They knew I had a boyfriend named Adam but they didn't know I was living with him. And they asked questions that I thought were stupid and invasive. How did this Adam plan to support a family? Had I met his parents? What sort of people were they? I didn't answer because I couldn't. I hung up. I called back and we argued some more and my mother cried and they hung up. A week later my father sent me a check of one thousand dollars which was a lot of money for them and I didn't cash it. They didn't even talk about coming to the wedding, which was a grim little civil ceremony. A couple of Adam's friends came and when we left the courthouse they threw breadcrumbs instead of rice because, they said, birds sometimes choked on the rice. I thought it was great that I was marrying into a community of people that worried about birds. We all laughed and pretended that we were having fun and it was great to be so off-beat, so creative. Adam's parents came. It was the first time that I met Andrea and Mark, but they were very correct, smiled their thin disapproving smiles, kissed me on the cheek with very dry lips and took us out for a wedding lunch at Locke-Obers. Mark gave Adam an envelope and I knew that it answered my father's question about how Adam would support a family. I went back to my classes and continued working until Donny was born.'

'And then?' Daniel asks.

'And then Adam and I were home together all day and I was out of love. Because it was really hard to stay in love with a man who spent most of the day drinking very small glasses of vodka and blaming everyone for what was not happening in his life. He blamed his publisher for not promoting his book, his agent for not getting him a better contract, his parents for his lonely childhood, his disloyal friends who stopped coming around because Donny's crying and the stink of his diapers annoyed them. And he blamed me for getting pregnant. He discovered that he really didn't want to be married after all and he certainly didn't want to be a father. We quarreled and made up and then we quarreled and didn't make up. And the blame game went on and on and he drank more and more. Finally, we had a kind of terminal argument. It was a day when Donny was really sick and I had to take him to the pediatrician. He yelled that I cared more about Donny than I did about him and that crazy outburst made me realize that we couldn't go on. I told him he had to do something about himself, about our lives or I would leave. He began to cry then and said there was no way he could plan a future if he couldn't confront his past. He talked about having it out with his parents, of driving to his mother's house in New Hampshire. His father was there. It was the day scheduled for their usual monthly visit and he had to go. "Not today," I said, because he was already drunk. But he didn't answer me. Instead he called his father and he was talking to him when I left to take Donny to the pediatrician. He was gone when I got home. I knew he was on his way to New

Hampshire. And, of course, I knew that he was too drunk to drive. I wasn't even surprised when the phone rang. His father told me that Adam was dead. 'Gone' was the word Mark used, the only word he could manage because he was crying. I picked Donny up and said, 'He's gone. Your daddy is gone.' I hung up the phone and wondered who Adam was blaming when he died. Maybe me. I actually blame myself. Sometimes. Maybe, if I hadn't forced an ultimatum on him, if I hadn't said the things that I said, if I hadn't made him cry, if I had wiped away his tears . . . I was an awful person to think that. Awful not to be crying myself. Awful that I didn't cry for him then and I don't cry for him now.'

She leans back in her chair, exhausted now, staring past Daniel who takes her hand and holds it tightly.

'No,' he says firmly. 'You are not and could never be an awful person. And you know yourself that you are in no way responsible for his death.'

He speaks decisively and, wondering on what he bases this instinctive reassurance, he breaks off a bit of the biscotti and presses it with his thumb into a design on the tabletop, a habit that always annoyed Laura. Ellen passes and he asks for the check. Wendy stands, picks up her broad-brimmed lavender sun hat, waves to Ellen and waits for him in the doorway. Her long shadow falls in a dark velvet swathe across the sun-swept street. Her eyes are dangerously bright but she does not weep. He is moved to a sudden and inexplicable sadness.

They return to the craft shop and Wendy selects four cans of paint in different colors and four brushes suitable for outdoor use.

'This should keep the boys happy,' she says, and he nods.

They drive back to the inn in silence, conscious that too many words have already passed between them that afternoon.

SEVEN

As the afternoon wanes and the sun begins its long, slow descent, the teenagers who have spent the day at the lake make their way across the lawn dragging their wet towels and ragged blankets. They form an uneasy quartet, Paul and Annette walking together, their sun-brightened faces wreathed in laughter; Jeremy, Tracy and Richie trailing after them, Richie, breaking into a run and jostling Annette as he races past her. The small boys abandon their fort, carefully situating their freshly painted stones so that they will be in readiness for the next day's play.

Nessa Epstein reluctantly rises from her chair, marks her place in her Ruth Rendell novel, Bruno Bettelheim having been cast aside, and makes her way to the kitchen. Simon is already there, the wicker basket open, the small plates snug in their clever, gingham-lined compartments, the serving dishes spread across a counter at a remove from the areas where the chef is preparing salads for dinner. Louise Abbot hovers near Simon, removing a large dish she does not deem clean enough and washing and drying it before setting it down.

'You know, Simon, I'd be glad to let you have plates and glasses. You don't have to bring that basket,' she says as she has said every year.

Like her in-laws before her, she does not really approve of the late-afternoon cocktail party on the lawn that Simon Epstein organizes annually, imitating his own parents' Mount Haven custom. However, since the laws of New Hampshire prohibit the drinking of alcohol in public rooms, she accommodates him.

'I know, Louise. But this basket is kind of my toy. You'll indulge me, won't you?'

He turns to her, smiling his trademark smile, and Louise blushes.

'Yes. Of course. You know I will.'

Nessa flashes Louise a commiserative glance. Who could not indulge Simon when he smiles so charmingly and speaks so appealingly? The basket is Simon's conceit, an artifact of his marriage to Charlotte who had thought it a ridiculous wedding present and laid no claim to it in the painful ritual of divorce when possessions were divided, mysterious preferences expressed for ceramic candlesticks or cheese boards of walnut wood. But then, Nessa acknowledges, all marriages are strangely anchored by possessions and memories, and so many are dangerously vulnerable. She thinks of Daniel Goldner and Laura, of their unlikely togetherness and of the inevitable sadness of their parting. Poor Daniel, poor Laura.

She knows that there are those who marvel at her own marriage, but then she and Simon had been conditioned, following as they did in the footsteps of their past failures, her inappropriate lovers and the deterioration of his first marriage. They had been older, their life lessons well learned. They allow each other their disparate idiosyncrasies. They are graceful in compromise, always aware of their luck at finding each other.

Nessa had already danced at the weddings of all her friends and admired their newborn babies, convinced that her turn would never come, that she was not sure she wanted it to come.

One after another, her lovers had disappointed. But her life was full, her career successful and she knew herself to be happier than many of her married friends. Simon, in turn, had stumbled through the desert of a marriage grown loveless and lonely. And yet, against all odds, they had met and, against even more improbable odds, they have made each other happy, despite their disparities of style.

Nessa drives her battered, messy van and Simon drives his snappy, impeccable sports car. He dresses carefully, his shirts meticulously ironed, his pants sharply creased, never a button missing, never a shoe un-shined. He makes his own arrangements for the care of his wardrobe, making stops at the laundry, the dry cleaners, the neighborhood cobbler. He is a man who sits on corporate boards and leads graduate seminars. His appearance is important to him.

Nessa's own clothes are a colorful rumpled jumble, tossed carelessly into closets and drawers or sometimes simply plucked up from the floor. She selects her loose dresses and her shirts and skirts of gossamer fabrics because they are comfortable and she moves easily in them, skirts flaring over her ample waist, sneakers tied with different colored laces, sandals more often than not unstrapped. She prefers walking barefoot, padding across the rubber carpeted floors of her Magic Mountain Nursery School or gliding through her kitchen. She loves the feel of the cold ceramic floor against the soles of her calloused feet as she cooks her extravagant unplanned meals.

Because they are so unalike, meticulous Simon and careless, indifferent Nessa, their marriage bewilders their friends and acquaintances, but they themselves are not perplexed.

'We're like reverse magnets,' Nessa once told Paul who commented on his father's neatness, her own congenital disorder. 'Opposites attract, you know.'

Paul had nodded although he did not know. He only knows that his mother makes his studious, introspective father laugh out loud, that his father makes his mother smile, that her face glows when she sees him, that sometimes before dinner they dance to slow show tunes, her head resting on his shoulder, his fingers entwined in her unruly auburn curls. He has no other friends whose parents dance in the quiet of their own living rooms and he counts himself fortunate.

Nessa opens the huge inn refrigerator and studies the shelf Louise allotted to her for her Fairway purchases. She hands Simon the containers that hold the different olives and watches as he arranges them artfully on the large white plate.

'How did your meeting with Mark Templeton and Michael Curran go?' she asks.

'Fairly well, I think. Templeton may come through with some venture capital. A good deal for both of them.'

'Good,' she says.

She is proud of Simon for getting involved, for making his expertise and advice available to Michael Curran whom she likes and who always reminds her of the child who appears inevitably in every nursery school class, frightened and wary, certain of failure and rejection. She is partial to such children and always proud that they leave her class standing taller, bolder at play, gay in song.

She places the cheeses on the counter. Simon begs some lettuce leaves from the chef and positions the golden cheddar and the pale Stilton on the greenery. She is glad that she remembered the tapenade that Tracy favors and the bruschetta that Richie eats voraciously, although she really does not care very much about pleasing Richie. He is so very adept at pleasing himself. It is not that she does not like her stepson. It is that, for reasons inexplicable to herself and certainly never articulated to Simon, she does not trust him. She wonders idly if her stepchildren (she hates that word) will really stay at the inn for so long a stretch and whether Charlotte, their mother, will make an appearance. Probably not. Charlotte will most likely be off on a junket to an exotic location, choosing a five-star hotel as her base.

Simon sets out an assortment of flat breads and crackers.

'That's an awful lot,' Nessa observes.

'Well, you know, first cocktail hour of the vacation. Everyone around. Probably everyone wanting to join us. Better to set out more rather than less.'

'Of course,' Nessa agrees, although she prefers it when the group that assembles on the lawn before dinner is smaller. But Simon is right. The first day is always an ice-breaker with everyone mingling. Later there will be more discrete pairing, absences because of day trips or evenings out.

She holds the door open for him as he carries some of the food out and within minutes Paul and Annette dash into the kitchen, wearing fresh clothes, newly showered, their hair damp, their skin rose gold after hours reveling in the lakeside sunshine. Her heart soars because they are so aglow with youth and energy and her heart breaks because she knows how vulnerable they are, her son and this slender girl who places her hand ever so lightly on his arm.

'Can we help you, Mom?' Paul asks.

'Sure. Paul, can you manage some of these bottles?'

Simon has brought the drinks of summer – vodka and gin and Aquavit, the very same drinks his parents served during their stays at Mount Haven Inn. There are containers of juice and baskets of potato chips and pretzels for the children.

'And Annette, can you take the basket? And maybe the plate with the crackers.'

'No problem.' Annette smiles.

She is a very pleasant girl, Nessa decides, the daughter of very pleasant parents, although strangely, Jeff Edwards had been alone on the lawn all afternoon, reading beneath a tree and then going off for a walk with Helene and Greg, even though Nessa suspects that he is not overly fond of his wife's sister and her husband. Susan Edwards had appeared briefly afterward, perhaps in search of Jeff, perhaps to monitor Matt who was, after all, happily painting the stones for the fort with Donny and Cary. Susan confided that she was working on a translation, an important work with a pressing deadline, a novel by Juliette LeBec. It surprised Nessa that Susan was working during this vacation, something she had never done before. She had once asserted proudly that she and Jeff had made a pact never to work during these August weeks. But Nessa asked no questions. It is really none of her business.

She takes a tall bottle of tonic water, a container of orange juice and another of tomato juice out of the refrigerator and, hugging them to her chest, carries them out to the lawn. It does not bother her at all that her magenta shirt is moist and darkened by the bottles' condensation. She smiles gratefully at Michael Curran who hurries to relieve her of the bottles.

Simon is busily arranging the food on a small wooden table while the other men assemble the Adirondack chairs in a large circle. Daniel Goldner emerges from the kitchen with a bucket of ice. He fills a glass of orange juice, adds a few cubes but no liquor and hands it to Wendy Templeton. Nessa wonders how he could have known that Wendy would not want vodka. The older Templetons settle themselves in the chairs that afford the best view of the mountain. Mark Templeton pours himself an Aquavit in a large glass with a great deal of ice and fills a small glass to the top with vodka which his wife drinks rather too quickly. Daniel Goldner watches her, thinking of Wendy's description of Adam's drinking, how he spent entire afternoons filling small glasses with vodka. He watches as Adam's mother drains her glass, leans across the table, spreads a piece of brie on a cracker and replenishes her drink.

The other guests slide into their chairs and their conversations are the casual and pleasant exchanges of acquaintances thrust together in comfortable and finite intimacy.

They speak and fall silent at will, luxuriating in their leisure, bending forward to idly spread cheese across a cracker, to add ice to a glass. The chaos of the world is at a distance. They are on vacation.

They have all changed into slacks against the very slight chill of evening, oddly enough each of them choosing light fabrics of brown and gray, the colors of the soft-winged moths that will soon flutter against the shades of their lamps. Their colorful cardigans litter the grass. Andrea Templeton, however, wears a silk pant suit the color of silver. The fabric shimmers as she refills her glass for the third time. Her husband watches her, and Wendy averts her eyes.

The sky darkens slowly. Donny, Cary and Matt abandon croquet and dash across the lawn in a game of tag, Donny's laughter trebling musically above the shouts of his friends. Wendy smiles, her son's happiness triggering her own. Daniel Goldner moves closer to her, whispers something in her ear and she smiles yet again. Andrea stares at them and refills her glass. But before she can lift it to her lips, Mark's hand shoots out. With deliberate swiftness, he knocks her drink to the grass and vodka petals the silver silk of her slacks with leaf-shaped stains.

'Mark!' Andrea's voice is shrill with anger.

'Clumsy of me,' he murmurs as Nessa darts forward with napkins and Simon picks up the glass.

She stares at him and trains a thin smile on the others.

'If you'll excuse me, I shall have to change,' she says and walks unsteadily back to the inn.

Daniel feels Wendy stiffen and too swiftly she moves toward her son. She places her hands over his eyes, calls gaily, 'Guess who?' and hugs him as he squirms away. Daniel realizes that she is, in fact, trying to shield Donny from his grandparents' discord.

Wendy need not have worried. Mark Templeton walks across the lawn and then looks up at the inn, perhaps searching out the window of his own room where, despite the fact that darkness has not yet fallen, a small lamp glows. Andrea is there and he knows exactly what she is doing.

Subdued, they acknowledge that the party is over. Nessa and Simon fill their picnic basket and the vacationers assemble in the dining room for dinner, heralded as always by the jangling of the bell.

They gather in the lounge after dinner and once again arrange themselves in small groups. Annette and Paul continue to work on the jigsaw puzzle, their heads bent close together, his cheek brushing hers as he reaches for a long rectangular-shaped piece.

'Lincoln's hat,' he says triumphantly.

Nessa, Wendy and Helene immerse themselves in a Scrabble game.

'Doesn't your sister want to play?' Nessa asks. Susan has long been a regular at the Scrabble table.

'She's trying to finish a section of the translation she's working on,' Helene replies. 'It's a very important book. Juliette LeBec,' she adds importantly although she had never heard of Juliette LeBec before Susan mentioned her. She waves to Greg who ambles toward the dart board.

In a badly lit corner of the room Jeff and Simon are hunched over a chess board while Michael Curran, seated at a bridge table, works at complicated spreadsheets, his laptop open, alternating between tapping his keyboard and making notations with a sharply pointed pencil. The small boys, as always, are lined up at the pinball machines, pumping in their quarters and shouting at each other as each game concludes. Richie is teaching Jeremy and Tracy the intricacies of shooting pool, chalking his cue with expert ease. Tracy, who knows how to play, glares at her brother and Jeremy wonders how old Tracy Epstein is. He calculates. Jeremy is a junior in high school, she is a college sophomore. Two years, he figures. Maybe three. Not such a stretch. His aunt Helene is two years older than his uncle Greg.

Andrea and Mark Templeton, seated in the two shabby armchairs separated by a single reading lamp, turn the pages of their very thick books. Mark is immersed in the Einstein biography and Andrea is trying hard to concentrate on *Barchester Towers*, which she selected because it was so long. Andrea prizes books for their length, rewards herself with a drink as each chapter comes to an end and congratulates herself by indulging in a very good cognac on completing each heavy volume. She thinks Mark ignorant of this regimen. He tolerates her drinking, but that tacit acceptance has grown strained since Adam's death. She wonders if he blames her for Adam's drinking. She feels a surge of anger as she recalls how he had jostled the drink out of her hand. With that gesture, he had violated the mutual complicity, the defined parameters of separation, which have for so long protected their marriage. Fragile from the outset, it had always been in need of support.

Their courtship had been brief, encouraged by both their families. An excellent social fit with economic perquisites. Andrea and Mark seemed well matched to others and they each thought the other to be an appropriate and attractive choice. They came together as strangers, totally unaware of each other's frailties and strengths. Such was the pattern in their elevated social circle in which two handsome young people from good families routinely married and lived comfortable, unquestioning lives.

They discovered, early on, that if they were to continue to live as man and wife accommodations would have to be made. They were not happy together but knew that they would be even unhappier apart. Divorce was not an option that they considered. Their families' finances were intricately enmeshed and they enjoyed their social position. They were fond of each other and reasonably happy. Perhaps not 'happy' but managing. Andrea drank and she was an unrepentant drinker, given to melancholy and rage.

They decided on an unorthodox course. Mark bought a home in New Hampshire and Andrea delighted in furnishing it, delighted in living there alone while he continued to live in their New York town house. When necessary, she came to Manhattan to host a dinner party or to stand beside him at a business reception, always elegantly dressed and softly spoken. He in turn journeyed north every several weeks to spend time with her. And he was similarly safe, no longer subject to the embarrassment of her unpredictable outbursts at dinner parties, in the lobbies of theatres and concert halls.

'Andrea prefers the country while I love the city,' he explained to those who expressed mild surprise at their living situation, and to a certain extent that was true.

He was a venture capitalist, a denizen of Wall Street where he spent his days energized by the vagaries of the financial world, basking in his own shrewdness. He reveled in his evenings in the smoke-filled lounge of the University Club, dinners with powerful men who ordered thick steaks and sipped from tumblers of golden bourbon as they chewed the thick meat, and lathered layers of butter across their baked potatoes. There were occasional brief affairs, often with the wives of acquaintances who had opted for 'accommodations' similar to his own. And of course, he and Andrea still shared a bedroom and now and again came together as man and wife. Their families expected a child to be born and, ever obedient, they complied.

Mark went to New Hampshire more often after Adam was born but their lives remained essentially unchanged. Andrea furnished and refurnished their large home and had a small coterie of friends. She drank her wine, supervised her staff, slept after lunch, took care of their son and sipped vodka when Adam was in bed, a book in her hand, music on her stereo. They were mutually satisfied. Divorce was messy. Also lower class. These were not words they said aloud. She and Mark congratulated themselves, periodically, on having arrived at an arrangement that suited them both.

They had not thought about whether it suited Adam although he seemed happily unaffected by their odd life. His boyhood was uncomplicated. In an era when so many children were sent to psychologists, Adam was considered well adjusted. There were a few isolated incidents during his adolescence but then adolescence was always complicated. They ignored his moods, his occasional irrational angers. Always a good student, he excelled at Harvard and published his first novel, an account of his post-university odysseys, which won minor critical praise. They were pleased by his success and rewarded him with a generous allowance. It did not occur to them that the novel, which concentrated on the loneliness of an orphaned child, reflected his own incipient loneliness. It was fiction after all.

They acknowledged that Adam was overly secretive about his life but then they asked very few questions. They had not known of Wendy's existence until the week before Adam invited them to that sad little wedding. Her pregnancy had come as a surprise. Still, they were understanding, accepting. They increased Adam's allowance. Andrea enlarged their wedding picture, taken by a friend on the steps of the courthouse, and framed two copies – one for the New York apartment, the other for the New Hampshire house. Similarly, she displayed Donny's baby pictures in both homes.

But Adam's death, of course, changed everything. His marriage, the accident that claimed his life, and the child he had left behind, stripped them of all contentment. Rereading his novel with these new insights, they discerned the truth, revealed as it was on every page. They could no longer rationalize the life they had created for him. Their culpability was evident although they did not speak of it, not even to each other.

The New Hampshire house, which had been Andrea's refuge and the lonely fortress of Adam's childhood, was a grim reminder of his wasted life, and their own careless contribution to that sad and terrible waste. They deeded that home to Wendy and Donny and fled to California, to a house large enough to allow them to continue living their separate lives. Wendy continues to receive the allowance once sent to Adam.

They seldom mention Adam by name, but they devote all of August, the month of his birth, the month of his death, to his memory and to Wendy and Donny, the wife and son he left behind. Both Andrea and Mark find this ritual sufficient. It defines them as bereft parents and connects them, however briefly, to their grandson and to their son's widow, for whom they feel a remote fondness.

Their covenant remained unbroken, the latitude they allowed each other untroubled. Andrea, elegant as always, filled her small glasses with vodka and Mark, as always, controlled and removed, observed her in tolerant silence. But that silent truce seems to have worn thin for reasons neither of them can understand.

They sit now with their books, enmeshed by accusations as yet unarticulated, and watch as Liane Curran selects a dart, stands next to Greg and takes aim. Not quite a bull's-eye. She sighs in disappointment.

'I used to be really good,' she says to Greg.

'You have to lift your arm just a little higher.'

He lifts her arm, positions it, then angles the dart between her fingers.

'Take a half step forward and then throw.'

She hesitates, unwilling to move her arm, to relinquish the touch of his very soft hand against her flesh. Leaning closer toward him, she inhales the oddly pleasant odor of his sweat and knows that he, in turn, must surely be aware of the mingled aromas of her floral blended perfume and her almond-scented shampoo.

'Now!'

She obeys and the feathered dart sails through the air and punctures the heart of the board. The small boys, who have gathered to watch, applaud.

'We want to play. We want to play. Please, Uncle Greg.' Matt is imploring, insistent. The other boys echo his plea.

'Please. Teach us,' Cary and Donny ask in unison.

Wendy looks up from the Scrabble board. 'Is it safe?' she asks.

'Oh, it's fine,' Nessa assures her with the casual authority that commands the trust of the parents who enroll their children in her nursery school.

Wendy waves her consent, triumphantly moves her tiles on to a triple word and wonders where Daniel Goldner is. She is still surprised that she revealed so much of her life to him but she forgives herself. She is, after all, on vacation, a time when the norm is, by very definition, vacated, the vigilance imposed by the regulated routine of daily life abandoned. In the ambience of leisure, thought and word relax. That is why she had spoken as she did to Daniel, whom she hardly knows. She arranges and rearranges her letters, bitterly amused that she has blindly selected an A, a D and an M. With one more A she would have had Adam's name.

'Can I try, Mom?' Cary asks Liane.

'I'm OK with it,' she replies, relieved that Michael does not look up from his spreadsheets. He is, in all things related to Cary, much more cautious than she is.

'Jeff? Is it OK for Matt to play?' Greg calls.

'Sure.' Jeff captures Simon's knight with his bishop and smiles apologetically. He had assumed that Simon would be a more formidable opponent, but then so many of his assumptions have been proven wrong. He had, after all, assumed that on an evening as clear as this he and Susan might take a long walk, that he might give voice to the shadowy doubts and fears that have haunted him over the past several months. But Susan had hurried upstairs right after dinner, and he knows that she is engrossed in her translation. *That damn translation.* He sits back and watches Polly cross the room, hugging her heavy text and glancing at him nervously. Too quickly, he averts his eyes and studies the chess board, although he is aware that Polly is seated nearby, that the top buttons of her shirt have come undone and the rose-gold rise of her breasts is brushed by lamp light. His throat tightens and he shifts his chair so that she is out of his line of vision.

It is Simon's move and he fingers his remaining knight, looks up to smile at Daniel who has wandered into the room and moves on to observe the action at the dart board.

The small boys encircle Greg who sinks to his knees and shows them the darts.

'They're not toys,' he says. 'They're sharp. Very sharp. Look.'

He selects one and pricks his finger. A droplet of blood bubbles up and the boys look at it in fascinated fear. The slightest cut terrifies them, exposing as it does the mysterious fragility of their bodies, the streams of crimson liquid that course beneath their skin. They marvel at Greg's courage as he dismissively dabs at the tiny puncture with his handkerchief.

'So never fool around with them. You understand?' He speaks sternly, his voice trained by hours standing before restless students in crowded classrooms.

They nod solemnly, their heads bobbing, bright hair falling across suntanned brows.

Watching them from across the room, Nessa is almost moved to tears. They are so beautiful, so innocent. She feels impelled to rush toward them, to hold them close as she had held Paul as a toddler, as she still comforts the children in her care. She shakes her head and turns back to her Scrabble tiles, although a story is fermenting, a children's book to add to her popular series, *The Games We Play*. She has already written about the urban games once played on the sidewalks of her city, a group of competitive little girls jumping rope, two sets of siblings vying for a hopscotch championship, chalk drawings on harsh cement pavements. Why not a game of darts in a basement rec room? Swiftly, she turns a page on the scoring pad and draws the three small boys gazing so fixedly at the feathered darts.

The boys line up, Matt first. His uncle places a dart in his hand, positions his arm, tells him to look straight at the board, straight at the bull's eye. Matt thrusts himself forward and throws but the board is too high and he misses.

'Stupid of me. I have to lower the board for you guys,' Greg says and goes off in search of a hammer and a nail.

Matt picks up the fallen dart. 'Let me see it.'

'No, me.'

Donny and Cary clamor for a turn but Matt sprints away from them, holds the dart up high, then mischievously whips around and tosses it. Donny moves forward, Wendy screams and for the briefest of moments all movement and sound freezes until with startling suddenness, Daniel Goldner hurls himself at Donny. They crash to the floor as the dart sails past them and embeds itself into the floor.

Wendy hurries to her son who shakes off her embrace, turns away from the fear on her breath.

'I'm OK, Mom. Leave me alone.'

'I'm sorry, Mrs Templeton. Really, I was just kidding around.' Matt Edwards fights his own tears, both ashamed and angry.

'Come on, Donny. I'll give you one of my quarters for the pinball machine,' he says in atonement.

'Me too. I'll give you one,' Cary adds and the boys scuttle away, relieved to escape the accusing stares and fears of the grown-ups.

'Thank you,' Wendy says to Daniel, and turns to Andrea who stands beside her now, her lips pursed, her pale eyes cold as marbles.

'I was surprised you allowed him to play such a dangerous game. I would never have allowed Adam to go anywhere near a game like that,' the older woman says.

'Really? As though you ever knew where he was going and what he was doing,' Wendy replies.

Her face is flushed, but her voice is steady. It is the first time she has ever spoken in such a manner to Adam's mother and her words, cruel as she knows them to be, are strangely cleansing. She stares unflinchingly at Andrea who blanches and turns away. Mark takes his wife's arm and, without looking at Wendy, walks very slowly to the door, almost colliding with Susan Edwards who is on her way in.

'Matt,' Susan calls. 'It's bedtime.'

The other mothers glance at their own watches.

'Cary.'

'Donny.'

The maternal tones are stern and the small boys surrender to their own exhaustion and trail their mothers to their rooms where the beds are already turned down, and pajamas are laid out on the linens that smell of an unfamiliar detergent.

A restlessness overtakes those who remain. Games are abandoned, the jigsaw puzzle left undone. The teenagers huddle and then announce that they are going for a walk but within minutes they hear Richie rev his motor. Nessa goes to the window and sees that Annette sits beside Richie in the open-top roadster, her fair hair whipping her narrow face as he accelerates. Tracy, Jeremy and Paul race after them, laughing and calling their names. She glances quizzically at Simon who shrugs.

'It's all right,' he says. 'They're just having fun. You don't have to worry about Richie. He's a terrific driver.'

She does not tell him that it is not Richie who concerns her. Her worry is focused on Paul, who has, for this brief hour, lost his Annette, but she knows there is nothing she can do to protect him and it may be that he does not require protection. She goes to the table and glances at the jigsaw puzzle on which he and Annette are working. She writes a note – *Work in progress. Leave as is* – so that the cleaning staff will not disturb it. That much she can do.

Slowly, the room empties. Good nights are exchanged and they ascend the staircase. Michael Curran carefully folds his spreadsheets and places them in his attaché case. Helene and Greg Ames walk upstairs hand in hand. Polly concentrates on her text and sighs deeply as Jeff Edwards salutes her with a dismissive wave.

In their room, Jeff undresses swiftly and slides into bed next to Susan.

'You're finished early,' he says although it is, in fact, not all that early.

'I'm making good progress,' she assures him softly.

'Good. Very good.'

'Matt told me about the dart. He was really frightened.'

'Nothing happened. Almost doesn't count,' Jeff says, but his words are heavy with warning. Something could have happened. An 'almost' can become a reality. A near-miss on a highway could become a fatal accident. Brakes can fail. Their lives are shadowed by 'almosts', every hour pregnant with danger. Their son, their sweet, playful, fearful Matt, could have blinded another boy and spent the rest of his life haunted by guilt.

'Thank God.' Susan's voice is frightened and he knows that she now shares his awareness of lurking dangers, large and small, careless actions, careless words. How vulnerable they are, how cautious they must be.

He pulls Susan close in protective embrace, his mouth upon hers as though to quiet the words he does not want to hear. Their hearts beat in familiar unison as love and fear meld. Afterwards they lie awake in the darkness, until the sound of wheels on the driveway, and the slamming of the front door of the inn give proof that Annette has returned, that their family is intact and safe.

EIGHT

The passing days of that first week of vacation assume a slow and easy rhythm. The guests of August adjust to the finite luxury of unstructured hours, unstructured days. Small alliances are formed. Wendy and Daniel stake out an isolated corner of the lawn where he works on the proofs of his novel and she sketches, her rainbow-colored pencils spread across a weathered picnic table.

Michael Curran and Mark Templeton study the *Wall Street Journal* which Michael buys each day. There is urgent conversation as Michael opens his laptop and Mark studies the screen, now scrolling forward, now backward. Mark makes calls on his cell phone. Michael sweats profusely until Simon joins them, opens his notebook, speaks very softly. The pantomime is repeated each morning. It is understood that something is happening of considerable importance but nothing has yet been arranged. Mark is holding back. Liane observes her husband nervously. She wants him to stop sweating. She wants their future to be assured.

The women go for morning walks in odd couplings – Liane and Helene, Nessa and Susan. Andrea takes solitary strolls, elegant as always in pastel-colored linen pant suits with broad-brimmed sun hats to match. They return with armloads of flowers which they arrange in Louise's unmatched vases, their faces bright with pleasure. Only Andrea plucks a single blossom, a sprig of primrose, a regal iris, which she places in her own crystal bud vase on the center of her table.

Later in the morning, couples amble hand in hand down to the lake or cut across to the road that leads to the cemetery.

The teenagers sun themselves lazily, swim with effortless grace and, with startling suddenness, pile into rowboats and paddle vigorously across the quiet waters.

The small boys build adjuncts to their fort, create pathways of twigs and stones, furnishings of logs and rocks and suddenly quarrel with bitter intensity. Donny and Matt allied against Cary. Cary and Donny angry with Matt. The late-morning spats morph into peace by the afternoon, one parent or another driving the boys to the village for an ice cream or an impromptu visit to the hobby shop. Now and again Paul Epstein engages them in a board game of his own creation, using Harry Potter characters. The boys cluster around him, willing acolytes fascinated by their mentor's profound understanding of how Harry and Hermione negotiate their way through Hogwarts. Paul improvises a script, playing the part of Harry, and presses Annette into service as Hermione. Jeremy, Tracy and Richie, sprawled out on the lawn, watch them, smiling cynically. They have graduated from childhood and are bemused by Paul's tolerance of little kids, by Annette's complicity, although Annette seldom lingers after a perfunctory reading of her lines. Richie is teaching her to drive and she sits beside him in his small roadster and practices shifting gears, starting and cutting the engine, his hand guiding hers.

Nessa notes that often in the late afternoon, the young people clamber into that car, which has room only for four, and head into town, more often than not leaving Paul behind. It is then that her son seeks out Greg Ames and the two of them play their guitars together, Greg teaching Paul new chords, as Helene watches her husband, her eyes newly soft, a smile playing at her lips. Nessa finds Helene's expression oddly familiar, reminiscent of women she has known who have reached a decisive turning point in their lives. This new serenity of Helene's reminds her of friends long since vanished from her life, of the young mothers of her nursery school children who share small happy confidences with her or, occasionally, sad revelations.

'We've decided to move to the country.'

'We've decided to have another child.'

'We're going to separate, just a trial time apart.'

'We've decided to divorce.'

She mentions this to Susan Edwards, who sinks into a lawn chair beside her one day just before lunch.

'Helene looks as though she's come to terms with something, as though she's made some sort of decision,' she observes.

'My sister doesn't make decisions,' Susan replies. 'She drifts into them. She drifted across Europe and then she met Greg and she drifted into marriage. He became a teacher and so she drifted into teaching. It's worked for her. I'm the list maker, the organizer. The planner. And right now I'm not all that sure it's worked for me.' Her voice is heavy with a sadness that she herself does not understand.

'She may have changed. Maybe she's taken a page out of your book. And you could change. Maybe take a page out of her book. It happens,' Nessa observes, but Susan is no longer listening. Her gaze is fixed on the tennis courts where Simon and Jeff, neither of them accomplished players, are indulging in a leisurely volley as Polly, her arms laden with newly laundered white tablecloths, pauses to watch them. Polly turns suddenly and, seeing Susan, she blushes deeply and hurries into the inn.

'She's just a kid,' Nessa says. 'A town kid with a sick mother and a depressed father striving toward a better life.'

'Yes. I know,' Susan replies. 'I just hope it's not my life she's fantasizing about.'

Simon and Nessa carry their picnic basket out to the lawn late each afternoon but the group that joins them dwindles and varies. Daniel and Wendy occasionally join them but Andrea and Mark Templeton sit by themselves, all but concealed by the copper beech tree that dominates the far corner of the lawn. Their backs are toward her but Nessa is reasonably certain that the oversized soft leather handbag Andrea carries (she has several in different pastel shades and alternates them each day to match her outfit) contains a bottle of vodka and the small glasses Louise has reported missing from the kitchen. Andrea always pauses as she glides across the lawn to plant a light kiss on Wendy's cheek. She is demonstrating that there is no aftermath of antipathy since their angry exchange. She is not a woman who can cope easily with confrontations.

The evenings pass quietly. The Scrabble and chess games resume seamlessly and the jigsaw puzzle inches its way to completion, Paul and Annette uttering small yelps of excitement as a complicated section is completed. Greg idly strums his guitar, the dart board is approached and abandoned, the small boys chase fireflies.

Jeremy, Tracy and Richie disappear, sometimes briefly, sometimes for hours. Nessa supposes that they are smoking down at the lake, maybe pot, maybe cigarettes, or perhaps having beers at the small village tavern. She is relieved that Paul is not with them, relieved that Simon seems unconcerned. It pleases her that Annette lightly touches Paul's hand as she fumbles for one puzzle piece and then another.

On such an evening, at the end of the week, Louise Abbot joins her guests, her apron discarded, her hair twisted into a chignon that she has copied from Andrea Templeton. Room is made for her at the Scrabble table.

'Evan loves Scrabble,' she says as though mentioning the name of her husband will compensate for his frequent absences.

The other players, Nessa, Helene and Liane, nod.

'I'm glad to have the night off,' Louise says. 'I was going to bake blueberry pies but I never got to the blueberry farm.'

'That's what we ought to do tomorrow,' Nessa says. 'We ought to go and pick blueberries for you, Louise. We'll do it tomorrow.'

The others nod vigorously. It is indeed time to leave the inn, to indulge in a new adventure. Good for the children, something for the teenagers to do, good for all of them to feel the sun on their faces, the fruit plump beneath their fingers. Liane wonders what she will wear. She knows the dangers of blueberry fields. She does not want her new clothes to be ripped by brambles or stained with juice, but she smiles with practiced enthusiasm.

'It should be fun,' she says.

'Are you in, Daniel? Wendy?' Nessa calls across the room.

And Daniel, who remembers picking blueberries with his parents during the August vacations of his childhood, nods, and Wendy, who is in the market for new memories, raises her hand in agreement.

'After breakfast then,' Nessa decides, and she smiles broadly as she puts down a seven-letter word across a triple space and earns herself eighty-seven points. As she herself often says, she is not a competitive woman, but she does love to win.

It rains fiercely during the night but they waken the next

morning to the brilliant sunlight that often follows nocturnal mountain storms. The lawn is bathed in radiance and dancing sun beams spangle the windows. Polly's face is aglow after her walk to the inn and her bare arms flash golden as swiftly she places platters of pancakes and French toast on the tables. Susan thinks of a single sentence in her translation in which LeBec writes '*le soleil rayonée le sensualisme*'. She had translated it, hesitantly, to read, 'the sun radiates sensuality' and, looking at Polly, she recognizes the truth of LeBec's observation.

'I think I'll give the translation a pass this morning and go to the blueberry farm with you,' she says, touching Jeff's arm lightly. She will not forego the radiance of this day, the warmth and excitement of sensual sunlight.

'Great.' He pours another cup of coffee and she adds the cream and one teaspoon of sugar to it, carefully leveling it in the breakfast habit of their early courtship and of the vanished leisurely mornings of the first years of their marriage. It is an assertion of a kind. Of such small gestures, the basketry of love is tightly woven. She wonders if those words are her own.

They gather on the driveway to decide on how to arrange the cars. The smaller boys clamor to go together in one car and they pile into Nessa's messy van where they know no complaint will be registered if candy wrappers are scattered on the floor or if juice spills on the upholstery which is already stained beyond repair. Wendy and Daniel will travel on Daniel's motor-cycle. Wendy has succumbed at last to his assurances that it will be safe and has strapped on the helmet, absently plucking out the long blonde hairs that cling to the lining. Laura's hairs, she realizes. Andrea Templeton approaches her just as Daniel revs the motor.

'I thought we would go to the nursery today and select the plantings for Adam's grave,' she says.

'Maybe in the afternoon,' Wendy replies.

She has not forgotten that within days it will be the anniversary of Adam's death. The tenth anniversary. After a decade, does the statute of limitations on grief expire? The thought shames her. In atonement she summons up a mental image of Adam as she first knew him, the Adam who had so tenderly dried her hair the night of their first meeting, who had recited poetry to her in the half light of dawn, the Adam who was Donny's father.

She tightens her grip around Daniel's waist and does not look back as they speed down the sun-ribbed road.

All the young people pile into Richie's car, Annette's long legs dangling out the window as she sprawls across Paul's lap. Tracy leans forward and toys with the radio, searching for a station that plays jazz.

'Not that. No classical. No news.'

They laugh as she spins the dial and Annette waves her long legs as Richie accelerates and the roadster hurtles out of the driveway. Paul Epstein's hand rests on her head.

'Dangerous,' Susan Edwards murmurs. 'No seat belts. Five of them in that tiny car.'

'They'll be all right,' Helene assures her sister. 'Greg and I did lot of stuff that was way more dangerous back in our glory days. Right, Greg?'

She is thinking of how they hitched through Greece, then drove a beat-up hulk of a car through Tuscany. It broke down just before Siena and they hiked into the village in the dead of night. Danger meant excitement, freedom of a kind, membership in the community of the young and the daring. Danger meant an escape from her memories of her mother, from the real domestic hazards of her childhood. It is not something that Susan understands. Susan, who was in search of a home, in search of family and stability, married Jeff straight out of college and spent the days of her young womanhood translating textbooks and keeping house. Susan had not known the danger, nor had she harvested the memories. Helene, who envies her sister in so many things, pities her for that loss.

'Right,' Greg agrees. 'Where did we bum a ride on an ox cart?'

'Sicily. It must have been Sicily.'

'I never had any glory days,' Liane says wistfully.

She is pale on this golden morning and she has dressed with uncharacteristic carelessness, the brightly colored polished cotton shirts and the hip-hugging Capri pants abandoned in favor of jeans and a loose white shirt. Her hair, un-teased and un-lacquered, is caught up in a loose ponytail. Nessa, who

notices such things, thinks that Liane looks both sad and frightened. She wonders if the deal Simon has been trying to broker
for Michael with Mark Templeton has fallen through. Perhaps
that is why he too has stayed behind, explaining that he had to
be on hand for a conference call.

Liane follows Greg and Helene into the back seat of the
Edwards' car.

'Michael's not coming,' she explains. 'Mark wants to go over
some data with him. It's important. Really important. Some
very big deal they're working on.'

Her heart beats too rapidly. She fears to think of how desperately important it is, how their entire life lies in the balance.
She herself has not yet assimilated that knowledge, so new and
so terrifying.

She had told Michael about the planned berry-picking excursion
the previous night.

'I can't go,' he had said. 'I have to go over some stuff with
Mark Templeton and with Simon.'

Anger had gripped her and she crept into bed beside him,
simmering with fury. As they listened to the rain dance its way
across the copper eaves, the cumulated disappointments of recent
days, of months and years, boiled over into a litany of complaints.
She shot them at him like bullets.

Michael was spending too little time with her, too little time
with Cary, she felt herself neglected and bored. This was not
what he had promised her, not what she had signed on for. Her
plaintive accusations spattered forth in rhythm with the falling
drops.

He had turned to her, his face a death mask of sadness, his
voice an angry hiss.

'You don't understand what's at stake here, Liane. Do you
think I enjoy working during vacation? But I have no choice.
Understand this. I have a negative cash flow. We've been living
on plastic for months. We're surviving because I refinanced the
house. We could lose everything. *Everything.* I need Mark
Templeton. I need the capital he can pump in. And I need Simon
Epstein who's helping to persuade him that my software is a
good investment – which it is if only I can get it off the ground.
So stop complaining and let me do what I have to do, goddamn

it! For once, think about me and not just yourself and what you want and what you need and what you don't have. It was to give you everything you wanted that I went out on my own.'

'But it was what you promised me.' She murmured her defense as a single shaft of lightning streaked across the sky. 'I thought you could do it. I thought you wanted to do it.'

But he turned away and lay rigid beside her as the rain intensified and the wind moaned in the darkness. She wept then although she did not know if her tears were for him or for herself or for their son, asleep in the alcove, who now and again laughed sweetly in his sleep. She wakened early and, although Michael still slept, she moved closer to him and brushed his eyelids with her lips, a new and unfamiliar sympathy dislodging contempt. But he did not waken.

Liane stares out of the car window during the brief drive to the berry orchard. She does not look at Helene and Greg, who sit very close to each other. They are trying to remember a song learned in Italy, and they laugh as Helene sings the first line and he hums the second. Susan wipes a scrap of egg from Jeff's lip. Liane closes her eyes.

These small marital intimacies of touch and song deepen Liane's feeling of aloneness on this sun-washed day. She is seared with jealousy and pretends not to hear when Helene asks her if she has ever picked blueberries before. She does not tell Helene that from earliest childhood she had picked the blueberries that grow wild along the coastal shore because her family could not afford to buy fruit. She shrinks from the memory of that poverty and trembles at the thought that she might sink into it yet again.

The cars from Mount Haven Inn pull into the parking lot of the blueberry orchard simultaneously. Richie's brakes squeak and he blares his horn. The teenagers disentangle themselves and laughingly fumble for sandals and sneakers. The small boys argue shrilly about who will pick the most berries. Matt and Cary remember that the previous year it was Donny who triumphed, but they also remember that his mother had helped fill his sack.

'It wasn't fair. It was cheating,' Cary says.

'OK. I won't let her help me this year.'

Donny is indifferent. He scurries away from his friends as Daniel's motorcycle pulls up and his mother slides off. Her face is radiant, her dark hair cascades about her shoulders when she removes the helmet.

'That was great,' she says. 'That was fun.'

She speaks with amazement, as though bewildered by the thought that fun has re-entered her life.

'Was it exciting, Mom? Can I try it? Please? Please?' Donny grips her hand, proud of his mother, exhilarated by her daring.

'Maybe one day, honey.' She leans down and kisses him, a mistake she realizes at once. She has, yet again, embarrassed him in front of his friends.

'Don't turn him into your companion,' her therapist had warned her. 'It's a danger with single mothers of sons.'

She sighs. All the days and nights of her motherhood are fraught with danger.

'Damn Adam.'

The thought, unbidden, shames her and Daniel, as though sensing the sudden shift of her mood, places a protective hand on her shoulder. She shakes it off impatiently and does not look up at him.

The owner of the orchard, a florid-faced, lank-haired woman, her hands stained blue, berry juice spattered across her oversized overalls and her long-sleeved army shirt, distributes large plastic sacks.

'You've got acres and acres to choose from here,' she says. 'And it's been a good season. You're in luck. Fill as many sacks as you want. A dollar a sack. You can stay close or spread out. But someone go along with the kids.'

Richie breathes into his clear plastic sack and laughs as it inflates into a transparent oval balloon that he twirls about his head. Annette claps her hands in appreciation. Nessa wonders why her stepson's smart-aleck playfulness annoys her and, with her usual honesty, recognizes that it is because of Annette's applause. She wants Annette to admire Paul, to be vested in him, because she knows that he is already vested in her. She does not want this girl, this very nice girl who delights her son, to be bewitched by Richie, who drives a roadster and blows plastic bags into the shape of a huge condom.

She shrugs and volunteers to supervise the boys and Liane offers to join her.

The teenagers race toward a distant field, Tracy and Annette sprinting ahead with Paul, Richie and Jeremy doing stag leaps behind them. Their long golden limbs are dappled by flickering shadows. They disappear into the overgrown foliage, their laughter trailing behind them.

Susan and Jeff head toward a favorite patch, revisited year after year, and Helene and Greg trail after them while Daniel and Wendy make their way toward a distant, overgrown thicket, its deep green leafage pebbled with blue fruit.

They begin to pick slowly, the work evenly divided by tacit consent. The berries are plump, small, thin-skinned globules exploding with juice. They grow in thick clusters and fall easily from the branches into Wendy's deft fingers. Daniel holds the bag open and she drops her harvest into it and slowly increases her pace, stripping one branch bare and moving on to the next. Fat bumblebees hover lazily over the laden bushes, their bodies swollen, their wings, delicate as cellophane, barely moving as they settle briefly, now in one patch, now in another. Their muted humming fills the air. The bees circle lazily and, with odd suddenness, take flight.

Wendy pauses to watch them and absently nibbles at the berries in her hand. Daniel reaches into the sack and crams an entire handful into his mouth. Juice trickles down his chin and Wendy, her own lips stained blue, laughs and moves toward him, fumbling in her pocket for a tissue. She reaches out to wipe his chin and, yet again, he places his hand on her bare shoulder. The warmth of her skin causes his fingers to tingle. They stand motionless for a brief moment beneath the verdant canopy of the tall, entangled bushes and then he pulls her toward him and kisses her hard, hears her gasp and feels the softness of her mouth against his own. Her slender body, yielding and pliant within his embrace, unlike Laura's dancer's body, surprises him. He remembers the tautness of his wife's trained muscles, the tight strength of her arms. Sadness pierces him. Gently, he releases Wendy. Startled, she steps away from him, her arms limp, as though she cannot think of where to place them.

'I'm sorry,' he says.

'Nothing to be sorry about,' she replies. 'A kiss. It was just a kiss. It was nice. It was good. It tasted like blueberries.'

They return to work, easily reclaiming their rhythm, berries falling softly upon berries, their eyes riveted to their work. His face is flushed. Hers is pale.

'Too soon,' she murmurs when the sack is full. 'Not your fault. Not mine. It was just too soon.'

'No. It's because I'd forgotten.' His own voice is hoarse with regret.

'Forgotten what?' Expertly she knots the bag and licks her fingers.

'I'm not sure.'

He looks hard at her, at her fine-featured face and dark eyes, at a heart-shaped green leaf that is entwined in her long dark hair, and realizes that while it was Laura he had thought of as he held her close, it was tenderness and the gentleness of touch that he had forgotten. He has been for so long without them. He cannot explain that to Wendy because she is right. It is too soon. They are, both of them, too vulnerable. Wordlessly, he places his hand on her head, threads that stray leaf between his fingers, and together they emerge from the shadows of the grove into the dazzling sunlight that sweeps across the orchard.

'It will not always be too soon,' he says, and she nods.

NINE

The group are all energized by the berry-picking excursion. They return to the inn waving their bounty, the clear plastic bags filled with the plump blue fruit. Richie and Jeremy whirl them about and race across the lawn in hot pursuit of Tracy and Annette who laugh tantalizingly and hug their own bulging sacks. They fall to the grass at last, all four of them, their lithe young bodies forming a pyramid of golden limbs and shining hair, the berries amazingly intact. Paul Epstein, who has trailed behind them, helps Annette disentangle herself and brushes stray blades of grass from her bare arms. He trembles at the smooth touch of her flesh.

The adults smile at their gaiety, Susan placing her hand on Jeff's arm, Simon holding Nessa close, recalling the wild exuberance of their own youth. The day has been a good one. They are all filled with a zest for new adventures, an urge to explore the New Hampshire world beyond the precincts of Mount Haven Inn. Fresh horizons beckon.

Colorful tourism brochures litter the lawn where Simon Epstein once again hosts his pre-dinner cocktail party. Greg and Helene study a map of Route Nine, the antique highway, circling shops that sound interesting. Liane tentatively suggests going to the outlets in Concord, but a glance from Michael silences her. She looks at him worriedly. Did the conference call go well? He has not told her and she dares not ask him. She wonders if it is a good sign that Mark Templeton has selected a chair close to Michael. She smiles brightly at the older man, offers him a cracker thinly coated with cheese and refills his glass of sparkling water. It does not disturb her that he barely acknowledges her solicitude. She has not forgotten how to be the invisible but accommodating secretary. She was good at her job, very good.

The smaller boys clamor for an excursion to a water park. Susan herself has no wish to go to the water park. The next

chapter of the LeBec novel is especially difficult and she longs
for the silence and solitude that will allow her to transfuse the
lyrical French into an English that will retain the author's
rhythmic cadence. If Jeff agrees to chaperone the trip to the
water park she will be free to work for much of the day.

It is agreed that he will take all three boys, that their mothers
will go to a craft fair nearby and that they will all meet for a
picnic lunch at the state park where a white-water stream rushes
over outcroppings of white rocks.

'If you don't mind,' Susan says, choosing her words carefully, 'I'll stay here. I kind of just want a lazy day.'

Liane and Wendy shrug indifferently but Jeff stares hard at
her.

'Sure,' he says, an unfamiliar harshness in his tone.

Richie promotes the idea of a sea-plane ride over Lake
Winnipesaukee. Enough room on the plane for five.

'Paul, Jeremy, Tracy, me and Annette. It's pricey but we can
split the costs and then meet you guys at the state park.'

Richie drapes his arm over Annette's shoulder in a proprietary
gesture and Paul winces.

Nessa turns away. The mothers of the younger boys
may protect their sons from white-water danger, but she cannot
protect Paul, her vulnerable adolescent son, from the pain of
rejection.

She herself, she announces, looks forward to spending a few
hours at the used bookstore a few miles down the road. She
has, in the past, found long-out-of-print children's books for
the library of her nursery school and she enjoys studying the
work of illustrators of generations past. She has, she acknowledges, incorporated some of their muted colors and classical
formats into her own whimsical work. To her surprise, Andrea
Templeton asks if she might accompany her.

'I know that shop well,' she says. 'When we lived up here I
went there often, sometimes with Adam, sometimes alone. Have
you ever gone there with Donny, Wendy?'

'No,' Wendy replies, her voice flat although she flushed at
the mention of Adam's name. 'It is a bit out of the way for us.
As it must have been for you. All those years ago.'

'All those years ago,' Andrea repeats and the two women,

the bereft wife and the bereft mother, look hard at each other, exchanging the calculating stare of adversaries competing in the difficult and uncertain game of mourning and memory.

'You'll be all right on your own, Mark?' Andrea asks.

'Well, I won't be entirely on my own. I'll be working with these young men. Michael has an interesting project underway but there are some glitches we have to iron out. Good of you to take the time to work on it, Epstein.'

He mispronounces Simon's name, elongating the last syllable but no one corrects him. Simon shrugs his shoulders. It is a casual slur that is familiar to him. It did not disturb him in his younger years and he is too secure now in his professional achievement to take issue with it. He is Jewish. So what?

Liane touches Michael's hand, almost faint with relief. They are all right then. The project is not dead.

'What about you, Daniel?' Simon asks.

He is, as always, concerned about his childhood friend who is weathering the transitional loneliness that had haunted Simon all those years ago, during that bleak period after his divorce from Charlotte and before Nessa came into his life. He smiles at Nessa, her face so bright in the pink radiance of sunset, a diaphanous robe of daring floral design flowing over the softness of her body, her long toes, their nails preposterously painted with stars and peace symbols, scissoring cool blades of grass. His own luck at finding her, at claiming her, amazes him. He hopes that Daniel, talented gentle Daniel, will find a woman like his Nessa, so comfortable in her own skin, so sensitive to the needs of others.

'I need a day to work on my page proofs,' Daniel says stiffly. 'I'll be fine.'

He does not look at Wendy, who betrays no disappointment. She is not surprised that Daniel has chosen not to join their outing. They moved too swiftly, presumed too much. She rises from her seat and glides across the lawn to a clearing where she watches the slowly setting sun turn the wine-dark lake the color of molten gold.

This is what vacations are for, Wendy thinks, moments like this, frozen in time, a precious suspension of all obligations, a surrender to the solitary magic of watching shimmering diamonds of fading light dance across darkening waters. Days remain for the soothing of small hurts, for gentle exchanges over fragrant cups of coffee. She smiles at Daniel as she returns to her seat and he, relieved, smiles back at her.

At dinner that evening Nessa tells Louise that they will need a large picnic lunch.

'No problem,' she assures them. 'Evan will drive it out to the state park. We do it for our guests all the time.'

It occurs to Nessa that Evan is absent from the dinner table and that he had not appeared at breakfast, but she asks no questions. Louise Abbot has made her own bargain with life and requires neither advisors nor intermediaries.

The sky is overcast the next morning but Louise, who as always has been up since dawn, assures them that the weather forecasters predict a clearing before midday. She offers them this news as she places the large bowls of scrambled eggs on the table, as though it is her role as innkeeper to dispense good weather just as she supervises their meals and the cleanliness of their rooms. She does not take her place at the table. Another waitress has disappointed and Louise is once again filling in. It is Daniel Goldner, as always, who expresses his concern.

'Don't work too hard, Louise,' he cautions, and she smiles gratefully at him and disappears into the kitchen.

Polly carries in the carafes of coffee and places a plate of toast next to Jeff Edwards.

'Whole wheat,' she says. 'I think that's what you like.'

'Actually Dr Edwards prefers not to eat bread in the morning,' Susan says crisply as she pushes the plate away.

Polly blushes and hurries to another table.

'That was rude and unnecessary, Susan.' Jeff's voice is cold and monitory, the tone he uses in the operating room when a scrub nurse hands him the wrong instrument. 'She was only trying to be helpful.'

'She presumes,' Susan replies tightly.

'Susan, really. She's a kid, a waitress,' Helene interjects.

Susan frowns and turns her attention to Matt who has been watching his parents, glassy-eyed with fear. He hates it when their voices are edged with irritation. He wonders why it is that his mother and father no longer laugh together, why his mother is not coming to the water park, why she is so often annoyed with Polly who tries so hard to be nice to them. He wishes that he could ask Jeremy and Annette these questions, but his older brother and sister barely notice him. It seems to him that they have drifted out of the world they once shared with him – the child world of games and giggling and of swift teasing quarrels easily resolved. They have aged into a mysterious realm whose borders are closed to him. Annette stands in front of the mirror, endlessly brushing her hair, applying lipstick, practicing her smile and, suddenly, without warning, breaking into tears. Jeremy slams doors, scowls as he listens to music on his iPad, and texts his friends ignoring their replies.

Matt eats the toast that his mother lathers with jam and wishes that his aunt Helene would mind her own business.

They rush from the breakfast tables to their cars, eager for their adventure to get underway. The boys' backpacks, over-flowing with towels, changes of clothing and goggles, are stowed into Jeff's station wagon. Susan supervises the buckling of seat belts and decides that if Jeff asks her, just once more, to join them, she will agree. But he says nothing, nor does he kiss her, as he climbs into the car. Her heart sinks. She remembers the early days of their marriage when he never left the apartment without holding her close, the later years when his lips brushed her cheek as they parted, even more recently when he briefly cupped her chin in his hands before going off.

There is a change, even a fissure, she acknowledges, but it is not irreparable. Most of the translation is done; this last difficult chapter will be completed today and she will be free. The last sun-bright days of August at Mount Haven Inn will work their magic as always. She and Jeff will relax on the lawn, stroll down to the lake in the cool of the evening, come together in velvet darkness with passion and tenderness as their children sleep in the adjoining room.

Helene is right. She is foolish to worry about Polly. She's just a kid and Jeff is just being kind. Stupid of her to read anything more into it. She walks hurriedly back to her room, eager to begin her work, French and English phrases already whirring through her mind. She does not turn back and so she does not see Jeff lift his arm in a brief and tentative wave.

The young people dash to Richie's car, Tracy perched on
Jeremy's lap in the back seat, Paul balancing his camera beside
them, Annette seated beside Richie, bare armed and bright eyed.
Paul's eyes are glued to the nape of her neck, bewitched by the
tendrils of hair that dance across her rose-gold skin. She laughs
at something Richie says and moves closer to him. Richie
switches on the radio and Beyoncé's voice fills that little car.
Annette's shoulders sway to the music.

Richie drums the steering wheel and sways toward her.
Tracy shifts position slightly, her leg sliding over to rest on
Paul's.

'My brother's a jerk,' she whispers, and Paul looks at her in
surprise. He does not think Richie is a jerk. He just wishes that
he'd never come to stay at Mount Haven Inn, that he was not
teaching Annette how to drive, sitting too close to her, and
making her laugh at his stupid jokes.

He has never been at ease with Richie and Tracy. His
half-siblings, who move easily through their mother's glam-
orous world, are only a few years older than him but they
are cool collegians while he still drudges his way through
high school, juggling his book bag and guitar. They discuss
their courses, invoking writers he has never heard of and
disparaging others whom he thinks are terrific. They treat
Paul with casual indifference, although Tracy adds an iota
of kindness to their odd emotional mix. He smiles gratefully
at her now as Jeremy allows his arm to rest loosely around
her waist.

'And my sister's a pain,' Jeremy whispers. 'Don't let her fool
you. She can be a real tease.'

Paul shrugs and, as though on cue, they all begin to sing,
their mournful mocking chorus oddly in tune.

Wendy and Liane drive up the mountain road in companionable
silence. Wendy's sketchpad and her drawing pencils are on the
back seat and now and again she parks at the side of the road
and swiftly sketches a regal tree, a copse of conifers, a slender
birch bent by the wind.

'I want to do a series of sketches of New Hampshire trees,'
she explains to Liane. 'I'll draw the same trees through all the

seasons, branches heavy with snow in the winter, just budding in the spring, full leafed in summer, their leaves turning at the onset of autumn.'

'Like now,' Liane says, looking up at a brace of maples, their foliage already scarlet-edged and brittle.

Her eyes drop to Wendy's sketchpad and she marvels at how Wendy has captured the intricacy of the branches, the strength and steadiness of the trunk. She wonders why it was that she had always so resented Wendy Templeton. She is actually very nice, not at all snobby.

'Will you sell them when you're done?' she asks.

'I think I'd like to try to put them together in a book,' Wendy replies. 'Maybe find some text to go with each drawing. People are always looking for nice gift books and a publisher made me what seems like a pretty good offer.'

Liane looks at her in surprise and Wendy smiles.

'I know. I'm not supposed to be thinking about money. After all, as everyone surely knows, Donny's grandparents are very generous, actually too generous. Writing checks to us makes them feel good, I suppose. But I've had enough. I want to stop being their charity case. My watercolors are selling well and I've started teaching workshops. I can support myself and Donny and that is what I want to do.'

This outpouring of confidences embarrasses Liane. Wendy calmly replaces her pencils in their case, sprays fixative over her drawing. It is odd, she knows, to have imposed such intimacy on Liane whom she hardly knows, but she is pleased to have spoken her thoughts aloud. It vests them with reality. It is a rehearsal for the conversation she wants to have with Adam's parents.

'Mr Templeton is being very helpful to my husband,' Liane says awkwardly.

'Yes. Being helpful to your husband and working with Simon Epstein gives him something to do. He's bored. He doesn't really want to be at Mount Haven Inn, you know. No golf course, no cocktail lounge, no gourmet food. He'd much rather be at a five-star hotel on Hilton Head Island. And, of course, so would Andrea.'

'Then why do they come here?' Liane asks. 'Year after year.'

She does not add that she herself would prefer to spend August at a five-star hotel.

'A pilgrimage of a kind. A way to get rid of guilt that they never acknowledged. Andrea claims that it is their way to reconnect with Adam, their son, my late husband, although they hardly connected with him when he was alive. And they claim that they want to spend quality time with Donny, although they hardly know him. They've never thought to invite him to California, to travel with him. They didn't know how to be parents and they don't know how to be grandparents.'

There is no bitterness in Wendy's tone. She decides with some satisfaction that her therapist would be proud of her. She had spoken openly to Liane as she had spoken openly to Daniel Goldner. Perhaps, at her next therapy session it will be mutually concluded that she has assimilated her anger and safely reached the relatively safe shore of honesty. She brakes suddenly as a fawn darts across the road and a doe chases after it, bleating with maternal ire.

Liane is silent, reluctant to venture into hazardous emotional terrain, fearful that any response she makes will be both naïve and inadequate. Why, she wonders, should Andrea and Mark Templeton feel guilty about their son's death? But it is not a question she can safely ask.

They drive the rest of the way in a companionable silence, broken only by brief discussions of their sons.

'Does Cary enjoy sports?' Wendy asks. It worries her that Donny is indifferent to the team activities offered at his school.

'Not so much, but I don't really care,' Liane admits. 'I'm just glad that he does well at school and that he has a couple of good friends. He's super at computer stuff. Like his father.'

She feels a swell of pride. It is Michael's acumen and tenacity that Cary has inherited. She has always known that Michael was smart, very smart. He is too good at what he does and too hardworking to lose even at this treacherous high-tech business gamble. Mark Templeton and Simon Epstein would not be investing time and perhaps money if they didn't think Michael's project had merit. And even if this software design fails, he has other ideas. He is always thinking, always working. And, she acknowledges, she has been of little help. No help.

Michael's angry words resonate in her memory. *Think about me for once and not just yourself.* He had spoken a truth she cannot deny. She can help him and she will. She can get a job. Like Wendy, she can earn money, she can assert her independence.

She opens the car window wider, breathes in the sweetness of the late-summer air and feels a new lightness. She has slipped free of the heavy cloak of envy and disappointment that has weighed her down for so many years. She does not deny that she married Michael for the life she thought he would offer her. And yes, she had been disappointed but always aware of his devotion, of his determination to please her, of the tenacious love he lavishes on their son. And on her. That awareness has shocked her into an amazing revelation. She has come to love her husband. Really love him. She will take up his challenge and think not only about herself but about him and about Cary. They will manage. They will more than manage.

She smiles happily as Wendy pulls into a sprawling meadow dotted with brightly colored tents and long display tables of the itinerant artisans. They wander from display to display. Wendy buys a tie-dyed T-shirt for Donny, a silver pin for Andrea. Liane pauses to watch a leather worker fashion a wallet of the softest deer skin. She buys it, not blanching at the price. It has been years since she has given Michael a gift and she thinks of how his face will light up with pleasure when she gives it to him.

To his surprise, Jeff enjoys the water park. The three boys require little supervision. They dart from water slide to waterfall bright with rainbows. They jump into the largest swimming pool, shouting with joy, and he follows after them sharing their exuberance, balancing each boy in turn on his shoulders and tossing them into the clear blue water. He challenges them to race after him as he swims in lane, slicing easily from one end of the pool to another, then sliding beneath the water, reversing his stroke to surface first beneath one boy and then another. They giggle excitedly and flail their arms and legs, evading his underwater pursuit.

He remembers how he and Susan, during the distant days of their courtship, had raced against each other in ocean and pool, both of them accomplished swimmers, delighting in their half-naked bodies, their sunlit limbs sleekly wet. With startling clarity, he recalls how, on one such day, at a favorite beach, he had pulled Susan down beneath the gentle waves and kissed her hard, then held her weightless body close, so that they moved in tandem, entwined as one. They had surfaced, spewing out the saltwater, choking with laughter, holding hands loosely as they raced back to their blanket. Susan wore her hair long then and sea salt had sparkled in her curls like bright bits of mica that vanished beneath his stroking fingers.

He yearns for her now with a piercing desire sharpened by memory.

He will not allow all that they have shared to vanish because he has been so weary, because he has allowed himself to be numbed by domestic routine and overwhelmed with sadness, which he knows to be peculiar to surgeons who have all too many encounters with death. Andrew, a colleague, has spoken to him of burnout, an exhaustion that followed him from the operating room to his home and eventually resulted in his divorce. 'I will not let that happen to us,' Jeff vows silently.

The mischievous laughter of the three boys, the rainbow prisms in the waterfall and fountains, the breathless fun of it all, has revitalized him. He and Susan will talk tonight, really talk. About her work and his. About their children. About their separate fears and all that has come between them. They will seize these last days of August, these wistful waning weeks of summer, and use them to build battlements against the demands of the seasons to come, the chill of autumn, the icy thrust of winter.

'Hey, guys,' he calls to the boys. 'Time to get dry, get dressed. They're waiting for us at the park.'

The youngsters shout their protests, swim away, swim back and, still laughing, emerge from the water, stand beside him beneath the frigid outdoor shower, towel themselves dry and swiftly dress, eager to sprint off to the next adventure. They sing nonsense songs as Jeff drives to Granite Creek Park, a sylvan clearing carved into the foothills of the White Mountains. Jeff parks in a shaded area and is surprised to note that there are so few cars in this popular family destination. The boys tumble out and a state trooper approaches.

'A rough current in the creek today,' he says. 'Keep an eye on your kids.'

'Hey, we're good swimmers,' Cary calls out.

'Great swimmers,' Donny adds.

'I'm Mark Spitz. Want to see my medals?' Matt laughs and the trooper grins.

'I guess you've got your work cut out for you,' the trooper tells Jeff.

'I guess I do. Thanks, Officer.'

Jeff wonders where the others are. He had expected Richie and his passengers to be late. The Epstein kids are notorious for never being on time. But it surprises him that Wendy and Liane have not arrived, nor has Evan shown up with their picnic lunch. He shrugs and spreads a blanket across a huge flat boulder that overlooks the roiling white waters of the creek below. Turbulent waves break against the rock formations that jut their way out of the stream, jagged stepping stones across the narrow waterway. Daring youngsters, their wet hair plastered against faces bright with sunlight and excitement, leap across the stony parapets, shouting triumphantly as they negotiate their way across and back again. A freckled boy, making his way across a sharp crag, lifts his foot high and his orange water shoe soars through the air and down into the water. Within seconds it is swept away. The boy shrugs and leaps onto the next flinty outcropping.

'Hey, Dad, can we go down there?' Matt asks. 'We want to climb the rocks like we did last year.'

'The current wasn't this strong last year,' Jeff says.

'We'll be really careful, Dr Edwards.' Donny adds his plea to Matt's, his voice respectful, hopeful. 'We won't climb any of the really big rocks and we won't go near the water. Honest.'

Jeff smiles. He likes Donny, the boy who has no father of his own to cajole.

'We'll stay together,' Cary adds. 'We'll be buddies like when we swim at day camp. It's safest that way. That's what our counselors said.'

'All right,' he agrees at last. 'I'll be watching. But stay close. No jumping into the water and be sure to watch your footing. Wear your sneakers.'

'But they'll get wet,' Cary protests. His sneakers are new. His mother impressed upon him how expensive they were and how it was important to keep them clean.

'They'll dry off. If your mother gets mad blame me,' Jeff tells Cary. 'I'll explain.'

Neither he nor Susan has ever really liked Liane Curran.

'Showy,' Susan has called her. 'Superficial. All those stupid matching outfits and brand names. Materialistic.'

But Liane has changed over these past several days. She is softer, Jeff thinks, as though she is ready to discard some of the defensive armor she has always worn during their shared vacation weeks. Her self-protective silence is much diminished. She is newly open, newly relaxed. He has the feeling she will not be unduly upset if Cary's sneakers are sullied.

'And make sure the laces are tightly tied,' he cautions them severely.

They toss their T-shirts on to the blanket and dash off. It pleases him to see that Matt is the tallest of the trio and that he runs the fastest, his laughter ricocheting back to his father. All to the good, Jeff thinks. He has been worried about his younger son, so sensitive to his parents' tensions, so newly isolated by his older siblings' rush into adolescence, their quarrels and their bickering. But here at Mount Haven, among his friends, Matt's latent sadness has all but vanished.

Jeff watches as the three boys reach the water's edge, as they plan their ascent, carefully, and then as a team, leap from rock to rock.

He glances at his watch. Where the hell are all the others? He is not concerned that Liane and Wendy are late. Women at a craft show linger, examining one display after another, hesitating over each purchase. He and his brother-in-law Greg have often downed at least two beers while Susan and Helene wandered through malls or antique stores. He wonders if Greg and Helene are planning to join them for the picnic lunch. If so, they too are late. But now he is really worried about the older kids. He never should have agreed to let Jeremy and Annette go off in Richie's roadster, too crowded, too unsafe. He turns away from the creek and stands and trains his gaze upon the parking area as though his stare will summon the missing vehicle.

'Dr Edwards! Dr Edwards!' Donny and Cary shout in unison, their shrill voices tremulous with terror.

He wheels around and sees them waving frantically, pointing down to the stream. His heart stops. Matt is caught in the current, a captive of the rushing waves; he flails his arms desperately, kicks wildly and still the current carries him inexorably further downstream. Jeff rushes forward, his heart pounding. He straddles the precipices that lead downward but suddenly his foot is wedged tightly between two rocks. He struggles to break loose, his eyes fixed on his son who is no longer fighting the current but is being tossed, rising and falling, his body now submerged, his head barely rising to the surface.

'Oh, God!' shouts Jeff. 'Matt! Matt!' His throat grows hoarse with terror, his heart beats in wild tympanic rhythm.

He wrenches his foot free, ready now to rush to his boy, but even as he sprints forward he sees a slender woman dive from a long rocky parapet. Her descent is swift; her body, like a carefully aimed jackknife, slices through the foaming waves below and she splashes into the water only millimeters away from the struggling boy. She swims with swiftness and power toward Matt, grasping him beneath his chin, pulling him free of the current, and then with steady stroke carries him to the safety of the pale-pebbled shore. She sets the boy gently down and brushes her rose-gold hair from her eyes. She looks up and Jeff, weak with relief, sees that it is Polly, mysteriously and improbably arrived from Mount Haven Inn, who has saved his son's life.

He hurries forward, breaking through the small crowd that has gathered. A woman drapes a towel about Polly's shoulders but Matt lies inert, his eyes closed, his lips a deathly blue. The blond father of three small girls rushes over and kneels beside him, his arms pounding the boy's chest, breathing into his mouth, each motion rhythmic, each breath measured. The crowd is silent, as though a single word, a single untoward movement will break the lifesaving momentum. The three small girls weep silently. Their mother fingers her cross, her lips moving soundlessly. Jeff thinks that his heart will split open and then suddenly Matt's lips part and he spews forth a spray of water followed by a green froth of vomit.

'Good,' says the tall man who speaks with a guttural accent. 'He lives. The boy is OK.'

He turns then to his own daughters and it is Jeff who kneels beside his son, wiping his face clean, smoothing his hair, murmuring his name in a mantra of gratitude.

'Matt! Matt! Matt!'

Donny and Cary hover close by, trembling children, stripped of gaiety and bravado, the innocence and joy of the earlier hours shattered by their friend's dangerously close brush with death.

'Will he be all right, Dr Edwards?'

'Is he really OK?'

Their voices are tremulous.

'He'll be fine,' Jeff assures them.

'I'm OK,' Matt says in a hoarse whisper, forcing himself to smile. He is a child whose rueful apologies have always been accompanied by a smile.

Jeff passes his hands across his son's torso, his legs, his arms; his touch is that of a father-surgeon, sensitive to any bruise, any irregularity of bone and muscle on that lithe young body he has cared for from the very moment of Matt's birth. He fears that he will weep but instead he smiles. He turns to Polly. 'I don't know how to thank you.'

Polly blushes. 'I'm just glad I was here.'

'I'm sorry, Dad,' Matt says. 'I didn't mean to go near the water. I thought I could make the jump between those rocks.'

'It's OK,' Jeff says. 'Next time you'll think again.'

He lifts his son and carries him in his arms to the huge flat boulder still spread with the faded blanket that had once draped his marriage bed, trailed by Polly and the other boys. Jeremy and Annette, who have finally arrived, hurry toward them.

'What happened, Dad?' Annette asks, but before he can answer them, Wendy and Liane, ashen with anxiety, race up to join them.

'We heard there was an accident, a drowning,' Wendy gasps. 'That's what they were saying at the car park.'

But even as she speaks Donny rushes into her arms and she encircles him into the safety of her embrace.

'Mommy.' Cary thrusts himself at Liane, burying his head between her breasts.

Suddenly, inexplicably, he bursts into tears.

'A near accident, Matt. No drowning and he'll be fine,' Jeff assures them. 'Thanks to Polly.'

She blushes and Jeff sees that she is shivering. He shrugs out of his own sweatshirt and bundles her into it.

'I'm OK, I'm fine.'

Still shivering, she points to a copse of spruce saplings.

'The picnic hamper should be there. That's where I set it down when I couldn't find you. I hope no one's taken it.'

She is once again the concerned employee worrying about the needs of the guests of August. Paul and Richie retrieve it and carry it triumphantly back to the blanket.

'There's a cooler in the van up there in the parking lot. Mrs Abbot sent drinks and fruit and stuff.'

Jeremy and Annette scurry off and return, balancing the Styrofoam cooler between them as Liane and Wendy distribute the sandwiches and salads. They discover, much to their surprise, that they are ravenously hungry. They eat with an astonishing rapidity, each taste life-affirming. They laugh as a bottle of orange juice is spilled, as a canister of coleslaw is overturned. They have cheated death and can mock the messier vagaries of life.

The boys describe Polly's daring dive. They draw close to her. They are, all three of them, in love with her at this golden moment. They will not soon relinquish the memory of her amazing mid-air grace, her fearless dive into the menacing rapids.

Polly explains that Louise Abbot had counted on Evan to deliver the picnic lunch.

'When he didn't show up she asked me to drive out here with it.'

'A good thing she did,' Wendy says.

'A damn good thing,' Jeff agrees.

'What's with that Evan?' Liane wonders. 'He's hardly been around lately.'

'He's weird. He's always been weird,' Tracy Epstein says. 'My dad always said so. And Daniel can't stand him.'

Tracy, they all know, is a third generation Mount Haven Inn vacationer. Her grandparents, like Daniel Goldner's parents, and then her parents, Simon and Charlotte, spent all their Augusts there. Tracy finds it oddly comforting that her father chooses to return to the inn with Nessa and Paul. It gives her a sense of continuity. Her parents' divorce has not exiled her from the summer landscape of her childhood, from the anecdotes scavenged during late-night eavesdropping and squirreled away for future processing. All the nuances of the Abbots' lives are familiar to her. She knows about Louise's teenage pregnancy and about the stillborn babies. She can understand why her father and his friend Daniel hold Evan and his phony pastel-colored crew-neck sweaters in such contempt.

Still, Tracy's words make the others uncomfortable. There are things that should not be discussed in front of Polly who is, after all, Evan Abbot's employee. But Polly is indifferent to Tracy's revelations. She knows where Evan Abbot spends his time and with whom. She has seen him often enough on the UNH Durham campus and he is seldom alone. But she says nothing and snuggles deeper into Jeff Edwards' sweatshirt, inhaling the scent of his body, running her fingers across the ragged cuff of the sleeve.

She wonders if she should mend it before returning it to him.

They clear the remnants of the picnic away and Polly murmurs that she should be getting back to the inn.

'Mrs Abbot needs me to set up for dinner,' she says sleepily, aware for the first time of how the plunge into the creek exhausted her. She rubs her neck, murmurs something about a pain in her back.

'A muscle strain,' Jeff says. 'I'll call the inn and explain. You should rest for a while.'

He calls Louise on his cell phone, leaning against the spruce. He tells her what happened.

'But don't tell my wife,' he cautions. 'Matt is fine but I don't want her to worry.'

'Of course.' Louise's reply is vague, and Jeff knows that she is now wondering where she can find another waitress to help her that afternoon.

He returns to the blanket where both Polly and Matt have fallen asleep. Wendy and Liane are reading, looking up now and again at their sons who are gathering branches to construct yet another fort. Richie has produced a Scrabble board and a lazy game is in progress. Jeff too stretches out on the blanket. They luxuriate in the lassitude of this late-summer afternoon. All danger has passed and the sun, having reached its zenith, is bright upon their faces.

Susan Edwards sighs with relief, snaps her laptop shut and closes her dictionary. The chapter is complete and she is satisfied with her translation. She struggled with the cadences of Pierre's voice as he confronted his wife, Jacqueline, his long-smoldering resentment boiling over into a barely contained fury. Susan wrote and rewrote. LeBec's lyrical tone was stubbornly resistant to an English rendering but at last she had gotten it right. That was what marriage was sometimes like, she thought. Slights and moods, words unspoken, angers contained, toxic combinations that inevitably simmer and overflow. But it is also inevitable, she assures herself, that heat cools, that even caustic stains fade and are wiped away, leaving only the palest of scars. LeBec is pessimistic but Susan, her translator, is optimistic. She pities Pierre and Jacqueline but she does not pity herself or Jeff. All that has been constrained between them will be remedied. She glances at her watch and sees that she will have time to shower and wash her hair before everyone returns from the day's outing. She decides that she and Jeff will not have dinner at the inn but will drive instead to their favorite restaurant in Portsmouth where pale-green linen cloths cover the tables and the narrow room is candle lit.

'Wine, a really good Sauvignon,' she decides as she shampoos her hair, using the expensive lavender conditioner that Jeff is partial to.

'Sole almondine,' she thinks as she towels herself dry and contemplates her scant vacation wardrobe, selecting at last the one dressy outfit. 'Casual chic,' the salesperson had called the pale-blue silk trousers and matching top. She slips it on, loving the feel of the fabric against her skin, loving the way the long string of faux pearls dangles so elegantly against the Grecian folds of the loosely cut tunic. How fortunate that she remembered to bring her high-heeled white sandals. How fortunate that her ankles have remained slender. She applies her make-up carefully, even adding eye shadow, closing her lightly colored lids against the memory of Jeff's angry stare when she declined to join him at the water park. But this is vacation. There is always time during vacations to banish harsh angers, to soothe small irritations, small disappointments. She was, of course, foolish – foolish and stupid – to speak so sharply to Polly, but that is a mistake she will not make again. Helene was right about that.

Dressed at last, pleased with her image in the mirror, she glides out to the lawn where Nessa and Simon are setting out their usual array of summer drinks and snacks. Michael Curran is, as always, hunched over his spreadsheets and across the lawn Andrea and Mark Templeton recline in their Adirondack chairs, each desultorily turning the pages of the very large books they seem to carry with them everywhere. Susan wonders uncharitably if they choose their reading matter for its heft.

'You look fantastic, Susan,' Nessa says.

'Well, I thought we might go into Portsmouth for dinner tonight. Don't you and Simon ever feel like just getting away?' she asks.

'Not really. This is our getaway, I suppose. Simon's always off to some academic dinner or some board cocktail party and sometimes it's sort of necessary that I go with him. Not my scene as you can probably tell.'

She threads her fingers through her unruly mass of auburn hair, tied back with a strip of tie-dyed fabric in tones of purple and blue that do not match her loose orange and yellow mumu. She kicks at the newly mown grass with bare feet, her toes painted green, the lacquer dotted with pinpoints of pink.

'So being up here, where I don't have to bother with that sort of thing, is my getaway.'

'I can understand that,' Susan says and helps Nessa arrange a cluster of grapes around a brick of brie.

They all look up as cars make their way up the inn's driveway. Richie's roadster pulls in first and Annette jumps out of the driver's seat flushed with excitement. 'Richie let me drive,' she shouts. 'I even passed another car.'

Tracy has driven the inn's van, Jeremy beside her, Paul straddling the rear seat. Paul presents his mother with a bouquet of wildflowers and Susan wishes that Jeremy had thought to do the same for her. But Jeremy, she acknowledges, is simply not that sort of boy. Wendy and Liane arrive with their sons in tow. The boys have slept during the ride and they wipe their eyes and squint against the early evening light. And then at last Susan sees Jeff's car and she runs toward it, aware of the silken fabric that flares about her legs, aware of the way the breeze ruffles her hair.

Matt opens the back door and hurtles toward her.

'Mommy, guess what happened,' he shouts, eager to share the dangers of his day with his mother, eager to hear her re-assurances, to see the lines of love glide across her face.

But she barely looks at him. Her gaze is fixed on Jeff, who emerges from his car and then holds the passenger-side door open for Polly. Polly, who wears his sweatshirt, whom he gingerly supports, his arm around her waist.

Susan feels the blood rush to her face. Her fists clench.

'What's going on, Jeff?' she asks.

Helene, who walks up the driveway just then, recognizes the icy edge in her sister's question. Susan has spoken in their mother's voice, the voice of the maternal inquisitor whose every accusatory question was born of her own unrelenting and frozen anger.

Susan has not, after all, escaped their childhood unscarred.

'Why is Polly wearing your sweatshirt? Why is she with you? Why are you holding her that way?' Susan's voice rises dangerously.

Polly pales, trembles and rushes into the inn. Jeff stares at his wife, his eyes narrowed, his face fiery with a fury he can barely control.

'She's wearing my sweatshirt because she got soaked to the skin diving into dangerous waters to save our son. I was supporting her because she strained her back in the process. What the hell is wrong with you, damn it!'

He strides past her and she stands very still, shamed and angered. She knows herself to be ridiculous in her pale-blue silk finery. She realizes that the other guests have moved away from her and are clustered about the redwood table where Simon Epstein carefully measures out drinks and Nessa, sensible, sensitive Nessa, perhaps to divert attention away from Susan, points skyward where a flock of geese is already scissoring their way south. Only Helene remains beside her, placing a comforting arm on her sister's shoulder. Angrily, Susan shakes it off and Helene too walks away.

With a great effort, Susan turns her attention to Matt. Frightened by the sharp exchange between his parents, he nervously prattles on, telling her how he almost drowned, how Polly had saved him. Cary and Donny chime in to report that they had thought he was dead, that a blond man had breathed into his mouth, that they were all scared.

'Really scared,' they shout in unison and then, because they are boys bred to resilience, they laugh wildly at their own unfounded terror and run up to their rooms, to find their quarters which they pump with ferocious optimism into the pinball machines.

In bed that night, Jeff lies rigid, staring up at the ceiling while Susan curls up, facing the wall, clutching a corner of the light blanket which provides little warmth against the encroaching nocturnal chill. Summer is drifting to a close, the cool days of autumn approaching too rapidly.

TEN

As though exhausted by the complications of their excursion into the White Mountains, a new and surprisingly pleasant lassitude overtakes the guests of August. They stake out sovereign territories beneath the wide-branched trees and place their chairs on discrete islands of shade.

Andrea Templeton chooses a seat near the playground area where Matt, Donny and Cary are constructing a waterfall, piling rock upon rock and pouring streams of water from juice bottles down into a pool they carefully dug. Their game defies the danger of the previous day, neutralizes their fear. They are in complete control of the elements. It is Donny whom Andrea watches closely. She searches her grandson's face, straining to see her son in the set of his mouth, the sharpness of his features, but Donny is his mother's son. It is Wendy's coloring he has inherited, her sharp features, her olive skin and dark eyes. Adam is not restored to her through this grandson she hardly knows. But then, she thinks sadly, had she really known Adam? She sighs, opens her book and struggles to remember where she stopped reading the previous day.

Simon Epstein, Mark Templeton and Michael Curran commandeer a redwood table on a far corner of the lawn and set up a command center, laptops and spreadsheets, their cell phones and Blackberries near to hand, as though at any moment a crisis may arise and be averted. Michael holds a pen and as Simon directs, he corrects numbers on his printouts. Mark Templeton looks on, his hands loosely clasped, his lips pursed, indifferent and powerful, a financial regent in his impeccably ironed oxford blue shirt and chino trousers, sharply creased, because Andrea hung them so carefully in his garment bag. He is grateful to Andrea for such small attentions and he frowns as his grandson, Donny, runs past him in dirt-spattered jeans and an oversized T-shirt. Wendy should dress her son more carefully. Andrea, he is certain, never allowed Adam to run about like a ragamuffin, but then he cannot really be sure about that. He cannot really remember Adam as a small boy. Nor as an adolescent for that matter.

Helene and Greg Ames spread a blanket beneath an elm tree and Greg lazily plucks at his guitar. Louise has suggested a sing-along for the after-dinner hour and he is trying to decide what songs to play. Helene lies on the blanket, her head resting on his thigh, an unopened book in her outstretched hand. She stares at the inn, worried about Susan who did not come down to breakfast. Jeff himself ate little, drank too much coffee and offered monosyllabic replies to his children's strangely awkward chatter, erupting with uncharacteristic anger when Jeremy and Annette bickered over the last piece of coffee cake.

'Is Susan all right?' Helene had asked tentatively.

'Fine. She's fine.' His reply was terse, his face tense. He turned away from Matt, who stared at him anxiously.

It strikes Helene as odd that she should be worried about the sister who had always worried about her. She averts her eyes from the inn. Susan will come down when she is ready. It is a good sign that Jeff has placed two chairs together. He sits in one, piles his medical journals on the other. He will, of course, move them when Susan joins him. She closes her eyes as Paul Epstein, his own guitar in hand, settles down beside Greg. Annette approaches with her mandolin in hand.

'Want to learn those chords?' Greg asks.

Paul nods and Helene drifts into a light sleep as they softly sing a chorus of 'On Top of Old Smokey'.

Nessa and Wendy carry their pads and drawing pencils down to the lake. Two swans have mysteriously arrived and they are eager to sketch them. Nessa will do a whimsical drawing geared to her child readers. She will, she thinks, turn the fairy tale upside down and write of a majestic swan transformed into a mischievous duckling. Compassionate humor will triumph over beauty. Wendy, so accomplished in landscapes, will work in the style she has been studying in her Audubon text.

Intent on their project, they are surprised to discover Daniel seated on the sanded log smoking his first pipe of the day. The fragrance of his tobacco mingles sweetly with the pungent odor of damp earth and waterlogged flora.

'I'll share the bench with you,' he offers.

'No thanks. I want to get the shadows at the far shore,' Nessa says, and she walks across the lake front, settling down on a boulder near the dock.

'Not too subtle, is she?' Wendy asks. 'Determined to leave us alone together.'

'Nothing subtle about Nessa,' he agrees. 'That's what Simon loves about her. She's big-breasted, big-hearted, open, honest, comfortable in her own skin, at peace with her own eccentricities. Everything that Simon's first wife, Charlotte, wasn't.'

The swans glide closer to them, their long necks held high, their coal-black eyes regally surveying their aquatic kingdom as they continue their tandem sail across the sun-bright waters of the lake.

'Swans mate for life, I think,' Wendy says. 'No first marriages for them.'

'Lucky, or maybe not so lucky,' Daniel replies and she begins to draw, fearful that she has gone too far, that her words have hurt him.

'Simon has a theory,' he continues. 'He sees life as a series of chapters. One chapter ends, another begins. He talks about his own life – "the Simon and Charlotte chapter" – followed by "the Simon and Nessa chapter". He assures me that I'm just at the end of one chapter – the "Laura and Daniel chapter" – and I'll soon tumble into an entirely new chapter.'

'One with a happy ending?' Wendy asks and smiles. She begins to draw the swans who are now very still, only their wings ruffling the lake waters, creating gentle wavelets.

'Happier at least than the Daniel and Laura chapter. My wife – she is, I suppose still my wife – is a dancer; I think I told you that. And very beautiful. I may not have told you that. It's no longer very important to me.' He puffs deeply on his pipe and Wendy concentrates on her drawing, unwilling to look up and see the sorrow on his face. 'Tall, taller than me,' he goes on. 'Her hair is the color of honey.'

Wendy thinks of the blonde hairs that had clung to the motorcycle helmet he had placed on her head. Tendrils the color of honey. She selects a drawing pencil of deep orange and draws the swan's beak.

'Yes. Almost that color,' Daniel says, looking down at her work, and she blushes.

He tells her then about the night in the Hamptons, of his anger and aching sadness, of his fury and his sense of loss, and even as he speaks he wonders why he is revealing so much of himself to this lovely young woman whom he scarcely knows, but whose body had melted toward him in the shadows of bushes heavy with berries the color of the sky.

She listens calmly, as calmly as he himself had listened to her own story, to her bittersweet memories of the young writer whom she had loved and who had morphed into the alcoholic husband she could no longer love. She had spoken oh-so-softly of the father of her son, killed in an accident on a cool August afternoon on a roadway not far from the lake where they now sit staring out at the beautiful white birds who mate for life.

He sighs, his narrative done.

'I suppose my story isn't all that unusual. Infidelity is the norm for some people. Women claiming absolute freedom is something that's happening. Laura and Daniel – an ordinary tale, a very ordinary chapter . . .'

His voice trails off. He is embarrassed, suddenly, to have said so much – too much, he is sure. Wendy no longer looks at the swans. She looks at him.

'Ordinary isn't the word I'd use,' she says.

'Oh. What word would you use?'

'Sad,' she replied. 'What happened to you was sad. Being betrayed is sad and dealing with that betrayal is sad.'

He recognizes the very words he had spoken to her in the café, the solace he had offered, now in turn, offered to him. He turns to her, no longer embarrassed, no longer ashamed, and sees that her dark eyes are bright with tears. Gently, he pulls her toward him, gently his lips find hers, gently his hands crown her head, his fingers thread their way through her silk smooth hair. She leans into him and he welcomes the soft compliance of her flesh against his own. They remain in a sweet embrace as the swans stretch their long white necks and, with measured grace, glide to the opposite shore.

*   *   *

Polly arrives on time the next day, but Louise looks at her sharply and sees at once that she is pale, that there are dark circles beneath her eyes.

'Are you feeling all right, Polly?' she asks.

'Fine. I'm just worried about my mother. And I had a little trouble sleeping. I think I might have strained my back but it's fine now.'

'Why don't you take the morning off? Sit in the sun for a few hours.'

'Are you sure? Can you manage alone?' Polly is surprised. Louise is not often solicitous of those who work for her.

'Of course I'm sure.' Louise's reply is abrupt. She is uneasy with gratitude.

'All right.'

Polly retrieves her physiology textbook. She is grateful for these bonus hours, pleased to be able to sit outside on this sunlit morning, glad that she wore the sleeveless pale-green dress that exposes her arms and shoulders to the golden warmth. She heads outside toward a secluded area of the lawn but Jeff Edwards calls to her.

'Polly, do you have a minute?'

She hesitates and then walks toward him. He sweeps his journals off the chair beside him and motions her to sit.

'I wanted to ask you how you were feeling today. And I wanted to explain my wife's behavior yesterday. She's been working too hard. She's very stressed out. She didn't mean anything by what she said.'

His own words, so patently false, embarrass him but how else to account for Susan's wildly accusatory questions? Polly is owed some explanation, some apology. He cannot, of course, speak to her of the true origins of Susan's words, of the tensions that haunt their marriage, the exhausting routine of their days, the incessant demands of their children, Jeremy and Annette's constant bickering, Matt's watchful uneasiness. Jeff acknowledges that the dreams of their courtship, of the early years of their marriage, are tarnished, that age has diminished their energy, narrowed their horizons. He flinches from the memory of his wife's words whispered into the darkness last night. *I was frightened.* He too is frightened but he cannot put a face to his fear.

Polly, innocent, hard-working Polly, radiant with youth and hope, her future charted but still unrealized, would be unable to understand that inexplicable fear that crushes reason. It is triggered by the sadness of middle age, moods that darken with the encroachment of evening. In truth he does not understand it himself. He knows only that he and Susan are adrift in a season of uncertainty. Their phone rings with news of death and divorce. They attend more funerals than weddings and shudder with fear when minor pains and illnesses ambush them. They frown into the mirror when they notice the new laugh lines that crinkle about their eyes, the new strands of silver that shimmer in their hair. They are newly aware of their own mortality, of tomorrows fringed with uncertainty. None of this can he share with young Polly who smiles shyly at him now.

'That's OK,' she says. 'Everyone gets upset when they're tired.'

She opens her textbook and searches for her place.

He glances down at it. 'There's an easy mnemonic for that stuff. I'll help you with it. But it's too gorgeous a day to worry about bone structure. How about a walk? If you're not too tired?'

'I'm not too tired,' she replies, and with those words the weariness she had felt since waking falls away. He strides forward and she rises from the chair, leaves her textbook forgotten, and follows after him, trailing in his shadow and then, quickening her pace, she walks beside him.

Helene turns her attention from Greg and Paul, who continue to strum their guitars. She shades her eyes and watches as her brother-in-law helps Polly over a stile. They walk, as though jointly balanced on ribs of sunlight, toward the meadow. Helene sighs and goes over to their abandoned chairs. She straightens Jeff's journals and moves Polly's textbook to a bench a few feet away from the chair that is too close to his.

'Poor Susan,' she thinks for the second time that day.

Jeff and Polly progress in silence, their arms swinging but not touching, a slight breeze brushing their sunlit faces. They pause and look up as a red-winged blackbird soars with heart-stopping grace and disappears behind a drifting cloud. Jeff plucks a long blade of grass.

'It almost matches your dress,' he tells Polly.

She does not reply but her hands tremble and her cheeks grow hot. Impulsively she removes her sandals and dances barefoot through the wild meadow and he, without thinking, races after her. He is infused with her energy. He feels himself a young man again, dashing through the bright fields of summer, in pursuit of a barefoot, golden-limbed girl whose hair falls in loose swaths about her laughing face. Susan's angry words, still sour in memory, have ignited a desire he never acknowledged. He will resist it. Of course he will resist it. Polly is only a few years older than his daughter and he is a man who loves his wife.

But his body betrays him. He races after her, catches her, touches her shoulder, inhales a familiar scent. Jean Nate again, the toilet water favored by Susan during their courtship. It is, he knows, the young girl's gateway aroma, so light and sweet, its black-capped green bottle holding out a promise of sophistication, of romance, of sex, tentative and tender. The aroma dizzies him with its reminder of Polly's age and his own.

'Polly,' he says softly and she turns to him, her face radiant with anticipation. His arm is outstretched. Within seconds he will draw her closer, within milliseconds his lips will be soft against hers. His throat is dry, his arm paralyzed. What is he doing? What the hell is he doing?

'Dad!' Matt's voice rings out loud and clear across the meadow. 'Hey, Dad.'

Jeff turns and his son sprints toward him, followed by Cary and Donny.

'Hey, Dad, we want to take a rowboat out but we need an adult to be with us. Cary's dad is working and Donny can't find his mother. Can you do it? Please, Dad.'

He turns from his son to Polly.

'Go ahead. The kids need you. I'll see you at lunch,' she says, and the relief in her voice matches the sudden lightening of his heart.

Swinging her sandals, she turns back to the inn and he trails after the boys who break into a run. He sprints along with them although by the time they reach the lake he is breathing hard and his pulse is racing dangerously.

Polly returns to the inn and goes at once into the kitchen. Louise, who is counting out cutlery, glances at her, taking note of Polly's high color and seeing that her hair, pulled back earlier, now falls loosely about her face. Bending to mop up a damp spot on the floor, she sees the grass stains that streak Polly's slender feet.

'I'll fold the napkins,' Polly offers.

They work side by side in silence and then, with a startling abruptness, Louise turns to her, her face grim, her tone monitory.

'Be careful, Polly,' she says. 'Be very careful.'

'I don't know what you're talking about,' Polly protests but her cheeks burn and a napkin slithers to the floor.

'I think you do.' Louise's tone is flat. 'Your life can be changed in a morning, in an hour, in minutes. Everything you dreamed about, everything you worked for, can disappear. Believe me. I know. Don't be foolish. Don't be stupid. You've worked too hard, Polly. Don't lose everything . . .'

Her voice trails off.

'You have no right . . .' Polly begins, impelled to anger, but she looks at Louise and sees that the older woman is very pale, that the cutlery she holds clatters on to the counter, that tears glint in her faded blue eyes.

Wordlessly, she fills a glass with water. She hands the glass to Louise, goes into the dining room and begins to set the tables.

ELEVEN

The sing-along is a success. Greg and Paul each play solos and then ease into a duet. Annette strums along on her mandolin. Their audience is relaxed, attentive. Nessa sprawls across the couch, her head resting on Simon's lap, smiling because Paul's music always makes her smile.

Andrea Templeton notes disapprovingly that Nessa has painted her toenails silver with rainbow-colored stripes that match her loose wide-sleeved mumu. So inappropriate, she thinks as she pulls her needle angrily through her needlepoint. Her mood softens as Greg and Paul play a new arrangement of 'Foggy Foggy Dew.' The song had been a favorite of Adam's, she remembers, happy to have retrieved that one lonely memory of her son. She sings along softly and sees that Wendy, who sits beside Daniel Goldner, is also singing. He taps his foot in rhythm to her voice. Andrea frowns.

Mark, however, is silent. He does not know that his son had a particular fondness for that song but he does know that the teacup from which Andrea now and again takes small sips surely contains vodka. He will not confront her with that deception. They have not spoken of the incident on the lawn, of the inexplicable (to him as well as to her) fury with which he had jerked the drink from her hand. Her anger and his regret have diminished over the passing days and they have retreated again into the complicity of silence which has for so long sustained their marriage. He watches as she lifts the cup yet again and wonders for how long he will have to sit through this damn sing-along. He wonders too how many sips of vodka it will take for Andrea to achieve the numbness of thought and feeling that she craves, that she has always craved. He is, however, grateful, as always, that she is now a quiet, unobtrusive drinker as opposed to her behavior during the early days of their marriage. The New Hampshire solution had, in retrospect, worked well after all. No divorce, a minimum of drama-infused scenes, their marriage in survival mode. He is satisfied, he supposes, or would be if they could forego the inevitable August pilgrimage. But Andrea is right. It is a social imperative, an obligation.

The entire group sings 'On Top of Old Smokey' and Matt, Donny and Cary, giggling and red-faced, rehearsed by Greg and encouraged by Paul and Annette, sing 'If I Had a Hammer' and invite everyone to join in the chorus. With easy spontaneity, they all link arms and sway as they sing.

'I'd hammer out freedom, I'd hammer out love between my brothers and my sisters all over this land.'

They smile at each other. This is a moment that will be frozen in memory, a vacation evening to recall through the lonely wintry months to come, this hour of easy comfortable fellowship, their voices raised in song in a lamplit pine-paneled room. Matt seeks out his mother who is in one corner of the room and then his father who crouches on the floor, directly in front of the makeshift stage. He wills them to move closer to each other, to exchange glances and smiles, so that he might be reassured that everything is all right between them, but they remain in self-imposed isolation. He turns away and joins the small energetic chorus in singing the final refrain. They then segue into solos.

Liane surprises them by singing a haunting love ballad, her voice trembling with a sweetness Michael does not recognize. Paul accompanies her on the piano as Greg and Helene glide across the floor in a slow dance.

Watchful Nessa sees that Richie's arm rests on Annette Edwards' bare shoulder, sees that he draws her closer. Annette moves imperceptibly away, but her color is high and she sweeps her long silken hair back so that her fingers lightly touch Richie's hand.

There is applause, a call for an encore, and Liane obliges with 'Dancing in the Dark'. Wendy and Daniel now dance with easy grace, as though they have been partnered forever. Nessa, in Simon's arms, moves with the light-footedness peculiar to many heavyset women. Jeremy and Tracy waltz across the floor but Susan Edwards does not move from her chair and her husband stares out the window where the branches of the elms tremble against the gust of a sudden wind.

Richie and Annette leave, having offered to help Louise Abbot set out the apple cider and cookies she traditionally provides for the sing-alongs, a custom that fits into her concept of what should be done at a country inn. But before going into the kitchen they wander outside and look out across the lawn, listening to the wind, welcoming its cool caress across their faces. Richie turns to Annette and again he draws her close. This time she does not pull away. His lips find hers, his tongue rakes its way about her mouth, a mingling of moistures. He kisses her once and then again but when his hands touch her breasts, she thrusts him away.

'No,' she says. 'I'm sorry. No.'

'Why not?' he asks harshly. 'Why the hell not?'

It is not a question she can answer. Instead, she dashes into the kitchen and reluctantly he follows her. Tease, he thinks, Goddamn tease. He should have known better than to start up with a high-school kid.

The music trails them into the kitchen where Louise has already filled the pitchers with cider. Paul at the piano and Greg on the guitar play old-time show times. Helene and Susan sing as they did when they were teenagers, vulnerable sisters then, singing their way free of the strangling net of their mother's misery, of her silent and inexplicable rage. The soothing duets of their sad adolescence are a legacy they reclaim.

Susan sings 'Some Enchanted Evening' by herself as Helene hums.

'My mom has a really good voice,' Annette tells Richie, hoping that he is not angry with her.

'Oh yeah. Good for her,' he answers, his voice heavy with indifference.

She turns away as he lifts the tray that holds two pitchers of cider and carries it out without looking back at her. He's done with her.

She arranges the cookies on a paper doily and hopes that she will not cry.

It rains that night, a fierce, relentless late-summer storm, the heavy downfall an ominous reminder of the season's treacherous ending.

Louise Abbot moves through the deserted dimly lit kitchen, clearing the counters, filling the huge urn with coffee ready to be brewed at first light. She worries that Evan does not have his rain gear and chides herself for the foolishness of that worry. She places a battered pot on the kitchen floor to catch the rain drops that drip through a leak in the roof. The building needs a new roof, she knows, but she wonders if they can afford it, wonders if it is even worth doing. The life of the inn is uncertain. Reservations are down and even regular guests have not booked for the coming season. It is not even certain that the guests of August will return. It is a frightening thought and so, swiftly, she reassures herself.

Oh, but they are loyal that August contingent; they have long been loyal. All will be well. It had been such a good evening. The singing, the dancing. They will surely remember that.

She draws the kitchen curtains against the weeping rain and goes upstairs to the loneliness of the large double bed that had belonged to Evan's parents. She lays awake, as she often does, indulgent in her imaginings, the fantasy of her girlhood still held close, the life plan upended by carelessness and harsh reality. She hopes that Polly understood her warning.

At the edge of sleep, she visualizes the ghostly apartment in Boston she had once thought to make her own. She would have furnished it with a beige couch, many colorful cushions, a low teak coffee table. Sometimes she adds a desk with a shaded lamp for the papers she carries home from the office where she is an executive secretary. She has always loved the sound of those words. *Executive secretary.*

She would have given small parties in that pleasant room. There are nights when she imagines Daniel Goldner arriving as a guest at such a party, carrying flowers, yellow roses which she will place in a blue ceramic vase. She will welcome him, welcome her other guests, and pile their coats on her bed, covered with a madras spread. Smiling sleepily, she reminds herself that it is a bed bought new. In her entire life, Louise has only slept on beds handed down from others.

On this rainy night, infused with nostalgia after the sing-along, she places an imaginary crystal bowl on her imaginary bedside table. Soothed and satisfied by her illusory conjectures, she adds Evan's pillow to her own and falls asleep.

Annette Edwards also lies awake and listens to the tympanic patter of the rain drops against the brittle leaves of the giant oak tree just outside the window.

'Jeremy.' She calls softly to her brother, across the flimsy curtained partition that separates their beds.

'I'm sleeping, Nette. Let me sleep,' he replies drowsily.

He has not been sleeping. He has been remembering how he held Tracy Epstein close, reliving the magic moment when he felt the softness of her breasts against his body as they danced with such ease. He wonders if she would rebuff him if he really put a move on her. He wants a kiss, just a lousy kiss. She could give him that. She's probably done a lot more with other guys. She's in college, after all. So what if he's a couple of years younger than she is? They've been getting along great, really having fun, and he wants to have a memory of this vacation, a small triumph to be revisited over the coming months. He imagines himself lying in bed on winter nights thinking of Tracy's lips soft upon his own, her hands gliding slowly across his body. He will remember always that her hair smells of citrus and her chin dimples when she smiles.

Tracy. He mouths her name soundlessly into the darkness.

But Annette is persistent. 'I just want to ask you something,' she says, and the hesitancy in her voice surprises him. They are twins who once spoke to each other in their own secret language, anticipated each other's thoughts, but those days have vanished. They have bickered their way into independence, learned how to tease and provoke. But their sensitivity to each other's moods lingers. He hears her pain.

'What do you want to ask me?' His voice is gentler now.

'Do you think Richie is a nice guy?'

He does not hesitate. 'No. I think he's a jerk. A conceited jerk. Even Tracy thinks that and she's his own sister. You know who's a nice guy? Paul's a nice guy. It's hard to think that those two guys have the same father. Richie and Paul.'

'Yeah. Paul is a really nice guy,' she says thoughtfully, calmly, and within minutes they are both asleep.

Nessa and Simon sip their tea in the soft glow of their bed lamps and speak in the relaxed marital shorthand peculiar to their late-night exchanges.

'Cheese,' she says sleepily. 'And olives. Kalamatas.'

'Tomorrow. I'll zip into the village. The deli. Probably in the afternoon,' he assures her.

He is irritated that his pro-bono advice to Michael Curran is taking up so many mornings because Mark Templeton, that arrogant bastard, is being so difficult. Curran's software is a terrific opportunity for venture capital investment, yet Templeton keeps upping the ante. Simon has sat on boards with men like Mark, petty corporate tyrants who confuse their wealth with actual power. Simon is not surprised that elegant Andrea Templeton is a secret drinker and Templeton's daughter-in-law and grandson keep their emotional distance from him.

'Brie. And Gouda,' Nessa adds and segues on to another topic.

'I'm worried about Paul. You know, the Edwards girl. He really has a thing for her.'

'I know. Richie's in the equation. Not much we can do about it. They'll be all right. They'll sort it out. All kids go through that sort of thing.'

'I suppose.'

She will go no further. She does not discuss the children of his first marriage with Simon. She will not say that she fears that Richie is very much his mother's son, that he has inherited Charlotte's false values, her careless indifference to the needs of others. Simon knows that she fears for Paul who is so gentle, so sensitive, so new to desire, so very different from his older half-brother. But this is a subject on which they must remain silent. He is father to both boys.

He sets his empty teacup down and turns off his bedside light.

'What about Wendy and Daniel?' Nessa asks, gravitating toward safer territory.

'She would be so good for him.'

'Too early for Daniel to get involved,' Simon says carefully.

'He's so newly burned. No time yet for him to heal. It wasn't easy with Laura. And they're not even divorced yet. He's still in no-man's land.'

'I like Wendy.'

'I do too. But I don't think either of them are ready for anything permanent.'

Nessa nods. Still, she decides that she will invite Wendy and Donny to spend a weekend with them in New York. She will organize a dinner party. Or perhaps a brunch. A brunch would be more casual, less obvious. And afterwards she and Simon and Wendy and Daniel will walk through Central Park. She imagines the four of them kicking their way through swaths of autumn leaves. The plan contents her. She is a generous woman. Her own happiness is not sufficient; she would share it with others. She wants Daniel, their dear friend, Simon's surrogate younger brother, to be happy. She wants to hear Wendy laugh.

She too sets her cup down and turns off her own light. Simon draws her close and rests his head on her shoulder. They lie quietly and listen to the storm which has intensified.

Helene and Greg, awakened by the clap of thunder, hold each other close.

'I loved tonight,' she murmurs.

'Good vibes,' he agrees. 'Nice music. Nice dancing.'

'I love the way you look when you play.'

'And I love the way you look at me when I play.'

That exchange of looks has been there from their very first meeting. They were vagabond Americans then, self-designated bohemians, drawn to each other amid the merriment of an Irish pub. He had looked at her, she had looked at him and they were together then and thereafter.

She snuggles closer to him. It is wonderful to be warm and dry, safe from the storm, safe from fear and loneliness. His finger traces the curve of her lips and her body arches against him with feline grace.

'Wait,' he says warningly.

He knows her to be uncertain. Do they really want children? Will she be a good mother? She knows him to be patient.

But tonight is different. He senses that at once.

'No. No need to wait,' she says. 'I'm done waiting.'

The exposed fragility of Susan's marriage has caused her to fear for her own.

They come together as twin bolts of lightning flash across the sky. Their passion is purposeful, their pulses race, their limbs entangle, their breath commingles. Exhausted, satiated, they lie hand in hand, cocooned in joy, thrilled by their new and wondrous togetherness.

In the room across the hall Susan and Jeff lie in wakeful uneasiness. Their eyes are closed, their bodies rigid. They make no move to draw closer to each other in this, the largest double bed in Mount Haven Inn. Raindrops drizzle down the windowpanes and Jeff rises and pulls the gossamer white curtains closed. Susan says nothing. She is thinking about the chapter she recently translated in which LeBec's characters, Pierre and Jacqueline, recognize the vulnerability of their marriage and Pierre reflects bitterly that, in fact, all marriages are dangerously fragile. Susan had struggled with the very concept, struggled with the translation of LeBec's phrasing of Pierre's meandering thoughts, rendered in an archaic French. Even as she tapped her hesitant translation on to her keyboard, she had argued against the thought. Pierre was wrong, she had told herself.

All marriages are not fragile. My marriage is not fragile. She had felt her family immune to the epidemic of divorce that had swept across Matt's grade during the past winter. Matt had returned home to report on the splits, sad-eyed and worried. Russ's father had moved to another city. Eddie's mom had taken him and his brothers to live with her parents. Eugene spends three days with his mother and four with his father.

'It's so scary,' Matt had said.

'Don't be scared,' she had assured him. 'We're fine. We're great. You never have to worry about your family. Daddy and I love each other. Forever.'

'*All marriages are not fragile,*' she would tell LeBec defiantly.

Now it occurs to her that her mental and vocal protests were dangerous. She had tempted fate and Jeff's heart is sealed against her. Weighted with misery, she falls asleep at last. But Jeff tosses and turns until the first light of dawn streaks its way across the sky.

Wendy springs into wakefulness as a streak of lightning flashes across the sky. She has always been intrigued and excited by summer storms and, after checking on Donny, shrugs into her dressing gown and heads downstairs.

Next door, Andrea Templeton is awake. She's always found it difficult to sleep during a storm. Adam too had always been frightened by wind and rain and often, during his boyhood, he had crept into her bed. Too often, she supposes, she had rebuffed him and sent him back to the loneliness of his own room. Familiar guilt settles heavily upon her. She had tried, she has tried to assure herself, but she knows that she had not been a good mother.

Suddenly Donny calls out, his voice thick with sleep. She waits for Wendy to go to him but when he cries out again, she tiptoes into the adjoining room. Wendy's bed is empty and Donny is now peacefully asleep, the smile of what must surely have been a happy dream playing on his lips. His cry must have been an utterance of joy.

Relieved, she glances at the table on which Wendy's sketchpad lies. She flips it open and studies the rough drawings of the swans. Grudgingly, she admires them. Wendy must have studied Audubon's technique. She is progressing beyond the watercolor landscapes which, Andrea admits, are very pleasing. She closes the pad and centers it carefully on the table.

'Where is Wendy?' she wonders, although she is fairly certain that she knows.

She returns to her own room, fills a glass with vodka which she drinks as she stares unseeingly into the darkness. Mark, a light sleeper, wakens, watches her but says nothing. What, after all, would be the point?

Michael and Liane sleep peacefully, indifferent to the storm. Now and again, his arm brushes her shoulder and she smiles at his touch. His spreadsheets, bloodied with the red ink of Mark Templeton's pen, litter the desk. At each subsequent meeting Mark has made corrections, insisted on adjustments, raised questions about proven calculations.

Michael thinks his suggestions unnecessary, as does Simon Epstein, who is after all a world-famous economist, a financial guru consulted regularly by venture capitalists. But it is Simon, ever the pragmatist, who suggests that Michael acquiesce to Templeton's suggestions.

'All you need is his capital. Say yes, pocket the check and do as you please,' he advised, and Michael supposes that he is right.

Still, although he gets up once in the night to close the window, he does not glance at his work. Time enough in the morning. He no longer feels the urgency that choked him with fear only a few days earlier. No matter what, he and Liane will manage, they will survive. She has offered him reassurances, even a plan. His wife, mysteriously and wondrously, is once again his own.

He covers Cary with a light blanket, returns to bed and drops a kiss on Liane's forehead, before drifting back into a sweet and dreamless sleep.

TWELVE

The new morning is sun-swept, the air sweet and fresh in the aftermath of the wild and cleansing nocturnal storm. The rain-washed lawn is a verdant expanse across which Donny, Cary and Matt dance barefoot before breakfast. Louise fills the vases with the last roses of summer; the delicate amber-colored petals pearled with drops of dew. The flowers and the promising brightness of the sunlight that emblazons the windows please the vacationers as they drift in for breakfast. Polly carries in one tray of pancakes, but another waitress serves the table where the Edwards family is seated in stiff and uneasy silence. Matt, tousle-haired, his feet deliciously cold, tries valiantly to coax them into laughter, telling jokes which evoke reluctant smiles.

'Want to go antiquing with us today?' Helene asks Susan. 'It would be fun for the four of us to do something together.'

She is eager to please her sister, to encircle Susan in her own newfound cocoon of contentment.

'Maybe,' Susan says.

'No.' Jeff's reply is flatly final.

Susan blushes and Helene looks away.

The dining room is abuzz with conversations about plans for the day ahead. Andrea and Mark decide to go to a nursery and select new plantings for Adam's grave.

'What do you think about a bonsai arrangement, Wendy?' Andrea asks.

She is careful not to ignore Adam's widow on such a delicate topic.

'Or perhaps a small hedgerow just bordering the grave.'

'I thought we'd put in some more bulbs. Daffodils and narcissi. The ones we put in last year were beautiful when they bloomed in the spring,' Wendy replies carefully. 'Crocuses maybe. Adam liked crocuses. He always bought potted crocuses for our apartment.'

That had never happened, but she takes malicious pleasure in inventing it. She wants to wound her husband's mother who had never visited their small Cambridge apartment, who had not been witness to the sad last weeks and months of Adam's life, who has no way of knowing whether or not crocuses had bloomed on their windowsill.

'You visited his grave in the spring?' Andrea has difficulty concealing the surprise in her voice.

'We go every spring, me and Mom. And sometimes in the winter,' Donny tells her. 'Last year we went on Thanksgiving morning.'

He is proud of these pilgrimages in retrospect, although in actual practice he resists them. He has no memory of the father who lies beneath the pale marble gravestone with its elegant cursive inscription. *Adam Templeton. Beloved Son, Husband and Father.* The year of his birth and the year of his death are carved beneath the letters. Donny has done the arithmetic and knows that his father was thirty years old on the day of his death. Always he runs his fingers across the carved inscription, unnerved to find granules of dark earth within the letters. Diligently, during each such visit, he helps his mother pull the weeds that stubbornly force their way around the plants set in place each August. Sometimes his mother cries and sometimes she is dry eyed. He himself has never cried. How can he weep for a father he never knew? He forgives himself for his lack of sorrow. It is enough that he accompanies his mother, no matter how reluctantly.

'On Thanksgiving morning,' Andrea repeats, her tone cold. 'An interesting choice of days to make such a visit.'

Wendy smiles bitterly. Does Adam's mother think she has a monopoly on grief, that her August pilgrimages must remain inviolate, that she and Donny have no right to visit the grave on their own? She turns to Donny.

'Do you want to go to the nursery with us?' she asks him.

'But he always comes with us,' Andrea protests. 'I can't think why you're giving him a choice this year.'

'Always does not mean forever,' Wendy replies as Donny crumbles his toast and builds a small hillock with the crumbs which he brushes angrily to the floor. His grandparents should not talk about him. Why don't they talk *to* him?

'I'm not sure what I want to do,' he says sullenly.

Only then does Mark look up from his perusal of the *Wall Street Journal* which Michael Curran dutifully delivers to their table each morning.

'Wendy, I think you know that it means a lot to Adam's mother that Donny come with us, that he help us make a choice about what we want to plant,' he says.

Each word is clipped. He is not a man who raises his voice. He has other ways of making his will known.

Wendy flushes, places her arm about her son's shoulder.

'It's OK, Mom. I'll go with you.'

Donny's response is swift. He would agree to anything to ease the tension between his mother and his grandparents. He does not point out that, in fact, in past years, his opinion was never solicited as they wandered about the nursery, studying shrubbery and bushes. He has long felt that a small tree should be planted just beyond the grave so that the marble slab might be shaded in the heat of the summer. And perhaps a small stone bench placed just beneath it so that his mother might rest on it when she visits. He has seen such benches at other grave sites. Perhaps today, he will mention both the tree and the bench. After all, his grandfather has said that he should help in their choice.

Paul volunteers to take Cary and Matt canoeing and he is surprised when Annette offers to join them. Richie frowns but says nothing. His cell phone rings. He glances at the screen and goes outside where the reception is better.

'Our mother probably,' Tracy says drily. 'She calls in the mornings. Before her meetings. Before her conference calls. Before she has to rush to the airport or speed to a runway show. We're like the stuffing in her sandwich – she fits us in between slices of time.'

Nessa thinks she should defend Charlotte, tell Tracy that her mother is really a very busy woman, that her job is time bound and weighted with responsibility. But she remains silent. It is not her role to run interference for her husband's first wife. Stepmothers must be careful, very careful.

Simon also ignores Tracy's comment. His own morning stretches pleasantly before him, Mark Templeton having announced that he would be unavailable to work on Michael Curran's project. Simon has a new idea as to how to proceed with young Curran's software, but he is granting himself a reprieve. For these next few hours, he will be neither an economist nor a business guru but a man on vacation, strolling at his own leisurely pace through a small New Hampshire village, making pleasant purchases, perhaps lingering in a café where the coffee is excellent and the scones are toasted and served with whipped butter.

'I'm going into the village,' he announces. 'Anyone want to join me?'

He turns to his wife, his daughter.

Tracy opts out. She has promised to play tennis with Jeremy Edwards. She leaves the dining room without waiting for Richie to report on his conversation with their mother.

'I want to visit my swans,' Nessa says.

She has roughed out the text of her book and emailed it to her editor who is intrigued by the idea of transforming the beautiful and graceful swan into an adorable mischievous duckling. The editor, an astute judge of children's yearnings, has raised the possibility of a series of upside-down fairy tales. Why not have a friendly wolf triumph over three arrogant and complacent pigs? A racing hare might outmaneuver the plodding tortoise. Perhaps Nessa will invent a version of Cinderella redux and focus on a beneficent stepmother who worries only about the happiness of her stepchildren. *'Mirror, mirror on the wall. Who is the best stepmom of them all?'* the editor has suggested.

Nessa finds the concept attractive. It amuses her to turn the improbable into a happy reality, a reflection of sorts of her own life. She knows that there is some wonderment that overweight, irreverent Nessa married slender, fastidious and successful Simon Epstein and even more wonderment that, in fact, they are living happily ever after. Yes, such a series could work. But first she must complete the drawings of the swans still in residence at the lake.

Daniel also declines a visit to the village. He is determined to finish reading his proofs. He is, as always, impatient with his own work. The novel is too calculated, too formulaic, written hastily because he needed the money. Laura's lessons,

her rental of a studio, her trips to dance workshops and audi-
tions in distant cities, her costumes, the long skirts in every
color of the rainbow, the leotards sculpted to hug her body,
the satin-stringed shoes, her very expensive macrobiotic diet
– it all meant a constant outpouring of money so he wrote
swiftly, almost recklessly. But now, with his life beginning
anew, he will be able to write according to his own lights, no
longer concerned with commercial success. It is a thought that
both pleases and saddens him.

Jeff and Susan carry their books out to the lawn. The white,
high-backed and wide-armed chairs they favor are still wet and
Jeff dries them with paper towels.

'Thank you,' Susan says.

Her expression of gratitude is overly formal and he acknowledges it with an equally formal nod. They take their seats and
turn to their books, not looking at each other, as alone in their
casual proximity as two strangers accidentally seated side by
side.

Polly stands at the kitchen window, looks out at them, then
turns away and helps Louise fold the newly laundered
tablecloths.

'Can you finish doing this?' Louise asks. 'I want to wipe off
the rest of the garden chairs.'

That, of course, is Evan's job, Polly knows, but Evan is still
absent from the inn.

'Evan's at some sort of language conference at the university,'
Louise says, as though reading Polly's thoughts.

Polly shrugs, indicating her disinterest. She has no time to
worry about Louise and Evan Abbot. She is consumed with
worry about her mother, so weak this morning that she could
barely lift her glass of orange juice, so frail that she leaned
against Polly to cross the room. Their family doctor is on vacation and the doctor filling in for him had not been available
when she called. His receptionist was indifferent. Twice, as she
cycled to the inn that morning, she was impelled to turn back
and make sure that her mother was all right. But she had
continued on, spurred by the thought that she might ask Jeff
Edwards' advice. He is, after all, both a surgeon and a
diagnostician.

But seeing him seated beside his wife on the lawn, the courage to do that deserts her. His wife would surely resent it. She looks out the window and watches Annette sprint across the lawn and pause to drop a kiss on her father's head, to accept his smile and casual wave. Polly wonders what it might be like to have a father like Jeff who understands his children, who cares so deeply for them, a man who has the luxury to sit quietly on a lawn chair on a summer day and turn the pages of a book.

When Louise leaves, Polly calls her own father, that sad and work-worn man, who tells her that her mother seems to be feeling better.

'She gets these spells,' he says. 'Don't be so scared.'

Polly does not tell him that cancer is not a spell because 'cancer' is not a word that they say aloud, fearful always that its very utterance will vest it with grim reality. 'Anemia' is the word they use because it is so much less frightening than 'leukemia'.

She hangs up as Liane Curran dashes into the kitchen to fill a thermos with cold water. It is the Currans who will join Helene and Greg on their antiquing junket. Susan looks up from her book, smiles too brightly and waves to her sister as Greg revs the motor and the two couples drive off.

The nursery that the Templetons favor is lively on this sunny morning. Diligent, optimistic gardeners wander through the outdoor displays of small saplings wrapped in burlap, tangled roots thrusting their way through the rough fabric. Sacks of bulbs are hefted and considered. Groups of laughing and chatting young mothers, their children trailing after them, select trays of russet colored zinnias to combat the dreary arrival of autumn.

Wendy looks at the carefree shoppers with a twinge of envy. None of them, she is certain, is intent on landscaping a gravesite. They will not carry their fragrant purchases to a cemetery. They are not planning botanical tributes to the dead. She wonders, not for the first time, why this yearly ritual is so important to Adam's parents. She thinks the answer may be compensation, for the scant attention they gave their son during his brief life. The thought is unkind, she knows, but she allows herself the luxury of malice. Her therapist has taught her that thoughts in themselves are harmless.

The owner of the nursery, a stout red-cheeked man who invariably has a twist of bright green leaves entangled in his thick white hair, greets them effusively. Andrea had been a faithful customer during her years in New Hampshire, and when Adam died he sent a large floral display to the funeral parlor. It annoys him that Adam Templeton's young widow only visits the nursery during August when she is accompanied by her in-laws. He assumes, with some bitterness, that she makes her own garden purchases at less expensive stores. Nevertheless, he smiles at her and her son although he directs his attention to the elegant elderly couple who will, of course, be writing the check.

'I thought you might be interested in a new ground cover,' he says. 'I would advise a new ivy. Very durable. The grounds keepers at the cemetery tell me it survives our terrible winters.'

'That sounds exactly right,' Andrea says. 'What do you think, Wendy?'

'Ivy strangles. And it's difficult to uproot.'

Wendy states her objection firmly, the first time during these annual nursery visits that she has opposed Adam's mother. Her therapist would be proud of her. She is proud of herself.

'I'd rather put in bulbs that will come up in the spring and maybe a hydrangea bush,' she adds.

'There are other ground covers.'

The nursery owner is persistent, but Wendy shakes her head. 'I want color,' she says. 'Adam loved flowers. Brightly colored flowers.'

She plays her trump card, certain that Adam's parents have no idea of either Adam's loves or his hates.

'Of course. Flowers. But I do think we should consider some ground cover. Perhaps not ivy. Salvia or ferns. Or a self-contained moss that wouldn't spread and would leave room for your bulbs,' Andrea counters.

'I don't think of them as *my* bulbs,' Wendy says.

'But you are being just a bit territorial, aren't you?' Mark Templeton says, his voice dripping sarcasm.

Donny grips his mother's hand and stares hard at his grandmother. She is so bossy. What right does she have to be so bossy? And his grandfather shouldn't talk to his mother like that. What does territorial mean anyway? And he has the right to say something. It is his own father's grave, after all, and they did say that he could choose.

'I want a tree,' he says suddenly. 'And a bench.'

They look at him in surprise.

'A small tree,' he amends.

'Actually a deciduous conifer is a good idea,' the nursery owner agrees. 'The needles provide some sort of ground cover that would shelter the bulbs.'

He points to a small pine tree, its branches darkly green.

'All right.' Andrea and Wendy speak in unison, relieved to have reached an agreement of sorts.

'And a bench?' Donny is newly insistent. 'A little one. Like the one down at the lake, you know. The one you sat on when you drew the swans.'

'That wooden bench?' Wendy asks.

'Most of those small benches at the cemetery are stone,' Andrea interjects, although the idea of a bench pleases her. Properly placed, it will dignify Adam's grave and Andrea has always chased after dignity.

'Actually, I know a carpenter who makes wooden benches for grave sites,' the nursery owner says. 'They are very graceful. People admire them.'

Wendy restrains her desire to laugh at the absurdity of mourners trekking through a graveyard and pausing to cast admiring glances at benches and monuments, but Mark responds with grateful quiescence.

'That sounds good,' he says. 'Yes. Let's have a well-crafted wooden bench.'

He wants this whole business of selecting plants to be over and done with. He is tired of playing referee to the emotional duel between his wife and his son's widow. The nursery owner is pleased. The carpenter is his friend and will be grateful for the commission. He has a catalog of his work which he shows them. A shape is selected. Briefly they discuss the kind of wood that will be used.

'A dark wood,' Donny insists. 'Like the bench near the lake.'

They nod in agreement, soothed by the compromise. Wendy

selects her bulbs. Andrea chooses the dwarf rosebush as well as a forsythia plant. They will collect their purchases in a few days' time. Adam's birthday. It has become their grim custom to attend to the landscaping of his grave on that day.

As they drive back to the inn, Andrea attempts a reconciliation of a kind with Wendy.

'I never walk down to the lake,' she says, 'so I'm unfamiliar with the bench Donny seems to like so much. And I haven't seen the swans. But I did admire your drawings. Have you been studying Audubon's work?'

Wendy looks at her sharply. 'When did you see my drawings?' she asks.

'I went into your room last night. I thought I heard Donny cry out. And your sketchpad was open on the desk.'

'I see.'

Wendy thinks to say that she makes a habit never to leave her sketchpad open, but she remains silent. The words unsaid linger heavily in the air, now grown uncomfortably warm as she drives slowly, much too slowly, back to the inn.

The antique shop is dimly lit and Helene and Greg, Michael and Liane speak very softly as they enter as though unwilling to disturb whatever ghosts might lurk in the shadows. They tiptoe past the large ancient golden oak desk awkwardly situated in the middle of the floor and cast bemused glances at the scrub board placed in a copper cauldron which, mysteriously, has been burnished to a high shine.

The proprietress, a wizened elderly woman, her sparse gray hair loosely knotted in a bun, her black dress rusted with age, looks up from the ledger on the counter, her face alight with pleasure, her blue eyes startlingly bright.

'Mr Ames. Mrs Ames. How nice to see you. I thought perhaps you'd skipped your New Hampshire visit this year. Did you enjoy the head vases you bought last year?'

She is a woman who prides herself on remembering the names of her itinerant customers as well as their purchases. Helene and Greg have visited her shop often, always buying small whimsical items. There was the ancient xylophone which Greg repaired with great care, coaxing a pleasant sound from its metallic keys, and a wooden paint box that Helene varnished and filled with tubes of oil paint and brushes, carrying it with her on their weekend rambles. The large ceramic bowl that sits on their dining room table; the small crystal based lamp beside Greg's bed; the battered metal measuring cups on their kitchen counter – all were purchased here and, of course, only last year they had carried home the head vases, unsmiling Victoriana relics that they had filled each week with colorful assortments of flowers.

'We love the head vases, Maria,' Helene says and Greg smiles in agreement, pleased that Helene has returned the compliment and remembered the proprietress's name. But then Helene always memorizes the names of her students, getting them right at the end of the very first week of school.

Maria beams, pleased to hear her own name spoken so pleasantly. It is, Greg thinks, not something that happens very often during the long days the elderly woman spends in this shop so crowded with abandoned treasures and orphaned memorabilia. He smiles at his wife and strides across the room to a corner where a zither rests atop a leather steamer trunk.

'These are our friends, the Currans,' Helene tells Maria. Liane and Michael smile shyly, uncertain as to how to respond to the introduction.

'They're also guests at Mount Haven Inn,' Helene continues. 'This is their first shot at antiquing.'

'Let me help you then,' Maria offers. 'Are you looking for anything in particular?'

'A bookshelf,' Liane says at once. 'For our son's room. He loves to read.' She smiles proudly and Michael looks at her in surprise.

From the earliest days of their marriage, she had always insisted on new furnishings. Quality had not been as important as the fact that everything they brought into their home was brand new.

'I had enough of living with other people's shit,' Liane had told him. 'My aunt's ratty sofa. An armchair our neighbors were giving away. Even my bed, my goddamn bed with its skinny mattress, was a hand-me-down from my cousin.'

He had struggled to understand this need of hers, as he had

always struggled to understand this pretty woman who had so miraculously consented to be his wife. And he had struggled to please her in this as he struggled to please her in all things. He lived in fear of her discontent. He understood the terms of their marriage. He had promised her so much and had delivered so little. Their house is small, their vacations modest, their evenings out few and far between. But all their furniture is new, paid for in instalments. Cary's room is furnished with a desk, a bureau, a bed, all discounted floor models bought on sale, crafted of plasterboard stained the color of stressed golden oak.

But now Liane adds to the surprises she has heaped upon him during this very strange vacation. She is contemplating the purchase of a used bookcase.

'There's a little bookcase in that corner,' Maria says, pointing across the room.

They make their way to where the bookcase stands. Although long neglected, it has three finely beveled shelves and the golden wood has a dull glow.

'I like this bookcase. I really do,' Liane insists. 'Is the price marked?'

Maria, who has been watching, glides over to stand beside them. In the end they settle on twenty-five dollars – the lowest price Maria will accept.

Liane is elated. Michael takes out his wallet and counts out the bills. Maria shakes hands with both of them. She too is pleased.

'I hope Mr and Mrs Ames find something,' she says to Liane. 'But I'm sure they will. Mrs Ames has a very good eye.'

'Do you know what they're looking for?' Liane asks.

'Oh, I imagine that they'll know when they find it.'

Greg and Helene move slowly through the second floor where Maria keeps larger items of furniture. Smaller pieces, which she has despaired of selling, are shrouded in protective covering. They have already set aside a very small faux Tiffany lamp and a set of onyx bookends.

'These will be pricey,' Helene objects, replacing the bookends.

'But if you like them.'

'Not really what I'm looking for.' Her head down, she walks to the cluttered far end of the room.

'What *are* you looking for?' Greg is growing impatient. He wants to claim his zither and see what he will have to do to repair the strings which he knows to be damaged. The thought of the instrument excites him. He imagines bringing it to class, showing it to his students, building a lesson about ancient instruments. He loves his work. In the beginning teaching had been a compromise, an acknowledgment that he could not support himself as a musician, that his and Helene's wandering days were over. But teaching delights and energizes him. One of life's surprises – but then life continues to surprise him. He thinks of the previous night and smiles at the memory of how Helene surprised him. He coaxes a chord from the zither, pleased at the gentleness of the sound.

'Did you find it, whatever it is?' he calls again.

Helene does not answer him. She is on her knees, burrowing through objects shrouded in dust cloths, spider webs clinging to her hair, but when she does reply, her voice resonates with triumph.

'Yes. Here it is! I found it. This is what I've been looking for. Remember? We saw it here last year. I'm so glad she didn't sell it.'

'What are you talking about?'

He strides over to her, kneels beside her, sees the smile on her face, sees her fingers sliding their way tenderly across the pale birch wood of the antique cradle which rocks gently at her touch. He does remember that cradle, remembers that they had looked at it the previous year and swiftly averted their eyes. But now he passes his hand over the mattress stuffed with corn husks and indented by the pressure of vanished infant bodies. He imagines a child of his own (of their own; swiftly he amends the thought) safely asleep upon it, deepening that indentation, a smiling and cooing baby with Helene's deep gray eyes and her dimpled chin. It will happen. He has no doubt now that it will happen, and that it will happen sooner, rather than later.

He helps his wife to her feet, lifts the cradle and carefully carries it down the stairwell. There is no need to discuss it, no need to bargain with Maria. They will buy it.

And they do.

*   *   *

Annette and Paul paddle across the lake. Matt and Cary are impatient passengers.

'You can try it on the way back,' Paul promises. 'If you'll be very careful.'

'You only get to almost drown once on a vacation,' Annette teases her brother.

'It wasn't my fault,' he protests. 'I didn't know about the current. There's no current here.'

That much is true. The lake is as smooth as silk, rhomboids of light dancing across the dark waters. The swans, still in residence, glide away from their fragile craft, hissing angrily at the invasion of their aquatic kingdom.

'There are wild blackberry bushes over there,' Paul says. 'My dad told me that he and Daniel Goldner used to paddle over and pick them. Do you want to try it?'

'Sure. We love blackberries, don't we, Matt?'

Cary is enthusiastic. He would agree to any suggestion made by Paul Epstein, who always takes time out to explain the complexities of the Harry Potter plots, and to help the younger boys create their forts. He has even taught them how to win extra games on the pinball machine, a skillful maneuver that outwits the 'tilt' button.

'I guess,' Matt says.

He doesn't want his sister to tease him. Annette can be mean sometimes, but he has to admit that she is being really nice today.

'But what'll we put them in? We don't have any bags.'

'Our hats,' Paul says and waves his own baseball cap.

'Sure. Why not?' Annette removes her denim cap, releasing her hair which falls in thick sheaves to her shoulders.

Paul's heart stops. He wonders whether a single strand of her sun-tinged curls would burn his fingers. He smiles at the foolishness of the thought. But she is beautiful, so beautiful. His heart pounds.

'OK then.'

They paddle the canoe to shore, jump out and tether it to a large rock. They see the berry bushes at once, the thick black fruit dragging down the branches.

'You guys pick over here,' Paul says. 'My dad told me that

there are more bushes further in. That's where Annette and I will go.'

'OK.'

Matt and Cary are already stuffing the sweet fruit into their mouths.

Annette and Paul follow a rough trail until they are no longer in sight of the boys. There is a profusion of bushes here but the fruit is sparser. They separate and concentrate on searching out laden branches, their heads bent, the sun sweeping warmly across their backs, the earth friable beneath their feet. Grackles quarrel noisily in a tangle of wild vines and fly away, soaring through the cloudless sky.

Annette and Paul move closer to each other, their hands touching as they both reach out to pluck berries from the same branch. They laugh, pick the fruit, reach up again, touch again. This time their fingers link. This time they smile. Their lips are stained black, a leaf is entwined in her bright hair. He reaches out, leans toward her, brushes it away and his fingers do not burn. His lips meet hers; their eyes are closed.

Reluctantly they open their eyes and, wordlessly, balancing their berry-laden hats, they make their way back to the small boys who are tossing unripened fruit at each other and laughing wildly.

True to his promise, Paul allows the boys to paddle back to the dock. He and Annette sit at opposite ends of the canoe, their faces lifted to the sun, their hands trailing through the cool, dark water. Now and again their eyes meet, and they smile shyly and swiftly avert their gaze.

The boys dash across the lawn, popping berries into their mouths. Annette and Paul follow them, walking slowly, their faces aglow, their eyes bright.

Nessa looks at her son. Susan closes her book and stares at her daughter. The two mothers nod to each other, silently acknowledging that their children have wandered beyond the borders of childhood.

THIRTEEN

The brightness of the morning lasts through the afternoon and the guests of August rush to exploit it. They gather at the lake and splash their way into the cool water, launch the canoes and rowboats and spread brightly patterned beach towels across the narrow shingle beach. They are seized with a new urgency to enjoy the last lingering hours of summer warmth.

Wendy and Andrea, however, seek out a shaded spot on the lawn and Daniel, carrying an oversized mailer that contains the corrected proof of his novel, strides toward them.

'I'm off to mail this monster to my editor,' he says. 'Want to ride into town with me?'

He smiles at both women but clearly his invitation is meant for Wendy.

'I wouldn't mind,' she says at once. 'You'll be all right on your own, Andrea?' she asks her mother-in-law.

Her words are more a statement than a question. She knows, and she is certain Andrea knows, that she doesn't give a damn about whether or not Adam's mother will be all right.

'I'm quite used to being on my own,' Andrea replies coldly. 'And of course Mark is right here.'

She points to the redwood table where Mark sits in conference with Michael and Simon. Once again the three men finger their smart phones and study the spreadsheets that have absorbed them since their arrival. Michael looks anxious. He bites his lip. Simon, in professorial mode, refills his pipe and flashes him a reassuring glance. Mark turns page after page of the proposal, his expression impassive, a seasoned poker player unwilling to reveal his hand.

'All right then,' Wendy tells Andrea. 'Donny is with the other boys and Paul Epstein and Annette Edwards volunteered to sort of be in charge.'

'I'm delighted that you are so concerned about your son,' Andrea remarks, her tone acidic, her gaze accusatory.

'Most mothers are concerned about their sons. Not all, but most,' Wendy says evenly and walks swiftly away as Andrea purses her lips and struggles to contain her anger.

Perched on the rear seat of Daniel's motorbike, the heavy helmet hugging her head, the light breeze brushing her face, she is relieved to be leaving the inn, to be free of Adam's parents, their judgments and expectations. She knows that her insinuating words have wounded Andrea but she does not regret them. She feels that she has been released from the intricate August dance of grief and memory that Adam's parents choreographed. Her arms are tight about Daniel's waist as he speeds down the mountain road toward the village.

At the small parking area just beyond the café they dismount and remove their helmets. Wendy's dark hair tumbles to her shoulders and she runs her fingers through the cascading curls in an effort to tame them. Daniel watches her, moved by the beauty of her slender hands. He wonders how those tapering fingers would feel if they were to move gently across his body.

It is a tenderness of gesture he has always craved, and which Laura, sensual Laura, proud of her well-trained body's strength and passion, had dismissed as foolish.

It was sensuality that ruled her and it was that very sensuality that had seduced him. He banishes the thought. He has grown skillful at avoiding thoughts and memories tainted with pain. He removes the parcel that contains his corrected manuscript from the pannier.

'You go ahead and get us a table. I'll go over to the post office and mail this monster,' he tells Wendy.

She nods and goes into the café which is strangely crowded.

'Wendy, it's great to see you,' calls Ellen, the proprietress, as she rushes up to her. 'I thought I'd be seeing a lot more of you during your stay at Mount Haven.'

'Well, things tend to get sort of complicated,' Wendy explains. 'But it doesn't look as though you've been short of customers.'

'Oh, we've been busy today. A bus load of international students from the university who were on some sort of organized trip. Hungry and thirsty but unfortunately short of dollars. We're doing a land office business in iced tea and lemonade. But of course I can always find a table for you.'

Smiling, she leads Wendy to a far corner of the room where a secluded booth for two is unoccupied. Wendy smiles gratefully and leans forward to smell the fragrance of the cluster of amber-colored rose buds in a slender green glass vase.

'Beautiful, aren't they?' Ellen says. 'And just a little sad. The very last roses of summer. What will you have, Wendy?'

'Oh, I'll wait to order until my friend gets here,' Wendy demurs.

'Your friend. That lean, dark-haired guy who was with you last time?'

'Yup, that lean, dark-haired guy,' Wendy agrees. It is an apt enough description of Daniel – one she has no trouble repeating. 'I'm surprised you remember him.'

'But I always remember men with deep eyes and sharp features,' Ellen counters easily. Wendy wonders how she could have forgotten that Ellen has the portraitist's gift for memorizing intriguing faces and, of course, Daniel Goldner's angular features, his brooding heavy-browed eyes, are indeed intriguing.

The crowded room is abuzz with conversations in a blend of languages. The students laugh easily, their faces animated. They clap as a waitress sets down a tray of drinks and pastries. They feed each other cream puffs and pluck sprigs of mint from tall golden glasses of iced tea and fashion them into mock moustaches. Two slender dark-haired girls flit from table to table, their hands outstretched. They collect bills and coins from their friends, curtsy gratefully and hand the money they gather to Ellen who thrusts it into her pocket without bothering to count it.

Wendy feels a pang of envy. They are all so daring and carefree, these visitors from other countries, geared for adventure, paying their way with laughter and charm. This was the kind of student life she might have known if she had not gone to a Cambridge party where Adam Templeton had accidentally spilled beer all over her brand-new blue sweater and then so very gently washed her face and claimed her love. She shakes her head vigorously, angered by her own foolishness, her pointless yearning for what might have been. She has Donny, she has her work, she is gaining recognition among galleries and collectors, and soon, very soon, she will have independence. This annual August charade with Andrea and Mark is coming to an end.

'Hey, why the head shaking? Why the frown?'

Daniel slides into the seat opposite her and smiles broadly.

'We're here to have fun. We're here to toast me for finally getting rid of that damn manuscript, the novel from hell. So what's with the mood?'

'Oh, nothing. Random thoughts.'

'The most dangerous kind.'

He leans back and glances around the café. He is, after all, a novelist, who automatically studies every new scene, registering nuances of atmosphere, oddities of furnishings, gestures and expressions that will mysteriously surface in narratives as yet unwritten. Suddenly, he sits up straighter, trains his gaze on a booth across the room where a man and woman sit very close to each other.

The woman is very young, blonde and fair-skinned. She wears tight jeans and a pale-blue turtleneck shirt. He cannot see her eyes but he is certain that the shirt was chosen to match them. She speaks earnestly to the man seated beside her, his hand holding hers, his thigh pressed close against her knee. He wears the student uniform of the Ivy League, the careless pale-green cotton crew-necked sweater, the well pressed khaki pants, his Jansport backpack leaning against the table. But he is not young. He is, clearly, too old to be a student, too old to be in such intimate contact with this slender golden-haired girl. His earth-colored hair is thick and brushed with strands of gray. Laugh lines curl about his eyes. He is Evan Abbot, Louise's husband who has been absent from the inn for so many days, a man masquerading as a boy, an aging husband who is the lover – or perhaps the would-be lover – of the sweet-faced girl newly emerging from adolescence.

Daniel is suffused with anger at Evan Abbot. He remembers Louise, whom he knew when he was a boy and she the unso-phisticated, hardworking teenager who always found time to be kind to him – more than kind. She had always managed to wait on his family's table, always brought him extra bowls of ice cream and spoke pleasantly to his parents who admired her work ethic and her energy. His mother had helped her fill out the application form to the business school in Boston. His father had given her books to read and tipped her very generously at the season's end. Her ambition had been modest and attainable.

An independent life in Boston at a remove from rural New Hampshire and her family's indifference and poverty of mind and manner. He knows why that dream remained unrealized. He knows that she was betrayed by her own innocence and Evan Abbot's carelessness. She is fettered to Mount Haven Inn, fettered to Evan Abbot, damn him.

'What's wrong?' Wendy asks.

She senses the change in his mood, the narrowing of his eyes, the angry purse of his lips.

'Across the room. That table in the corner. It's Evan Abbot.'

She follows his gaze and, as they both covertly watch, Evan Abbot leans even closer to his companion, encases her in an embrace and presses his lips to hers. She laughs. They kiss again. And then together they leave the café, his arm about her shoulder, his backpack carelessly swinging.

'The bastard,' Daniel says.

'It happens,' Wendy replies calmly.

She herself is unsurprised but Daniel, she knows, is new to the singles scene of mature adults where odd partnerships are briefly formed – older men with younger women, older women with younger men, the unhappily married seducing the unhappily single, naïve young girls in a foreign country experimenting with clandestine romance.

'It shouldn't happen to Louise,' he says. 'She's so damn good, so hardworking. Simon and I knew her when she was just a kid waitressing at the inn, saving up for a business course, planning to get an office job in Boston, planning to break free of her good-for-nothing parents. She wanted to live in her own apartment, wear suits to work, go to museums and concerts. A doable ambition. And then Evan Abbot got her pregnant and it was all over. She's stuck at Mount Haven Inn for the rest of her life and he has a free pass to be the perennial student, one advanced degree after another while she works her ass off.'

Ellen sets their coffees down. She has known without asking that Wendy would be having her usual cappuccino and biscotti and assumed that Daniel would have the same. They smile gratefully at her.

'Look,' Wendy says softly, 'I'm sorry for Louise. But that's her life and she's chosen to stay with Evan.'

'But a choice doesn't have to be forever.'

'That's true,' she agrees.

He has repeated the very words she spoke to Adam's mother that morning. Nothing is forever. Changes can be made. Choices can be reversed.

They relax then and sip their coffee, nibble their biscotti, venture amusing conjectures about the students who are slowly drifting out of the café. Was that couple French? Were those girls Italian? And are that tall blonde youth and that short, almond-skinned girl lovers? They laugh softly, pleased with their idle scenarios. Daniel's anger melts. Wendy's mood lifts. Against all odds, they are enjoying themselves.

On the ride back to the inn, Daniel decides that he will speak to Louise. He owes it to her to make sure she knows what Evan is up to. He wishes now that someone had told him about Laura, that it had not come as a shock to him, a shock that shattered any hope that his marriage might survive.

Once again, in the pre-dinner hour, Simon and Nessa carry their wicker basket out to the lawn and set a redwood table with their replenished stock of cheeses and olives, a chilled carafe of white wine, bottles of gin, vodka and tonic water. The lawn chairs are arranged in a semi-circle, the conversations are easy. They are all relaxed with each other, soothed into the luxurious lethargy that comes at the end of a sun-swept vacation day. Jokes are told, memories traded.

'Do you remember the year we hid the dinner bell?' Simon asks Daniel. 'I thought old man Abbot would go nuts.'

'I remember.'

They all smile, knowing that this year's adventure will feed the memory mill for years to come.

Paul wonders if Annette will remember the softness of his lips upon her own. He himself, he knows, will never forget it.

The juice runs out and Daniel volunteers to fetch another bottle from the kitchen. The wide-windowed room is a bustle of activity. Dinner preparations are underway, the cook furiously slicing and stirring, Polly and the other wait staff scurrying in and out of the dining room, their arms laden with table linen and cutlery. Louise is arranging flowers.

She turns to him and he sees that there are dark circles beneath her eyes. Her light-brown hair is damp and lank from her late-afternoon shower. Her navy-blue dress hangs loosely about her narrow frame. She has clearly lost weight. His heart turns as he remembers the young Louise, that pretty girl, light of step, bright-eyed and eager. She had been so like pink-cheeked Polly, who circles the dining room now, a small-town girl dancing toward her future, dreaming her way into another life. He hopes that Polly's luck will be better than Louise's.

'Can I help you, Daniel?' Louise asks, her voice as always soft, almost maternal when she speaks to him.

'The kids want some apple juice,' he says.

'In the pantry.'

He follows her into the small room stocked with kitchen provisions. Impulsively, he closes the door. She looks at him quizzically.

'What is it, Daniel?'

'I want to talk to you.'

'Oh?' She stands very straight as though braced for an assault of bad news.

'I was in the village this afternoon. At the Windermere Café. I saw Evan there.'

'He goes there sometimes. People from the university often go there.'

'He wasn't alone.'

'And?'

'He was with a girl. They were very much together. I thought you should know about it, Louise.'

'But I do know about it,' she replies, her tone steady. 'I've always known about it.

'This is a small town. Kids go off to the university. Adults take extension courses. They see Evan. They know what he's up to. They talk and eventually the talk comes back to me. So you're not telling me anything new. Of course there was a girl and of course they were very much together. There is always some girl, some woman, graduate, undergraduate. Summer session. Fall session. Sometimes a foreign student on an exchange program. I think Evan prefers foreign students because they leave. They go home to Copenhagen or Croatia and there's no trouble, no entanglements. Occasionally they write to him. I don't open the letters. I toss them out and after one or two tries they stop writing to him. The inn is of little interest to Evan. It is simply the home he has always known, the economic base that allows him to linger in libraries and seminar rooms, meeting new young women and garnering meaningless degrees and useless certifications which, nevertheless, fully satisfy him.'

'But, Louise, why don't you do something about it? You shouldn't have to live like this, working your ass off while Evan relaxes in a café with his latest squeeze.'

Daniel is angry, seriously angry. Evan and Laura, unfaithful spouses both, meld in the febrile outrage that causes him to raise his voice.

'And what do you think I should do about it, Daniel?' Louise asks wearily. 'What options do I have? I'm a high-school graduate. No skills. No family. I don't even know where my parents are. Not that they'd help me. Not that they *could* help me. The only thing that I know how to do is run this inn, to make sure we can survive year after year. That's what I've been doing for the last eighteen years. And just for the record, the inn was left to Evan and myself jointly. I could never afford to buy him out and he surely could not afford to buy me out. So I am stuck. I don't have the choices that you have. I don't know what happened between you and Laura, but you were able to cut loose and so was she. You both had careers, education. Simon divorced Charlotte, but they could go on to new lives. Divorce is a luxury. It's expensive. People in this town don't split. They shout, they slam doors, they drink, they cry but they don't divorce, or at least most of them don't. They can't afford to. And even if I could I'm not sure I'd want to divorce Evan. This sounds crazy, I know, but after all those miscarriages, those stillbirths, I realized that the only child I'd ever have would be Evan. We're not really husband and wife, haven't been for a long time. We're more like mother and son. I take care of him. I see that he's well dressed, well fed. I give him an allowance. I make sure he has enough money for his tuition, for his schoolbooks. I worry when it rains that he forgot his boots and his slicker even though I know he's probably dry enough in some girl's bed. I nurse him when he's sick. I get mad at him when he doesn't do his chores, the same chores he did when he was a high-school kid, and I say the same things his mother used to say. "Evan, why didn't you bring in the lawn furniture? Evan, please pick up the guests who went to Portsmouth for dinner." He brings me his transcripts the way kids bring their mothers their report cards and I congratulate him on an A in urban planning even though he'll never be an urban planner, a B-plus in Latin although I'm thinking *where the hell is he ever going to use Latin?* So that's where we are and that's where we'll be. Have I shocked you, Daniel? Do you think I'm some kind of an idiot for living this kind of life?'

He stares at her, startled by her honesty, astounded by her stoicism. But he is persistent.

'Have you and Evan ever talked openly about what he was doing, about what you felt? Because, Louise, you must have felt betrayed.'

He realizes how effortlessly he has projected his own feelings on to her, how much he wants her to respond as he did to Laura's betrayal. He would have her shout out her sorrow and her fury as he had done on that night in the Hamptons when the truth of his marriage at last became clear to him.

She nods. 'In the beginning. When it first began. One of my waitresses worked at a motel in Durham and saw him checking in with a graduate student. I was angry. I spoke to him. I cried. He cried. He said all the things small boys say when they want to be forgiven for something. *I'm sorry. It won't happen again. Forgive me.* So I did what all good mothers do. I hugged him, I let him hug me. I forgave him. And, of course, it happened again and again and again. And it will go on happening. But I don't accuse any more and he doesn't cry.'

Sadness muffles her voice but she stands erect, her eyes scanning the shelves so neatly stacked with cans and bottles, cartons and containers. A can of beans is out of place among cans of tomato sauce and she restores it to the proper shelf.

He is silent, defeated.

'But, Daniel,' she continues, 'I want to thank you for telling me. I know you thought you were doing the right thing.'

'I've always cared about you, Louise,' he says gently, his tone matching hers. 'I've always hoped that you would be happy.'

'And I cared about you. And more than that. You were my window into another world.'

She does not tell him that she has not abandoned that world – that it survives in her nocturnal fantasies. She will not reveal to him how often she lies half awake and mentally furnishes the apartment that will never be hers, how she welcomes guests to the parties that she will never give.

He sees that her eyes are bright with tears. He puts his hand on her shoulder and because he, the wordsmith, has exhausted all words, he leaves the pantry. She follows him a few minutes later and hands him two bottles of apple juice which he carries out to the party still in progress on the lawn.

The dining room is subdued that evening. The guests, by tacit agreement, ignore Louise's carefully programmed seating arrangements and settle into new configurations. They are sufficiently at ease with each other, after all the lazy days spent together, to select their own seats at will. Nessa and Simon join Susan and Jeff. It is Nessa's decision.

'I think maybe we can make them a little less tense. They seem really unhappy,' she told her husband, who offered no protest.

Simon is proud of Nessa's kindness. He likes the Edwards couple and he too has noticed the strain between them. As, of course, he supposes, so have all the other guests. There is little room for emotional privacy in their small vacation community. Everyone, after all, was assembled on the lawn, unwilling witnesses to Susan's angry accusations as Jeff and Polly made their way up the path.

Helene and Greg sit with Liane and Michael. Helene acknowledges that she is relieved to be sitting apart from her sister, that for this meal at least she will not have to jump-start conversations and fill in the awkward silences that are so upsetting to Matt. It troubles her to see her nephew dart anxious glances from one parent to another. She knows what it is like to be an unhappy child in an unhappy home.

Liane, still intrigued by their visit to the antique shop, wonders about the source of Maria's inventory.

'Where does all that junk come from?' she asks. 'Not that the stuff that we bought is junk,' she adds swiftly.

'A lot of it *is* junk. The shards of other people's lives, the remnants of death and divorce,' Greg says. The words come easily to him and he wonders if he can weave them into the lyrics of a song.

'Divorce,' Helene repeats, as though she can neutralize the word.

She glances over to the table where Jeff and Susan sit side by side, Jeff speaking to Simon, Susan speaking to Nessa, their eyes averted from each other. She visualizes her sister's beautiful home, so tastefully decorated during the glory days of their marriage. She imagines it empty, the furnishings divided and scattered, the golden oak rocking chair on which Susan had nursed the twins, Jeremy at one breast, Annette on the other, banished to the attic of an antique store. She thrusts the image away. Her sister is not getting divorced. Susan and Jeff will be all right. This is just a bad patch. They will get through it.

There is amused disapproval of the meal. Mark and Andrea Templeton glance at the tuna casserole and the salad of wilted greens and announce that they will drive into Portsmouth for dinner. Wendy declines their invitation to join them. Donny and his friends have arranged a game of darts with Greg and Liane offering instruction.

'It's a dangerous game,' Andrea murmurs.

'Life is dangerous,' Wendy replies flippantly and helps herself to a generous portion of the casserole. 'It's actually very good,' she says, tasting it. 'Even though there are more noodles than tuna.'

'Well, we don't come here for the food,' Mark says wryly.

'Why exactly do we come here?' Wendy murmurs as Adam's parents leave. She wonders if they heard her and decides that she does not care if they did.

'I think Louise is trying to economize,' Daniel tells her. 'Things are a little tough for her.'

It does not surprise him that Louise has not joined them for dinner. Polly called to say that her mother was ill and Louise, unable to find a replacement, rushes from table to table, her cheeks flushed, her hands laden.

'You spoke to her?' Wendy asks.

'I did.'

He is pleased that she does not ask him about their conversation, that she understands that there are confidences that must not be betrayed. He eats slowly, without pleasure, and concentrates on finding an answer to Donny's probing question about where JK Rowling gets her ideas.

'Like how does a writer know what he's going to write?' Donny asks.

'It's a mystery, actually,' Daniel acknowledges.

'You know my dad was a writer.'

Wendy looks at her son in surprise. Donny so rarely refers to Adam.

'I guess my mom likes writers,' Donny adds and dashes away from the table.

Matt and Cary have finished eating and the three boys dash to the pinball machine jangling their quarters.

'He's right,' Wendy says softly. 'I do like writers.'

'I'm glad.' His voice is husky with pleasure.

She drops her napkin; he picks it up and for a long moment their fingers are linked.

Tracy, Richie and Jeremy saunter over to announce that they are going into town for burgers.

'Want to come?' Richie asks Paul, pointedly ignoring Annette.

'Nope. I'm into noodles,' Paul says good-naturedly. 'I'm thinking of becoming vegan.'

'Of course you are,' Richie says. 'Go to Oberlin, eat tofu and play your guitar. You like tofu eaters, Annette?'

She ignores him but Paul shrugs indifferently. His stepbrother's taunts cannot upset him; he is inured by his memory of the morning's tenderness, when Annette's lips were so soft upon his own. Screw Richie.

Simon pulls out a twenty and hands it to Richie. The rivalry between his sons both amuses and troubles him. He wants to speed Richie on his way.

'That should be enough,' he says.

'Yeah. Thanks. And hey, Dad, Mom called today. She may be stopping by some time soon. She has a shoot at some resort in the White Mountains.'

'That's good.' Simon is non-committal and now it is Nessa who swiftly fills the awkward silence.

'It'll be great for you and Tracy to spend some time with Charlotte,' she says.

'Yeah. Great,' Tracy responds, her voice flat.

Susan and Jeff watch the interchange in silence. Tracy's sullenness and Richie's aggressiveness are not lost on them. The children of Simon Epstein's first marriage are casualties of his very amicable divorce. That is what she and Jeff would say to each other if they were in fact saying such things to each other, if they were not locked into the silence of anger and regret. Susan thinks back to her translation, of Pierre's warning words to Jacqueline. *Tout les marriages sont fragiles* – all marriages are fragile. She had rejected LeBec's words even as she translated them but now, with a heavy heart, she is reconciled to their truth.

They are all relieved when the meal ends, when they are free to abandon the dessert dishes on which sour scraps of rhubarb pie have congealed (although Daniel, loyal to Louise, fearful of hurting her feelings, has dutifully eaten his share) and they can retreat to the rec room. Paul and Annette return to their puzzle of American presidents. They sit very close to each other wearing expressions of great seriousness, of great concentration, as they search for the small pieces that will complete Teddy Roosevelt's moustache, while Susan, Nessa and Jeff play Scrabble and Michael and Liane, Helene and Greg supervise the game of darts with Matt, Cary and Donny.

As the evening draws to a close, cars draw up to the inn. A cab brings Mark and Andrea Templeton back from Portsmouth and they see that Andrea, as always impeccably groomed, leans heavily on her husband's arm as she makes her way unsteadily to the door. Wendy wonders how much vodka she drank before dinner and how much wine she drank with the meal. Not that it matters.

Richie's roadster roars up and Tracy and Jeremy get out but Richie turns the car around and speeds back down the drive. Simon frowns and then turns his attention back to the chess board.

Jeff watches as his son and Tracy walk across the lawn and wander down to the lake. Like Simon, he frowns and, like Simon, he says nothing. He is very tired but he will wait until he is certain that Susan is asleep before going up to their room.

FOURTEEN

With the dawning of each new day the air is increasingly cooler and by the late afternoon the women drape light wool cardigans over their shoulders. They sip white wine and watch the fiery sunsets of summer fade into the melancholy pastels of encroaching autumn. Already they are teased by the tensions of the lives left behind, so soon to be resumed. Susan receives an email lauding her translation but asking for minor changes. Nessa's editor has a new idea for the fairy tale series and calls to set up a meeting in the city. Simon dodges phone messages from the various boards on which he sits. Jeff receives a troubling report about a patient on whom he operated just before leaving for New Hampshire. But despite these small invasions the vacationers are intent on cramming as much pleasure as possible into these last days of leisure.

Michael takes Liane out to dinner in Portsmouth, choosing a very expensive French restaurant recommended by Simon. They sit across from each other at a candle-lit table spread with an immaculate white linen cloth, inhale the scent of the pale pink rose buds in the crystal vase and lift their wine glasses in a silent toast. Michael has ordered champagne.

'You remember that I promised you champagne,' he reminds her.

'Is it really happening then?' she asks.

'Mark Templeton is almost definitely on board. He's been in touch with his investors and he promises venture capital, more than I ever contemplated asking for. Simon says that his investors are actually getting a bargain. My software design has features that no other anti-virus program has, especially important in this crazy economy.'

He does not mask the pride in his voice, pride in his own work and pride in his ability to give her the things she has wanted since the day of their marriage. He no longer has to worry about losing her. He recognizes that she has changed but he has the additional assurance that she will be safely ensnared in the new prosperity that will soon be theirs.

She smiles at him and he sees the new softness in her eyes. She reaches across the table and takes his hand. Her touch is as light as a butterfly's wing. He marvels at how these vacation weeks have affected her. He wonders briefly, disloyally, if it is because he hovers so close to the material success she has always craved, but he dismisses the thought at once. It is enough that she looks at him with tenderness he had never thought to claim. His heart swells. He, the shy bespectacled boy, grown into the shy bespectacled man, stooped with worry, meekly petitioning for love, is, for the first time in his life, suffused with joy and gladness.

'I'm happy for you,' she says.

'I'm happy for both of us. And for Cary.'

'Yes. Of course. For Cary.'

They reach for the oversized red leather menus, hide their faces from each other as they study the choices, each unwilling for the other to see the tears that burn their eyes.

Plans are made for a final picnic at Franconia Notch. It is Evan, returned to the inn, proudly displaying a certificate validating his proficiency in international mediation earned during his summer seminar, who suggests the locale and volunteers to make the arrangements. Louise slides the certificate into a leather binder and displays it at the reception desk. Simon and Daniel smile at each other. They recall that Evan's parents had displayed his high-school honor society plaques and his letter of acceptance to Dartmouth on that same desk. Louise is simply continuing the parental tradition. Daniel overhears Louise on the phone assuring a caller that Evan is not at the inn.

'He is traveling somewhere, I believe. He'll be away for several weeks. Yes, I'll be sure to give him your message, Karine. I've written your name down. And your cell phone number. If I hear from him I'll tell him to call you.'

She hangs up, crumbles the slip of paper on which she has scrawled only half the numbers, spies Daniel and shrugs. He nods knowingly. She has made her peace. He will make his.

Evan maps out the route to Franconia Notch, speaks with a forest ranger who will do a nature tour with their party, and consults with Louise about the food and drinks they will need. He discusses the equipment they will take. Perhaps a soccer ball, the badminton set. He nods enthusiastically when Greg suggests that they transport the dart board and darts. The rec room has only limited space while an open field will allow them to aim at their target from a considerable distance. Cary, Donny and Matt jump up and down at the thought of demonstrating their new-found skill in the vast arena of mountain and forest.

'I know exactly the tree where we can set the board up,' Evan says.

He is in his element – pleasure and fun are his forte – and Louise, the patient, forgiving mother-wife smiles and makes up her list of picnic provisions.

Andrea Templeton receives a call from the proprietor of the nursery. The woodworker has completed the bench to be placed beside Adam's grave and the earth has been turned so that the new plantings can be easily set in place.

'That's wonderful,' she says. 'We'll go to the cemetery tomorrow just as we planned.'

The next day is, of course, Adam's birthday. Had he lived he would have been thirty-nine years old.

'Thirty-nine,' she murmurs, and fills a glass with vodka which she drinks very slowly.

'Thirty-nine,' Mark repeats. He goes to the window and looks down at the lawn where his grandson, dark-haired, dark-eyed Donny, is racing after his two friends, all three of them pursuing Paul Epstein.

'We should get an early start tomorrow,' Mark says to Wendy at dinner that evening.

'Tomorrow?' It is Daniel who asks the question, raising his thick eyebrows quizzically.

'Yes. Tomorrow. Why should that surprise you?' Andrea asks coldly. 'We always go to the cemetery on my son's birthday. But of course you would have no way of knowing that.'

She does not like this New York novelist who spends so much time with her daughter-in-law, who has so inappropriately inserted himself into a very private family conversation. 'Pushy,' she thinks. 'Very pushy.' She does not mean 'Jewish'. She is certainly not anti-Semitic.

'Tomorrow is the picnic at Franconia Notch,' Wendy says calmly. 'Lots of activities have been planned for the boys. Donny won't want to miss it.'

'And I'm not going to,' Donny says too loudly. 'We're going to have a dart contest. And climb a real mountain. And lots of other stuff.' His face is very red and his eyes are dangerously bright.

'I should think that showing respect to your father is more important than a picnic.'

Mark speaks with practiced severity. It is the tone he used with great success to intimidate recalcitrant employees and reluctant brokers. It allows for neither negotiation nor compromise. Donny's lip trembles and his hands tighten into fists.

Wendy's color is high but her voice remains calm. She pours a glass of lemonade for Donny and water for herself and Daniel before she speaks.

'I do know that it's important to you that Donny and I be there,' she says. 'But Donny really does not have to spend the entire morning there. He can come with us and then go on to join the others at Franconia Notch.'

'And how will he get there?' Andrea asks. 'I assume you'll want to help with the planting. It's what you've always done. What we've always done. For Adam. In his memory.'

Wendy stares at her, her mind an angry confusion of words she will not utter. Not yet. Not in front of Donny and certainly not in front of Daniel Goldner. Still, her thoughts gather in an angry avalanche that she can barely contain.

'Adam is dead,' she says. She does not share her cascade of angry thoughts.

The flowers, the bench to be set into place, are for us not for him. These macabre birthday pilgrimages to his grave are an act of atonement, an appeasement for an unacknowledged guilt, my own, I guess, and definitely yours. But Donny is free of that guilt. He never harmed the father he barely knew. Surely he is exempt from this annual rite of penitence with trowel and pruning shears as we kneel in the shadow of Adam's grave

plucking weeds and sliding green shoots into the friable earth.
She thinks all this as the silence between them thickens.

She finds voice at last, places a calming hand on her son's
shoulder.

'I'll work something out,' she promises.

'I'll pick him up at the cemetery and drive him to Franconia
Notch,' Daniel offers.

His suggestion comes with ease, as though he had discussed
it with Wendy, which he had not, and she looks at him
gratefully.

'That will be OK, won't it, Donny?' Wendy asks her son.

'I guess.' He drinks his lemonade, his eyes averted from his
grandparents.

'I'm not sure that's an acceptable plan,' Andrea protests, but
Mark looks at her warningly and they are all grateful when
Louise and Evan join them.

Evan, of course, can be counted on to direct the conversation
to himself, to the seminar he attended that summer, to the
courses he plans to take in the fall. All discussion of the visit
to the cemetery is tabled, Louise smiles and, like an attentive
mother, fills her husband's plate with the chicken breast he
prefers and the baked potato she prepared especially for him
because he does not care for the rice she has served to the other
guests. Daniel frowns and looks away.

The next day dawns crystal clear and everyone opts to go
on the picnic. Even Louise decides to join them, a rare excursion for her. She and Evan fill the inn's van with the picnic
food and sports equipment. It is a strenuous effort that they
accomplish alone because Polly is out again, caring for her
mother who has developed a dangerous fever. The guests pile
into their various cars. They are almost set to pull away when
Jeff Edwards' cell phone rings. His chief resident is calling
from the hospital to tell him that a patient of his has developed
complications and is being readmitted. What procedures should
he follow?

'Well you won't know until you examine him and make an
evaluation,' Jeff replies irritably. 'Call me after you've done
that. I'll be here.'

The patient in question is an elderly man of whom he is particularly fond and the surgical procedure to correct post-operative complications is delicate and may be life-threatening. Jeff can think of no other doctor on staff whom he would trust with such a complicated operation.

'You're not coming?' Susan asks him.

'I can't. I don't know what kind of cell phone reception there'll be up there and I'll need the car if I have to travel home and get to the hospital to handle this myself. You and Matt go with Helene and Greg and I'll catch up with you if I can.'

'If that's what you want.' Her response is flat.

'It's not what I want. It's what has to be done,' he replies briskly, aware that Matt is staring at his parents with that worried look in his eyes.

'All right then. Come on, Matt.'

Susan is pale, her voice tight. Jeff immediately regrets the harshness of his tone. He hurries after her, thinking to kiss her in apology, thinking to reassure his son, but she is already in Greg's car, the window closed, and Greg is maneuvering his way down the driveway. It is Matt who presses his face against the car window and waves to his father.

Jeff watches until the car disappears from sight. He drives his car back to the parking lot and finds a sheet of notepaper on Susan's seat that must have dropped from her open bag. It is covered with 'to dos' – each one numbered. A list, of course, one of her inevitable lists. He scans it.

1. *Sunblock for Matt. Sunblock for Jeff*
2. *Hair clips for Annette*
3. *Film for Jeremy*
4. *Souvenir gifts for Nancy and Sue Ellen*
5. *Marcia's birthday. Remind Jeff to call*
6. *Call the plumber for September appointment. Upstairs bathroom*

He smiles. Nancy and Sue Ellen are his nurses. Marcia is his mother. This list does not annoy him; it shames him. He would have forgotten his mother's birthday. He would have neglected his nurses. It reminds him of Susan's vigilance, her constancy of concern that anchors the family. She is the custodian of their needs – sunblock, hair clips, a blocked sink. How could he have forgotten how caring and careful she is, how mindful of what needs to be done, what needs to be purchased? Ruefully, he presses the paper to his lips and thrusts the list into his pocket.

He returns to the deserted lawn, alone and lonely. He realizes that he misses Susan, misses his family. It is a welcome realization. He will make amends. He and Susan will edge out of this inexplicable marital maze and find a pathway home. He takes the list out of his pocket and reads it yet again, this time with an appreciative smile.

Andrea and Mark, Donny and Wendy stand before Adam's grave. Walking through the cemetery, along the quiet pebbled paths lined with carefully pruned boxwood, they passed a stooped, white-haired woman kneeling and weeping beside a grave, her fingers fretting their way through a rosary. On an adjacent plot a young couple stood with their heads bowed before the very small marble footstone that surely marks the grave of a child. The man held a slender black leather-bound prayer book from which he read, his lips barely moving. His wife swayed and he reached out and held her close, continuing to read, his very soft voice matching the keening rhythm of her body. Wendy wishes that they themselves had the comfort of words of devotion, that there was something they could say that might assuage their grief, but they are not a family with such soothing resources. Instead, they stand together (yet separately) in silence, their heads bowed, Adam's bereft parents, his widow and the son who does not remember him, dry eyed and heavy hearted. It is Donny who steps forward and places his hand on his father's gravestone.

'I'm really sorry that you're dead, Daddy,' he says in his high, sweet voice.

Andrea gasps, Mark winces and Wendy places her arm about her son's narrow shoulders.

'We're all sorry, Donny, honey,' she murmurs.

And then, having admired the new bench, inhaled the smell of the wood, passed their fingers across the carpenter's skillful carving of Adam's name, they busy themselves with spades and trowels. Donny plucks up a few weeds and tosses them away just as Daniel walks up to them.

He greets Andrea and Mark with a nod, smiles at Wendy.

'Ready to go up to Franconia Notch, Donny?' he asks, and grins as Donny nods eagerly, waves to his grandparents and his mother.

'Here are the directions,' he tells Wendy. 'We'll see you there later.'

'Of course,' she assures him.

She watches them walk off, the tall man slowing his stride to keep pace with Donny, inclining his head to better hear the boy's excited chatter.

'How are they getting there?' Andrea asks suddenly.

'On Daniel's motorbike.'

'Is that safe? Don't you care that you're placing your child in danger? Wasn't it bad enough that you left him alone during that awful storm so that you could be with your lover? Now you allow him to ride off with that man on a motorbike.'

Andrea's voice is strident, accusative. She covers her mouth with her hand as though to silence herself. Her color is high as though her own words have shocked her. *Lover. That man.* However accurate they may be – and she believes that they are accurate – she should not have uttered them. She flinches from the disapproval she sees on Mark's face. She has not maintained her dignity, a great offense in his eyes and her own.

Wendy sets down her trowel, her eyes ablaze with anger, her heart beating rapidly. The unspent fury of years of silence washes over her in a massive wave and she struggles for breath, seeks to soar above it, but she knows that it will not ebb. Words spew forth in a voice that she does not recognize.

'I have never placed Donny in danger. And Daniel Goldner is not my lover. How dare you, you of all people, talk to me about endangering my child? Who are you to pass judgment on me? Do you know why we are here today, dutiful guardians of a grave? Do you know why Adam died?'

Andrea trembles and leans against her husband, who holds up his hand warningly, as though to silence Wendy, but she ignores him. She moves closer toward them, her rage replaced with sorrow. She speaks softly now, as though a harsher tone might shatter the brittle and dangerous words so long unsaid.

'It was because you were such lousy parents, because you didn't give a damn about Adam when he was alive. You, both of you, might as well have been behind the wheel of his car because in the end it was you who killed him.'

Tears streak her cheeks but she can breathe. It is as though a crushing weight has been lifted from her heart. Andrea and Mark stare at her, Andrea very pale, Mark's cheeks mottled, his arm raised as though at any moment he might move to strike her. Instead he looks hard at Wendy and when he speaks his voice is dangerously calm.

'You are saying terrible, unforgivable things, Wendy. I cannot imagine what you are talking about. You have no right to speak to us in such a manner.'

'Then I'll tell you what I'm talking about,' Wendy says, the evenness of her tone matching the calm of his. 'I am sure you know, Mark, that Adam was drunk when he died, that he lost control of the car because his alcohol blood level was sky high. And he was drunk because drinking was what he could do best. He learned the secrets of clever, secret drinking when he was still in grade school. Don't you think he watched you, Andrea, filling your small crystal glasses with vodka and, occasionally, even daring to use a water glass? How fortunate for you that vodka is colorless and that it doesn't stink. So Adam learned that one way to deal with misery, one way to deal with loneliness and fear, is to simply get numb, to drink and drink until it doesn't hurt any more. After all, that's what you did, and if it worked for you it could work for him. Adam remembered being all alone in that big house, that well-kept beautiful home. With you sprawled on the bed, too drunk to drive him to play dates, to after-school activities, but never too drunk to miss a hairdresser appointment or your facial in Portsmouth on the last Thursday of the month. Adam remembered that. And you were never too drunk to drive to New York and play the role of the perfect hostess when Mark needed you. Adam knew that his father, the venture capitalist, money manager to the monied, had to be the picture of propriety and stability.'

'I think you've said quite enough.'

Mark turns his back on her but Wendy will not be silenced.

'Mark, you had to know it wasn't enough to breeze up to New Hampshire every couple of weeks with expensive toys, with sweets and treats, just so that you could con yourself into believing that Adam was OK with the crazy life you and Andrea had worked out. You had to realize how sad and alone he was. How he had to find a way out of that sadness.'

'You don't know what you're talking about,' Andrea hisses. She clutches Mark's arm. Her cheeks are flushed and red hives of anger dapple her neck. 'Adam was fine. A terrific student. High school with honors, Harvard with honors. A novel published when he was only two years out of college. His life was on track. Until he met you. Until you tricked him into marriage like the manipulative little bitch you are.'

She is relieved to have at last given voice to that firm conviction, unarticulated over all these long and silent years. Adam's death was Wendy's fault; it is Wendy, that little nobody from nowhere, who is to blame for the loss of her son. That ungrateful bitch who lives in her house and cashes her checks. Exhausted, she sits down on the bench, her head resting against the deeply etched letters that spell out ADAM.

Wendy reaches into the basket of bulbs, selects one and places it tenderly in the earth before replying. Her voice is calm, her tone regretful. But she will speak. This is the hour of truth-telling.

'He wasn't fine. He wasn't all right. A boy who lives in silence, in isolation, is never all right. That's another lesson he learned from you. How to pretend to be fine. How to put on a show. He even pretended to himself. He wasn't an alcoholic, he told himself. He just liked a drink. Every now and then, until every now and then became every hour. You'd taught him the secret of very small glasses. You'd taught him the secret of vodka so he could pretend the way that you had pretended, the way you still pretend. And he sure as hell pretended to me.'

'You must have been singularly naïve,' Mark observes dryly.

'I was. Singularly naïve. Who was I? A scholarship student from a small Midwestern town. I was barely twenty years old. What did I know? What *could* I know? But I learned pretty quickly. I had married a writer who didn't write. He didn't know how to live in a family because he'd never lived in a family. He drank. He blamed everyone for everything that went wrong in his life, but he especially blamed you. And then he began to blame me, and I told him that I couldn't live like that. I couldn't live with the drinking; I couldn't live with the anger. Finally, I gave him an ultimatum. He'd have to do something or I'd leave him. I said that at about two o'clock on that August afternoon when Donny was playing with building blocks on the living-room floor. Adam was already drunk; he'd already dropped a glass and a shard of glass just missed Donny's eye. I didn't want him to blind our son. I didn't want him to destroy our lives. "Get help or get out," I yelled. He was scared because there was blood on Donny's cheek, scared enough to realize I meant what I was saying, scared enough to look hard at me and say that he'd do just that. He talked about rehab, about therapy, and then he said that his first step was going to be to drive up to New Hampshire and confront the both of you. He knew you were there, Mark. Your usual monthly visit. He wanted to tell you how you had screwed up his life. I told him not to go. I told him he was too drunk to drive and then I left because I had to take Donny to the doctor. I even took the car keys with me, but of course he had another set. When you called later that day, I let the phone ring three times, four times, because I knew what you were going to tell me. I knew that there had been an accident. And five minutes later I knew that Donny's father was dead and I was a widow.'

Tears streak her face. Her throat is dry. She does not look at Adam's parents who sit huddled together on the bench, Andrea blinking like a small child who has just walked out of the darkness into sudden and searing light.

'How dare you speak to us like that?' she asks, her voice broken now. 'After all we've done for you.'

'You did what you had to do,' Wendy replies. 'Donny is your grandson. You gave him a home. You bought your way out of guilt. But you won't have to make payments for much longer. I'll be able to support my son.'

She turns away from them, picks up the trowel and carefully, methodically, she sets the young plants in place. The nursery owner has already rooted the small conifer and she encircles it with tulip bulbs. Mark and Andrea do not move from the bench, their faces frozen into masks of grief. Her work done, Wendy stands and looks at them, pity and sorrow heavy upon her heart.

They drive back to the inn without speaking. It is quite possible, Wendy thinks, that they will never speak again. The charade of their relationship is over. Andrea and Mark leave the car at the entry to the inn without saying a word to her and she drives away without looking back. She wants to reach Franconia Notch in time for the picnic lunch. She is, quite suddenly, ravenously hungry.

Jeff Edwards, seated alone on the lawn, waiting for the phone call from the hospital, watches the Templetons enter the inn, watches Wendy drive off. An hour and a half later, he watches as the village's only taxi pulls up and Mark and Andrea Templeton, dressed for travel, emerge from the inn. Andrea wears the same silk mauve pant suit she had worn when she arrived and Mark has dressed carefully in his trademark beige linen jacket and well-pressed slacks. The driver hoists their suitcases and garment bags and drives away. The distinguished-looking, silver-haired elderly couple sit far apart on the rear seat of the cab and Jeff notes that they do not look at each other.

Franconia Notch does not disappoint. It is a wild wonderland of jagged mountain peaks standing vigil above patches of forest. Ancient rock formations jut their way out of sere earth to abut majestic pines. Mount Haven Inn vacationers split up to follow different trails and passes, each approach lined with trees, the sheltering canopies of leaves already laced with the early scarlet and golden borders of autumn foliage. Overhead flocks of Canada geese scissor their way south through the clear sky. Their wings beat their way through lazily floating white clouds gilded by sunlight.

Most of the hikers dutifully trek after the earnest forest ranger who conscientiously explains the geological origins of the rugged range. Susan barely listens. She keeps pace with Matt, who clutches her hand tightly as though the pressure of his touch might assuage the sadness he perceives in his mother's face. She remembers a camping vacation during the early days of her marriage, probably when Jeff was still an intern, when they had fearlessly hiked mountain trails. Jeff had led the way, now bursting into song, now pausing for rest on a sun-drenched boulder. She is sad that he is not with them. This is his kind of day. But he had little choice. She knows that his first responsibility is to his patient. She should have told him that she understood that much. She sighs and Matt tugs her hand.

'Don't be sad, Mommy,' he says.

'I'm not,' she lies and wonders why it is that only Matt, of their three children, is sensitive to the tension that has shadowed this vacation.

Perhaps it is because Annette and Jeremy have already plunged into the emotional whirlpool of their own yearnings; their parents are no longer the anchors of their lives. The dynamics of their family have changed, the dynamics of their marriage shifted. She should be neither surprised nor disheartened. Not after the months she has spent translating LeBec's portrait of a marriage and the novelist's reluctant, almost clichéd conclusion. *Plus ça change, tout c'est la même chose.* Everything changes, everything remains the same. Every marriage is fragile. Change, LeBec had emphasized, does not mean dissolution. Fragility does not mean divorce.

Susan bends, kisses the top of Matt's head and watches as her daughter and Paul Epstein veer off on to a narrow ridge, separating themselves from the rest of their group.

Pleased to be alone on this rough pathway, Annette and Paul walk hand in hand. Brittle, wind-tossed leaves flutter to the ground and a small heart-shaped crimson maple leaf settles in Annette's hair. Paul plucks it loose and puts it in his pocket.

'To remind me of you. In the winter,' he says, blushing at her gaze.

'I won't need a leaf to remind me of you,' she says softly.

She knows that this summer, these August days, will be her precious legacy through the weeks and months to come. Always she will remember this season of her awakening to tenderness, to the power of gentle touch, of a boy's soft voice, his hand resting upon her own as they stood together in a wilderness of berry bushes.

Paul says nothing. They have no need for words. Instead he stoops, picks up an acorn and hands it to her. She smiles and puts it in her pocket. Years later, probably, she will find it in the bottom of her jewelry box, a mysterious souvenir of these magic August days.

They return to the picnic area where the rest of the group has already assembled.

Energized by their hike, their faces ruddied by wind and sun, they all help Louise and Evan set out the food. Greg surveys the area and settles on a tree at a remove from the picnic tables. He hammers the dart board into place, checks the wooden box of newly sharpened darts and, satisfied, turns to Cary, Matt and Donny who have trailed after him.

'Ready for the big contest?' he asks.

'Aren't we going to wait for my mom?' Donny glances nervously toward the road leading to the parking area.

Daniel stands there, leaning against his motorcycle. He too is waiting for Wendy and they both smile as her car makes its way up the road. She gets out and Daniel notes at once the pallor of her face, the newly etched worry lines about her eyes. He waits as Donny rushes forward to hug her, to talk excitedly about the hike to the gorge, how he and Matt and Cary collected really cool rocks, how this was the greatest place he'd ever been. She listens, smiles and watches him dash back to his friends. Only then does Daniel go up to her.

'Did something happen?' he asks. 'Was it bad?'

'Yes. Something happened. And it was bad.'

'Perhaps not as bad as you think.'

'I told them the truth. A very dangerous thing to have done.'

'Are you sorry?'

'No. I'm relieved. It was time that they understood what it was like for Adam; time that they understood how wounded and vulnerable he was. I wanted them to know what it was like for me, for us and, I'll be honest, I think I wanted to punish them. I wanted them to acknowledge their responsibility. I broke their code of silence and talked about her drinking, about Adam's drinking. And I didn't let myself off the hook. I told them about the threat I made that very last day of his life. They will not forgive me for that and they know now that I have never forgiven them for how they failed him over the years. So it was sad. Very sad. Sad for me. Sad for them. And the end of our pretending to be a family. The masquerade is over.'

Her voice is calm but he sees that she is shivering although her pale-blue shirt is stained with sweat. He takes off his cardigan and drapes it over her trembling shoulders.

'You'll be all right,' he says.

'I know. I know.'

Together, but not touching, they walk back to the group at the picnic table and, without asking, he pours a cup of hot coffee from Louise's huge thermos and gives it to her, watching patiently as she drinks it down.

As the drink warms her, she looks up at him and sees the concern on his face.

This is what it is like to be cared for, she thinks as he takes his handkerchief and wipes a drop of coffee from the corner of her mouth. *A man offers you a hot drink and watches as you drink it.*

The picnic spread is ample. They are ravenous and they consume Louise's sandwiches and pastries with abandon. Evan is the jovial host, producing a carafe of newly fermented sparkling cider and toasting his wife and their guests.

'To next year,' he calls out, lifting his glass.

'To next year,' they echo.

It is their pledge, renewed each year, an oath of allegiance to these August days when memory and hope are magically commingled.

'Your in-laws didn't come with you?' Michael asks Wendy.

'I think they were tired,' she replies but she does not meet his eyes.

Liane looks at him with concern but he places a reassuring arm on her shoulder.

'It's all right,' he says and wonders if he is reassuring her or himself.

'Of course it's all right,' Simon Epstein interjects, his voice authoritative. 'Every kink's been worked out. Mark is going to back you. He'd be a fool not to. Hey, the check is in the mail. And if he doesn't kick in someone else will. I guarantee it.'

Michael laughs, embarrassed by his insecurity, and Liane

smiles. No need to worry. They are no longer adrift on the waters of uncertainty. They have landed on safe shores.

They follow Greg and the others to the tree where shafts of sunlight plunge through the thick-leafed branches and rib the punctured red and black circlets of the cork board.

The adults toss the darts first, laughing at each other's ineptitude, Nessa's dart hitting the tree rather than the board, Helene's landing in the outer ring. Evan triumphantly hits the treble ring. They laugh at each other's efforts. Tolerance and affection have been nurtured during these weeks of intimacy. Greg and Liane are, of course, the champions, easily meeting their mark. Paul, Jeremy and Richie achieve the bull's eye with laconic certitude. It is no contest for them. They have the ease and grace of youth, the amused admiration of Annette and Tracy who stand side by side.

But it is the youngest among them who triumph in the end. Matt, Cary and Donny, who could barely hit the board during the first days of this shared holiday, each in turn step up to the stone marker with confidence. Greg has taught them well. Their small bodies are perfectly pitched, their gazes do not swerve from the board. As Greg has instructed them, they finger the dart, straighten the feathers and toss with unerring accuracy. One by one, they shoot directly into the bull's eye. They turn to their audience; their smiles radiate shyness and pride. These vacation weeks have served them well. They have achieved. They have learned. There is a smattering of applause. Their mothers run toward them with congratulatory hugs. The sun shifts, the dart board is draped in shadows. Slowly, reluctantly, gear is packed, missing sweatshirts are found, final photographs are snapped as they prepare to return to the inn.

Jeff remains on the lawn until late afternoon when his chief resident calls to tell him that his patient's condition has stabilized and there is no need for him to come to the hospital. By that time it is too late for him to set out for Franconia Notch. He goes into the inn, finds the plate of sandwiches that Louise left for him, and eats without appetite. He looks at his watch and wonders when his family will be back. He misses them, misses Susan. There is so much he wants to say to her, so much he must explain.

He has been too hard on her, too hard on himself. He is suffused by a new and not unpleasant exhaustion that he recognizes. It is not unlike the fatigue of a patient recovering after a long illness, who can, at last, relax. They are safe, he and Susan. They are in recovery. They have simply gone through a difficult time. He reaches into his pocket and his fingers curl around the flimsy sheet of notepaper, the list, those small loving obligations she accomplishes so quietly. It is a talisman of her caring and he presses it to his lips.

As he sits in the vast empty kitchen, the phone rings. He does not answer. Louise, of course, will have the answering machine on and it is not his place to pick up. It rings again and again until at last the answering machine does kick in. He is on the way out of the kitchen when he hears Polly's voice shrilling into the machine.

'Louise! Evan! Someone! Please pick up. I don't know what to do. It's my mother. My mother! Mommy. Oh, Mommy.' Now her voice is muffled. Now he hears sobs and then again her voice, softer now, pleading. 'Help me. Someone please help me.'

He reaches for the phone, waits until she falls silent and then speaks with as much calm as he can muster.

'Polly. It's Dr Edwards. What's happening? Catch your breath. Speak slowly. I will help you.'

'My mom. I can't wake her up. She's in bed and I can't wake her up.'

'Polly, you must call nine-one-one. Can you do that? Call nine-one-one.'

'Nine-one-one.' She repeats the emergency number. 'But that's for the police. We don't want the police.'

He understands. Of course they don't want the police. This is New Hampshire where privacy is safely guarded, where people are fond of saying they keep themselves to themselves.

'It's for any emergency,' he explains. 'And I'll be there in a very few minutes. I'm leaving right now. I know where you live. Call nine-one-one, Polly. Tell them you need an ambulance. Take deep breaths. Drink some water and wait for me.'

He hangs up, relieved that his medical bag is already in his car, and rushes out. It will not take him more than five minutes to reach Polly's house. He presses down on the accelerator although he is certain that Polly's mother, that frail and sickly woman, is almost certainly dead. He pulls up in front of the house, grabs his bag and hurries inside, following Polly into the narrow dimly lit room.

He kneels beside the bed, its clean linen sheets already sour with the unmistakable scent of death. He does not even have to examine the skeletal yellow-skinned woman, her thin gray hair plastered to her skull, who lies motionless. Still, he feels for a pulse, listens for a heartbeat and holds a mirror to her lips, knowing full well that no breath of life will cloud it. Polly, in a pale-blue sun dress, hovers near him, her eyes red with tears that continue to fall as she sways from side to side.

'I called her. And she didn't answer. And then I tried to wake her up. And then I tried to breathe into her mouth. In and out. In and out. But she didn't move. Even though her eyes were open. See. They're still open.'

Jeff nods.

'It sometimes happens that way,' he says gently. 'You did everything you could, Polly.'

He leans forward and with practiced fingers, because he has done this so many times, he gently closes the fragile eyelids of the dead woman. As always, he is fearful that the delicate skin might crumble at his touch although he knows that of course this will not happen.

Carefully, he pulls a blanket over her face.

'Your father?' he asks. 'Where is your father?'

'At work. Or on his way home. I didn't call him. I didn't want to scare him.'

'Of course.'

There is the rumble of wheels, the trill of a siren. Jeff goes to the window. A police car has pulled up, followed by an ambulance. He speaks quietly to the officer, to the gangly acne-pocked emergency medical technician. He sits with Polly in the kitchen as the body is lifted, placed on a gurney and wheeled out of the house.

'She weighed nothing. Nothing at all,' the police officer muttered.

Polly weeps and weeps. 'I'm scared,' she says. 'I'm so scared.'
'It's all right. I'll wait here with you until your dad comes home,' Jeff assures her.
'I can't breathe,' she says plaintively.
'It's too warm in here.'
He stands at the door and watches as first the ambulance and then the police car pull away. Then he takes Polly's hand and leads her, as though she were a small child, out to the rickety front steps. They sit there, side by side, and because she is trembling, he places his arm about her shoulders.

They are still sitting there when the first cars headed for Mount Haven Inn head down the road. Susan, her face pressed against the window, sees them and her heart turns over in despair.

And Jeff sees his wife's frozen face and knows what she is thinking. But this is not a time for explanations, not when Polly cannot stop trembling and her breath comes in tortuous gasps.

'It will be all right. It will be all right.'
His reassuring words are meant both for Polly and himself.

FIFTEEN

The news of Polly's loss dispels the elation of the group's day at Franconia Notch. Nessa organizes a collection and they all write generous checks. Louise prepares a hamper of food which Evan delivers. He returns to report that everything is being taken care of. The neighbors are caring for Polly and her father and making arrangements. He mentions this with proprietary pride.

'That's how things happen here,' he says. 'This is New Hampshire.'

He is reminding the guests that they are, in the end, outsiders, unfamiliar with the customs of the small town where privacy is inviolate but community concern and action is a given.

'Is Polly all right?' Jeff asks.

Susan does not look at him. Carefully she butters a piece of bread for Matt. Carefully she fills her water glass. Her own thoughts shame her. She, who has always admired her husband's capacity for compassion, would have him be indifferent to Polly at such a time. She knows herself to be jealous without cause, and she knows too that Jeff is aware of that irrational jealousy. He has not, of course, said anything about it to her. That is not his way. He has, instead, retreated into silence.

'Polly's a strong girl,' Evan says. 'But it's hard to lose a mother.'

Helene and Susan exchange an uneasy glance. It had not been hard for them to lose their mother. They see themselves as the unnatural daughters of an unnatural mother, their lives crippled by her excesses. Even now, all these years after her death, they cannot forgive the dead woman for her cruelty to Helene, for filling Susan with fear and uncertainty. *Trust no one. Suspect everyone*, she had cautioned her elder daughter. That cruel maternal legacy had lingered, filling Helene with fear of replicating her sadistic harshness, frightening her out of motherhood. It has hovered like a cloud over Susan's happy marriage. That cloud has darkened dangerously during this long season of their discontent.

Greg, who loves his own parents, pities his wife and her sister. It occurs to him that they who never mourned their own mother may, perhaps, envy Polly her grief.

The somber mood in the dining room is deepened when they become aware of the inexplicable and abrupt departure of Andrea and Mark Templeton. Michael and Liane are visibly upset. So much time, so much hope, had been invested with Mark. Is it possible that he has simply abandoned the project? Michael confers with Simon who, in turn, is tight lipped and angry. He stalks out to send an urgent email to Mark Templeton but, of course, there can be no reply until the morning.

'I'm sure he must have finalized arrangements with his investors,' he tells Michael. 'He made a commitment. And like I told you, if he doesn't buy in, I'll find someone who will.'

Wendy, unsurprised but angered by her in-laws' departure, offers vague explanations.

'I think something unexpected came up regarding their property in California and they had to attend to it,' she says.

'But they didn't even say goodbye,' Donny says plaintively.

'They'll call you and explain,' she assures him, but she wonders if that will happen. Mark and Andrea are not in the habit of offering explanations. Still, she has no regrets. She said what had to be said. She and Donny will manage.

Louise sets the salad bowl on the table and motions the waitress to bring in the turkey platter. She does not tell Wendy that Mark Templeton had left an envelope for her at the reception desk containing a check that covered his family's bill for their stay and generous gratuities for the staff as well as a brief note. Mark claimed that they had neglected to cancel an important doctor's appointment and had to return home at once. He added a graceful postscript telling her how he and his wife had always enjoyed their vacations at Mount Haven Inn. He wishes her success in the future. It is, she realizes, a valedictory message. Mark and Andrea Templeton will not be returning to the inn.

'But they really should have said goodbye,' Donny insists.

'Probably there wasn't time. Probably they had to rush to catch a plane,' Daniel says gently as Wendy struggles to formulate another, more satisfying answer.

She recognizes that Mark and Andrea, faithful to the pattern of their lives, did not think of Donny. Their grandson had not entered their emotional equation. Only their anger had absorbed them. The impact of her words had been lost on them. They had abandoned Donny even as they had abandoned Adam all the days of his life. They would remain within their own comfort zone, living their own lie. Oh, there would be birthday gifts and Christmas packages for their grandson and, in all probability, a trust fund. The checks, she assumed, would continue to arrive on the fifteenth day of the month. As indifferent as they had been to Adam's life, they had been responsible; they had observed the necessary formalities. They had never forgotten his allowance, never forgotten his birthday. The Brooks Brothers parcels had arrived promptly each year. And that faithful remembrance had continued after his death with the remittance of financial support, birthday gifts, and Christmas packages to her and to Donny.

Wendy imagines them righteously describing their New Hampshire vacations to Californian acquaintances.

'Our son's birthday,' Andrea probably says. 'We spend time with his widow and his son. We visit his grave.'

She might even shed a discreet tear. Their friends, of course, will respect their grief, admire their courage. But the macabre reunions are over. Wendy wonders wryly how they will explain that to their friends. Perhaps they will say that they are old, they are exhausted. And yes, they are old, they are exhausted. Sighing, she turns to Donny.

'Daniel is right,' she says. 'Your grandmother and grandfather must have had a very good reason to leave without saying goodbye. They love you. You know that.'

She puts her arm about the boy, draws him close and knows that he does not believe her.

There are no Scrabble games that evening. Greg does not play his guitar and even the pinball machines and the ping pong table are abandoned. Death has come too close. A need for solitude is upon them. They find quiet corners and turn the pages of their books, now and again looking up, fighting against a fatigue that threatens to blanket them with a sleep for which they are still unprepared.

Annette and Paul finger the pieces of the jigsaw puzzle and then, by tacit consent, opt for a desultory game of checkers.

'Polly's like three years older than us,' Annette says sadly. 'She's in college. A sophomore. Maybe a junior.'

He nods. She is frightened and he is frightened. What happened to Polly might happen to them. They too are vulnerable to devastating loss. Parents die. Friends disappear.

Tracy and Jeremy drive into the village with Richie. They want to nurse beers, listen to music and forget that the wings of death have, for the first time, brushed so close to them.

Matt, Cary and Donny wander the room with their hands thrust into their pockets. They select a game from the shelf on which Louise stores the battered board games abandoned each year by departing youngsters. A piece is missing and they select another. The instructions are complicated.

'It's a stupid game,' Cary says. He tosses the cards into the air as Donny and Matt pelt each other with the plastic playing pieces. They are, for the first time since their arrival, in the throes of boredom. The lassitude of the adults is contagious.

'Aren't you boys tired?' Susan asks. 'You really had a very busy day.'

'Leave us alone. We're not tired,' Matt retorts angrily.

He seethes with rage at his mother who will not be happy, who will not smile at his father. She is placing them – all of them – in jeopardy. He knows what he fears and he also knows, for the first time, the liberating power of anger.

Susan blanches and turns away from her son, his mood so alien to his sweet nature. She shrugs into her cardigan and goes outside, grateful for the cold evening breeze that ruffles her hair, grateful for the narrow path of silver moonlight that she follows across the lawn. She looks up and sees that the light is on in their room. Jeff is up there, sprawled across the bed, staring at the ceiling. This is the posture he assumes in the aftermath of death. It is how she has always known that a patient of his has died despite all his efforts. She has learned over the years how to comfort him at such times, how to lie quietly beside him until the warmth of her body melts the fear and sorrow that grips him. But she will not do that tonight. Not tonight.

Michael checks his email again and again. His laptop flies open and shut with staccato precision.

'Stop that,' Liane says. 'You're making me nervous.'

He looks hard at her, sees that she has not turned a single page of the book she is supposedly reading, a tic that he has never seen before plays nervously at the corner of her mouth. His heart sinks. Is it possible that all the emotional gains of these past weeks will be lost if Mark Templeton has indeed withdrawn his support, if the venture capital is not forthcoming? The familiar, cold vise of despair tightens about his heart. Unable to sit beside his wife a moment longer, he seeks out Louise in her office.

'You're certain that Mr Templeton did not leave a message for me?' he asks.

'I'm certain,' Louise says. 'I'm sure he'll contact you tomorrow.'

But she is lying. She is certain that Mark Templeton will not call, will not write, will not email. He has, for whatever reason, severed all ties with Mount Haven Inn and the guests of August.

Michael returns to the rec room where Simon and Daniel are playing chess. He will not bother Simon again tonight. But Nessa, curled into the deepest of the worn leather chairs, barefoot as always, in a voluminous blue gown that matches the polish that dots her toenails, leans toward him.

'Simon will call California in the morning, Michael,' she says softly, and he smiles gratefully at her, envying Simon his wild-haired wife, who is so instinctively kind, so wonderfully indifferent to the judgment of others.

'I know. Thanks.'

'It'll be OK,' she adds.

'Yeah. I know.'

He glances across the room at Wendy, who has spent the evening with her sketchbook open but the charcoal stick is motionless in her hand, as though she cannot decide what she might draw next. Now and again she glances at Daniel. He in turn smiles at her, leans back, studies the chess board, and makes his next move. What will her own next move be, she wonders, and uses her charcoal stick to draw a whimsical question mark surrounded by stars.

'I'm bored,' Donny complains to his mother.

'You're not bored. Only stupid children are bored.' Her reply is automatic. He has heard it often enough before.

Louise brings a pitcher of cocoa, a platter of cookies. Like children in need of comfort, they sip the warm sweet drink, munch the cookies and then go to their rooms. They seek elusive comfort in their memories of the happy day at Franconia Notch. They are relieved that the evening of sadness and loss is over.

Daniel walks Wendy to her room. Once again they linger at her door. He cups her chin in his hands and looks down at her.

'We'll talk tomorrow,' he says.

'Yes. Tomorrow.'

A promise is hidden in the word which Donny, scampering past her into the room, overhears.

'Tomorrow,' he says mischievously. 'Tomorrow we won't be bored.'

'Right,' they reply in unison and, for the first time that day, the ache in Wendy's heart is eased.

They waken the next morning to a sky canopied with clouds, but slowly the sun works its way through and by mid-morning the lawn is sheathed in light. Determinedly, the guests of August take advantage of the new brightness, intent on scavenging the last scraps of pleasure from the waning days of their vacation weeks.

At breakfast Daniel announces his intention of riding his motorbike up a mountain trail. 'I want to see how she takes the ascent,' he says. 'Want to risk it, Wendy?'

'I'll pass.'

She smiles. 'But be careful,' she adds.

'Oh, Ma, chill out.' Donny grins at them, pleased to use the new expression the teenagers toss about.

Annette and Paul, Tracy and Jeremy play tennis, an energetic game of doubles. Bare armed, they hold their rackets high, and their sun-bronzed legs flash as they sprint from one corner of the court to another. Tracy's many silver bracelets jingle as she lifts her arm to lob a ball. The young people are energized, geared to the promise of the hours ahead, content with all that has passed between them during their brief time together. They have, however tentatively, made their way across secret boundaries. It is with ease that Jeremy hugs Tracy when she makes a point. With equal ease Paul kneels to tie the lace of Annette's sneaker when it comes undone.

Liane leans listlessly against a post and watches them. She wonders where Michael is. She has not seen him since they finished breakfast, since he went outside clutching his cell phone. He had asked Wendy for Mark Templeton's California number and Liane knows that he was intent on calling that pompous bastard, ignoring her suggestion that he leave that difficult call to Simon.

'It's my project, my future. Try – try really hard – to have some faith in me.' She had flinched from the sarcasm in his tone, from the hurt in his eyes and turned away. And now she cannot find him. He is not in their room, not on the lawn, not in the rec room. Cary and his friends run past her on their way to the swings.

'Cary, have you seen your dad?' she calls.

'He was walking toward the lake,' Cary replies.

'Hey, Liane, do you want to come into the village with us?'

Nessa and Wendy approach her. Their smiles are warm and welcoming. They offer her comfort, they offer her friendship, something she could not have anticipated at the onset of the vacation.

'We'll go to the flower shop and order an arrangement for Polly. The funeral isn't for a couple of days and we'll be gone by then,' Wendy says. 'And we want to get some treats for the kids. We'll have a little farewell party for them, lift their spirits.'

Liane does not say that it is their own spirits that are in need of lifting. Surely they share her regret that summer is ending and the obligations of a new season, with all its tensions, will soon be upon them.

'I was kind of looking for Michael,' she says.

'Oh, he's probably off somewhere with Simon,' Nessa assures her.

'I suppose,' she agrees and gets into Wendy's car.

But as they drive off she sees Simon leaving the inn. He is alone. So where is Michael? She should not have let him walk off without reassuring him that she did not care about his damn project, that she was prepared to help him through whatever difficulties might await them. But then, he had not waited for her reassurance. She supposes that she cannot blame him for having so little faith in her but she will make it up to him. The mental pledge relieves her and she joins Nessa and Wendy in a discussion of the most appropriate flowers to order and whether or not they should send a fruit basket as well.

It is Wendy, so familiar with floral death offerings, who instructs the florist to send a wreath of orange and gold chrysanthemums to be delivered to the church on the day of the funeral, the card to be signed 'From your friends at Mount Haven Inn'.

'Mrs Syms' funeral,' Nessa adds unnecessarily.

'Yes, of course. I know,' the florist says.

He is a sad-eyed man, his skin unnaturally sallow as though all pigmentation has been leached by the bright and fragrant blossoms he offers for sale.

Of course he would know. There are no secrets, no privacy in this small New Hampshire village. Wendy wonders, not for the first time, how many residents of the town where Adam grew up, where she and Donny now live, knew that Andrea was a secret drunk. The bottles of vodka and wine had to be ordered from the neighborhood liquor store and carted away by village workers. She brushes the thought away. Such conjectures no longer matter.

Their grim errand accomplished, they go to the small market and buy sweets and treats for the boys, deciding with carefree abandon on chocolate-covered pretzels, marshmallows to be roasted at a campfire on the last night of the holiday, and soft, rainbow-colored gum drops. Nessa stocks up on cheese and crackers, tries to remember how much wine they have left, and decides to add a bottle of Chablis, a bottle of Burgundy and a fifth of gin.

'Why not?' she asks her friends and they shrug happily.

'Why not?'

Their answer is light-hearted. They will themselves to happiness.

Carrying their shopping bags, they head for the Windermere Café and, as they pull into the small parking area, a low-slung red sports car speeds out without decelerating. The woman at the wheel waves apologetically, turns to the passenger who sits beside her holding a map close to her face, and drives toward the inn.

Nessa sighs. The driver, so indifferent to the rules of the road, is, of course, Charlotte, Simon's first wife. She should not be surprised. Richie did tell them, with that sly mischievous smile of his, that his mother would be coming to New Hampshire. Something about a photo shoot in the White Mountains which would give her a chance to see her son and daughter. Nessa marvels at how skillfully Charlotte manages to interweave career and motherhood. Never a wasted minute, never a wasted mile. But she does not pass judgment. It is not her way.

She hopes that Simon will not be disconcerted. It would have been nice for Charlotte to have given them some warning although, actually, what difference would that have made? And she wonders idly who was sitting beside Charlotte. Another editor or a model, she supposes. She says nothing to Wendy and Liane. She is unwilling to surrender the light-hearted mood they have managed to assume, unwilling to discuss Charlotte who always excites the curiosity of other women.

They manage to laugh a great deal over their cappuccinos and they consume an entire platter of freshly baked croissants, reveling in their truancy from their families and the ambience of the inn which, they silently acknowledge, is growing just slightly claustrophobic. Wendy orders two blueberry muffins, Daniel's favorites. She imagines his pleasure when she offers them to him, her own pleasure at the swiftness of his gratitude for the smallest of gestures. Carefully she places the wrapped muffins in the large pockets of her denim skirt.

Louise, having enlisted the aid of two high-school girls from the village to substitute for Polly, is busy with arrangements for lunch. There will be extra guests for whom she must prepare. Two new families, responding to the lower late-summer rates, have checked in. A committee, searching out a convention site for a sorority reunion, is arriving to evaluate the appropriateness of Mount Haven Inn.

Louise will see to the food and Evan will see to the charm. That is something at which he excels and which he enjoys. Already, like an eager schoolboy, he has changed into a crisp blue Oxford shirt and neatly pressed khakis. She is grateful for his presence, grateful too that the phone calls from the Danish graduate student have ceased as she had known they would. She and Evan will go on as they always have, sustaining the inn and sustained by it.

Methodically, she moves through the dining room, setting out vases of fresh flowers, placing the most generous arrangement on the table assigned to the convention planners. She glances out the window and sees that Simon Epstein, seated at one of the redwood tables, is still on his cell phone, his laptop still open. He has spent almost the entire morning making calls, checking and sending emails. But as she watches him, he looks up, frowns, sets his phone down, slams his laptop closed. He crosses the lawn and, because she can no longer see him from the window, Louise goes to the French doors and sees two women approach.

They move toward Simon with languid grace, their huge purses of soft pastel leather, one peach colored, the other lemon yellow, swinging at their sides. They are confident women, born to beauty, ever accustomed to the lightness of silk against their skin, at once aware of and indifferent to the admiration of others.

Their bright smiles radiate assurance, perhaps amusement. They, after all, have the advantage of surprise. Simon Epstein, when he becomes aware of them, lifts his arm in a feeble wave of welcome.

Louise, who has not seen either of the women for years, still recognizes them at once. The woman wearing a silk pant suit of the palest pink, her dark hair amber streaked and pulled loosely back into a seemingly careless knot, is Charlotte – once Charlotte Epstein, now Charlotte Evanier – whose name heads the masthead of the glossy magazine which Louise reads every other month when she goes to the beauty salon in Portsmouth. Charlotte's face is thinner than Louise remembers and singularly unlined. Botox, Louise thinks unkindly. The other woman, taller than Charlotte, her honey-blonde hair floating about her shoulders, wears a long yellow narrow-waisted skirt that flares about her ankles, and a white leotard that hugs her breasts and clings to her firm muscular arms. Laura, Daniel's ex-wife – or perhaps they are still married. Louise realizes that although Daniel invaded the parameters of her marriage, she never asked him about the status of his own. There is, and always has been, a basic inequity in their odd relationship. Innkeeper and paying guest – their roles limit their intimacy.

She watches as Simon kisses his ex-wife on the cheek, as he shakes Laura's hand. It is significant, Louise knows, that he does not kiss Laura. The three of them speak briefly and then Simon points to the tennis court where Richie and Tracy are now playing singles. Charlotte goes off to greet her son and daughter who rush toward her. She lifts her arms to embrace them, the wide sleeves of her pink jacket fluttering like the wings of an enormous butterfly, even as Simon and Laura stand in awkward silence on the lawn. Charlotte's bright-red sports car is taking up two spaces in the car park. Louise decides that she will ask her to park it properly. No, she will not phrase it as a request but as a demand. Charlotte has no rights here.

Wearily, she goes into the kitchen and tells the young waitress to set two more places at the Epsteins' table. Apologetically, she tells the chef that there will be extra guests for lunch. Apprehensively, she studies her room chart. If Charlotte and Laura ask to stay the night, where will she put them? She sets that task aside. She will deal with the situation if and when it arises.

Louise hears the roar of Daniel's motorbike but she does not go to the window. She does not want to witness Daniel's astonishment, or perhaps his dismay, at the unexpected arrival of his ex-wife.

She has no time to ponder it further. The sorority committee arrives, five florid-faced women, their expertly dyed hair lacquered into metallic helmets. Their outfits, L.L. Bean denim skirts and pastel shirts, are nostalgically collegiate. They are clearly reluctant to surrender the uniforms of their distant undergraduate lives. Their sorority pins and the pins of the fraternity men who, with trembling hands and rueful smiles defined their futures, surely nestle in corners of their jewelry boxes.

Louise welcomes them and introduces Evan whom they instantly recognize as one of their own. They dated boys and ultimately married men who look like him. They regret that their own husbands have not aged as well as this boy-man so oddly married to the dowdy innkeeper. Happily then, they follow him on the requisite tour. Louise watches as they linger on the lawn and admire the landscaping, the placement of the chairs so conducive to intimacy, so easily moved to accommodate a larger group. They wander down to the lake where he assures them that he will help them with a campfire around which they will sing their college songs.

'All the alumni groups we host love the campfires,' he will tell them, following the script Louise suggested when, in point of fact, the inn has hosted only one such reunion group. It is Louise's newest effort to increase reservations, suggested, of course, by Simon Epstein who has, with his business acumen, shrewdly assessed the financial situation of the inn and proffered suggestions.

Louise notes that a saltshaker on one of the tables is empty and she goes into the kitchen to refill it. When she stares out at the lawn once again, she sees that Simon and Charlotte, Tracy and Richie have settled into chairs at the picnic table, a broken family briefly soldered together. Laura and Daniel have disappeared although his motorbike is parked in its usual place. The red sports car is gone. Of course they have driven off in it. Louise wonders if she should remove the extra place settings but decides against it. Instead she loads a tray with a pitcher of iced tea and tall glasses which she carries out to the lawn.

Cary, Donny and Matt dash up to her.

'I'll ring the bell,' Cary shouts. 'It's my turn. Is it time to ring the bell?'

Louise nods. Simon glances at his watch.

'Actually it's not time yet. Another couple of minutes.'

The boys scoot away and he turns to his children.

'Do you remember how you two used to fight over whose turn it was to ring the bell?' he asks.

'No. I don't remember,' Richie says harshly.

Tracy shrugs. 'I think I do. Sort of.'

'But you must,' Charlotte says. 'You had such fun here.'

She smiles her brilliant smile, willing them to memories of happier times, but both Richie and Tracy shrug indifferently.

Simon lights his pipe and turns away. They have, these children of his broken marriage, managed to banish all pleasant recollections of a childhood betrayed by divorce. But then, had he and Charlotte stayed together (which they could not have done, which they should not have done) there would have been other emotional wounds, other repressed memories.

'We left our rackets on the court,' Richie says, and they return to the court where, by tacit agreement, they lazily lob a few more balls to each other.

Simon blows a smoke ring and Charlotte passes her finger through it, a half-remembered trick of their courtship.

'How does it happen that Laura came with you?' he asks.

'Well, Laura and I have stayed in touch over the years and my next issue is focusing on dance. The impact of contemporary choreography on contemporary fashion. That sort of thing. So I asked her to join the team as a consultant and of course that meant her coming along with me for the shoot. We'll catch up with the models and the photographers further north but it seemed like a good idea to stop here first. Simon, I really didn't know that Daniel would be here.'

'Didn't you? He did tell Laura that he'd be here,' he says, and she flushes, her automatic reaction when caught in a lie, he recalls.

But, as always, she manages a swift recovery and spins into self-justification.

'Still, it's a good thing that they have this chance to meet up, to talk, to maybe sort out their issues. Daniel didn't object when I suggested he take my car.'

She has, within milliseconds, established herself as a friendly enabler, perhaps even a rescuer of an endangered marriage. He imagines her planning a feature advising friends how to intervene when relationships are in danger.

Simon, so protective of Daniel, experiences a surge of anger. Charlotte had no right to make herself complicit, no right to organize this far from casual meeting.

'When did you become a marriage counselor?' he asks harshly.

'I have had some experience with a lousy marriage,' she replies, but the smile does not leave her face.

He is relieved when this dangerous interchange is interrupted by the screech of Nessa's impossible brakes just as Tracy and Richie wander back.

Nessa's battered station wagon pulls up and the three women tumble out and surge across the lawn, eager to display their frivolous purchases, to speak happily of the school of ducklings that had so cunningly crossed the road, delaying their ride back to the inn. They are, except for Nessa, taken aback by Charlotte's presence, although their recovery is swift. They, after all, have no emotional stake in her arrival.

'Charlotte,' Nessa says with her usual warmth. 'What a nice surprise, although Richie did mention that you might be in this area.'

She and Charlotte exchange air kisses. Tracy reaches for the lemonade and pours herself a glass without adding sugar. The bitterness of the drink reflects the bitterness of her feelings. She hates these displays of superficial affection between her mother and Nessa. She is impatient with the self-conscious cordiality so expertly practiced by her mother, her father and her stepmother who are forever ensnared in the trap of their shared parenthood.

'Divorce sucks,' she had told Jeremy Edwards as they lay side by side in their exhausted nakedness, after the second and last session of their pleasant sexual tutorials. She had not minded sleeping with him even though he was such a needy novice. It meant little to her, a lot to him and it was, in her mind, a vacation ritual, a rite of passage. She herself had made love for the first time in one of the inn's outbuildings, her partner a Dartmouth junior waiting tables that August whose name she has difficulty recalling.

'I don't know. My parents just don't seem happy together any more. At least not for the past couple of months. Sometimes I think it might be better if they split. Except that it would be hard on Matt. Really hard,' Jeremy had responded. 'You know what he asked us last night – what he asked me and Annette?

He asked if they were going to get a divorce and if they did could we all still live together in the same house because that's how it is for one of his friends, a kid named Eddie. This Eddie told Matt that his mom lives upstairs and his father lives in the basement and he goes back and forth. So Matt wanted to know if that's how it could happen for us.'

'What did you tell him?' Tracy asked.

'Annette told him that they weren't going to get divorced because there was no room in our basement for anyone to live there and then we all laughed and Matt went to sleep and Annette and I went for a walk. We're both kind of fed up with the way they're acting. First our mom's mad, then our dad's mad, but it's Matt we're really worried about.'

Tracy had liked him for worrying about his younger brother, for his honest acknowledgment that their parents' separation would be a matter of indifference for him and for Annette. They will be off to college next year. The days of their childhood dependency are over. If their parents do divorce (and Tracy doubts that they will) the twins will not be devastated the way she was, the way Richie was when their parents split.

They had been little kids then, years younger than Matt, when they listened to their parents' inevitable pre-divorce conversation.

'We both love you very much and we always will. We will always be a family,' Simon had said while Charlotte had smiled and nodded.

There had been no tears and each of them had received a gift. A stuffed lamb for Tracy who had, within the hour, torn a leg from the wooly white body and tossed the stuffing all over her room. Richie had received a beautifully crafted toy plane which he tossed from the window of their car the next day. Young as they were, they had made their statements. They would not be bribed into believing a lie. They would not be a family, not ever again.

Unlike Annette and Jeremy, she and Richie have no reservoir of familial memories to sustain them. Yes, she does vaguely remember ringing the damn bell at the inn, a meager droplet of remembrance that neither renews nor refreshes. She sips the lemonade, grimaces at its tartness.

'Would you mind pouring a glass for me?' Simon asks his daughter. 'And perhaps Liane and Wendy would like some.'

He stands, smiles at them and makes introductions, always a skillful host, an accomplished mediator, accustomed to navigating his way through uneasy situations.

'Charlotte, I don't think you ever met Liane Curran and Wendy Templeton. They're August regulars now, have been for the last couple of years. But that, of course, was after your time.'

The words fall flat, their hidden implication apparent. He flushes at the awkwardness of the phrasing. But how else could he have put it?

Your time, the years of our marriage when this inn was our shared vacation spot, when you yourself were a veteran guest of August, a role that ended when our marriage ended.

Such words, he decided, would be best left unsaid.

But Charlotte smiles without embarrassment. She holds out a hand to Liane and then to Wendy, automatically appraising each woman with her fashion editor's eye, registering clothing and make-up, recognizing that Liane's turquoise necklace and earrings are costume jewelry and that Wendy's filigreed bracelet is crafted of fine silver. She notices that Liane wears a wedding band, that Wendy's fingers are bare, and she toys with her own gem-studded ring, purchased at a very expensive jewelry shop the day her divorce from Simon became final.

'I'm really pleased to meet you,' she says graciously. 'I take it you're the mothers of those adorable boys who can't wait to ring the lunch bell.'

She smiles, inviting them to like her. Liane and Wendy force themselves to smile back.

'The dark-haired boy in the very dirty overalls is my Donny,' Wendy replies.

'The cute redhead is Matt Edwards. I think you might remember Susan and Jeff Edwards – he's a surgeon and she's a translator. They were here when we were.'

Again Simon flushes. Again he has blundered into the forbidden territory of their fissured past.

'Yes. I do remember them,' Charlotte said. 'They had twins. You kids used to play together.' She smiles at her son and daughter.

'Actually, we still play together, sort of,' Tracy says mischievously, and her brother looks at her warningly.

'So they still vacation here. And they've had another child.' Charlotte says this with some wonder, as though surprised that a marriage has actually survived through all these years, that a third child has been born. 'And a redhead at that.'

'The blonde one is my son Cary.'

Liane shades her eyes and stares across the lawn to the playground where the three boys are pelting each other with fallen leaves. She turns and her eyes rake the path that leads to the lake.

'Simon, have you seen Michael?' she asks.

'No. Actually, I was going to go off and look for him,' Simon says. 'I wanted to talk to him about some developments.' He turns to Charlotte. 'Liane's husband and I have been working on a business project,' he explains, and Nessa wonders irritably why it is necessary for him to offer her any explanation at all.

Liane stares at him. She wants to ask him if he was able to contact Mark Templeton, if the promised venture capital is still a reality, but she fears his answer. A new anxiety grips her. Where is Michael? She remembers the bitter set of his mouth, the fear that dulled his eyes when they spoke after breakfast.

'He hasn't been around all morning?' she asks.

'No. At least not out here. He may be in your room.'

'Yes. Probably. It was nice to meet you, Charlotte. Please excuse me. I really must find my husband.'

She walks too swiftly to the inn and races up the steps to their room. Even as she thrusts the door open, her throat dry, her heart hammering, she knows that Michael is not there. The bed is empty. His laptop is neatly placed on his pillow. She opens it, clicks on to her own email, fearful of what might appear, but the screen is blank and that, too, she sees as an ominous portent.

The group on the lawn is reconfigured. Nessa and Wendy sink into the chairs that Richie has brought over. Paul and Annette, their hair dampened by their morning swim, their glistening bodies wrapped in brightly colored beach towels, pause on their way up to change for lunch.

'Hey, Charlotte,' Paul says and holds his hand out to his father's first wife. He follows his mother's example, easy, unstressed acceptance. Charlotte has always been a peripheral presence in his life, almost a surrogate aunt who remembers his birthdays and sends him gifts on the holidays. He is untroubled by her arrival.

'Hey, Paul.' Charlotte is fully conversant with the shorthand language of the young. She acknowledges Annette as well.

'You probably don't remember me. I knew you when you were a little girl. How are your parents?'

'Fine,' Annette says automatically. She looks up at the inn's veranda where Susan stands alone. 'There's my mom.' She wonders where her father is and hopes that he has not gone to see Polly Syms. Of course, he is only being kind to her but still it's stupid for him to do things that upset her mother.

'I'm looking forward to seeing your parents at lunch,' Charlotte says, and the two young people nod and hurry in to change into dry clothing.

'Paul,' Simon calls after his son, 'did you guys see Michael Curran down at the lake?'

Paul wheels about, thinks for a moment and says, 'Yeah. Hours ago. He went off in a canoe. Did you see him come back, Annette?'

'I wasn't paying any attention,' she says and laughs.

Together they continue up the incline.

'You're not worried about Michael, are you?' Nessa asks.

'No. Of course not. But I have some news I want to share with him.'

They do not ask about the news, just as they did not question the reasons for the departure of Andrea and Mark Templeton, cognizant as they are that there are parameters of privacy in their small vacation community.

'Is Daniel around?' Wendy asks. 'I guess he's upstairs. His bike is here so I assume he arrived back intact.'

'Actually, he went off somewhere,' Simon says uneasily.

'Not on his bike?' Wendy is surprised.

'I lent him my car.' Charlotte smiles, inviting approval of her generosity.

'I see.' Wendy's answer is perfunctory and she asks no more

questions. She has no right, after all, to monitor Daniel Goldner's comings and goings.

Tracy and Richie register, with malicious amusement, that Laura's presence, her accompanying of Daniel, has not been mentioned. They are not surprised, inured as they are to their mother's skill at subterfuge.

It is, at last, time for lunch. The three boys march across the lawn proudly ringing the heavy bell, each taking a turn, and the guests drift into the dining room. Annette is relieved to see that her parents enter together although her mother is deep in conversation with her Aunt Helene while her father is listening attentively to her Uncle Greg. Still, they are together, and she knows for a fact that her father did not go to visit Polly Syms. He spent the morning with Jeremy at the used bookstore down the road where they picked up at least three Isaac Asimov titles, a passion that father and son share.

'And he found a really old copy of Molière plays in French that he bought for Mom,' Jeremy tells Annette. 'That's good, isn't it?'

She nods, recognizing the importance of Jeremy's question. They are, both of them, in search of small reassurances that the strain on their parents' marriage has eased, that all will, in fact, be well. They are Matt's older siblings, charged with the responsibility of offering him the fairy-tale ending, that they will all live happily ever after.

Wendy and Donny join Liane and Cary at their table. Liane is very pale but very careful to protect her son from the gathering darkness of her apprehension.

'I'm sure Michael's all right, Liane,' Wendy says softly when the boys are engaged in a passionate argument about the conclusion of the last Harry Potter book. She does not want Cary to worry about his father, but she does want to reassure Liane who jerks forward whenever the door opens, whenever the phone at the reception desk rings, an invasive sound that can be heard in the dining room.

'Of course he is,' Liane agrees. 'He often goes off by himself.'

That is not true, but she finds it a comforting allegation.

'And,' she adds, reassuring Wendy in turn, 'Daniel probably needed to get something at the outlets.'

'Maybe the lady he was with wanted to go shopping,' Cary suggests helpfully, having overheard his mother's words. He is tired of arguing with Donny, who has only read the Harry Potter books once while he has read each of them twice and the very first one three times.

'What lady?' It is Liane who asks the question while Wendy sits very still and lowers her fork, heavy with chicken salad, on to her plate. Her appetite is, quite suddenly, gone.

'The lady he drove away with,' Cary replies.

Wendy and Liane look at each other and then turn away, unwilling to trade fears, to share painful doubts, to ask Cary (and Donny, of course, who must have seen 'the lady') any questions although their minds are awash with them. Was the lady pretty? What color hair did she have? Did she and Daniel seem glad to see each other? They are wise enough to remain silent. These are not questions that one asks young boys.

'She looked like a nice lady,' Donny adds unhelpfully.

The two mothers are grateful when Nessa swoops down on their table. She is in her charismatic teacher mode, an exuberant pied piper in a diaphanous loose orange dress, a paper tiger lily crowning her untamed hair, Matt, Paul and Annette trailing behind her. She is organizing a scavenger hunt and Paul and Annette are heading up one team, Helene and Greg the second. And there are prizes. Great prizes.

'Are you guys in?'

Of course they are in. They dash after Nessa on to the lawn where Greg is already clashing away on cymbals improvised from frying pan lids purloined from Louise's kitchen.

'I'm going down to the lake,' Liane says quietly to Wendy. 'I'll row all the way across. And if I can't find him I'll have to speak to Louise.'

'I'll go with you,' Wendy volunteers.

'You know, Michael can't swim,' Liane says. 'Isn't that crazy? He never learned how to swim.'

Wendy does not reply. Liane does not expect her question to be answered.

Together they walk at a swift pace down to the lake, breaking into a run only when they can no longer be seen from the lawn. They are out of breath when they reach the dock. One of the three canoes is gone as well as one of the shabby orange life jackets that hang on hooks over the rough fencing that Evan built. Wendy does not mention the absent life jacket but she takes it as a good sign. A man in search of death would not strap an inflatable orange jacket around his body. But she does not say this to Liane because she knows that at this point no words will reassure.

They themselves don the life jackets and then they select oars and heft the heaviest of the row boats into the water. Wendy pushes it further out and Liane pushes it free of the dockside mud. Wendy leaps in. They each take an oar.

Surprisingly they are both accomplished rowers and well matched. The boat moves smoothly and swiftly across the dark sun-ribbed water. They row directly to the opposite side of the lake, the usual route for guests of the inn who know that the Abbots have water rights only to that particular area.

'Should we dock it and look around?' Wendy suggests.

'No point. There's no canoe.' Liane's reply is curt. 'Let's cut across and row east. Not much there. Mostly bogs. But let's try it.'

They turn the boat, rowing more slowly now, scanning the water, looking toward one side of the lake then scanning the other, leaving no expanse unobserved. They know what they are looking for. Canoes are light enough to float. Even over-turned canoes are not easily submerged.

Wendy, quite suddenly, rests her oar in the lock and carefully gets to her feet, her hand shading her eyes as she points forward.

'Look,' she shouts excitedly, and Liane's heart sinks.

'What? What?' Her voice rises in panic.

She turns and follows Wendy's gaze. There, on the surface of the lake, balanced on a rim of sunlight, floating downstream, is a glistening aluminum paddle, stamped with the Mount Haven logo.

'Michael must have rowed in this direction,' Wendy says as the shining paddle drifts from their view.

They do not speak as they raise their oars with a new urgency, intent now on moving with as much speed as they can muster. Within minutes they are in sight of an islet, an improbable rise of land in the heart of the lake, perhaps an artifact of the ice age when water rushed over the land to form this waterway leaving only this small patch of greenery. It is covered with wild shrubbery and shaded by an ancient dwarfed tree, a thick-leafed arboreal survivor. The aluminum canoe rests on its muddy shores, its shining hull entangled in an overgrowth of roots and trailing vines. Their hearts pounding, they row closer, their eyes raking the meager landscape for a sign of life. But all is still. There is no sound, no movement. Fear grips them. They row closer and suddenly the silence is pierced.

'Here. Over here!'

They lift their eyes and see that it is Michael Curran who stands on the shore, waving them forward.

'Michael. Oh, Michael!' Liane says. Her voice is but a whisper. 'Thank heavens. Thank heavens.'

Tears streak her face and she has difficulty controlling the tremor of her hand as she grips the oar and follows Wendy's rhythmic pace. Within minutes they have reached him; within seconds he has stepped through the muddy waters that rise to his knees and inched his way into the rowboat and then into his wife's outstretched arms.

'But why are you crying?' he asks in honest puzzlement as they reverse course and head back to the Mount Haven inlet.

'We thought – I thought . . .'

She hesitates, unable to give voice to the darkness of her imaginings. She cannot tell her husband, who now looks so endearingly young, his thick-lensed glasses vanished, his hair matted with leaves and his lips stained blue, that she had thought him dead, drowned, gone from her life.

'What happened, Michael?' Wendy asks. It is safe enough for her to ask the question. She has no vested interest in his answer.

'I took the canoe out. I just wanted a small getaway from my damn computer, a little exercise, a little quiet. I was tired of waiting for a phone call, an email from Templeton. So I took the canoe and paddled out here. I was tired, saw the island or whatever this is, and decided to give myself a rest. So I pulled in and while I was getting out of the canoe the damn paddle drifted away so here I was, marooned. I don't know for how long because I wasn't wearing my watch. But I didn't worry.

I had water in the canteen, and I kept cramming blueberries into my mouth. These damn bushes are full of blueberries.'

He grins ruefully at his own ineptitude, at his small adventure gone wrong.

'You were gone for hours and hours,' Liane says softly. 'I didn't know what had happened to you. I didn't know what to think.'

'And so you thought . . .' He hesitates over the words to come and looks at her in disbelief. 'You actually thought that because of that damn project, because Mark Templeton is probably pulling out, I'd do something drastic?'

He is pleased to have dredged up the word 'drastic'. It is safe enough. It encompasses and avoids.

She nods, both shamed and relieved to be thus exposed.

'Liane, would I do that to you? Would I do that to Cary? Never. Not now. Not before. Not ever.'

She shakes her head, acknowledging what she should have always known, what she should always have appreciated. Her husband, her Michael, is a man of commitment, of responsibility, a man who works hard and has, through the years of their marriage, survived disappointment, hers and his own. 'Before', he had said, and she understands what he meant by that. The years and years before these August weeks just past when hope and recognition had coalesced and ignited the love she had not known she possessed.

She takes his hand.

'I know, Michael,' she says. 'Of course I know. But I was worried. So worried.'

'But we're fine now. Everything is fine.' There is no uncertainty in his voice.

Back at the inn's dock, they tie the rowboat up and follow the path up to the inn. Because Michael is barefoot, he and Liane walk slowly, hand in hand, but Wendy strides ahead, leaving them behind.

She is alone then when she reaches the car park where Charlotte is getting into the bright-red sports car. Daniel stands beside the open passenger door and hands the seat belt to the slender woman whose honey-gold hair brushes her narrow shoulders. Wendy cannot see the woman's face but she knows that it is Laura, his wife, who engages his attention, his solicitude. She waits, unwilling to move forward, unwilling to have Laura's face planted firmly in her memory. It will be easier to resent a ghostly figure, a woman who places her fingers on her lips and presses them against the car window in mute farewell.

The red car skids down the road and Daniel watches until it can no longer be seen. He returns to the lawn and sits beside Simon who has turned his chair toward the sun, perhaps to avoid Charlotte's departure, perhaps to capture the last rays of that afternoon's brilliant light.

Wendy looks for Donny and sees that the scavenger hunt is still in progress. The participants, young and old alike, are scurrying across the lawn and in and out of the inn. They clutch Nessa's lists, intent on locating the odd array of objects she has specified. Donny, racing by with Cary, sees her and waves.

'We have to find a flag,' he shouts. 'We need a flag.'

'My mom has a scarf with an American flag on it,' Cary calls. 'Come on. I'll get it from her drawer.'

But he pauses briefly when he sees Wendy.

'Did my mom find my dad?' he asks. There is no concern, no anxiety in his voice.

'Yes. Yes, she did,' Wendy assures him. 'Of course she did.'

She watches as the two boys dash past her, envying them their careless optimism, their ability to lose themselves in this wild game of discovery, immune from the fear of disappointment and failure, having not yet experienced either.

She goes up to her room and sheds her waterlogged clothing. She takes a quick shower and slips on a cream-colored linen dress that she knows becomes her. She slips the blueberry muffin, still wrapped in a napkin, into her pocket. For the first time since her arrival at the inn, she takes pains with her make-up, using a coral lipstick, applying the slightest touch of blush. She acknowledges, as she brushes her long lashes with the very expensive mascara that was one of Andrea's last gifts, that she is doing all this in preparation for her conversation with Daniel. She knows herself to be competing with Laura, whose face she did not see but whom she imagines to be quite beautiful, a woman who dresses carefully and paints her face with a thespian's skill.

Wendy brushes her dark hair and twists it into a loose knot that rests gracefully at the nape of her neck. Only then does she go downstairs and wander out to the lawn.

She is intent on finding Daniel, sooner rather than later.

She does not have long to wait. He sees her, waves, murmurs something to Simon who smiles gravely, and then walks toward her.

'It's terrific that you and Liane found Michael,' he says. 'We were all getting a little freaked out.'

'You heard about it then.'

'News travels fast at Mount Haven Inn. No secrets here. All arrivals and departures known. Wendy, can we talk?'

Her heart sinks. She does not want to talk. She has already anticipated all that he might say. But she nods and smiles.

'That is what we were supposed to do today. We agreed on that, didn't we?' she says calmly.

'Yes. Yes, we did.'

He takes her hand, which lies limply in his own, and leads her to a secluded spot on the veranda. They sit side by side on the shabby canopied porch swing, its striped upholstery mended several times over. It was here, in its gentle sway, that as a small boy, Daniel had retreated for solitude and comfort, and it was on that swing that Wendy sat so often with Donny soothing him after a temper tantrum. She soothes herself now, pressing her foot so that it moves back and forth, back and forth, in the rocking rhythm of comfort.

Daniel does not look at her as he speaks. She suspects that he has rehearsed his words. She too stares straight ahead.

'You met Charlotte, Simon's ex-wife. Richie and Tracy's mother.'

It is not a question; it is a statement, an introductory sentence. But of course, he is a writer, skilled at introducing difficult dialogue.

'Yes.'

'Do you know that Laura drove up here with her?'

'I supposed as much.'

'Laura came because she's working on a shoot with Charlotte. But mainly, because she wanted to speak to me. She said it was important. We went out for lunch.'

'You don't have to give me any explanations,' Wendy says softly.

'But I think I do. You have a right to know.'

'All right then. What did she want to speak to you about? Not that it's any of my business.'

'Actually, I think it is your business. Because I made it your business. We told each other a great deal, you and I. And they were not casual confidences. At least not for me.'

'Nor for me,' she admits, and wonders why her hands have suddenly grown cold despite the warmth of the late afternoon. 'All right then. Tell me.'

'She wanted to talk about giving our marriage another chance. She's been unhappy. Lonely. She misses me. She misses us.'

'Did she cry?' Wendy asks dryly.

'She cried. Apparently she's been crying a lot. She said she was willing to change. That, in fact, she already had changed.'

'I see. She's given up casual lovers? She's willing to forego open marriage, weekend trysts?'

The cruelty of her questions surprises her but she grants herself the right to ask them. This much she has learned. Certain questions must be posed. Truth must be confronted.

'So she said. So she promised.'

'And you believed her. And you're going back to her?'

He shifts his weight, sets the swing in motion; he clenches and unclenches his fists. She looks up at him, sees the misery that masks his face. He answers her at last, his voice muffled with regret.

'Wendy, I really thought something important was happening between us. You're a wonderful woman. Brave and honest and talented. And beautiful. I thought you were beautiful the very first time I saw you, before we had said a single word to each other, before I realized that your beauty emanated from deep within you. I thought that we could leave the inn and then see each other through the fall and the winter, build something together. A loving friendship. A friendly love. I wanted that. I wasn't playing games. I saw a new beginning for you, for me, and I wanted that. But then I sat across the table from Laura this afternoon and I thought of all our years together. A lot of years. A lot of months and days and weekends and all those months and days and weekends crammed with memories. Not all of them good, but all of them part of my life. A trove of memories. I remembered all the things I knew about her, all the things she knew about me. She reminded me of some of them. She reminded me of all we had shared. And I listened. She said she truly believed that there was still hope for us and I thought that she could be right. You don't take all those years, all those memories, and toss them away. She wants to try, really try. I believed her. More than that, I realized that I wouldn't forgive myself if I didn't at least give our marriage a second chance. Can you understand that?'

His voice breaks and she fears that he may weep. She turns away. She does not want to see his tears.

'I can understand that,' she says and it is true. Wouldn't she have given Adam a second chance if he had lived, if his promise of change had come true? She cannot blame Daniel for taking a path she herself would have chosen.

'I won't lie to you,' she adds. 'I'm disappointed. I too thought that we could have a future. But there's no finger of blame to be pointed. We each have our own pasts, our own emotional baggage. And we were honest. With ourselves. With each other.'

'But we can be friends, can't we?' he asks.

'No, Daniel. It doesn't work like that. You know that. I know that.'

The swing glides slowly back and forth. They sit on in silence. He takes her hand and presses it to his lips, then walks away. She remains seated, her eyes closed until slowly, slowly, the swing at last comes to a rest.

Her tears begin to fall then and she reaches into her pocket for a handkerchief. Instead her fingers close around the blueberry muffin which she had thought to place in the pocket of her dress. She takes it out and sees that it has crumbled into tiny pieces. She tosses it to the ground and watches as a small flock of chirping birds descends and plucks up the pale yellow crumbs.

SIXTEEN

There is no cocktail party on the lawn that afternoon. Exhausted by the scavenger hunt, the adults are content to relax and watch the youngsters play with Nessa's whimsically chosen prizes. Plastic wands filled with magical fluid are waved aloft and rainbow prismed soap bubbles float through the soft summer air. The smaller boys delight in chasing after the colorful globules. The older group demonstrates its expertise by creating effervescent formations, bubble balanced upon bubble, until at last they are wafted away. There is much laughter as the airborne rhomboids evaporate, their rainbow-streaked beauty as ephemeral as the wistful dreams of these last blue and gold days of summer. There is also the swinging of yoyos and, finally, a game of wiffle ball with plastic bats slamming lightly against plastic balls.

Nessa controls the prizes in her usual languid manner. She is not surprised when Simon approaches Michael and the two men walk off together.

Liane watches them, certain that Simon is reporting on the conversation he surely had with Mark Templeton, perhaps sweetening the financier's betrayal. She hopes that Michael will thank Simon for all his efforts, for the time stolen from his own vacation, but she knows that Michael will not forget to do that. He is, in all things, appreciative. The smallest gestures invoke his gratitude. She remembers, with shame, how often he had thanked her for the slightest demonstration of affection, for any intimation of closeness. She sighs and turns to Wendy who has pulled up a chair beside her. She sees at once that all gaiety has faded from Wendy's face, although she forces herself to smile as Donny scores a hit and circles the improvised bases.

'Is everything all right, Wendy?' Liane asks.

'Actually no,' Wendy admits. 'But I'll cope. This will pass.'

She knows, from grim experience, that sadness does not last

forever, that cruel disappointment eventually drifts into the shadowy recesses of painful memory.

'And how are you? How is Michael? How are the both of you?' Wendy asks in turn.

'Things are better between us than they have been. Despite your father-in-law.'

'The bastard,' Wendy says calmly. It is liberating to speak honestly about Adam's father. The years of dissimulation are done with. They have skidded into an era of honesty.

The two women look at Simon and Michael who have paused at a far corner of the lawn and are now engaged in a conversation that entails much nodding. Almost in synchronized motion, each man pulls out a calculator and punches in numbers. They study each other's screens and shake hands vigorously. Simon walks briskly up to Nessa who is dispensing the last of her frivolous prizes, an assortment of hula hoops which are seized by the visiting sorority women who whirl about to much applause. Louise smiles, certain now that they will book the inn for their reunion.

Surprisingly, Wendy also springs up and lays claim to a yellow hoop. She is faster than the others, and there is much laughter as Donny snatches up a blue hoop and matches her speed, mother and son in tandem, playful dervishes laying determined claim to joy.

Michael strides toward his wife and sinks into the chair beside her.

'So,' he says, taking Liane's hand. 'It seems that miracles do happen, even in this lousy economy. Especially when you have a miracle-worker like Simon Epstein in your corner.'

'What happened?' she asks.

'Well, just as we thought, Templeton backed out. Nothing to do with the project, he assured Simon. Nothing to do with my software, which he agreed would be a great investment. He just didn't want any further involvement with anything to do with Mount Haven Inn. He claimed that he'd had a difficult time here and he wanted to put any memory of these weeks behind him. No matter the cost. No matter the investment of time. His time, my time, Simon's time. It's Simon's guess that something happened between him and Wendy. So he opts out. End of story.'

'But that's crazy. It doesn't make any sense,' Liane protests.

'People like Mark Templeton don't have to make sense. They think that they have enough power and money to do as they please – sensible, senseless, reasonable, unreasonable. They're exempt from excuses and explanations. In his case even from common courtesy. It's enough for him to say that he's out for whatever crazy reason that fits his scenario. The food at the inn, global warming, his reaction to Wendy. He doesn't even have to bother to tell us that he's out. He left it to Simon to chase after him.'

There is no bitterness in Michael's voice. He is a man who has always kept his expectations low. But a smile plays at his lips.

'Then what's the miracle?' Liane asks.

'Simon sits on the board of a major technology company. A giant in the field. They're in a position to fund start-ups and subsidiaries. He has a good relationship with the director of their research and development department and he knew they were looking for software similar to mine. So he took everything we worked on, emailed it to them and told them we needed an immediate response. Liane, it took them three hours to make an offer, to suggest a dollar package and schedule a conference where we'll sign on the dotted line. Simon and I crunched the numbers. Their offer is absolutely solid and it beats the venture capital amount that Templeton talked about. We're OK. We're more than OK.'

He springs to his feet, his face aglow with excitement. He pulls her up and, as the slowly setting sun pours its last radiance across the lawn, he holds her in a tight embrace.

Susan Edwards is awake before dawn the next morning. She moves soundlessly through the room where Jeff still sleeps, gathering her clothing. She washes and dresses in the dim light of the bathroom, then carries her laptop and the manuscript down to the rec room. She settles herself at a small table and scans her completed translation. She makes one correction and then another. This is her final draft. Daringly she changes the title. LeBec called her novel *Pierre and Jacqueline: Portrait of a Marriage*, but Susan revises the title page. *Pierre and*

Jacqueline: A Marriage Revealed. Revelation is exactly what LeBec accomplished. The French novelist stripped her fictional marriage bare, revealing both its weaknesses and strengths, sparing neither husband nor wife. In the end the weaknesses proved irrelevant. Its enduring strength was their love for each other, Jacqueline's for Pierre and Pierre's for Jacqueline. Susan supposes that the same holds true for Jeff and herself. She does not doubt her love for him and she hopes against hope that his love for her has emerged intact from the shadows of their discontents.

She sighs, writes a message to her agent, reviews the translation yet again before adding it as an attachment and presses the 'send' button. It is done and she sits back, relieved and relaxed.

She looks down at her watch and sees that more than two hours have passed since she began to work. The room is flooded with sunlight; the scent of coffee and freshly baked bread emanates from the kitchen. Their last full day at Mount Haven Inn has begun.

'Let's take one last walk this morning, Susan,' Helene suggests to her sister at breakfast.

Susan glances at Jeff. It has long been their custom to hike a mountain trail on their last vacation morning, but he pours himself another cup of coffee and says nothing.

'I'd love a walk,' she says hesitantly.

'You don't mind, do you, Greg?' Helene asks.

'No. I want to put my music together for the bonfire sing-along tonight.'

'Paul said he wanted to rehearse with you,' Annette volunteers.

Susan smiles at how the color rises in her daughter's cheeks and the softness of her voice when she mentions Paul's name. She is reminded of her younger self, of the days when she seized every opportunity to introduce Jeff's name into the most casual conversation, so overwhelmed was she by the miracle of their togetherness. *My boyfriend, Jeff thinks . . . My fiancé, Jeff says . . . My husband Jeff wishes . . .*

Those were the days when he called her 'Suse'. Never Susan. Never Susie. Always Suse. *My Suse*, whispered into her ear at night. *Sweet Suse*, murmured into the phone during their daily calls (because in those days they spoke every day, each invigorated by the sound of the other's voice). *Bravo, Suse* – his words of joy when the twins were born, when he held newborn Matt in his arms. She tries to remember now when he last called her Suse. She refills her coffee cup and turns to him.

'I'll go off with Helene then,' she says.

'Fine. I'll begin packing. We'll want to get an early start tomorrow.'

'Will we? Why?' she asks dryly, but he has already pushed his chair back and does not hear her.

The two sisters take the familiar path and walk slowly across the meadow where the tall grass is already dry, the green tendrils gilded in surrender to the dying season. The wildflowers, so abundant at the onset of their vacation, are now sparse and wilted, emitting a necrotic sweetness.

'Can you believe that we're leaving tomorrow?' Helene asks.

'I don't know whether to be relieved or sad,' Susan replies. 'It's been a complicated couple of weeks for us.'

'The Polly business?' Helene's question is cautious. She is always and forever the younger sister, conscious of boundaries, wary of trespass.

'The Polly business. The Jeff business. The Susan business. What I said. What I should have said. His moods. What he said. What he should have said. A lot of stuff to work out. *If* we can work it out.'

'You will.' Helene grips her hand, the small-girl gesture of reassurance resurrected. 'I have faith in you. And I hope you have faith in me.'

She smiles enigmatically, a smile Susan remembers, Helene's smile when she had a secret, a happy secret, ripe enough to be shared. Just as she had smiled when she told Susan about her scholarship to art school, when she won the grant that allowed her to go off to Europe. Just as she had smiled when she swooped down on Susan and Jeff and told them that she and Greg, her wonderful vagabond companion, had decided to get married.

Susan pauses, plucks a long stalk of grass and turns expectantly to her sister. 'Of course I have faith in you. But is there any particular reason you'll need it?' she asks, although she is almost certain that she knows the answer.

'I'm late. I've never been late before and now I am. And I'm pretty sure it means – and I want it to mean – you know . . .' Her voice trails off but her smile widens.

'Of course I know. It probably means that you're at least two minutes pregnant,' Susan says and embraces her sister. 'Oh, Helene, I'm so happy for you.'

'You don't think I'm nuts for thinking that so soon? I know that most of my friends waited for a couple of weeks at least before they even bought a pregnancy test. Which, by the way, I haven't done.'

'No. I don't think you're nuts. I believe in a kind of mystic instinct. I knew the very instant the twins were conceived, the same with Matt. Jeff laughed at me when I told him, but I knew both times and both times I was right. And I think you're right. And I'm glad, so glad. You'll be a great mother, a wonderful mother.'

Arm in arm, they continue on their way. They speak of how things will change, of how now, at last, Helene and Greg will decide on a house, on whether or not Helene will continue to teach.

'I'm so glad I saved our baby equipment,' Susan offers. 'I have a great bassinette.'

'That's one thing we won't need,' Helene says. 'We have a cradle. I bought an antique one.'

'When?'

'A couple of days after we talked. You remember how we talked that first morning. In the cemetery.'

'I remember.'

They are silent then. They have no need for words. They will not relive the past. They will not dwell on vanquished pain, on lingering fears now dispersed and etherized. They know that their mutual, hard-earned honesty was an exorcism of sorts for both of them. Now is the time to look to the future.

'Do you want a girl or a boy?' Susan asks playfully.

'It doesn't matter. I just want to be a good mother.'

'And you will be.'

There is no uncertainty in the assurance she offers her sister.

Their dark maternal legacy is nullified, both for Helene and for herself.

Susan smiles and realizes that she has known, from earliest morning, exactly what it was she had to do.

'Helene, I'm going to walk to the village. There is something I must take care of. You go back to the inn.'

'You don't want me to come with you?'

'No. This is something I have to do alone.'

'All right.'

Helene asks no questions. She kisses her sister's cheek and turns back.

And Susan, walking swiftly now, continues on, veering off on to the road that leads into the small hamlet. At the village bakery she inhales the hearty scent of newly baked bread, the sweet aroma of browning pastries and, at last, orders a selection of cookies and croissants.

'Would you like a pie? We have fresh baked blueberry and apple,' the baker's wife asks. 'I know you like the apple.'

She recognizes Susan from years past and knows her to be a guest at the inn. Susan, aware of that recognition, even comforted by it, nods.

'Which one will freeze better?' she asks.

'The apple. You should take the apple. That's what people always want somehow. You know – after.'

After. Susan is startled to hear the word uttered so knowingly. Does the baker's wife know for whom the pie is intended, that it will most probably be set out at the modest meal offered *after* the funeral? She answers her own question. Of course she does. Susan is a guest at the inn where Polly Syms works and her bakery order is surely a gift to Polly. There are no secrets in this New Hampshire village.

'All right then. The apple.'

There is an approving nod and Susan's purchases are carefully placed in stiff white boxes tied with red and white string. Susan pays and lifts her fragrant burden with great tenderness. The baked goods are heavier than she had anticipated and she shifts the boxes from one hand to the other as she walks to the rundown white clapboard house so oddly situated between village and woodland.

She lifts the tarnished knocker and brings it down gently as though fearful that the metallic sound might intrude on the muted sorrow within. The dingy curtain on the front window flutters briefly and then Polly opens the door. Her face is blanched, all rosiness faded from her cheeks, her expression dazed as though she is still bewildered by the dark reality of her mother's death. She blinks against the invasive brightness of the morning light and stares at Susan in surprise but says nothing.

'May I come in, Polly?' Susan asks.

'Yes . . . I suppose . . . Of course.'

She opens the door wider and Susan follows her into the house. A frail man, his gray hair matted, tightens the belt of his shabby brown bathrobe, rises from the sofa and shuffles into the kitchen.

'My dad,' Polly says and Susan nods.

'I hope you don't mind my coming,' she says. 'I'm very sorry about your mother.' She holds out the bakery boxes. 'I wanted to bring you something sweet.'

Her heart sinks at the absurdity of the gesture, the foolishness of her words. It is a ridiculous conceit to think that the offerings of cakes and cookies, the baskets of fruit and the boxes of candy that fill the homes of the newly bereaved, can assuage the bitterness of loss, the sourness of grief.

But Polly passes her hands across the stiff white boxes, feels the lingering warmth of the freshly baked pie and smiles gratefully.

'Thank you. Everyone's been really nice. Our neighbors. The Abbots – Evan and Louise came by and brought us lots of food. And Mrs Epstein, Nessa, was here. She gave me an envelope. Checks. Contributions from the guests. My dad thinks we should return it. He says that we don't need charity and we don't.'

'It isn't charity,' Susan protests. 'It's our way of saying thank you.'

'That's what Dr Edwards said. He was here yesterday.' She drops her eyes and Susan sees that her hands are shaking.

'I'm glad he came to see you,' she says reassuringly. 'He's very fond of you, Polly. And you know that our family, all of us, have a special reason to be grateful to you. You saved our Matt. I should have said this to you days ago. I owe you an apology, a very big apology. I am so sorry for what I said that day. It was really hurtful and wrong and very foolish of me. I don't know how to explain it. It's just that I was very tired and upset for all sorts of reasons. I hope you can forgive me.'

Again, Susan feels the inadequacy of her words, the weakness of her explanation, but Polly merely nods.

'It's all right. I understand. People say all sorts of things when they're upset and tired. I know how hard you work. I'm just grateful to Dr Edwards, but all I can think about now is my mother.'

She is weeping now and she points to an array of photographs set out on the coffee table which Susan notices for the first time. She stares down at a picture of a young girl who looks remarkably like Polly, full-featured and smiling. Next to it is a studio portrait of that same young girl, now a shy-eyed bride wearing a modest high-necked gown, and then a framed snapshot of that bride as a young mother with an infant on her lap, the infant Polly, of course, who grew into this hard-working, lovely young girl so determined to be a doctor.

They are carefully arranged, those camera-captured images of a life so newly vanished. Polly lifts them, one after the other, and presses them against her heart. It occurs to Susan that she and Helene had never studied photographs of their mother, not during her lifetime, not after her death.

'My mom. She was a really good woman,' Polly says softly. 'She worked hard, when she was still strong enough to work. She was a clerk in the insurance office in town. She put every penny she earned into a savings account for me. Because she wanted me to go to college. She was so proud when I told her I wanted to go to medical school. And now she'll never see me graduate. If I do manage to graduate.'

'You will graduate.' Susan speaks with authority. 'You'll finish college and you'll finish medical school. My husband says you're very bright, very talented.'

This is untrue. She and Jeff have, of course, never discussed Polly. They had perhaps feared that such a discussion would be fraught with emotional hazards – a dangerous confrontation with her irrational jealousy, his smoldering discontent. But the lie does not disconcert her. She plunges on.

'Polly, there are scholarships, fellowships. My sister and I both relied on them and we both worked our way through college. Our father died when we were young and our mother was a very sick woman.'

She hesitates. She cannot – will not – speak of her mother's death.

'It was very hard. I know how painful it is to lose a parent. But you'll recover from that pain. You won't forget but you'll recover. We all do. And you're a very strong girl, Polly. Strong and brave. You'll do what your mother wanted you to do. And your father will be fine. You'll see.'

She reaches into her pocket, pulls out a handkerchief and very gently wipes away the tears that streak the young girl's cheeks.

'Thank you,' Polly says softly. 'Thank you for coming. Thank you for talking to me.'

Susan opens the box of pastries and together they study the assortment. There are two chocolate croissants and they each take one and smile at the mutuality of their choice. In silence they eat the sweet cakes which, in fact, do assuage the lingering aftertaste of their shared and bitter grief.

The last afternoon of their vacation is strangely fractured for the guests of August. The adults pack sporadically, husbands and wives in shifts, unwilling to sacrifice the last bright hours of this final day. They flock to the lake where, amid much amusement, Michael Curran submits himself to swimming lessons following the instructions of Richie who captains his university swim team. He demonstrates, he commands.

'Kick!' Paul shouts and holds the older man afloat.

Simon's sons work in tandem, any uneasiness between them banished. There is great applause as Michael at last manages the dead man's float and a cheer when he dog paddles on his own. Liane leaps toward him, holding out a towel and planting an exuberant kiss on his cheek.

'Michael can swim. The summer's prime achievement,' Greg murmurs to Helene who smiles.

'I don't know. There have been a lot of achievements this summer.'

'And a couple of disappointments.'

He glances over at Wendy who is perched on a boulder, her sketchbook open, her drawing pencil poised, her eyes focused not on the laughing swimmers but on the two swans who float majestically by. She does not look up when Daniel wanders down to the small beach. She does not look up when he leaves.

'Wendy will be all right,' Helene says.

'Everyone will be all right eventually.'

'Susan and Jeff? I'm not so sure.'

She sighs, remembering their cool interchanges at lunch, Susan commenting on the egg salad, Jeff asking her too politely to pass the salt. Her sister and brother-in-law might have been strangers sharing a table in a crowded restaurant, so muted and restrained were their voices, so careful were they not to touch each other when, in fact, the salt was passed, the egg salad bowl emptied. Their children had watched them, wary-eyed and silent.

'They'll work things out, Susan and Jeff,' Greg says but there is no certainty in his voice. 'I just can't figure out what's going on between them.'

A cool breeze wafts across the lake and reluctantly towels are gathered, goggles are sought and found. Matt, Cary and Donny stick their brightly colored Styrofoam surf boards in the shed, covering them with a tarp so that they will be preserved and ready for use in the year to come. They share the innocent certainty peculiar to the very young that their lives will continue on a set course, that their August vacations will forever remain unchanged.

'Next year you'll learn the crawl stroke, Dad,' Cary says, and Michael smiles.

'Sure,' he says. 'Next year.'

He looks at Liane and she nods. His words are a promise, a contract of a kind.

The vacationers rush to their rooms to change into dry clothes. Unwilling to waste any part of this last golden afternoon, they once again assemble on the lawn. Jeff, his medical journal in hand, settles down to read in his usual chair.

'Where's Susan?' Helene asks him.

'Packing.'

He opens the journal and turns to an article that does not interest him. He knows that his answer was curt, almost rude, but he does not want to discuss his wife with her sister. What, after all, would he say? His own feelings are in confusion. He feels himself sinking in a quicksand of indecision. Should he, shouldn't he? He struggles to grasp the elusive verb to append to the 'should' and 'shouldn't' of his dark imaginings. Should he, shouldn't he . . . *what*?

Helene walks away and he allows the journal to slip from his hand on to the grass.

He watches as Richie and Jeremy set up a volleyball net. Tracy and Annette dash across the lawn dribbling a ball. He stares at his son and daughter, startled by Jeremy's height, by Annette's beauty, thrust back in memory to the day of their birth. He acknowledges that he is a father ambushed by his children's sprint out of childhood, a husband bewildered by his wife's moods and his own. He is, in fact, a middle-aged man uneasily balanced on the high wire of indecision, the personification of a cliché he has long rejected. Midlife crisis. The words are both apt and repellent. He smiles bitterly and leans forward as Tracy tosses the ball into the air.

'Game time,' she calls. 'Guys against gals. Who's in?'

Liane darts forward.

'I was pretty good in high school,' she says and joins Tracy and Annette.

Daniel and Simon take up positions but Nessa settles lazily on to a chaise.

'I'm out. Definitely out,' she says. 'Are you out?' she asks Wendy, who sinks into a chair beside her.

'On many counts,' Wendy agrees.

Nessa looks at her. 'Who knows?' she asks. 'Nothing is forever. Things happen. Simon and I still want you to visit us in New York. Spend a weekend. A week. Whatever. Whenever.'

'I'd like that. And so would Donny. You know, he adores Paul.'

'Good. That's settled then. No bridges burned?'

'No. No bridges burned.'

But she does not look at Daniel nor does he look at her.

Jeff, strangely energized, springs to his feet. 'Can you use another player?' he asks.

'Great,' Richie says, and motions him to a position.

Jeremy and Annette flash each other looks of shared annoyance. They do not want their father, who has not played the game for years, to embarrass them. Their annoyance intensifies when their mother, who has been standing on the porch, calls out that she too will play. Susan is, in fact, dressed for just such a game in white shorts, a white T-shirt, white sneakers, a white baseball cap, the immaculate uniform of an athletic vacationer. She is emancipated. Her translation is shooting its way through an electronic world. She is free to spend this sun-bright day sprinting skyward in a game that was so much a part of her past. Hers and Jeff's.

She smiles at him across the net, willing him to remember the days of their courtship when they played barefoot on public beaches with friends long vanished from their lives. She remembers still his soaring leaps to spike a ball, her successful and unsuccessful intercepts, their joint collapses on to the burning sand, choking with laughter, their limbs entwined.

'We were happy,' she wants to shout out to him. 'We can be happy still. I'm sorry. I'm sorry.'

She would apologize to him for breaking their vacation pact, for her irrational jealousy, although she now recognizes that it was nourished by her mother's cynical warnings repeated year after year, and by Jeff's own irritability and distance over the last several months. She acknowledges that she herself was seared with pain but she cannot yet forgive herself for the hot spurt of anger and suspicion that ignited her words that had singed Polly so unfairly. She had apologized to Polly but Jeff has no knowledge of her words of regret; she has not told him of peace offerings tendered in white cardboard bakery boxes. Her sadness remains unmitigated; her questions remain unanswered.

'What has happened between us?' she would ask Jeff. 'That I should think such thoughts? Can we go back to where we were?'

But Jeff kneels to tighten the lace of his sneaker, ignoring her smile, indifferent to the plea in her eyes. He nods to Greg and Paul who have abandoned their guitars for the game.

Other guests join the teams, pleased to feel themselves part of the vacation community. The sorority women warm up by chasing each other across the lawn. Donny, Matt and Cary take up positions on either side of the net ready to retrieve a ball hit too widely.

They play with great exuberance. The ball soars, expertly passed by the women and thrust back by the men who rely on individual strength rather than cooperative effort. Nessa watches this dynamic with wry amusement.

'This is classic,' she murmurs to Wendy. 'The gals rely on each other but each guy insists on demonstrating his own mojo. What macho idiots.' But her laughter is forgiving and affectionate.

The game proceeds. The players rotate positions. The score is almost tied and the momentum builds. The serves are powerful, strategically aimed and the returns are hard-fought and swift. Richie scrambles from left to right, from rear court to net, intercepting the ball again and again, sending it in soaring flight over the net.

'Hey, Richie, I was right there,' Paul protests as Richie sprints in front of him.

Richie does not answer but lurches forward to launch the ball to the furthest corner of the opposing team and gain a point.

'Dig that, Annette,' he shouts as she struggles unsuccessfully to keep the ball in play.

Simon looks at him warningly. He knows that his older son is reminding the girl who rejected him, who so improbably chose Paul instead, of his strength and power. Richie is, in this as in so many other ways, Charlotte's son.

Annette ignores him. She prepares to serve and Paul notes that her sweat-stained pink T-shirt clings to her body, clearly defining the rise of her breasts. Drops of perspiration bead her lips and he wonders if they would taste of salt if he licked them away. The thought both excites and embarrasses him, and he turns his concentration back to the game.

Her serve is directed at the third line of players and once again Richie darts forward. His response carries the ball only as far as the net and it is Jeff who leaps forward and spikes it over in a forceful thrust. Susan dashes forward, her arms raised high, prepared to make the save, to prevent the ball from plummeting to the ground. She is unprepared for the fierce velocity of Jeff's spike and the ball hits her in the face with powerful impact. Viscous scarlet blood rushes from her nose and mouth, streaking her snow-white shirt. She falls to her knees, gasping and crying.

'Susan!' Helene screams.

'Mom!' Her children, their voices a chorus of concern, kneel beside her. Matt grips Helene's hand.

And then Jeff is at her side, gently nudging his children away. He rips off his shirt and uses it to wipe the blood away. His knowing surgeon fingers probe the bones of her face, resting briefly on her nose from which the blood still streams. He slides them across her cheeks, her chin, and trembles with relief. Nothing is broken. He lifts her slightly, tilts her head back and presses his fingers firmly against her nostrils, cauterizing and staunching the flow.

'You're all right, Suse. Nothing is broken, darling. You're fine, just fine, my love. I'm sorry. I never should have hit the ball so hard, but I didn't see you coming. Suse, my Suse, can you hear me?'

Her eyes remain closed and he fears that she may have suffered a concussion. Or perhaps something worse. He is a physician, familiar with the worst. Head injuries that result in comas, that trigger dormant aneurysms. Nausea overwhelms him. He fears that if he were to vomit, noxious globules of fear and regret would emanate from his mouth. He struggles for control.

'Suse. My Suse.' The loving nickname he has not used for years springs again from his lips.

'Mommy! Mommy! Wake up! You're scaring us.' Matt's voice is shrill with fear, insistent.

'Suse. Suse, darling. Can you hear me? Please, please answer me.'

Her face is contorted as she struggles to concentrate on his question, to obey his command. Her eyelids flicker open, close, then open again. She emerges from the darkness, feels Jeff's hand on her own, grasps it tightly.

'Yes. I hear you. I'm all right. Matt, I'm fine. Mommy's OK.'
The bleeding has stopped. Jeff helps her to sit up.

'Easy now. Don't try to stand.'

He presses her head against his bare chest, inhales her scent, his heart pounding. His mouth still sour with residual fear.

She smiles weakly, relieved because the pain is receding, relieved because she heard his voice, his breathless and tender plea. 'Darling,' he had called her. 'My love,' he had said. '*Suse.*' She is, once again, his Suse. They are all right; in spite of everything they are all right and they will be all right. She is at one with LeBec. Like Pierre and Jacqueline, her ghostly fictional companions, she and Jeff will bear testimony to the fact that not all fragile marriages eventually shatter into irreparable shards. Some survive. No, she corrects herself. Many survive.

She turns to Jeff, remembering the game. 'Did you make the point?' she asks. 'Who won? The guys or the gals?' The players, who now surround her, are restored to merriment. They burst into laughter.

'We're calling it a tie,' Greg says.

They are still laughing, both teams and their boosters, as they move across the lawn to the redwood picnic table where Nessa is setting up the last pre-dinner cocktail party of the summer.

SEVENTEEN

Dinner on that final evening of their vacation is, as always, a festive occasion and, as always, the guests dress with considerable care. The women glide through the room in pastel-colored dresses of gossamer fabrics, shawls and cardigans of the lightest of wools draped over their shoulders. Tracy and Annette wear loose snow-white cotton dresses that offset their sun-burnished skin. Tracy's silver bracelets jangle musically as she waves to Jeremy across the room. The men are oddly self-conscious in their soft collared shirts, chinos and blazers. They are, however reluctantly, easing their way back into their urban uniforms. Cary, Donny and Matt have been coaxed into freshly ironed shirts and long pants. There is much amusement when it is noticed that the trousers of all three boys have grown too short during their stay.

Louise follows the tradition of Evan's parents, and puts forth a special effort for this valedictory meal. There is a rich creamy mushroom soup, roast beef, a rice pilaf, and a chocolate mousse for dessert. She is dressed as she was on the morning of their arrival. Her black linen dress is newly pressed and its white collar and cuffs are freshly washed and ironed. She and Evan circle the room, the proud host and hostess, stopping at each table to speak to their long-time guests, their long-time friends.

Louise now knows that she will welcome them again next year; their reservations have been duly made and recorded, and that new certainty has brought color to her face, a spring to her step. The new families have also committed for the season to come and the sorority women have confirmed their reunion booking. The survival of the inn is less tenuous than it was. The waitresses circle the room filling the wine glasses with a very good Burgundy, Nessa's annual contribution.

Simon Epstein rises and proposes a toast. 'To our August hosts, Louise and Evan Abbot, who make their home ours for these happy weeks we spend together each year.'

There is applause, a lifting of glasses, pleasant smiles.

Evan, not to be outdone, offers a toast in turn. 'To the guests of August, our dear and welcome friends.'

They stand and raise their glasses to the Abbots and then to each other.

After dinner, they change into jeans and sweaters for the bonfire. Glowing flashlights in hand, they walk through the smoky darkness of autumn's onset, down to the lake where the bonfire is already ablaze. Tongues of flame leap skyward, sparks dance across the moonlit water. The adults settle into the white Adirondack chairs, ranged in a circle around the fire, while the young people sprawl across the blankets spread on the ground. Cary, Matt and Donny chase after each other, darting across the narrow beach, perching atop canoes and row boats.

Greg and Paul, guitars in hand, sit side by side on a boulder and begin the sing-along. It is a repertoire barely altered year after year. 'On Top of Old Smokey,' 'Foggy Foggy Dew', 'Barbara Allen', 'If I Had a Hammer'. Theirs is a muted chorus and they smile as they sing. Annette lightly strums her mandolin.

Louise passes the basket of marshmallows and Evan the long, sharpened sticks for spearing. They plunge the sweet white circlets into the fire, watch them blaze and blacken, greedily eating them before they are sufficiently cool. They grimace and happily do it again.

And finally, Evan begins the fireworks display. The sky becomes a riot of color; sprays of red, white and blue, shooting arrows of green and orange, beams of gold light up their faces. They lean forward, their eyes following each luminous arc, surrendering to enchantment. Michael puts his arm about Liane's shoulder and a flashing red rocket bathes her face in a rosy glow. Susan leans against Jeff and looks across the dancing flames of the slowly dying fire at Helene who rests her hand so very lightly on her abdomen. Daniel stands alone and then he is not alone because Wendy is beside him, her hand resting on his.

'I was wrong,' she says softly. 'We can be friends.'

They stand side by side as the last of the lights shoot their way across the darkness in a rapid blaze of glittering silver and sparkling golden stars. There are gasps of delight and Tracy and Jeremy, Paul, Annette and Richie spring to their feet and form a single unit, their arms about each other's waists, all rivalries abandoned, all tensions forgotten in the magic of the moment.

Bathed in this final and glorious light, the guests of August, each separately, and all together, acknowledge the joys and sorrows of the weeks they shared, the hopes realized, the disappointments accepted. They have, during these shared weeks, been brushed by death and gifted with friendship and love. This season has ended but there will be new beginnings.

Simon and Nessa lift their voices in song and Greg and Paul add their gentle accompaniment.

'Should auld acquaintance be forgot,' they sing in unison, 'and never brought to mind. Should auld acquaintance be forgot in days of auld lang syne.'

One by one, humming and singing, they turn on their flashlights and make their way up the incline and across the lawn to the shelter of Mount Haven Inn.

Lightning Source UK Ltd.
Milton Keynes UK
UKHW011930260321
381049UK00002B/23

9 781780 296630